SINFUL DESIRE

LAUREN BLAKELY

Book 2 in the NYT Bestselling *Sinful Nights* Series

Also by Lauren Blakely

The Caught Up in Love Series (Each book in this series follows a different couple so each book can be read separately, or enjoyed as a series since characters crossover)

Caught Up in Her (A short prequel novella to
   Caught Up in Us)
Caught Up In Us
Pretending He's Mine
Trophy Husband
Playing With Her Heart

Standalone Novels (Each of these full-length romance novels can be read by themselves, though they feature appearance from characters in Caught Up in Love)

Far Too Tempting
Stars in Their Eyes
21 Stolen Kisses

The No Regrets Series (These books should be read in order)

The Thrill of It
Every Second With You

The Seductive Nights Series

First Night (Julia and Clay, prequel novella)
Night After Night (Julia and Clay, book one)
After This Night (Julia and Clay, book two)
One More Night (Julia and Clay, book three)

Nights With Him (A standalone novel about Michelle and Jack)
Forbidden Nights (A standalone novel about Nate and Casey)

The Sinful Nights Series

Sweet Sinful Nights
Sinful Desire
Sinful Longing (November 2015)
Sinful Love (2016)

The Fighting Fire Series

Burn For Me (Smith and Jamie)
Melt for Him (Megan and Becker)
Consumed By You (Travis and Cara)

DEDICATION

This book is dedicated to my fabulous ladies, Laurelin, Kristy and CD, and, as always, to my dear friend Cynthia.

AUTHOR'S NOTE

Every effort has been made to present Las Vegas as readers know it, in its glittery, sinful, neon glory. However, some street names and details about where the characters live or have lived beyond The Strip have been fictionalized for the sake of the story.

Chapter One

The light was playing tricks on him.

The golden haze of the late afternoon sun, and its halo glow, was some kind of illusion. No way, no how, was it possible for anyone to be so gorgeous that she actually shimmered.

Mirage was the more plausible explanation for the platinum blonde stepping out of the Aston Martin at three o'clock in the afternoon on a Thursday in July, looking as if she belonged in a gangster movie. She was the woman they all fought over. The woman who brought the men to their knees.

From the pinup dress, to the pouty lips, to the gleaming car that stretched a city block—or so it seemed—she was…

Glamorous. Sultry. Voluptuous.

Ryan's fantasy woman.

No question about it.

This was lust at first sight. Pure, unadulterated lust knocking around in his chest and threatening to make matters in his charcoal gray slacks harder than he needed them to be right now.

But he was willing to deal with that problem because the woman could not be ignored. A groan rolled around in his throat as he stared shamelessly over the top of his aviator shades. He walked along the palm-tree lined sidewalk that framed police headquarters, cycling through his best opening lines, even though he had a hunch a woman like that—a woman who wore a black dress with a cherry pattern and bright white sunglasses—had heard them all. Busty and bold enough to pull up to Vegas's municipal building at midday looking like sin come to life, this woman wasn't going to be wooed by lines or a standard *come-here often?*

With one hand on the car door, she glanced to the left, away from him, and pushed her sunglasses on top of her hair. In her other hand, she held a phone, a notepad, and a pen. She bumped her rear against the car door, shutting it with her ass.

What a lucky car door.

He half wished she'd drop the pen, just so he could swoop in and pick it up. Bend down, grab it before it rattled to the street, and gallantly present it.

Then he'd get her number with that pen. She'd be the type to push up the cuff of his shirtsleeve and write it on his arm.

He scoffed at himself. As if that would work. But something had to, because the clock was ticking, and he was ten feet from this heavenly vision. Checking his watch, he saw he had two minutes to spare before he met with the detective. He could do this. He could meet her in 120 seconds.

The sun pelted its hot desert rays at him, radiating off the sidewalks, as he ran a hand along his green tie and cleared his throat. She looked up from her phone, and instantly they locked eyes. Hers were blue like the sea. As she caught his gaze, she arched an eyebrow.

This was it. No time for lines. Just fucking talk to the gorgeous creature. "Seems I've been caught staring," he said as he reached her, claiming a patch of concrete real estate a foot away.

"I'm afraid I'm guilty on that count, too," she fired back, her voice laced with a torch-singer sultriness, her words telling him to keep going.

She had the pen in her hand and she twirled it once absently.

He tipped his forehead toward it. "Incidentally, I'm astonishingly good at picking up pens that beautiful women drop outside our fine city's government buildings."

Her lips twitched. *Red*. Cherry red and full. He wanted to know what they tasted like. How they felt. What she liked to do with them.

She brought the pen to her lips, danced it between them, raised her eyebrows in an invitation, and then let it drop. It clattered to the sidewalk. "Is that so?"

The pen was like a promise. Of something more. Of flirting, and then flirting back. Of phone numbers to follow. And then some. Oh yeah, so much and then some.

"That is so," he said in a firm voice, bending down to pick up the writing implement, just as Sinatra's 'Fly Me to the Moon' crooned from her phone. He rose, and she was tapping her screen, sliding her thumb across it.

"Must answer this. But thank you so much for the pen. By the way, I like your tie." She reached out to trail a finger down the silky fabric, her hand terribly close to his chest. Then she held up that finger, asking him to wait.

"So good to hear from you," she said into the phone, keeping her eyes on him the whole time. "I can't wait to see you tonight at the gala at Aria," she said, arching an eyebrow at Ryan as she emphasized that last word. "It's going to be a fabulous event and we'll raise so much money. My only hope is there will be some gorgeous man there in a green tie who can afford a last-minute ticket."

He shot her a grin—a lopsided smile that said yes, the man in the green tie could absolutely afford a ticket.

He nodded his RSVP to the gala. She waved goodbye and walked down the street.

Suddenly, Ryan had plans that night.

* * *

Ryan wondered if everyone he encountered today had been hired from Central Casting. Because the detective was straight out of a script. If there was a dress code for police detectives, rule number one must be: thou shalt not tightly knot a tie. John Winston had taken that to heart and was sporting the slightly-loosened look, as if he'd been tugging on his navy tie all day, frustration increasing as he questioned belligerent suspects. Then there were the other hallmarks of the job, from the striped button-down with the cuffs rolled up, to the paper cup of deli coffee on the desk in his office. Even the stubble seemed to have been custom ordered to fit the part of homicide detective.

Funny how people could look like their jobs. Briefly, Ryan wondered if the blonde was a movie star. He wouldn't be surprised.

"Thanks for coming in," Winston said, shutting the door to his office behind them. Glass windows looked out over the rest of the department, and a sea of half-empty desks. Ryan wasn't sure if that meant business was good or bad in homicide. "Have a seat." The man gestured to a frayed brown office chair. "Ordinarily, I'd chat with you in a witness room, but they're all full right now."

So it was a busy day here.

"This works fine for me. What can I do for you?" Ryan asked as he sat down, eager to glean any details he could about the reopened investigation into his father's murder.

Winston had called earlier in the week and asked him to come in. To help shed some light on the case, the detective had emphasized. "You're not the target of the investigation. This isn't about you. But you are a potential witness so I'd like to talk to you," Winston had said on the phone.

Ryan was flying solo here today. Bringing a lawyer in for routine questioning would make it look as if he had something to hide. He *did* have something to hide, but he didn't need an attorney by his side to keep the vault in his brain locked tight. That had been sealed for eighteen years, and no crowbar would get it open, so he wasn't worried.

He was, however, damn curious. He wanted to know what Winston knew about his family. About his mother in prison. About his father, six feet under. Ryan quickly scanned the detective's desk for any clue as to who John Winston was—a family photo, pictures of the detective with his kid, maybe even some sports memorabilia. But there were no telltale signs, save for an autographed baseball in a plastic case amidst a neat desk covered only with newspapers and a stack of Manila folders.

Ryan was left to his own devices to construct his character bio for John Winston, and he certainly didn't need a photo on the desk to know the chances were good that Winston was a cop because his dad had been one, or because someone he cared about had been a victim of a crime.

That was how a man usually went into this business. He wasn't judging Winston. Hell, Ryan fit the bill himself. He ran a private security firm, and he matched the job profile for that profession. Given that his father, Thomas Paige, had been gunned down in his own driveway when Ryan was fourteen, his job motivation was no mystery to anyone.

The detective grabbed the chair opposite Ryan. "I appreciate you coming in," Winston said, as he held up a digital recorder. "I'm going to record this. Standard procedure whenever we talk to someone." Ryan nodded as Winston set the recorder on his desk. "And, please, I'd like to keep what you say just between us. We're going to be talking to a lot of people, and I want you to feel free to speak about what you know of your parents, and for others to do the same. I'm just hoping you might be able to answer a few questions that could help us in this investigation."

"I'll see what I can do," Ryan said, shooting him a smile. *See? Nothing to hide.* "You've got us all curious. Not gonna lie—we were pretty damn surprised when you showed up at my grandma's house and told us the case was being reopened. Last thing I expected to hear. What have you got?"

The shooting was eighteen years ago, and his mother was doing hard time for it. She'd gone to trial quickly for murder for hire, along with the gunman, and both were behind bars. Ryan was dying to know why after eighteen years a closed case had gotten hot again.

Winston clucked his tongue and held out his hands wide, as if he was saying he was sorry. "I'm not really at liberty to say yet, since nothing has been confirmed. But some new evidence has come to light, and we're trying to determine the validity of it."

"New evidence about my mother's guilt, or innocence?"

Dora Prince had steadfastly maintained her innocence. Of course, there was hardly an inmate in any prison anywhere who didn't. Still, she was *his* mother, and he wanted to know if there was truth to her claim. He'd love to believe her. Hell, he'd be beside himself to learn his mother wasn't a killer. He'd held on to the possibility for as long as she'd been locked away, grasping it tenaciously, never letting it go, waiting for a moment like this. For the chance that she might not have done it. That he wasn't raised by a murderer. He dug his fingers into his palms in anticipation.

But the expression on Winston's face was stony, his eyes hard. "New evidence about the crime," he said, giving nothing away. "I know you were fourteen at the time, but is there any chance you remember some of the people your mother was associating with then?"

A muscle in his jaw twitched. The answer was yes, and the answer was no. Ryan knew more than he should, but not enough to make sense of what his mother had given him, and he sure as hell didn't want to say the wrong thing. He bought himself some time. "Can you be a little more specific?"

"We want to know who she spent time with. Beyond Stefano," he said, dropping the name of the shooter, who was also behind bars.

"I'd just finished eighth grade." Ryan was keenly aware of his own body language, of how he was sitting, how he was trying to strike a mix of casual and interested. Even though he was innocent, even though he didn't have first-hand knowledge of the murder, he had intel about his mother that he didn't intend to share, and that made him hyper-vigilant. *Never say a word.* He'd taken that directive from her to heart when he was younger, and as the years went on, too. Besides, what he knew would have no bearing on his mother or her freedom. But rather than focus on the classified documents inside his head, he narrowed in on the truth as he answered. "I didn't have a great sense of the conversations she was having with that guy or any others— beyond the customers who came to our house to pick up clothes and costumes."

Winston nodded and rubbed a hand over his chin, slowing as he seemed to consider. "We just want to get a better understanding of everything that happened. Something that might seem innocuous to you could actually wind up being a key piece of information for us. Were there new people in her life? Did she have any new friends?"

Ryan's senses tingled as his analytical mind played connect-the-dots. "Does this mean you think there were others involved?"

Winston leaned forward, resting his elbows on his thighs, the classic pose for trying to get somebody to open up. "Listen, I'm really just trying to get a better picture of what her life looked like at the time of your father's murder. Trying to understand who she was involved with. It could be relevant to the investigation." Winston made an encouraging gesture with his hands. "The customers you said would come over to pick up clothes—was there anyone new in the months or weeks prior?"

Ryan scrunched up his forehead, rewinding time. "Around then she was sewing leotards for a local gymnastics team. She tailored dresses for some of the girls in the neighborhood going to prom. She joked once that she had so much leftover fabric that she was going to start making dog jackets," he said, and Winston's lips quirked up in the barest grin.

"I like dogs," Winston said.

"Same here."

"Any idea who her clients were? Beyond the gymnastics folks? Her friends?"

"Sorry. I honestly didn't keep track of who her friends were," Ryan said, speaking the truth, the whole truth, and nothing but the truth.

"Listen, if anything comes to you, I'd greatly appreciate if you could share it with me," Winston said, turning off the recorder then pushing back from his seat and standing up.

Ryan tilted his head. "What is it you're looking for, detective? It would help me if I knew what sort of info you think would be useful."

"Honestly, *anything*," he said, emphasizing the last word with a touch of desperation. "Even if it seems like nothing —even if it seems like the smallest piece of evidence," he said as he opened the door to his office and escorted Ryan through the main office, which reeked of the late afternoon scent of TGIF even though it was Thursday, as weary cops and detectives finished phone calls, shuffled papers, and glanced at the clock as if they were all counting down the minutes 'til quitting time.

Ryan couldn't blame them. He was eager to end this workday and get on his phone to sort out his new evening plans at Aria. He said goodbye to the detective and left, returning to the blanket of heat outside, where he dropped his shades over his blue eyes and scanned for the Aston Martin. The car was still there, but the blonde was gone.

Damn. He wouldn't have minded another chance to drink her in. She would be a balm after that conversation with the detective, which had stirred up too many memories and far too many buried emotions. The past was such a thorny son-of-a-bitch. Diving back to his younger years was not a favorite hobby of his. Those days were messy and dangerous, and he wished he could leave them behind him.

He'd never been able to, though. They had dug claws into him. Grown knotty roots inside his head and his heart.

All the more reason to focus on the things that would take his mind off his obsession with the past.

Like tonight, and the chance to see the sexy blonde again. As he walked down the steps, he wondered briefly what kind of business she had at the municipal offices. One thing he was fairly certain about—she probably wasn't talking to homicide detectives about an eighteen-year-old case.

A case he'd love to know more about. What he wouldn't give to know what was inside John Winston's head.

CHAPTER TWO

Sophie knocked twice on the glass window. John looked up and flashed her a brief smile. Such a hard worker. Always had been. Always would be. He'd be burning the midnight oil tonight, either here at the station or at home.

Her brother, at thirty-three, was two years older than her, and she hadn't been surprised to find him bent over his desk, one hand pushed through his dark blond hair, the other flipping through some papers. Probably some case he was hell-bent on solving, since that pretty much described her brother's single-minded mission in life.

He came to the door and let her in. She'd just finished her phone call with her friend Jenna. Well, that call had then morphed into another one with her ex-husband Holden, but she always loved chatting with him, so the pair of them had kept her occupied as she'd strolled outside, gabbing with some of her favorite people.

"Hey you," John said, and dropped a quick kiss on her cheek.

"Hey you to you," she said, her voice bright and bubbly because she was still in a fantastic mood thanks to Mr.

Green Tie. She was hoping that handsome man—wait, make that *devilishly* handsome, because he'd had a wicked glint in those dark blue eyes—would pick up the trail of breadcrumbs she'd left behind. The way Mr. Green Tie had looked at her on the street…she'd never felt so deliciously naked while wearing clothes. A man like that, bold enough to walk right up and talk to her…he was exactly the kind of man who would show up tonight at Aria.

The kind of man she'd never experienced.

But wanted to.

Oh, how she wanted to know what a direct, confident, and forward man was like.

Anticipation knitted a path up her spine. She barely knew the guy, had uttered all of ten words to him, but Sophie thrived on moments like this. Moments that could unspool into decadent possibility. She had a feeling about him. A good feeling. A sexy feeling.

Okay, fine. She supposed it was entirely possible he could be a serial killer or an axe murderer.

But that was highly unlikely.

And it wasn't as if she'd stupidly invited him to a deserted house at the end of an isolated road. She'd invited him to a ballroom event at Aria that cost a pretty penny for a ticket, where security would be top-notch because the attendee list had the sort of net worth that required it. Not that money was indicative of a man's character or date-ability, but she'd been able to tell by the cut of his pants and the silk of his tie that he would be able to afford the ticket.

The ticket was a pre-screening. A show of faith in his interest. A sign that he'd jump through the first hoop to see her.

She crossed her fingers that he'd show.

"You're in a good mood," John said then grabbed her arm protectively. He tipped his head to the chatter and hum of the men at the desks behind her. "And get in here. Everyone is staring at you. Don't you own a jacket?"

She laughed with her red-lipsticked mouth wide open, and shook her head. "It's July. It's close to a hundred degrees outside. Why on earth would I wear a jacket?"

"Why on earth do you insist on wearing a dress everywhere you go? It doesn't even have sleeves," he countered as he tugged her into his office and shut the door behind him.

"Thank heavens for the lack of sleeves." Sophie raised her chin up high. "And you never know who you might meet. I certainly don't want to be wearing a sweat suit when I meet the future love of my life."

"Perish the thought," he muttered.

Her eyes widened. "I might bump into Mr. Right anywhere."

He scoffed and waved broadly at the offices and desks behind her. "You better hope you're not meeting the love of your life here."

But really, you never knew. Her mother had run into her father at a fruit stand in a farmer's market on the outskirts of town when she was buying a pineapple from him. They'd known each other in high school when both were involved with other people, and then they'd bumped into each other again twenty years later. They'd locked eyes across the citrus, and the rest was history—thirty-five years of an insanely happy marriage and two kids. Sophie could recall many nights when she'd sneak out of bed as a kid and find them slow dancing in the living room to Ella

Fitzgerald as a breeze blew through the gauzy curtains, looking so in love.

A love launched by a pineapple.

"In any case, Captain John Buzzkill Winston," she said, fishing around in her cherry-red purse to find what she'd come for, "here is the transponder to get into my building." She pressed the flat white object into his palm. "Just wave it at the gate, and you can get into the garage. I have two spots. Use 121 or 122."

"Thank you," he said, tapping the device. "Fucking termites. I really appreciate you letting me stay with you. I'd stay with one of the guys…"

She cut him off. "You'll do no such thing. Men who live alone live like pigs. Think of it as a vacation at the Ritz. Or really, the Veer," she said, since Sophie lived in a penthouse condo at that luxurious building on the Strip, and it was as close to the Ritz as one could get. "I'll be leaving at six-thirty sharp for the benefit. You sure you can't come?"

"No time for a benefit."

She pouted. "But you look so cute when you clean up," she said then squeezed his cheek.

He hissed.

"Oh, you don't scare me with your hisses. You might scare all those poor little suspects you question, but I know you're just a hushpuppy underneath."

He rolled his eyes. "You're killing me."

"I know. It's so much fun to embarrass you. I think when I leave, I'm gonna shake my rear a little bit. Would that make you crazy? If all your fellas stared at your little sister?"

He held up a finger warning her not to. "You know they all lust after you. Don't, Soph. Please."

Oh, but it was too fun to needle him like this. "Don't try on my shoes tonight while I'm out. Just promise me that," she said as she opened the door, then pressed her fingers to her mouth in an "oops" gesture. He huffed, and she walked out, winking at the mustached man at the desk a few feet away. "Hi Gavin. Don't you work too hard."

"I promise I won't, Sophie," he said, then followed her with his puppy dog eyes. "That is, if you'll finally go out with me."

She clasped her hand on her heart. "Oh, Gavin. You know I want to. But John just won't let his little sister date one of the guys he works with."

Gavin frowned, as he always did when she playfully said no, since he always asked.

Sophie said hello to another guy she knew. "Hey there, Jason. You look handsome today. Say hello to Evie and the boys from me."

Jason gave a quick salute. "I will. She said to tell you she loved your peach pie recipe."

"I am so pleased to hear that. My sweet mother left that one for me. It's divine," Sophie said, then blew a big communal kiss off her palm for the whole lot of them. As she pictured the red lips floating through the air, she caught one last look at her brother. He scowled from behind the glass in his office.

She winked then walked out.

Sophie Winston was a certified flirt. She hadn't always been one. Growing up, she was one hundred percent geek. But those days were gone, and now she could be *this* woman. The one who finally flirted. Flirting was like champagne to her—it gave her a rush, and she loved it. Besides, it let her bide her time. Until it could be more than flirting. Until it could become the real thing.

Maybe someday she'd meet someone who she'd want to do more than flirt with, who'd want her in the same way. She wasn't entirely sure what that would feel like, but she knew she craved that kind of connection. She wanted it all the way...but she'd also happily take the physical side of the equation for now, if the opportunity arose.

She'd had a mere two lovers in her life, but she knew what she wanted.

She knew what turned her on.

As she returned to her car and started the engine, an image of that man in the green tie slipped into her mind. Of the way she'd felt when he'd stared at her—as if she were being hunted. How she loved that kind of hungry gaze. How she longed to be the prey.

A man who stared at her that way was enough to make her get down on her knees, and that was exactly where she wanted to be.

* * *

As Johnny Cash leapt high to catch a Frisbee in midair in his backyard, Ryan scrolled through the search results. The sun inched closer to the horizon, pelting bolts of pure summer swelter from the sky. He'd already taken a dip in his pool to cool off when he'd arrived home a few minutes ago, and the blue water had done the trick...momentarily.

After quickly tracking down the gala details on his phone in the parking lot, and snagging a pricy ticket for a benefit to raise money for a new children's wing at a local hospital, Ryan had headed to the gym for a quick workout. With five miles on the treadmill as he answered emails from clients, and several rounds of weights under the belt, he had some time now to dig deeper about his possible date tonight.

To learn more than simply the name of the event.

His black and white Border Collie mix raced to his side, nudging Ryan's bare leg with the purple Frisbee, which was etched with teeth marks around the rim. Johnny Cash was addicted to this Frisbee. Ryan understood deeply the dog's single-minded focus. His intensity. His drive.

"Ready for another?"

The dog thumped his tail on the emerald-green grass. From under the relative cool of the big yellow umbrella on the deck of the pool, Ryan cocked his arm and Johnny Cash took off racing, barreling to the far corner of the yard, around the water, and past a cluster of palm trees that shaded the edge of his property. Ryan tossed the Frisbee then glanced down at the iPad again, hunting for any clue that might yield a name for the bombshell.

She'd said something on the phone about raising money, so perhaps she worked for the hospital, heading up its fundraising, maybe. He scanned the event page more closely. Tonight's fete was a silent auction with drinks and hors d'oeuvres, as well as a performance by a well-known Vegas torch singer. All the town's glitterati would be there. Probably even some of Ryan's clients, since the security firm he and his brother ran had contracts with many of the city's top spenders.

Those were the only details he found.

He shrugged as he reached the bottom of the page and came up empty-handed in the information department. But he didn't need her name to know he wanted to see her again. He'd already plunked down his cash for the entrance fee in the hope he'd spend time with her tonight. He was rolling the dice big time, but he had a feeling, just from those fifteen seconds on the street that the—

Wait.

There it was. In small print. On the bottom of the page.

The gala had been organized by...*noted Vegas philanthropist Sophie Winston.*

His dog returned to his side, depositing the Frisbee demandingly at Ryan's feet, but he couldn't pull his eyes off that name, wildly rolling and rattling around in his brain like pinballs bouncing off flippers.

Could she really be related?

Nah.

He was getting ahead of himself.

"It's just a common last name, right?" he said to the dog. Johnny Cash panted, then eyed the Frisbee. A reminder. Didn't matter to the dog what the woman's name was. *Throw the damn Frisbee.*

He picked up the purple disc, chucked it across the yard once more, and peered again at the screen through his shades. His fingers tingled, itching with possibility.

Winston.

Sophie Winston.

Showing up at the same building where John Winston worked.

The same John Winston who knew why his father's murder investigation had been reopened but wouldn't pony up the details.

Winston. Winston. Winston.

Take a deep breath. Maybe the detective just happened to have the same last name as the woman Ryan wanted to get his hands on.

He popped open another browser window, plugged in her name and John's together, and soon the all-knowing Google revealed that the woman who'd invited him to the fete was the detective's sister.

"Huh," he said, staring at the screen in a sort of awed silence. As his dog scurried back to him, Ryan kneeled down and patted his head. "What kind of lucky son-of-a-bitch am I?"

The dog panted and Ryan imagined he was saying, "The luckiest."

He scratched the dog's chin. "I can't be that much of an asshole to hope she might know something, can I?

The dog had no answers. Instead, he nosed the Frisbee.

Not wanting to deny his best friend and confidant, Ryan pointed to the pool, then threw the Frisbee into the glistening crystal-blue oval in his yard. The dog splashed loudly, then paddled to the shallow end in hot pursuit of his favorite thing.

As Ryan returned his focus to the screen, he told himself to slow it down. Just because Sophie-come-hither-to-my-party-tonight-Winston was the detective's sister didn't mean she was going to serve up details of the case to him. Hell, she probably didn't know anything. He didn't share the details of his job with his sister, so it was foolish to think John had told her the things Ryan was desperate to know.

Besides, he was interested in the woman because there'd been some kind of fuse lit between the two of them this afternoon, and far be it from him to deny that kind of heat. He wasn't some fool who believed in love at first sight. He had no interest in love, nor any faith that it existed. He did, however, believe in the almighty power of lust.

Ryan had been invited to spin into Sophie's orbit, and that was precisely where he intended to be tonight. But he didn't like to be unprepared. He vastly preferred arming himself with data and details, so he spent a little more time with Google and Sophie, learning she possessed a hell of a lot more than a beautiful body.

Apparently, she had quite a large brain, too.

She wasn't simply "noted Vegas philanthropist Sophie Winston."

Several business news articles told him what else she was, and it shocked the hell out of him.

Never ever would he have pegged her as a goddamn tech millionaire.

He zeroed in on a well-known tech blog and read its coverage of the sale of an Internet start-up to an online search giant several years ago.

Stanford graduate Sophie Winston sold the encoding compression start-up InCode in a deal rumored to be valued at $100 million. She launched the company while finishing her computer science degree at Stanford, and oversaw two rounds of venture capital funding for the technology, which has been used by networks and broadcasters, and in enterprise applications. Her brother was the original investor, having provided the initial seed funding from his savings, she has said. Winston tells us she is "delighted" with the acquisition, and plans to step down as CEO, return to her hometown of Las Vegas, and begin charitable work. "I'm thrilled that InCode will be in good hands, and am eager to return home to be with my family."

Ryan whistled in admiration. The sound caught the attention of his sopping wet dog, who cocked his ears as he trotted to Ryan.

"Guess what, Johnny Cash?" he said, as the dog shook the chlorinated water from his fur at Mach speed. Ryan stepped away, making sure the tablet screen wasn't in the line of fire. "Seems I was wrong when I thought she was a movie star. The woman's a retired Mark Zuckerberg."

He chucked the disc into the pool, and his dog raced after it, launching into the deep end.

But maybe that wasn't the best comparison, because there was nothing unfeminine about Sophie. She was all woman, and all sex appeal, and he intended to find out tonight what made her tick.

Because his desire for the beautiful—and evidently brainy—blonde had nothing to do with the fact that she might be privy to things he wanted to know. Nothing at all. It had everything to do with how she looked in that dress, and how insatiably curious Ryan was to learn how she looked out of it.

He was living for that moment, and that moment only.

CHAPTER THREE

Sophie was late.

Sophie was often late.

Being on time was so hard when there was makeup to do, and hair to blow-dry, and chandelier earrings to locate in the bottom drawer of her jewelry chest (when she *swore* she'd left them in the top drawer), and stockings to pull on just so, inch by delicate inch, because you didn't want them to rip.

Stockings took time to do right.

Hers were positioned properly with the garter attached at her thigh.

She'd be wearing them even if she didn't have that little, fluttery hope of a hot man in her crosshairs. She wore them because she loved stockings. Stockings were sexy, and being sexy was fun. After years upon years of donning jeans and hoodies and knit caps because that was what the "nerds" wore and she'd desperately wanted to look the part —since being a woman in the tech field had already made her stick out like a sore thumb—she relished looking like a woman. She'd shed the old Sophie when she left the land of bits and bytes behind her, that man's world of dressed-down anti-fashion.

Now, with her new focus on philanthropy, dressing up was not only embraced, it was essential.

The panties though...those were just for her.

She had on her favorite pair, though nearly every pair she owned was her favorite. La Perla had a way with silk and satin and beads and pearls that made every slinky bit of fabric enticing. Tonight's panties were black like her dress, and sheer, with a slim, crisscross tie up the side.

She smoothed a hand over her dress, gave herself one more quick once-over in her full-length bedroom mirror, then snagged her purse from the middle of the cranberry-red comforter on her bed. She swiveled around, ready to go, then sneaked one more final glance.

Just to make sure that the piece of hair above her ear hadn't fallen out of place.

Nope. All was well.

Wait.

Did she have any lipstick on her teeth? She bared her canines and was satisfied. Everything was in order. She headed down the hall to the wide-open living room with its floor-to-ceiling windows, which boasted her favorite view in the universe—Vegas, lit up and neon, bright and bold, her favorite city in all its unabashedly sinful glory.

She paused in the living room, one hand on the back of the soft chocolate-brown couch, wondering if she'd remembered to put fresh pillowcases for her brother in the guest room at the other end of the condo.

A flicker of tension skimmed through her veins.

She knew she had. This was just a momentary bout of OCD making her doubt herself.

She stood stock still, tapping her fingers against her forehead. She could recall perfectly having placed new linens on the bed just this morning. The gray-and-white striped ones. Masculine and perfect for John.

She headed for the front door. But it *was* always better to be safe, right? Checking and double checking, and then checking one more time in that final quality assurance test —well, that was what had gotten her far in life. She'd been notoriously thorough as a student and as a computer scientist, a trait stemming from her drive to *just check once more*. Tugging on her skirt and gathering up the soft material, she race-walked down the opposite hall, turned the doorknob, and breathed a sigh of relief as she took in the sight of the bed, as crisply made as a hotel room in the Bellagio.

Okay, she could go now.

She made her way to the front door and gripped the handle when she was nearly knocked on the floor by the unexpected force of the door opening.

"Oh!"

"Shit. Sorry, Soph. I thought you'd be gone by now."

She waved off his worry. "I should be. Running late."

He narrowed his eyes. "Were you checking everything three times?"

"Only your room," she admitted in a low voice.

He clasped a big hand on her shoulder. "Don't worry about that stuff. Besides, I'll happily sleep on the floor, or an unmade bed. You don't have to check to make sure everything is perfect for me," he said softly, then gestured to her right ear. "But you might want to check on your earring. Looks like one is about to pop out."

Lifting her hand to her ear, she felt the edge of the earring slipping from her earlobe. She peered in a small mirror by the door, catching the reflection of a framed photograph of her parents from across the room, her heart lurching briefly at the image, and how much she loved and missed them. "I thought you were working late," she said as she repositioned the jewelry.

He shrugged. "Yeah, but I figured it'll be nice and quiet at your place, and you'll be out so I can work on the case here."

"Close to solving it?"

He scoffed. "Not even remotely. Talked to some guy today who I'm sure knows something, but he won't let on what it is."

"What do you think he knows?" she asked, turning away from the mirror to face her brother, who was unknotting his tie and tugging it off.

"Something that would help me find the other guys I think were involved."

"What kind of case it?"

He laughed. "You're not getting that out of me."

"I know. I just like asking, because it's funny to see how many ways you can say *no comment*." John never gave up details. He always spoke vaguely about his work so she could never connect the dots. Not that she wanted to. She vastly preferred operating on her side of the world, entertaining the wealthy and privileged and encouraging them to dig deep into their pockets to help those who needed it most—the children, the ill, the underprivileged, the animals who needed a voice. She'd helped raise money and fund new programs for all those causes, and she intended to do just that tonight for the hospital.

* * *

Sometime later, after the silent auction of a painting by Miller Valentina—donated on behalf of a New York-based couple who'd said the piece had given them so much already, and they wanted to give back—Sophie walked to the podium in the ballroom and thanked the sea of glittering guests in their shimmery dresses and crisp suits.

"I am so unbelievably thrilled to share the news that, thanks to your generosity, we've raised well above our funding goal for the new children's wing, which will provide state-of-the art care," she said, surveying the tables in the ballroom as the crowd clapped in recognition of the good news.

The man in the green tie hadn't made it, and Sophie simply told herself *c'est la vie*. She didn't know anything about him, and it had been silly to want a stranger so badly. Besides, he'd never truly said he was attending. He'd simply nodded when she'd made that leading comment during her phone call to Jenna. He was probably a decadent flirt, too, just like her. Better to move on, and better to rid her chest of this tinge of sadness.

Besides, she had a busy agenda for the rest of the evening. "We would not have been able to do this without your generosity," she said, beaming at the guests. Her heart was full, bursting with joy over their willingness to give. "But don't think I'm going to let any of you gorgeous people—and for the record, you are all my favorite people—slip away this evening. We have Heaven Leigh here with us, and if her voice doesn't make you want to snuggle up to your date, then I don't know what will. She'll be on in five minutes."

Sophie's assistant, Kelley Jeffers, caught up with her as she walked through a small section of the wings backstage.

Ever efficient and always prepared, Kelley tapped her clipboard. "You have forty-five minutes until we need you on again to close out the event with the awards."

"Perfect. I'll grab a drink and mingle."

"Be sure to be backstage at nine forty-five so we can stay on time."

"Absolutely," she said then headed to the steps, ready to chitchat and socialize. As she reached the ballroom floor, though, she nearly froze.

She wasn't sure if she saw him first or merely sensed him. If perhaps her body had installed some sort of homing beacon to detect the presence of Absolutely Delicious Male in the ballroom. She turned her head, and goose bumps rose on her bare arms as she drank him in.

In the distance, he leaned against the big doorway to the ballroom, looking cool, sexy and debonair, wearing a dark gray suit that fit him like a glove—tailored, and snug where it needed to be, revealing strength and tone. His light brown hair was messy, but not sloppy. It was the type of hair that was too thick to be contained, that couldn't be combed into submission, but instead simply invited fingers to run through it.

But then, if she was doing things right, her hands wouldn't be free.

Across all the tables and chairs, past the dazzling chandelier lights, beyond the sea of designer dresses, he locked eyes with her.

His seemed to say *I'm here for you. I'm coming to get you.*

She flashed a smile, aware that it was a high-wattage one, but then that was how she felt—bubbly, buoyant, and powered by the thrill of possibility. She hadn't misread the moment outside the municipal building. The chemistry had been electric and instant—and intense enough for him to come calling.

As she walked around the dance floor to find her way to him, a flash of gray hair appeared in the corner of her vision. Next came a phlegmy clearing of the throat.

Oh dear.

Not now.

Please not this second when her hormones were beating a path to Mr. Hotness Whose Name She Didn't Know and Liked It That Way.

One of her regular donors placed a clammy hand on her bare arm—Clyde Graser, pushing eighty, sweet as could be, and more generous than virtually anyone.

He was also terribly out of touch with women.

"Sophie, how are you, my dear?"

He received one of her brightest smiles. "I'm very well, Mr. Graser. So good to see you."

After a minute of small talk, he cleared his throat once more, a sign he had something important to say. "My grandson Taylor is coming back to town. He graduated from Harvard Law earlier this year and has been hired into a corporate practice here. I have a hunch the two of you would get along swimmingly, and I would love to introduce you to him."

A newly minted law school graduate was probably all of twenty-five. Divorced and thirty-one, Sophie had a clear cut-off. You had to be over thirty to ride this ride. She simply wasn't into cradle-robbing.

"I'm sure he's lovely," she said, doing her best to be kind but evasive.

Clyde's matchmaking effort wasn't the first she'd had to deflect. These sorts of offers had been happening with increasing frequency since she and Holden had divorced two years ago. With the money she'd socked away from the sale of her company—even after Holden's cut of the profits— and the work she did now, many of the city's old wealth wanted her for their sons.

She wanted no such thing.

"Wonderful. Then I'll bring him to the Beethoven concert," Clyde said. The law firm Clyde had founded was a lead sponsor of that upcoming charity event, and Sophie hoped to convince him to pour even more of his corporate cash into a community center that was being refurbished in a section of town that had been a hotbed for a local gang many years ago—a street gang that had been rising up again, which made it all the more important to revitalize the neighborhood.

"I can't wait," Sophie said as Clyde walked away.

Then her pulse suddenly quickened.

She knew.

Knew the sexy man had to be mere feet from her. She knew it by the way the little hairs on her arms stood on end. Sophie and this man were two elements smashing into each other and setting off sparks. There was no other explanation, because she'd never felt this kind of intense desire for someone she'd just met.

It was a riot inside her body.

He placed a hand on the small of her back—gentle, terribly gentle, and it unleashed an electric charge in her. "Can't wait for what?" he asked.

Oh God, his voice. His deep, sexy voice that was an aphrodisiac. It was the opening act in the seduction of her.

"For the evening to turn more exciting," she said as she came face-to-face with the man she knew nothing about.

He was the sexiest stranger she'd ever met, and he wasn't going to be a stranger much longer.

"Looks like I arrived just in time. Because that's exactly what I intend to do."

She arched an eyebrow. "Excite me?"

The first notes of a sexy ballad sounded from the stage. "Yes. That's why I came here," he said, gesturing to the throngs milling about around them. "Right now, however, I'd like to monopolize you on the dance floor, Miss Sophie Winston."

"You know my name," she said, shooting him a look that said she was impressed.

"I do," he said, holding her captive with his dark blue eyes. "And I'd like to get to know more than your name."

"That sort of intel might be obtained with a dance," she said, clasping his hand and letting him lead her to the dance floor as the lights dimmed and the song wrapped itself around them.

CHAPTER FOUR

As the slinky, silky Vegas nightclub singer belted out a bluesy number from the stage, the lights in the ballroom dimmed. They turned the bright, silent auction that Ryan had caught the tail end of into a sultry, nighttime affair. The chandeliers flickered, and violet lights shone on the dance floor. Men in tuxes and women in evening dresses moved and swayed; the event reeked of old money and new money, mingling together. This was the cocktail mix of the Vegas built on the bedrock of Rat Pack era casinos, stirred up with the cool swagger of the sleek, skyscraper crowds of today.

Ryan led Sophie to the dance floor, threading their way through the glitz and glam of the dolled-up and dressed-up. She kept her eyes on him as he dropped a hand on her elbow, leaving his palm on her back.

Her skin was so soft. So bare. So fantastically naked in this backless dress as he pulled her near and they began to dance.

"So you made it," she said.

"I would have been here sooner, but I had to walk my dog."

She burst out in surprised laughter. "Really?"

"You don't believe me?"

"It's not that I don't believe it. It just came out sounding like an excuse," she said as they swayed in time to the jazzy number from the red-sequined woman on stage.

"He's a very demanding dog. Have you ever met a Border Collie mix? They can be quite needy. And I like to make sure he's happy."

"How good of you to think of him."

"I was thinking of you, too," he said, his eyes fixed on her as he spoke. "I couldn't get you off my mind."

"Is that so?" she asked, but her smile made it seem less like a question. "I figured I'd read you wrong."

"You didn't expect me to show up?" He spread his fingers across the bare skin of her back. Goose bumps rose on her flesh.

"One never knows if a man has it in him to respond to an invitation on the street," she said coyly.

His spine straightened, and he stood even taller. "When a woman like you tells a man she wants him, that man should do everything in his power to show up."

She moved closer, her sky-blue eyes sparkling with mischief. "I don't believe I said I wanted you," she whispered.

He bent his head to her ear, catching the faint scent of her perfume. Something vaguely tropical. Something that suggested hot summer nights. He wanted to run his nose along her skin and inhale her. A groan worked its way up his chest. "You didn't have to say it," he said.

She shot him a sharp stare, but she didn't let go of him. "My, my. Aren't we a little over-confident?"

"Am I?" he asked, letting go to spin her in a circle then tugging her back as the music rose to a crescendo.

"Perhaps I just wanted to make sure the ballroom was full," she said, gesturing to the crowd. "Maybe that's why I invited you."

"Is that what you wanted? One more attendee at your event?"

She swallowed and parted her lips. "Maybe I want other things."

She pressed her hand against his shoulder, and the pressure from that slight touch sent electricity flying through him. He stopped swaying and dipped her, holding her in that pose, her back bent in an arc, her body draped over his arm, trusting him. "Tell me, Sophie. What other things do you want?"

He watched her like that as he waited for her answer. Her eyes never wavered from his. There was no shyness in her gaze, no nerves evident in her expression. Only confidence, which was so damn alluring. She licked her lips then answered, "A man who can figure *those things* out."

Oh, hell yeah. This woman turned him on fiercely. She was direct and naughty at the same time. He raised her up. Her full breasts were flush with his chest, and he was sure he could spend hours worshipping them. Or biting them. Or fucking them. "I can figure out all those things you want. I can deliver all of them, too. But right now? Here on the dance floor? I presume this is when you need me to role play at being a perfect gentleman," he said, casting his gaze briefly at the crowds dancing alongside them.

"So you wouldn't be a gentleman if we weren't in front of all these people?"

"I would absolutely not be a gentleman at all," he said, letting his hand travel along her back. "But for the moment, you have your donors here to entertain."

She raised her chin and looked at him studiously. "You did your homework, Mister—" Then she laughed and cut herself off, placing a finger over his lips. "Don't tell me your name. I prefer to think of you as the Man with the Green Tie. So we can pretend we hardly know each other. We can be strangers."

"Strangers can make the best lovers."

"Are you? A good lover?"

"I don't really think you want me to answer that question."

"Why on earth wouldn't I want the answer to that?" she asked, toying with his tie, her voice a purr that lit up his organs, setting every last part of him on fire.

He shook his head. Pressed his lips near her ear. Whispered. "I think you'd rather I show you."

She gasped, an enticing sound that ignited him. His body was strung tight, like a snare drum. He was torn between wanting to pounce on her now, and drawing out the anticipation. Making her want him. Making her beg. He was willing to bet she was a marvelous beggar, that she could get on her knees and say *please* in a voice that snapped all his restraint.

"Show me," she whispered, then her eyes floated closed as he touched her, fingertips brushing her back. They traveled higher, and she arched into his hand, like a cat being pet. He reached her hair, winding a loose, blonde strand around his index finger, cataloguing the expression on her face, the way her features were so soft, so open—her lips parted, her eyes closed, her breath gentle.

He let her long curls fall through his fingers as she molded to him.

Then he showed her what else he liked. That he wasn't soft. That he wasn't gentle. With his fingers gripping her hair, he tugged.

Hard.

Her eyes snapped open, and they blazed at him. "That wasn't gentlemanly."

"I know," he said, her hair still twisted in his fist. "And you liked it. Now, have you got any more questions about how I am in bed?"

She gulped. A touch of nervousness seemed to flicker across her eyes. "Not at the moment." She blinked and seemed to rearrange her features as he let go of her hair, smoothing it out as it fell along her neck. "So tell me, Mr. Green Tie, what did you learn about me when you went hunting for information?"

He learned she shared DNA with the lead detective re-investigating his father's murder. But that wasn't exactly information that needed to be served up for small talk. "I learned you know everyone here, and can convince anyone to contribute to a worthy cause. Lots of money. Insane amounts."

She pursed her lips together. "That does sound like one of my skills," she said playfully.

"I learned you do it because you can. Because you made your mint already and now you give back."

"True, true. Does that bother you?"

"That you made a mint?"

She nodded. "Yes. That can intimidate some men. When a woman is successful."

He scoffed. "I'm not easily intimidated. And I happen to think successful women are"—he moved in closer, his lips daringly close to hers—"incredibly hot." He skimmed his hand from her shoulder down her arm, unable to resist touching her. "But that's what I learned from your bio, Sophie. I know other things about you, just from these last ten minutes."

"What do you know?" she asked as the singer began a new tune, and the purple lights swooshed across the dance floor.

He ran a fingertip along her wrist, her chest rising as she drew in a quick breath. "That you like being touched."

She nodded. "If a man knows how."

"That you like to play games."

She frowned. "You make that sound bad."

"Games aren't bad." He lowered his voice to a whisper. "I bet you like to play pretend. Make believe. Role-play."

"I have an idea," she said in a purr, as she roped her hands around his neck then trailed her fingertips across the back of it, her touch a jolt of pleasure. "We could pretend, say, that we just met, and I'm curious about the man who has been in my thoughts. All I want is a little something. A little bit of intel to round out the picture. How about this for a simple question? Since you know what occupied my time in college, why don't you tell me what occupied yours?"

This was easy. He could tell her his college major without giving up too much. "History."

"Why history?"

"I like to understand what motivates people. Why they do what they do."

"And did you learn what motivates people?"

"Usually it's a desire for property or money."

She smiled ruefully. "Sounds about right. What about sports? Did you play sports?"

"Yes. Hockey. Right wing."

"Did you cause fights?" she asked, curiosity dripping from her voice.

He shook his head, his lips in a smirk, proud to be able to say no. "I was the one who stopped the fights."

Her eyes widened. "Interesting. Why is that?"

"I like to be in control."

She inched her hands up toward his hair, and he grasped her wrists and returned them to his shoulders. "What line of business are you in?" she asked.

"Security."

"What do you do in security? Watch over banks? Guard the mall?" she said, lightness in her tone.

He laughed and shook his head. "No. I run a security company. Does that turn you on?"

"If you're asking if your job turns me on, the answer is no. And that's because I don't find jobs a turn-on *or* off." She danced her fingers down the front of his shirt. "I find men who know what they want a turn-on."

"I know what I want."

"You do. You want me."

"So fucking much," he growled. He tugged her in closer, aligning his body to hers, letting her feel how he wanted her already. A sexy sigh escaped her lips as he brought her near to him. She fit in his arms perfectly. Like that, they danced and moved under the dim lights to the next few songs, chatting about Vegas, and the event, and the silent auction, as he asked her questions about the gala and the hospital it benefitted.

"See? You are a gentleman. Asking a woman questions. Getting to know her," she said, then touched a lock of his hair that had fallen on his forehead. He caught her arm, his fingers wrapping tightly around her flesh. He bent his head and brushed his lips against her wrist.

Their first kiss, and he was nowhere near her lips. But the skin of her arm had that same sultry, sexy scent as her neck. He let his lips linger on her wrist, then let go. "You taste fantastic," he said, holding her eyes, letting his meaning register.

"Do I?"

"Yes. You do. I bet you taste delicious everywhere."

She waved a hand in front of her face. "It's getting awfully hot out here. I'm afraid I might combust if we stay on the dance floor like this." She tipped her head to the bar. "Drink?"

He nodded and pressed his lips briefly to her neck, dusting a kiss on her collarbone. A soft moan floated to his ears. He was going to have a field day with Sophie Winston. She was a dream—every touch, every taste and she murmured, she sighed, she moaned.

He hadn't even properly kissed her yet.

They threaded their way to the bar where he asked for two champagnes. As he reached for the flutes, a woman in a high-necked maroon dress and a severe bun zeroed in on Sophie, commanding her focus to ask her opinion on how the children's wing should be decorated. As that woman finished, another darted in, declaring that she knew a building contractor, and she could up her donation if that would help secure the contract. Sophie was gracious with all of them, but after a few minutes she tossed Ryan a *save me* glance.

He stepped in next to her, handed her a glass of champagne, and flashed a smile at the two ladies. "I hope you'll forgive me for interrupting, but I have to leave shortly, since I've been called to the hospital to do an unplanned surgery."

The woman in maroon shot him a curious look. "Oh, you're a surgeon?"

He nodded. "I am. And I need two minutes with our Sophie before I have to begin a bone graft."

The other woman eyed his champagne. He quickly thrust it at her. "Please. Take this from me. I can't drink on surgery nights, of course. I don't even know why the bartender gave it to me. But I hate to be rude," Ryan said, shaking his head as if he couldn't bear the thought of turning down the man tending bar.

"Of course you don't want to be rude. You're a respected surgeon," the second woman said in a commanding voice.

"And we don't want to be rude either," the maroon woman added. "Please. Go on. We don't want to keep you from the bone graft."

"Thank you so much," he said and turned to leave, the beautiful bombshell by his side, her lips pressed together so she wouldn't laugh.

"Bone graft?" she whispered from the side of her mouth as they walked off.

"I suppose bones, and the hardness of them, must be on my mind." Then he shrugged. "Besides, I needed to come up with something or we'd never have a moment alone."

"You want to be alone with me?"

"Isn't it abundantly apparent?"

"From the hardness of your bones? Why yes, it does seem quite abundant," she said with an amused expression as she cast her eyes to his pants.

He stopped at the side door, away from the crowds. He lowered his voice, and spoke in a rough, husky tone. "You turned me on from the second I laid eyes on you this afternoon. You are gorgeous and beautiful, and everything about you arouses me. *Abundantly.*"

Her chest rose and fell and she exhaled heavily. "Oh God," she whispered.

"Can you get away?"

She squeezed her eyes shut and shook her head. "I have to present a few awards on stage in—"

Out of the corner of his eye, Ryan spotted a woman in a sharp black dress marching purposely in their direction. She pointed at Sophie.

"I think someone's looking for you."

The woman stopped when she reached them. "Sophie, you have seven minutes before we need you on stage again."

"Thank you so much, Kelley."

The woman spun efficiently on her heel and walked off.

Sophie turned back to him. "I can't get away."

"No. You can't. Let me walk you backstage so you don't miss your presentation."

CHAPTER FIVE

The black curtain hugged the small stage, shielding them from the crowds still dancing and enjoying the music. Here, off to the side, in this section of the wings, Sophie was all alone with her stranger.

His eyes roamed her body. The look in them was predatory. He stalked her, and she backed up, step by step in her heels, until she hit the black wood wall. "You have six minutes now before you go out there," he said in a hungry voice, his fingertips brushing the fabric of her dress along her thigh. "Do you know what I can do to you in six minutes to make you feel amazing?"

The temperature inside her shot sky high. A pulse beat between her legs. She was hot and she was wet. She'd been turned on ever since he'd asked her to dance.

"What can you do?" she asked, feeling both utterly vulnerable and completely aroused. It was a matchstick combination for Sophie.

"Do you want me to tell you?" He roamed his hand up her leg, reaching her waist, making her shudder.

"I do," she said breathily, her body on the cusp of something intense. Something she wanted desperately.

"What I've been thinking about since I met you." He raised his hand and cupped her cheek. His touch was both gentle and possessive. "First, I'm going to place my hand on your beautiful face, and your knees will go weak, because I'll finally be touching you the way you've been fantasizing about since this afternoon," he said, his hot breath painting her skin.

"That's cocky."

"It is," he said with a nod as he ran his thumb along her jawline. "But it's also true. From the moment I met you, I knew I'd have my hands on you. You knew it, too. Felt it, too."

She nodded as she trembled from the trace of his finger. "I did feel it."

He brought his mouth to her ear and spoke softly. "If I ever do or say something you don't like, tell me. Or smack me. I only want to bring you pleasure." His words were both sexy and earnest. The combination sent flutters through her belly. "Immense pleasure."

"You already are. So tell me something else that's true. Something else you know," she said, loving the hot, dirty way he talked to her as he touched her.

"I'm going to look into your eyes like I want to take you," he said, his eyes blazing with desire. "That look will drive you wild. And you'll swallow nervously because you don't know me, and it's odd wanting a stranger as much as you do." He was reading her like a teenage diary. On the one hand, she was nervous. She didn't know him at all. But she was also aroused beyond words. Beyond reason. Beyond any normal limits.

For that same reason—because she didn't know him.

"Then, you'll run a hand down my tie," he told her, and she reached out instantly, doing exactly as he said, loving the directions he gave. Sophie craved this kind of interaction. She wanted a man to command her. So much time was spent deciding, and doing, and planning. It drove her brain batty, and she longed for this kind of release from her days.

"Do you know why you're so fascinated with my tie?" he asked huskily, his eyes pinned on her. He practically fucked her with his gaze. It was so intense. His confidence set her on fire. It torched a path across her body, sizzling her skin.

"Tell me," she said, eager for more of his words. "Since you seem to know me so well. Tell me."

He brushed the backs of his fingers against her cheek. Oh God, she was dying for him to kiss her. She was so eager to feel those lips. To taste him.

He grasped a wrist with one hand, yanking it up his chest and loosely wrapping the end of his tie around her hand. "You want me to tie you up."

"How do you know that?" she asked, her voice stripped to the bones. He knew her. He read her. He could sense everything she wanted. He crowded her against the wall. Heaven Leigh belted out her song on stage. The inky black of the backstage cloaked them.

"Am I wrong?" he asked, arching an eyebrow. "If I'm wrong, tell me and I'll walk away."

She shook her head. "Are you going to take it off? Tie me up?" she asked in a voice that hardly sounded like hers. It belonged to the part of her that had been untended for years.

He grinned wickedly. "No. I have other ways to tie you up," he said, and in a flash, he gripped her wrists in his big strong hands, wrapping his fingers around her, binding her as he yanked her hands behind her back. Heat flared in her body, spinning through her, settling between her legs. Her gorgeous, sexy panties were so damp right now they were useless.

She ached for his touch. And she could do nothing but wait for it since she was his hostage.

He was so strong she couldn't wriggle away if she wanted to. His thumbs dug into her wrist bones, pinning her hands above her ass, rendering her helpless. The pressure from the twist in her arms bordered on pain, and felt oh so good.

There was no space between the two of them. Only breath. Only words and his bare, husky voice. "Do you know what else I've been thinking about all day?"

She shook her head.

He inched closer, his mouth mere centimeters from hers. Her lips parted, so ready for him. God, she needed him to kiss her. Needed it badly. He was making her wait for it. Making her nearly ask for it. His mouth hovered so close she wanted to dart out her tongue and lick him. Draw him to her. His forehead brushed hers, and her breath fluttered.

Somehow, she managed a *please.*

"Please kiss you?" he asked. "Is that what you want me to do?"

She nodded, too turned on to form another word, even a yes.

"That's exactly what I've been thinking about all day," he whispered.

Then he kissed her, and he wasn't gentle. He wasn't sweet. He was rough as he claimed her mouth, kissing hard. She moaned as he drew her bottom lip between his teeth then fused his mouth to hers.

His stubble rubbed against her chin. She'd have whisker burn later. She longed for the redness, the proof, the evidence of a bruising kiss.

The kiss lit her up. She felt it everywhere—in her toes, in her hair, in her belly.

And, deliciously, between her legs.

She ached for him there. She angled her hips closer as they kissed, desperately seeking contact from him. God, how she wanted him. And she didn't even know his name.

But he knew her body.

He knew her desires.

He held her hands so tightly they might as well be cuffed. In a flash, he changed his grip, wrapping both her wrists in one hand, keeping them pinned behind her back. He moved his free hand to the front of her dress and found his way up her skirt. He broke the kiss as his fingertips brushed above her knee, touching her stockings and her garter. "Are you wet for me, Sophie?"

"Yes," she said on a pant.

"Are you hot for me?" he asked, racing closer to her heat.

"God, yes."

"Was I wrong about anything I told you?"

She shook her head. "No."

"Do you still want to ask me if I'm a good lover?" He flicked his finger against her clit. Ripples of pleasure spread through her body. She inhaled sharply and bit her lip so she wouldn't cry out loud.

"No. I don't need to ask you," she said as he stroked her through her black lace panties.

"Are you sure?"

"I'm sure," she whispered as sparks shot through her bloodstream.

"Why not?" he asked, as if he were truly so damn curious.

"Because you're showing me."

His fingers glided across the wet panel of her panties, stroking faster as she rocked into him. He kept a firm grip on her wrists as she greedily sought his friction. "That's right," he said roughly. "I'm showing you, Sophie. I'm showing you exactly what I can do to you."

He stopped momentarily. Her eyes widened. A trace of fear zipped through her. Fear that he might not let her come. "Did you want to question me again?" he asked, taunting her. "I can stop if you have questions."

"No," she said, her breath staccato.

"Good. But I want to question you."

"Anything," she panted. "Ask me anything."

He fixed her with a serious stare. "Are you sure you want to go out on stage having just come all over my hand?"

"Yes," she said, begging.

He leaned in closer to her ear. "I can't hear you. Say it again."

"Yes, God yes."

He ran his fingers across the wet lace. He narrowed in on her where she wanted him. She was so close to the edge, and she needed him to keep touching her. She needed his fingers flying across her clit. Touching her until she fell apart.

"Beg for it," he commanded.

"*Please*," she whispered in his ear, her knees shaking, so desperate was she for release. "Please make me come."

He rubbed fast and expertly, and she rocked into his hand as bright white fireworks blasted in her brain, radiating throughout her body. Faintly, in the back of her mind, she heard the song nearing the end, and she knew she'd have to come in seconds to make it to the stage on time.

But seconds were all this man needed.

"I want to taste your lips as you fuck my hand," he said, then dropped his delicious mouth to hers once more, kissing her fiercely as she rode his fingers. He wasn't even touching her flesh. He was getting her off through the lace. He was that good. She was that turned on. The tension in her body escalated, rising up like a rollercoaster car nearing the top of the hill. Then she reached it, hovered for beautiful seconds in that suspended state of bliss, then raced downhill as if it was an orgasmic joyride. As her own pleasure crashed into her, he ravaged her mouth with his lips, swallowing her moans, tasting her cries, and somehow it felt like kissing was coming, and coming was kissing.

Only it was more. It was being held back. And that was a hint of all that she craved.

She blinked and breathed hard as he pulled away. He arched an eyebrow, and let go of her wrists. Her skin burned from his grip. She shook her right hand.

Gently, he brought her wrist to his lips. He kissed her softly, reminding her of the first time he kissed her hand on the dance floor as he erased the sting, his lips traveling across the same territory where he'd held her tight moments ago.

"Better?" he asked quietly.

She nodded as he gave the same treatment to her other hand. All these sensations both rattled and delighted her—she didn't know what to make of this man, and how he could talk and touch so rough and harsh in the heat of the moment then become so sweet in the afterglow.

He lowered her hands to her sides then tucked a loose strand of her hair behind her ear. "Beautiful," he said, his eyes softer now as he looked her over.

She smoothed a hand over her dress. Her legs felt wobbly. Her heart roared loudly. Her body still sang.

Clapping echoed loudly from beyond the curtains. The song was over. "Thank you so much," the singer said from the stage.

He tipped his head. "You better get out there."

Nerves took off inside her, then a blast of anger. She was not going to be dismissed. This was not going to be a one-time thing. She grabbed his tie, tugged him close. "Name. Tell me your name."

She expected a sly remark. A hint that gave little away.

"Ryan," he said with a glint in his dark eyes.

She scoffed. "Your name's not Ryan," she fired back as Heaven Leigh said her goodbyes.

"Why not?

"Ryan's a nice guy name."

"Are you saying I'm not a nice guy?"

She shook her head, and curled her hand around his shoulder. "You're not a nice guy at all."

He brought his palm to his chest. "I'm hurt. I'm a terribly nice guy. I saved you from those women who wanted to monopolize you at the bar. And I kissed you when you came so no one heard how orgasmic you were."

"Then why are you leaving?"

"Because you have to go," he said, nodding to the stage.

"And why are you giving me your first name only?"

He brushed his lips against her ear. "What are you doing on Sunday at seven p.m.?"

She practically held her breath at the possibility unfurling before her—that she might see this man another time. "What should I be doing Sunday at seven p.m.?"

"Be at Caesars. Outside the Fizz Bar. I want to see you again." He paused then added, "*Badly.*"

She smiled. She wanted to see him, too. "I'll be there."

She ran her hand along her skirt once more then gently touched her hair, making sure it was still in place. Her heart sped up in worry. She grabbed Ryan's strong arm. "Wait. Is my lipstick smeared?"

He shook his head. "No. It's all gone." He brushed the pad of his thumb along her cheek. Softly. "But you look perfect. Every single thing about you looks perfect."

"Thank you," she said, taking a deep breath as she left.

She walked on the stage, flashing a big, bright smile to the crowd. She thanked Heaven Leigh for singing and then talked about how talented the woman was. As she spoke, she scanned the crowd and caught a last glimpse of the man in the suit, the man who'd made her come backstage. He was on his way out, but he stopped briefly and watched her. He didn't wave. He didn't chuckle. He didn't make a single gesture to say they had a secret.

But the way he stared made her tingle all over, and the way his lips curved up in a grin said he knew he had that effect on her, and that he had every intention of doing it again.

CHAPTER SIX

Ryan gripped the large tree trunk that had fallen on the roof, as his brother finished slicing through the last section of the wood. The chainsaw buzzed loudly in the midday air, then Michael turned it off.

Ryan let go of the wood. Grabbing the waist of his faded gray T-shirt, he wiped the sweat from his brow. His skin was baking under his shirt.

"You think it feels hotter since we're closer to the sun? Being on the roof and all," he asked his brother.

"Absolutely. It's a proven scientific fact that working on someone's roof equates to a ten-degree increase in temperature," Michael said as he set the chainsaw on the tiles, resting it by his feet so it wouldn't topple into the yard.

Ryan rapped his knuckles against the pile of wood they'd chopped from a large tree branch that had fallen on their friend Sanders's roof during a recent windy night. "Now we just need to get this over to green recycling and we're good."

Sanders Foxton was a friend of their father's from long ago. Nearing retirement and damn ready for it, Sanders was a mechanic at the limo company where their father had worked the last few years of his life. Thomas Paige had been on the job the night he was killed, chauffeuring a group of teenagers around town for their prom, first delivering them safely to the dance, then to their homes. Then he'd returned to his house in his own car and was shot four times in the back in his driveway after midnight.

"Did you meet with Winston?" Ryan asked, as they walked to the edge of the roof, stopping when they reached the ladder resting against the house.

"Yeah. But I'm not supposed to tell you a word about what was said," Michael said, miming zipping his lips.

Ryan laughed. "He said that to me, too. But what are the chances that we aren't going to tell each other?" he said, though sometimes he wondered if his siblings had kept secrets from him, as he had from them. Would John Winston be privy to those secrets if they had them? "So what did he ask you?"

With his sunglasses shielding his light blue eyes, Michael answered matter-of-factly. "Same as before. Any new friends. Anything I remember," he said, repeating what the detective had said to Ryan. "But he also asked about Luke."

The hair on Ryan's neck prickled at the mention of their mother's lover, a local piano teacher. "What about him?"

Michael sneered. "Wanted to know what I knew about their relationship. Like I had a clue about the affair. I mean, what the hell? Isn't that the point of an affair? It was all in secret." He made a gesture with his fingers as if he were digging and hiding something.

"Did Winston say he thinks Luke was involved?"

Michael shook his head. "Nah. That man just asks questions. Didn't share any details. And I have no idea if Luke was part of it. They cleared him at the time, so who the heck knows?"

"Got any new theories on why they reopened the case?" They'd already speculated for hours after the detective showed up at Shannon and Brent's wedding celebration at their grandmother's house a week ago and dropped the bomb about the investigation's new life. "It's frustrating that they know something but won't tell us."

Michael pushed down his sunglasses, meeting Ryan's eyes. "Here's the thing. I watch enough police dramas to make a guess. And it's this—I bet they think someone else helped plan the murder."

"You think Mom will get out of prison?" Ryan asked, his voice rising with a touch of hope that he knew would piss off his brother. Michael had cut off their mom. He didn't visit her. Didn't talk to her. Wanted nothing to do with her. Her guilt was crystal clear to Michael.

Ryan understood why, but the world wasn't black and white to him. He'd seen and heard other sides to the story. The side their mom hadn't told anyone else. He couldn't let go of the dream that she'd been framed. That he and his siblings weren't born to a killer.

Michael lifted his chin and scoffed. "Her fingerprints are all over everything. She's not fucking innocent. But there might be someone else who's guilty, too. Murder for hire isn't a to-go order. You don't walk into a store and order a hit with fries on the side." Michael shook his head, as if to chase the thought away. "Now let's get this wood down to your truck."

That was apparently all the discussion Michael wanted to entertain about the investigation. But Ryan wasn't ready to drop the subject. He rarely wanted to drop the issue that had gnawed at him for eighteen years. "You learned that from your police shows?" he asked, teasing his brother.

"Ha ha." Michael rolled his eyes.

"Besides, when do you even have time to watch TV? You're always working."

"That's because my business partner is busy wining and dining," he said, staring sharply at Ryan.

Ryan blew on his fingers as if they were too hot to handle. "What can I say? One of us needs to seal the deals." He pretended to cast a fishing rod and reel in a big one. "Can I help it if I'm just a good people person who knows how to win them over?"

Michael shook his head and laughed. "Get your ass off the roof. I'm hot, and I need a beer."

Ryan hefted a few chunks of wood under his arm. "You let me know when the next episode of *CSI* helps you solve the mystery, 'kay?"

Thirty minutes later, they'd finished loading up the bed of Ryan's truck with the chopped-up tree trunk.

"Damn back," Sanders muttered, one hand parked on the side of the truck door, the other patting his spine in frustration. "But I appreciate you coming by to help out. Couldn't do this without you guys, clearly."

"You know we're always happy to help," Ryan said.

At sixty-one, Sanders was seven years older than their dad would have been if the two men still went out for beers, or to shoot a round of pool as they had done regularly the last few years of his dad's life. But all that time Sanders had spent as a mechanic bent over hoods or under the engine, had taken its toll on the man. With a bad back, and his own sons living in Arizona, he leaned on Ryan and Michael for heavy lifting from time to time. They were happy to help, especially since Sanders had looked out for them. Though they had grandparents who'd raised them during high school, Sanders had remained a close friend, stopping by, checking in, and making sure they knew how to change a tire and check the oil pressure—his way of passing on a part of Thomas Paige after he was gone.

"Let me treat you to a beer," Sanders said, clapping Ryan on the shoulder.

"I'm always game for a brew. And Michael was already hankering for one."

Sanders waggled the salt-and-pepper eyebrows that matched his hair. "Wait 'til you experience the AC in my house. It was on the fritz and I fixed it myself the other day. Replaced the air filter. See, I still can manage a few things all by my studly self."

Ryan laughed. "I bet the missus was impressed that you didn't have to call us on the AC problem," he said as they walked across the front lawn.

The older man winked. "Truth be told, she likes it when you come over. Between you and me, I think she's got a crush on the whole lot of you. Probably had eyes for your dad, too," he said with a no-big-deal shrug, and Ryan couldn't deny that he enjoyed the free and easy way Sanders had of talking about his father. Some people were afraid to mention the deceased. They tiptoed around the family history.

Not Sanders. He talked openly about Thomas Paige, and Ryan had always liked that.

"That wouldn't surprise me," Michael said with a wink. "Our good looks did come from him."

The air was heavy with silence for a brief moment. Because the natural next thing to say would be to mention the traits that came from their mom.

Ryan broke the silence. "Hey, is your wife still pissed about your speeding ticket? You do know they have apps now that tell you where the speed traps are," he said as they reached the side gate to the backyard.

Sanders rolled his eyes. "I know, I know. What can I say? I was getting tired and was eager to get home so I gunned the engine. The highway looked free and clear. You'd think four decades of driving would have taught me better." Ryan had been ribbing Sanders ever since he was nailed by a state trooper in California a month ago. First time ever that the normally cautious driver had landed a speeding ticket.

"They have coffee for that problem. The falling asleep at the wheel one," Michael said as they reached the deck.

Sanders's wife Becky stood by the sliding glass door, shielding her eyes as she waved. "I've got cold beer for my favorite handymen," she said.

"You are the best, Mrs. Foxton," Ryan said. "I'd give you a big hug, but I'm sweaty and gross."

"I'm not," Michael said, elbowing Ryan, as he moved in for an embrace. "I'll hug you."

Sanders stepped in front of both of them.

"Now, now. Keep your mitts off my woman. She'll be liable to leave me for one of you," Sanders said with narrowed eyes. "I'll be the only sweaty man touching her." He draped an arm around his wife and planted a kiss on her cheek. She smiled at him then led them into the house.

Cool air blasted Ryan's hot skin. "This is heaven," he said with a relaxed sigh.

Becky handed beer bottles to Ryan and Michael. "Glad you like it here."

"Now it's really heaven," Michael said, then knocked back some of the beer.

Sanders squeezed his wife's shoulder possessively. "Only four more months 'til I can spend my days drinking beer and sitting on my ass on a lounge chair on the pool deck as we circle the Bahamas."

Becky smiled. "I can't wait. We're going on a cruise for three whole weeks. It's been a dream my whole life."

"Just make sure they don't make you do time for your speeding ticket," Ryan joked.

Sanders seemed to tense, his spine straightening over those words. "Course not. It was just speeding."

"Let's not talk about the trip to California right now," Becky said in a quiet but firm voice that brooked no argument. She turned away, her shoulders rising and falling as she took a deep breath. Ryan glanced briefly at Sanders, who was rubbing his wife's arm, then to his brother. Michael shrugged a shoulder.

Ryan had no clue why the speeding ticket had touched such a nerve for Sanders and Becky.

But the weird glances, the needy reassurance, the mix of worry and admonishment—those were all reminders of why he steered clear of relationships. They were trouble. Women needed soothing and tending to, and those were just not things Ryan was good at.

He was, however, quite good in other areas, and there was a woman who seemed fond of those skills. A woman he'd be seeing tomorrow.

He couldn't fucking wait.

* * *

Ever dapper, always elegant, Holden played the final, jubilant notes in Beethoven's ninth symphony on the grand piano.

Sophie tapped her fingertips against the black lacquer at Holden's apartment overlooking the Mandalay Bay pool. Several stories below, hotel guests drank towering drinks and splashed in the cool water.

"Ta da!" Holden declared with a flourish as he finished the piece, then stood up and bowed deeply. Sophie clapped and shouted *bravo*, giving a one-woman ovation that was loud enough to be worthy of many.

"Thank you, thank you, to all my adoring fans," he said, then blew air kisses to the fictional crowd.

Sophie wrapped her arms around him in a hug. "You're going to be amazing. Though that's not a surprise in the least."

"You really liked it?"

"Liked it? I absolutely loved it. It was…" She let her voice trail off as she searched for just the right word to describe his musical talent. She brought her fingers to her lips like a chef pleased with a dish. "*Magnifique.*"

He sighed happily and beamed, placing his hand on his chest as he mouthed *thank you*. He wore tight blue slacks, loafers, and a crisp, striped button-down. Her ex-husband had achieved some sort of pinnacle in male fashion—he never dressed down.

He was a lot like her.

That was the problem in their marriage.

He was a tad bit too much like Sophie.

He liked clothes, he liked shopping, and he liked kicking back on the couch and gabbing over a glass of chardonnay and a pint of ice cream. No, he wasn't gay. But he wasn't entirely straight either. Which might not make sense to most people. In fact, Sophie hadn't tried to explain the demise of her marriage to "most people" because, one, it was none of their business, and two, they wouldn't understand.

Best friends in high school, she and Holden were perfect for each other. She was the computer geek; he was the music geek. Together, they were two peas in a pod, driven by their passion for machines or instruments. They connected, they laughed, and they had a grand old time. Their easy way together reminded her of what her parents had so nearly missed, if fate hadn't drawn them together again twenty years later.

Sophie had seen the love her parents had, and she didn't want to let it pass her by. Or to wait twenty years for it. So after college, she married her best friend.

It sounded like a great recipe for a successful marriage. Everything between them had gone swimmingly as husband and wife, except in the bedroom. They'd learned they wanted different things from a lover. Fine, lack of bedroom chemistry wasn't the barometer for the success or failure of a marriage, but Sophie didn't excite him, and he didn't excite her, and the things they tried to spice up their love life fell flat.

For instance, the time she'd asked him to pull her hair and talk dirty to her, resulted in him calling her a *hot bitch* a he tugged gently on her strands. He broke into peals of laughter, clutching his belly as he said, "I'm sorry. I just can't say things like *I want you on your hands and knees now, woman.*"

That was where she wanted to be, though.

And that was where he wanted to be, too, because he'd inquired casually one evening over their second pinot noir if she might want to try pegging. They could even go shopping right then, he'd suggested.

Her eyebrows had shot into her hairline as she'd uttered a resounding *never.*

A few weeks later, he'd wanted to know if she'd be willing to have a threesome with another guy.

"Would I be the sandwich filling?" she asked.

He shook his head and tapped his chest. He would be the middle man.

Yup. Her ex-husband went both ways, and when he went, he submitted. Which meant they didn't, and wouldn't, and couldn't ever gel. There was simply no room for two submissives in a marriage.

But was that the right word for her? She didn't really know if the term fit her since she'd never been in that type of relationship. Her experience was limited to Holden and to a college boyfriend who'd been rather "fratty" in bed.

Still, she knew what turned her on. She knew what she fantasized about.

Being dominated. Being taken. Being tied up. Even if she'd never fully experienced that type of lover, she was sure of what made her blood heat up and her body spark. Fantasies tripped through her mind late at night in bed, alone, and they often involved being pinned.

Bound.

Tied.

After struggling to make it work between the sheets, she and Holden had both agreed they'd be better off friends than lovers. The transition away from him wasn't wholly easy, and there had been times when she'd felt unsure of herself and her femininity. But she and Holden made a pact to stay the close friends they had always been.

A talented pianist, Holden had both toured the world and played piano in recording sessions for commercials and jingles, and would be joining the symphony at the concert she'd arranged in two weeks to raise money for the community center. "Do you think Clyde will try to marry you off again at the concert?" Holden asked.

Sophie wrapped her fingers around the edge of the piano. "He's bringing a boy-child to the event. I have no doubt he wants to pawn me off on his lawyer grandson, and he thinks if he can just get us in the same room that we'll fall madly in love."

Holden shuddered dramatically. "Being the *glamorous divorcée,*" he said, stopping to sketch air quotes as he used the moniker that a Vegas high-society blog had bestowed on her, "isn't all it's cracked up to be, is it?"

She swatted his shoulder. "You're a glamorous divorcé, too."

"Oh yeah. They're lining up in droves for a piece of me," he said with a wink.

Piece of me. Her mind flashed back to a few nights ago at Aria, and to the commanding way Ryan Whoever He Was had controlled her pleasure backstage. A frisson of longing raced through her. She craved his touch again.

"Hello? Did you just drift off to la-la land?" Holden asked, waving his hand in front of her.

She blinked, and grinned, caught in the act of remembering a hot encounter. "I did. Because I met someone the other night, and we had a fantastic time."

Holden patted the piano bench. "Sit. Tell me everything."

Sophie sat on the bench and recounted the details. Not all of them. Not the particularly naughty ones. But the tidbits about how they met, and how he showed up at the gala, and how she barely knew anything about him.

"Which I like," she added. Perhaps she liked it so much because it was the opposite of her experience. She'd known everything about Holden, she'd gone in with her eyes wide open, and they hadn't worked out.

She knew virtually nothing of Ryan. Maybe the change was what she needed. To go into this thing blindfolded.

Wait. Add that to the list of things she wanted to try. *Blindfold.*

"Be careful," Holden said in warning. "He could be anyone."

"That's why it's fun."

"That's also why it's dangerous."

She nodded. "I know. I like danger."

"I just don't want to see you get hurt," he said, patting her knee.

"It's only fun and games. I'm not interested in anything more. In fact, I hope I never learn his last name," she said as she crossed her legs and kicked a foot back and forth, demonstrating how completely content she'd be in that scenario.

Even though, truth be told, she was terribly curious about the man behind the orgasm.

CHAPTER SEVEN

So many sartorial choices.

On the one hand, this sun-yellow dress hugged her hips quite nicely.

On the other hand, the red one with the tiny white polka dots did offer a nice little cleavage peek-a-boo.

As Sophie tapped her finger against her lips, weighing the options for tonight in her perfectly organized, neatly arranged, color-coordinated closet, her phone buzzed from the back pocket of her capris. She was at home, so jeans were acceptable.

She grabbed it and spotted an envelope icon popping up at the top of the screen. Probably nothing that needed her attention now, midday Sunday, especially, since she had a whole sea of clothes to consider in the middle of her walk-in closet, which was something of a sanctuary in her home.

Because…*walk-in closet.*

Complete with carpeting and ample shelves for shoes.

Enough said.

Absently, she ran her thumb across the screen, noticing the time as she scrolled. Seven more hours until her date.

Four hundred and twenty minutes. Twenty-five thousand and two hundred seconds.

Whoa.

Was that her date's name in her email?

Perhaps this email warranted her undivided attention after all. As she opened it, her belly flipped, her body lighting up simply from the intoxicating memory of his backstage skills.

from: guywithgreentie@gmail.com
to: Sophiefashionista@gmail.com
date: July 14, 11:58 AM
subject: Question

Are you afraid of heights?

A grin spread quickly across her face. She hadn't expected to hear from him until she saw him this evening. He must have found her email address on her Facebook profile. She liked that he'd been hunting for her. She liked it a lot.

from: Sophiefashionista@gmail.com
to: guywithgreentie@gmail.com
date: July 14, 12:01 PM
subject: Lovely to hear from you too…

No. Should I be? Are you, say, taking me to the moon?

from: guywithgreentie@gmail.com
to: Sophiefashionista@gmail.com
date: July 14, 12:08 PM
subject: I couldn't wait 'til tonight...

I will indeed be taking you on that kind of a trip.

from: Sophiefashionista@gmail.com
to: guywithgreentie@gmail.com
date: July 14, 12:10 PM
subject: Glad to hear you're counting down the hours...

How can you be so confident?

from: guywithgreentie@gmail.com
to: Sophiefashionista@gmail.com
date: July 14, 12:14 PM
subject: Six hours, forty-six minutes

Because I've already taken you there.

from: Sophiefashionista@gmail.com
to: guywithgreentie@gmail.com
date: July 14, 12:19 PM
subject: Wait. I know what you have in mind.

Admit it. We're going for a hot air balloon ride over the Strip, right?

from: guywithgreentie@gmail.com
to: Sophiefashionista@gmail.com
date: July 14, 12:21 PM
subject: Nice guess, but…

Or maybe I plan to take you on the rollercoaster at New York, New York.

from: Sophiefashionista@gmail.com
to: guywithgreentie@gmail.com
date: July 14, 12:25 PM
subject: Flaw in that plan

Then why are we meeting at Caesar's?

from: guywithgreentie@gmail.com
to: Sophiefashionista@gmail.com
date: July 14, 12:31 PM
subject: The plan for tonight is perfect.

To throw you off the scent of my plan. Because I suspect you like surprises. And rollercoasters, too.

from: Sophiefashionista@gmail.com
to: guywithgreentie@gmail.com
date: July 14, 12:32 PM
subject: I like the best laid plans…pun intended

So now we're going for a rollercoaster ride. Excellent. I'm clapping with glee.

Incidentally, I'm quite loud on rollercoasters.

* * *

Good thing he was alone in his office.

The subject line made him groan.

The prospect of hearing her orgasmic cries of pleasure at full volume had his dick knocking against his fly. Closing his eyes briefly, he imagined the sounds she might make, the cries and moans and gasps he'd elicit from her. She'd be sweet music to his ears.

Now, he was hard as steel. Fucking great.

He was tempted to take matters into his own hand. But he was a thirty-two-year-old man, not a teenage boy ready to jack off to the slightest provocation from his computer screen. Ryan was patient and controlled, and as much as he wanted to experience those *best laid plans* he didn't intend for *that* to happen tonight. Not for lack of desire. But because anticipation was the most powerful kind of foreplay. Waiting, teasing, and wanting made the *doing* better.

It made the fucking practically divine.

He'd only intended to send one note to make sure she could handle heights. But that one note had turned into a volley that made him even more eager to see her. Each appearance of her name in his email inbox turned him on. As he finished up some work, they continued to ping-pong over cyberspace.

from: guywithgreentie@gmail.com
to: Sophiefashionista@gmail.com
date: July 14, 12:35 PM
subject: If your intention was hardness, well done.

I have not yet had the pleasure of hearing the highs you can hit vocally. You came quietly the other night.

from: Sophiefashionista@gmail.com
to: guywithgreentie@gmail.com
date: July 14, 12:38 PM
subject: That's how I like it.

And is that something you wish to know? My vocal range? Rather than my silent cries of pleasure?

from: guywithgreentie@gmail.com
to: Sophiefashionista@gmail.com
date: July 14, 12:41 PM
subject: High C, I'm betting

It's not just something I wish to know. It's something I intend to discover tonight.

from: Sophiefashionista@gmail.com
to: guywithgreentie@gmail.com
date: July 14, 12:44 PM
subject: Bet on several full octaves

I suppose it is in your hands then to find out how high I go.

from: guywithgreentie@gmail.com
to: Sophiefashionista@gmail.com
date: July 14, 12:49 AM
subject: My ears are eager now

Hands, maybe. Could be other parts of the anatomy.

from: Sophiefashionista@gmail.com
to: guywithgreentie@gmail.com
date: July 14, 12:51 PM
subject: And other parts are more eager?

Now, Ryan, I don't know that we're going *there* just yet.
I might want you to work more for that.

from: guywithgreentie@gmail.com
to: Sophiefashionista@gmail.com
date: July 14, 12:52 AM
subject: Eager and at attention

Going where, Sophie? Where are we not going? Can
you spell it out?

from: Sophiefashionista@gmail.com
to: guywithgreentie@gmail.com
date: July 14, 12:54 PM
subject: B-E-L-O-W-T-H-E-B-E-L-T

That. Part. The one I felt pressed against me, hard as a
rock.

* * *

Sophie had moved to her comfy, king-size bed, a book in one hand, the phone in the other, ready for the zing that ripped through her body with each note from Ryan. As she peeked at her inbox periodically, in between reading a biography of Mick Jagger, gooseflesh rose on her skin from the excitement of the back and forth. Ah, to flirt like this. Everything inside her tingled, as if she'd just drunk champagne and had become as effervescent as the drink.

Another note appeared, and she set down Mick's story, flipped to her belly, kicked her feet in the air, and continued the email foreplay.

from: guywithgreentie@gmail.com
to: Sophiefashionista@gmail.com
date: July 14, 12:58 PM
subject: T-O-N-G-U-E-S?

Or maybe we will be going to places that make you sing like you're high up at the top of the rollercoaster. Perhaps, I should amend my plans for tonight and take you on that rollercoaster ride after all.

On second thought, I'm just going to keep the plans to myself and surprise you.

from: Sophiefashionista@gmail.com
to: guywithgreentie@gmail.com
date: July 14, 1:01 PM
subject: Like I'm going in blindfolded

I like rides.

from: guywithgreentie@gmail.com
to: Sophiefashionista@gmail.com
date: July 14, 1:06 PM
subject: My favorite accessory

Speaking of fashion, wear a skirt tonight.

She laughed out loud at the last email. As if she'd wear anything but a skirt. She was about to reply with something saucy when another note dropped into her inbox.

from: guywithgreentie@gmail.com
to: Sophiefashionista@gmail.com
date: July 14, 1:07 PM
subject: Name, rank and serial number

On a more serious note, it's not right for me to know your name and occupation and you to not know the same. Not in this day and age. So, here's me.

Sophie hovered her index finger over the link at the end of the note.

The game had been fun, almost like a masquerade ball. Now, he had changed the game and removed his mask. Asking her if she wanted to look.

How could she not?

Sophie was a cat in front of an open box. The cat had no choice but to slink inside, and explore its contents. That man had sparked her mind and ignited her body, and hell, it was natural to want to know more about him. So from the cozy cocoon of gold and cranberry-red pillows on her bed, she clicked on the link to his company.

Sloan Protection Resources.

The web site had a rugged, sturdy and masculine look with black and gray colors and imposing fonts. Completely fitting with what it was selling—armed private security, event security, bodyguards, guard dogs, and more. The "mission" on the home page read: "We provide secure solutions to a wide range of individuals, corporations, nonprofit organizations and government customers. We are committed to helping businesses and individuals operate in a safe and secure environment that will enable them to prosper."

Interesting.

Sophie vaguely wondered if any of her event organizers had relied on Sloan Protection Resources. Or if some of her wealthiest benefactors did. She suspected the answer was yes, and that she and Ryan Sloan trafficked in the same circles even though they hadn't met until the other day.

She clicked on the About Us section, and was greeted by a photo that made her heart stutter and other parts heat up.

The picture was of two strong, tall men—clearly related —in suits, with arms crossed and serious looks on their faces. Sophie's eyes were drawn to Ryan, with his light brown hair, a slight wave to it, his eyes like night, and the firm, strong, toned body that the suit didn't even try to hide. That man just knew how to wear sharp-dressed garb. He was tailor-made for the part of strong, sexy businessman.

A murmur fell from her lips as she brushed her fingertip across his image. He was so fucking hot.

Clicking on his name, she jumped to another page and found his bio.

Ryan Sloan is one of the founders of Sloan Protection Resources. A native of Las Vegas, Ryan attended University of Michigan where he played for the hockey team. After graduating with a bachelor's degree in history, he spent five years in the army, completing his service as a captain, like his brother Michael. The two of them founded Sloan Protection Resources six years ago. Together they are committed to ensuring the highest level of safety for clients, and rely on trained teams of former law enforcement, military, and security professionals who are state certified and skilled in the latest tools and tactics.

Sophie's grin spread along with a burst of warmth through her chest. That was just…sexy.

And hot.

And so very dominant.

from: Sophiefashionista@gmail.com
to: guywithgreentie@gmail.com
date: July 14, 1:28 PM
subject: The more you know…

Thank you. And your bio sure makes you sound hot. Good thing I know you can back it up with your talented fingers. And possibly other instruments. See you tonight.

from: guywithgreentie@gmail.com
to: Sophiefashionista@gmail.com
date: July 14, 1:37 PM
subject: Five hours, twenty-three minutes

Still can't wait.

from: Sophiefashionista@gmail.com
to: guywithgreentie@gmail.com
date: July 14, 1:41 PM
subject: One more thing…

What if I don't wear a skirt?

He never answered her last note.

CHAPTER EIGHT

Sophie was early for once.

Only because she told herself over and over that their date started an hour sooner. She'd even set the alarm on her phone to leave her building at five-thirty, which gave her the necessary thirty minutes to walk to Ceasar's and make it to the Fizz Bar, and then keep herself entertained outside it playing the slots as she waited.

She didn't want to be late for her date, so she'd tricked her own overactive mind.

Now, the little hand on the clock had landed on seven. On the dot.

"I see you didn't take my advice to heart."

At her perch at the Wizard of Oz slot machine that had been occupying her restless fingers and seconds-counting mind, Sophie's lips quirked up in a wicked grin as the deep, sexy voice of her date landed in her ears. She turned around and drank in the sight of Ryan Sloan, who looked just as lickable minus the tie and tailored suit she'd seen him in for their first encounter. Tonight he wore crisp, charcoal pants that showed off a fantastic ass, the kind you could bounce a quarter off of, and a white button-down that demanded to be unbuttoned. Such a simple look, but such a sexy one. Casual, but classy.

"Perhaps I was feeling a little defiant," she said playfully, taking the time to cross her legs and show off the skinny jeans that she wore, in direct disobedience of his skirt request.

For some reason the prospect of going against his fashion wishes had felt like naughty mischief, and naughty mischief was irresistible.

She looked away from him and pressed the button once more on the one-armed bandit, hoping for a trio of glittery red slippers. "Over the Rainbow" played as the reel spun, and Sophie awaited her line-up, eager for a winning jackpot. No such luck. Sliding into place were a tin man, a lion, and a wicked witch, who cackled in mockery. Sophie pouted. "I guess my luck has run out on this machine. Are you a bad luck charm?" she teased as she glanced up at her too-handsome-to-be-believed date.

Ryan's hand came down on her neck firmly, but his voice matched her light-hearted tone. "I don't mind your defiance," he said, returning to her earlier comment. "As long as you don't mind having to wait longer now for all the good things I have planned for you."

Instantly, her brain was awash with images, fantasies, and filthy scenarios she'd only dreamed of. She wanted *all the good things*.

"What sort of good things?" she asked, shivering as he touched her, his big palm wrapping around her neck. She closed her eyes as he traveled up to her nape. He threaded his fingers in her hair, gripping her locks. She tensed. His hand was sending a message, one that his mouth made abundantly clear when he bent his head to her ear and spoke.

"The kind that a skirt makes possible," he said as he tugged her head back so she had to stare up at him.

"You don't like the way I look in jeans?"

"I love the way you look in anything because you're extraordinary to look at, and even more phenomenal to touch. But I especially like the *access* your skirts give me." His lips were mere millimeters from her ear. He flicked his tongue against her earlobe, and she gasped. Then he drew the soft flesh into his teeth and bit. A burst of excitement whipped through her from his touch. Holden had never bitten her like this. Not with a sense of ownership.

Ryan ran a hand along the bare skin of her arm, on display in her black blouse with cap sleeves. The sheer material revealed a tight, lacy camisole underneath, which pushed up her breasts, showcasing ample cleavage.

"Maybe I wanted to make sure you didn't forget about other parts of me," she said, casting her gaze down her chest, letting him follow.

Ryan laughed deeply then shook his head, seemingly in admiration of the view. He let go of his firm hold and kissed her neck, a soft and unbearably sexy kiss. She nearly squirmed on the plush red stool parked in front of the gambling machine. "Sophie, there's not a chance in hell I'd forget those gorgeous breasts, and I plan on getting better acquainted with them. Maybe even fucking them," he said, as he dragged a finger along the bare flesh of her chest, and she nearly moaned out loud at the prospect of being fucked in the valley of her breasts by this dirty, dominating man. "Would you like that?"

She nodded as heat flared through her system. "I believe I would," she whispered.

"Excellent. Because I believe I would like to do that to you. There are many things I want to do to you, and I always want you to feel good."

"I'd say you're meeting your goal because so far it's all good," she said, pausing before she added, "*Quite* good."

He grinned. "And you should always tell me what you like and don't like. Does that work for you?"

"Yes." Anticipation bloomed inside her as they made some sort of impromptu pact, it seemed, to govern their pleasure.

"And I'll do the same," he said, bending closer to her head as he ran his nose along her hair, inhaling her scent. He murmured as he touched her, then kissed a curl on the side of her face. "Like right now when I tell you I really don't like that you didn't listen to me. And do you know what that means?"

She raised an eyebrow. She'd never experienced this sort of cat-and-mouse play before. By wearing jeans in defiance, had she violated some unwritten rule of the tie-me-up-and-take-me game? A squadron of nerves docked in her belly, and she wished she had more experience with men like Ryan. Her knowledge of the opposite sex was woefully limited, and while she wasn't innocent by any degree, she felt a bit like a wide-eyed woman recently freed from an unusual marriage and thrust into an unknown battlefield with this intense, commanding man.

That was the point, of course. Still, she was a traveler wandering through a lush new land without a map.

Whether she'd been *disobedient* or not, this back-and-forth they had going was intoxicating, especially since they were in public, ensconced in the middle of the Caesar's Palace slot machines, amid the whir and jingle of imaginary coins falling as gamblers hunted for payouts in the games of chance.

The cowardly lion roared idly from her game, trying to entice her to play another round. She ignored it.

"No. Tell me tell me what it means," she said, turning to face him and running her lacquered fire-engine red nails along his arm. She could feel the outline of his muscles, his strong biceps, his steely forearms, through the fabric of his shirt. "I'm dying to know."

"You want to know?"

She nodded, keeping her gaze firmly fixed on his. His midnight blue eyes were hungry. He looked as if he wanted to eat her. "Are you going to spank me?"

"Would you like that?"

A shiver of anticipation ran across her skin. "I think I would," she said in a whisper.

He knitted his brow. "You think? You don't know?"

She shook her head, biting her lip. "I've never been spanked."

He let out a low whistle of regret. "That's a damn shame, because you have a highly spankable ass. But this is music to my ears, because I fully intend to break it in," he said as he moved his hand down her back along the fabric of her shirt, heading in the direction of her, evidently, quite spankable ass.

"I suspect I'd like your hands on my ass," she said, and he groaned—a sexy, dirty rumble that turned her on. "So are you going to spank me on the rollercoaster? The hot air balloon? Or your secret hidden jet that you'll be piloting tonight?"

"None of the above. You're going to have to wait for all the good things now. That's what happens when you don't listen."

"Ah, so that's my punishment for my impudence. How long must I wait?"

He offered her a hand and pulled her up from her stool. "Until you're wearing a skirt," he answered crisply, and her eyes lit up as she stood facing him. She thrilled inside that he'd called her on this. The stern look in his gaze said he was serious, and that he could wait for her to change. He'd be waiting a lot less than he thought.

"Right now though, I want to spend some time getting to know you. That's why I bought tickets to the High Roller," he said, mentioning the Ferris wheel nearby. "So I can chat with you as we ride. Because you're far too classy a woman for me to get you off in front of all the other people riding in our pod."

"Why thank you for opting not to get me off in a pod. But you know it's become a *thing* in Vegas now, trying to have sex on the Ferris wheel."

He nodded. "Yeah, and most people get busted. There's a difference between trying to get a tacky, tasteless notch on your public sex belt, and knowing how to pleasure a woman in public so that you're the only one who knows she's about to fall apart in your arms."

"And I trust you know the difference?"

He cupped her cheek, drawing her face near to his so his nose touched hers. How was it possible that touching noses was sexy? Even an Eskimo kiss from this man made her sizzle. Then his words scorched her imagination as he said, "What I know, Sophie, is exactly what I want to do to you. And you'll just have to wait to find out."

He grazed his lips against hers, and she murmured as she melted into his touch. Their first kiss at the gala had been hungry and demanding. Ferocious and possessive. This was a soft, slow, unhurried kiss. It was an exploration, as his mouth caressed hers and her body turned soft and pliant under his touch. His kisses were velvet. They were melting chocolate. They were delicious appetizers at the most fantastic restaurant, the kind that made you roll your eyes in pleasure and want so much more.

His touch turned her into a weak-kneed, hazy-headed, buzzing-head-to-toe woman who wanted him. As he laced his fingers through her hair and held the back of her head in his hand, she gave herself over to him, letting him have her however he wanted.

When they separated, he whispered. "But kisses in public are good. They show everyone you're with me tonight, and that turns me on—having you with me." His tone, too, sounded thoroughly possessive. Then he laughed. "Which means I better sit and play a round, otherwise I'll be walking around with a raging hard-on."

He parked himself on the stool. In a flash, he pulled her back to him so she was seated on his lap. "Mmm," she said, wriggling against his erection. "Not sure this is going to help get rid of the issue."

He gripped her hips, the pressure pulling her down against his dick so she could feel his hard length lining up perfectly against her ass. Damn, he felt good.

He stretched out his arm and pressed the button on the machine. "Maybe you're *my* lucky charm."

She crossed her fingers in the air as they waited for the reel to roll through thousands upon thousands of permutations, and Sophie rocked her rear, subtly, but insistently, against his crotch. His breath hitched. He dug his thumbs harder into her hip bones, as if he needed to hold on to survive having her on his lap.

The reel slowed. One ruby red slipper. Then another. Sophie's shoulders tensed in anticipation and hope. "Please let it be another slipper," she murmured. She sighed when a witch's broom busted their chances. "Damn," she muttered.

"I don't mind losing. We can just play here all evening because I like the way you feel sitting on me."

"You'll get no complaints from me. But we don't want to miss the High Roller."

He glanced at his watch. "We have time."

They played a few more rounds, losing every one. But it didn't matter, because his arms were wrapped around her waist, and he held her close in his lap, a delicious start to her second rendezvous with this man who was not as much of a mystery as he'd been the first night, but who was now even more enticing. Perhaps it was knowing his name, or maybe it was the email exchange earlier. It might even be the naughty compliments he never ceased raining down on her. Any and all of the above drew her in.

"How's your dog?" she asked as the sound of a tornado grew louder from the machine. Dorothy's home was churning in the cyclone during this spin.

He chuckled. "You remembered I have a dog."

She rolled her eyes. "Of course I do. You had to walk him. He's a demanding Border Collie. Is he totally adorable?"

"Ha. I suppose. Mostly I just think of him as badass."

"Got any pictures?"

He shook his head. "No, but if you're a good girl, I'll send you one."

"All the more reason to be good," she quipped. "What's his name?"

"Johnny Cash," he said, with the swagger it called for.

"That is a cool name."

"He is a cool dog. Loyal. Smart. Devoted. And a great listener."

"Sounds perfect. How'd you pick it?"

"My dad's favorite musician."

"Is your dad in town?"

Ryan shook his head. Sophie looked back at him. A kind of darkness had descended over him. She processed quickly that he hadn't used a verb when talking about his father. "Oh, I'm sorry. Is he gone?"

Ryan nodded.

She sighed wistfully. "Mine, too. Both my parents died two years ago."

He squeezed her arm affectionately. "Sorry to hear that."

"Actually, they were both older. Not terribly old, but late seventies. They met in their late thirties and had us in their early forties. They died within three months of each other. They were ridiculously in love even till the end."

"I can't imagine," he said, his voice hollow. The empty sound made her want to ask why he couldn't imagine loving someone until the end of your life. But it was too soon to press. Besides, she wasn't even sure she wanted to know his answer. Better not to go there. She danced away from this topic, returning to more comfortable second date terrain as she pointed at the pair of flying monkeys that had landed in the last spin, alongside a shiny red apple.

"So, Ryan Sloan, former army captain, now head of Sloan Protection Resources…Flying monkeys." She tapped the screen. "Your verdict—are they fearsome or comical?"

He laughed, and in that sound the tension deflated. "Absolutely fucking terrifying. When I was a kid I ran from the room every time the flying monkeys came on." Then he squeezed the side of her rear lightly. "We should head to the High Roller."

She stood up from her seat on his lap and held up a finger. "Give me two minutes."

With her purple leather purse on her shoulder, she popped into the ladies room at the other end of the slots, shimmied out of her jeans, and slid into a short, flowy pink skirt that hit her just above the knees and offered a perfect amount of lift if she twirled. She folded her jeans in half, then tightly rolled them and stuffed them into a side compartment of her purse.

She returned to Ryan.

And twirled once.

His jaw dropped when he saw her change-up.

"See? I'm not all naughty. I can be a good listener," she said with a flirty tilt of her head, as she jutted out her hip and ran her hands along the outside of the pink skirt with the white polka dots.

"You're the perfect amount of naughty," he said, his voice smoky as he drank her in from head to toe, from her black patent leather heels with the strap across her instep, to the bare legs, to the revealing blouse. "You're going to be rewarded so well for doing as you were told."

CHAPTER NINE

With a hand on her lower back, he guided her past the lines at the High Roller Ferris Wheel and straight to the head of the VIP queue. One of the highest Ferris wheels in the world, the ride circled to more than five hundred feet in the air and offered a majestic view of the skyline and bright neon lights of the city.

The attendant opened the door to one of the space agey, glass-encased pods. Ryan and Sophie weren't alone in the spacious capsule with the panoramic view, but it wasn't crowded either. They staked a claim at one end of the oval, and Ryan leaned his hip against the railing, facing his date.

His stunning, gorgeous, sexy, naughty, and sweet date.

Soon, the observation wheel began to move, slowly rising higher as each capsule filled with passengers on the first revolution. "Hope you didn't mind too much that I sent you my bio. That, coupled with my dog's name, means you know everything there is to know about me," he joked.

"Absolutely. I can't think of a single other thing that I'd be curious about."

He wiped a hand across his brow as if to say *whew*. "Okay, so we're done then with the résumé basics and we can move on to favorite TV shows and movies, then?"

She laughed, a bright and pretty sound that seemed to match her personality and her bold sense of style. Not that he was well versed in women's fashion, but the way this woman dressed caught his eye and sparked his imagination. She had a va-va-voom look to her that was his kryptonite. She was all gorgeous, sexy, voluptuous woman, and knew how to show off her assets.

He couldn't look away from her if he tried.

"Actually, I think someone's favorite show can be quite telling. I wouldn't mind knowing yours," she said, then did that utterly sexy thing she'd done at the slot machine, where she ran her hand along his arm. Okay, it wasn't like some signature move or anything. But the combination of her long nails, the glint in her blue eyes, along with the wild flirtatiousness in her tone, turned him on something fierce.

As she'd done from the second he met her.

"*Top Gear*," he answered easily.

"You like fast cars."

He nodded. "I do. And it's just a kick-ass show."

"I bet you'd like to drive my Aston Martin someday," she said, brushing her fingertips over his bicep now.

He nodded eagerly. "I'd love to get behind the wheel of that baby. What about you?"

"My favorite show?"

He shrugged happily. This was a simple enough topic. "Sure. Tell me."

"*Mad Men* for the fashion," she said, counting off one finger. "Dancing competition shows because they're gorgeous to watch. And *Orange is the New Black* because it reminds me to always be a good girl."

He forced a laugh at the last one and decided not to touch it, even though he was tempted to make a dirty comment about being a good girl. But he couldn't chance any conversation drifting into this territory—the behind bars territory. He returned to the middle choice. "My sister is a choreographer. She's done some work on a reality dance show."

Sophie arched an eyebrow. "Ooh! Which one?"

"*Dance All Night*," he said, naming the show that Shannon had worked on.

Her eyes lit up. "Get out of here!" She slugged his arm.

He ran his hand over the spot where she'd hit him, pretending it hurt. "Ouch."

"I'll kiss it and make it better," she said, planting a quick kiss on his arm. Damn, that felt good, even through the fabric of his shirt. She raised her face. "I absolutely adore *Dance All Night*. Tell her that her work is amazing. Please, please, please tell her that. There's a one-night reunion show coming up, and I already have it marked on my calendar to make sure I don't schedule anything else that night."

Ryan's grin spread, anticipating Sophie's next reaction. "I know about the reunion. She's choreographing that, too. My sister is Shay Sloan. She runs Shay Productions," he said, using Shannon's business name. Their capsule reached the midway point in its rise. More hotels and landmarks came into view, dotting the darkening sky with their blazing lights—the top of the Stratosphere, the Eiffel Tower on The Paris, and the pink neon edging The Flamingo.

Sophie grabbed his arm, wrapping her fingers around it and squeezing hard. "Are you kidding me? I *love* her shows. I've seen the live ones, too. I saw her show at the Wynn. Please tell her I'm a huge fangirl."

"I will," he said, and the words surprised him. He didn't usually discuss his romantic life with his sister, or his two brothers, either. He didn't usually date anyone long enough to mention her to the most important people in his life—his siblings. So it was odd that he'd easily entertained the thought of telling Shannon about Sophie's adoration of her work. Odder still—talking about his family with Sophie didn't make him want to run for the hills. Even when they'd landed on the topic of his father earlier, he hadn't shut down as he normally would. Because Ryan didn't share pieces of himself with women. He didn't like to get close. He didn't do relationships.

It was weird not to be breaking out in hives right now.

"I wish I knew how to dance," Sophie said wistfully. "I have absolutely no skills in that arena whatsoever. I'm pretty sure I can't even manage a basic foxtrot."

He leaned in and whispered, "Confession: I don't even know what a foxtrot is. Besides, I think you danced pretty damn fine with me the other night."

"Dancing with you was easy. I just aimed to press my body as close as I could."

"Good rule of thumb. Keep it up, because you feel spectacular pressed up against me," he said.

"Imagine how spectacular I'd feel…" she began, then let her voice trail off as she danced her fingers down the front of his shirt and whispered, "…*naked.*"

He drew in a hiss and narrowed his eyes. "You are too tempting." It was a warning, even though it was an invitation, too.

"I think you like being tempted by me," she answered, licking her lips.

The pressure in his pants said he liked it far too much. He was so damn hard there was no breathing room for his dick. Especially when his eyes landed on her pouty red lips, which would look so good wrapped around him. Her red lips meeting his dick... He nearly groaned out loud. He wanted that so badly. Wanted it from her. He couldn't imagine anything hotter than her gorgeous head bobbing up and down between his legs.

He shoved a hand through his hair, as if that would reroute his brain and discourage this inconvenient erection. "Talk about something else," he instructed with a huff.

She nodded. "So you've got one sister, and you have a brother, too, your bio said. Three of you?"

Ah, nothing like family to make an erection vanish. He held up four fingers as the pod rose higher into the night, creating the illusion of floating above the brightly lit city and its landmark skyline. "Shay"—he used his sister's public name—"and Colin are twins. There are four of us. Michael and I run the security firm. Shay is the choreographer, and Colin is a venture capitalist. He lives here, too."

"You all have fascinating jobs. That's so cool. And sounds like you're close."

He nodded. That was the understatement of a lifetime. In spite of his secrets, the four of them were as tight as any set of siblings could ever be. Their history, and their tragedy, had cemented their bond. The four of them had come to rely on each other, as well as the grandparents who had raised them after their mother was sent to prison.

"We're very close," he echoed, twisting his index finger around the middle one as if to show the connection between the Sloans.

"I'm close to my brother, too. Especially since it's the two of us now. He's here in Vegas as well."

"Oh, is he?" Ryan asked, keeping his voice even and normal, as if he'd just learned this fact for the very first time.

"I basically adore him, even though I love to give him a hard time about his job and his co-workers."

"Bet he enjoys that," he said with a wink, feeling only the slightest bit weasely. But she'd offered up the brother details; he was merely making a safe remark that didn't give himself away.

Sophie laughed. "Drives him crazy. He's a detective with Metro so it's all very macho and guy-centric at his office."

Ryan drew on his best *isn't that interesting* face. "That must be an intense job."

"Intense definitely describes John. He's a total workaholic. Honestly, he doesn't even have to work as much as he does. He chooses to."

"What do you mean? Doesn't have to?"

"He was my primary investor. He funded my company with his savings account. Basically everything he'd ever had as a kid—from the jobs he worked, from his neighborhood lemonade stand, from money gifts from relatives on birthdays—everything. He put it into my company when I started it—he was the seed investor. So when I sold it, he profited, too. I joked that he could retire like me, but he said *never.* He has too much work to do putting criminals behind bars."

A tight line of tension coiled through him. Ryan wasn't a criminal, but he'd been born to a woman branded as one. "He sounds pretty driven," he said, doing his best to refrain from prying. The less he said the better off he'd be if Sophie ever found out he'd had business with her brother. Not that she would. He didn't date anyone long enough to meet her family.

She lowered her voice to the barest thread as they reached the top of the observation wheel. "John had a good friend who was an innocent bystander, shot in a drive-by gang shooting when we were younger."

"That's terrible," Ryan said, a dose of rage coursing through him. He knew far too well what it felt like to lose someone to a bullet. "How old?"

"David was fourteen when it happened. Same as John," she said, her voice breaking a bit. "He was a good friend of all of ours."

Ryan gripped her hand tighter, and then instinct told him to drop a quick, comforting kiss on her forehead. Her skin was so soft. "I'm sorry," he whispered. "I was fourteen when—"

He cut himself off. Damn near kicked himself, too. What the hell? Ryan didn't go around offering up bits and pieces of his family story. He didn't run the motor mouth and say *I was fourteen when my dad was killed by a gang gunman, too.* He'd already shared more about his father than he ever did at this point. He couldn't believe he'd been about to say more.

Something about this woman, maybe her willingness to share little details of her life, was working its way under his skin and tricking him into offering up more than he liked to.

Good thing Ryan had no intention of getting any closer to her, or to any woman. Closeness led to commitment, and commitment led to resentment, and resentment led to losing your parents when you were fourteen. And that led to your head and your heart being fucked forever by not knowing who to trust, or who to believe. To your mother telling you over and over that she didn't do it even as the cops arrested her, and the jury sentenced her for murder for hire.

And worst of all, it meant your father became just faded photographs and memories that blurred around the edges. Ryan was left with only faint reminders of camping trips with his dad, and days spent traipsing around Vegas with him, checking out the new additions to the Strip.

"Fourteen when…?" she asked leadingly. "Oh, when your dad passed away?"

Sophie was giving him a way out, unknowingly providing a safe landing. Hell, he needed one, given the way his mind had been spiraling, turning his insides into a treacherous knot. He nodded. "And your brother lost his friend around that age?"

She clasped her hand over her mouth and squeezed her eyes shut. Uh-oh. He must have said something wrong. "Oh God. I'm so sorry," she said when she opened her eyes. "I didn't mean to imply David was killed. I should have been more clear. David's paralyzed, though, which is still pretty sad."

"Yeah. Definitely. And all because of a drive-by shooting," he said, shaking his head in disgust. No faking emotion there.

"It was some kind of retaliation shooting over territory. That's what really drove John to become a detective. Our dad was a fruit salesman, of all things," she said with a laugh. "Fruit salesmen don't usually have cops for sons. But then this happened to John's best friend, and it led him to want to clean up the streets."

Ryan couldn't help but wonder if John had a personal stake in the investigation of his father's murder, if the gang connection had caught his eye because of his own goal to rid the town of street gangs. If that was the case, John must be betting on his dad's murder having deeper threads to the Royal Sinners.

Shit.

His gut churned, his emotions yanked in too many directions. Desire to know more warred with the need to backpedal from this discussion.

"That is some heavy stuff," he said, staying vague. Even if he wasn't poking and prodding, he should know better than to try to pry. Than to try to glean a little bit of intel about the detective.

But when your mom's in prison, and your dad's in the ground, and the men in charge think someone else might be involved, you don't always do the right thing. Sometimes you poke. "I bet he has some stories about what he's seen," he said then wanted to zip his mouth closed for having led the witness.

"He hardly tells me anything. But when he does it's usually laced with skepticism," Sophie said, tucking a strand of hair that had fallen loose behind her ear. So strange to have this conversation there in the tourist attraction wheel circling the city, surrounded by people chattering and watching the night fly past the glass windows.

"Why's that?"

"Detectives are naturally skeptical. It's their job."

"Ah. Of course," he said, and a bead of guilt gathered in his veins as he let Sophie continue to talk freely.

"Think about it. They spend their days getting lied to. Lied to by suspects. By criminals. Even by family members. Almost all of the people they interact with hold back. No one ever offers a full truth to a detective. If someone rolls over, for instance, he's only ever doing it to protect himself, because he has information that might lessen his own crime. Not for altruism." She pinned him with a sharp gaze as she made her point, and the guilt inside him stirred. "Or take the case of the drive-by shooting. When detectives questioned the people who lived in the house that was the target, they said they knew nothing and heard nothing, even though there were bullet holes in their window. But the gang guys, they protect each other, and they fight their battles with each other, not with the cops. Even witnesses who have some key piece of information will usually only offer it up if it helps them. It happens all the time. Just the other night John mentioned he'd talked to someone who he was sure knew some key details, but the guy wouldn't tell him."

Was John talking about him? Giving Sophie details of the case? The possibility was so damn enticing. He was dying to know. But guilt knocked louder inside him, telling him to stop hurtling down this path of deception with Sophie. She hadn't a clue that he was likely one of those witnesses her brother didn't trust.

He needed to focus just on the woman, and forget this tenuous link between brother and sister, woman and cop. Besides, he had friends in the District Attorney's office. His hockey buddy Marshall from high school was now an assistant D.A., and now that Marshall was back in town from his vacation, Ryan didn't need to sniff around this gorgeous woman and take advantage of her open heart.

He stared off in the distance, the city turning blurry as his eyes went out of focus, and he shoved off the questions about Stefano, and people his mother associated with, and anyone else who might have been involved in the murder. He blinked, refocusing to the here and now. To the best second date he'd had in ages. To the only one in a long time that made him want to have a third date.

"Do you like it up here?" he asked.

"The view is amazing," she said, as she gazed at the endless sea of neon and night.

"I fucking love Vegas," he said as he wrapped his arms around her waist, and rested his chin on her shoulder, drinking in the aerial show.

"You do?"

He nodded. "Yeah. This city will chew you up and spit you out or it will embrace you and lift you up. Vegas always gives you the choice—to crawl in the gutter or soar in the sky."

"I choose soaring in the sky," she said softly.

"Me, too."

They soared, high above the city they both called home, hovering in the summer night sky as stars winked on and skyscrapers raced to the heavens. He loved this city. He loved his home, with all its troubles, and problems, and crimes. Maybe he wasn't that different from Sophie's brother. He wanted Vegas to be all that it could be.

He did his best to make that happen, too.

She craned her neck to look up at him. "Would it be too bold to say I wanted you to kiss me again right now?"

"Kissing you is becoming a favorite habit of mine."

And so he kissed her. A lingering, luxurious kiss as the capsule swooped down toward the ground. But soon the kiss climbed the heat scale, and by the time the observation wheel had completed its rotation, lust had camped out in his body, and desire was ruling the rest of the night.

Good thing he'd booked a limo simply to drive around town. He needed to get her in it, stat, and get her naked. Then, he'd regain some of the control he'd felt slipping away during all that talking.

CHAPTER TEN

The gleaming white limo waited in the portico. The driver wore a black cap. A soft blue light glowed along the wood paneling of the bar where the champagne chilled.

That was all Sophie saw in the three seconds after he shut the limo door before he pounced on her.

There was no other way to describe it.

She was pinned on her back on the leather seat. His palms were planted firmly by her sides, and he stared at her hungrily as sexy techno music played from a speaker near the bar.

"Are you still mad at me about the jeans?" she asked, her breathing coming quickly. The car began to hum as it pulled away from the hotel, vibrating gently as it rolled along the Strip in Sunday night traffic.

"Do I look mad?"

"A little."

"Does it turn you on if I'm angry with you?"

"Yes."

"I'm not mad. Because you have this," he said, lowering his hand between her legs and fingering the hem of her pink skirt. "If you hadn't brought it I wouldn't do what I'm about to do. I'd send you home hot and bothered. Instead, I'm going to reward you."

"How will you reward me?" she asked, as anticipation flared through her nervous system. This moment was the cusp—the tantalizing precipice before they ignited. The way he gazed at her like a predator sent her temperature rising. She wanted him so much. She wanted whatever he planned to give her.

"This," he said, crushing her mouth in a kiss that scorched her body. He lowered himself onto her, and she moaned loudly, ready to offer a prayer of thanks to the universe for the delicious weight of his body. He was strong, and cut, and she hadn't even seen him with a shred of clothing off, but she knew from the feel of his arms and the firmness of his ass that his body was going to be the most fuckable one she'd ever laid eyes on.

Not that she'd glimpsed many, but who cared? It didn't take a rocket scientist to know he was hard everywhere, and it turned her on beyond all reason, past all normal levels of arousal. She'd dreamed about this kind of chemistry, about giving up control, and it was even better than she'd imagined. His commanding touch set her mind free.

His mouth was a hunter, taking her lips, marking her as his. He kissed her ferociously, and she could barely move underneath him, nor did she want to. He'd somehow immobilized her with his arms, with his weight, with his hard cock that rubbed against her.

She'd never felt like this with her ex. Never. Their kisses had been playful and fun. They'd been two puppies tussling. Being kissed by Ryan was a mad claiming. His hand slinked down her side, and she gasped in pleasure, and that sound was swallowed up by his insistent lips on hers once more.

When he reached her ass, he squeezed one cheek, so hard she yelped. Then, in a flash, he'd moved from hovering over her to sitting. He pulled her on top of him so she straddled his legs, facing him.

"Change of plans?" she asked in between breaths.

"No," he said, pushing her skirt so it bunched up at her hips. "This is what I have planned." He gazed at her panties. Candy pink with a delicate heart-shaped bow. He ran his tongue over his top lip as he stared at her legs.

"They match the skirt," she offered, as if this detail were somehow vital.

"That they do," he said, and then she cried out as his hand landed on her ass. The sting radiated throughout her cheek.

"Did it hurt?"

"A little."

"But did you like it?"

She nodded. "A lot."

"Good. Because I loved it, too." He rubbed his hand gently across her rear, soothing out the sting. "God, your ass is fucking perfect," he whispered, with a kind of reverence that she'd never heard before. It thrilled her.

She tensed in anticipation as he lifted his arm again, and then his palm landed hard on her rear once more. She yelped as the sharpness spread. "Did that feel good too?" he asked.

She nodded on a pant, as he smoothed his hand against her backside.

"Then let's see how you like it when it's flesh on flesh," he said, as he gathered the edges of the pink lace and tugged it inward.

Her eyes widened in shock as it registered fully what he was doing. He'd turned her panties into a thong, wedging the material into a tight thread between her legs, so the front rubbed her clit, and the back exposed her cheeks.

She trembled as she waited for another smack. "Is this for not wearing a skirt at first?"

With his left hand, he gripped her chin roughly. The callous touch sent hot sparks down her belly on a mad dash to between her legs. "This is what you wanted, Sophie. You wanted to test me. To see what I'd do. And I'm doing it. Because you wanted to know how it feels to have this perfect fucking flesh owned by a man who loves taking charge of you, and who is consumed with spanking this gorgeous ass."

She almost asked *how did you know*? Instead, she asked something she longed to hear to answer to: "Do you love it?"

"I am fucking obsessed with it," he said, his voice hot and filled with lust—a lust she'd inspired in him. That knowledge lit her up. Somehow, she was this man's desire. She seemed to drive him wild. She quivered, waiting for the next swat as he licked a path along her neck up to her ear, whispering with a dirty sort of awe, "I'm obsessed with your ass. And your tits. And your body. And your lips. And your face. And I want to mark this beautiful, round, sweet ass with my palm."

He let go of her chin and looked in her eyes. He tugged her panties, the tight fabric hitting her clit, setting off a chain reaction as he cracked his hand so damn hard on her ass that she flinched.

And gushed.

Oh God. She was so fucking liquid. She was so immeasurably turned on from all these new feelings crashing into her, colliding inside her body in sweet, filthy bliss. Her eyes fluttered closed as the sharp sting rippled through her. He rubbed his palm against her rear to erase the pain, and she whimpered at the quick shift from harsh to gentle.

Then she moaned loudly, because his hand was inside her panties.

"I need to know if you love it like I do," he said, and his fingers glided across the evidence. He groaned appreciatively.

"I do," she said. "I do, I do, I do."

"Yes, you fucking do," he said, sliding his expert fingers over her, touching her bare flesh, feeling her heat. She shuddered as he slid his fingers through all that wetness, then once again as he landed a biting slap on her rear. Heat pooled between her legs from the hit, turning her into an inferno. Sophie was learning that all her fantasies, all her dreams, all her wild imaginings of pain and pleasure were not only coming true, but she liked it.

No, she *loved* the mix of hurt and heat, of a sharp sting and a hot kiss. The evidence was on his fingers.

He gripped her hips and lifted her off him, laying her flat on her back again on the plush leather seats of the limo. She vaguely wondered where they were on the Strip, but she didn't care enough to sneak a peek out the window, not with her body vibrating with this intense need to be touched.

"Where's your purse?" he asked, glancing around.

She furrowed her brow, thrown off by the odd question. "My purse? It's over there," she said, pointing to the other side of the long car and the bench where she'd left her bag.

He stretched out and grabbed it.

"Why do you need my bag?"

"Do you trust me?" he countered, running his thumb along the slim strap of her purse.

She hardly knew him. But she'd already let him spank her, so she supposed in the context of the situation, the answer was that she did. The car slowed in traffic as she gave him her one-word answer.

"Yes."

His lips curved in a small smile, and he dropped a quick kiss on the hollow of her throat. Then he grabbed her wrists, held them together, and positioned them above her head, so she was stretched out. He wrapped the purse strap around her wrists. When she turned her head to the side she realized what he was doing. He was tying the strap on her wrists to the seat belt buckle. Next he reached for the hem of her skirt and gently adjusted it over her ass. She wasn't sure why he was covering her backside, until he tugged her legs while ensuring her punished ass didn't rub against the leather. He pulled her along the seat, making her arms go taut. She'd become a straight line under his control, bound to his choices, yet somehow safe in his arms.

The prospect electrified her. All the planning and decisions and choices she managed all day long disappeared with this kind of letting go.

She breathed harder, lust and desire pent up inside her.

He kneeled at her feet on the end of leather seat, his hands wrapped around her ankles. "I want to tie these gorgeous feet up, too." He bent his head to her legs, dusting the bare skin of her calf with a kiss. Her hips shot up.

"Oh God, please touch me," she cried out.

He turned to her other leg, kissing her there, too, then biting down on her flesh.

"I can't fucking resist," he said, and grabbed her panties, yanking them hard down her legs. "I want your hands *and* your feet tied. Say you want it, too."

"I do, I do," she said quickly, the words spilling out.

With arms that moved like lightning, he had her pink lace at her ankles, and he turned the fabric in a knot, twisting the delicate lace. "I'll buy you new ones. Just like this. Because these are so fucking hot I have to tie you with them.

"Please tie me up," she said, squirming now, her body so damn desperate for his touch. "I don't care about the panties."

He finished his work on her ankles, and raised his head to meet her eyes. "You're so gorgeous, Sophie," he said, raking his eyes over her body. She was still fully clothed in her black blouse and pink skirt and black strappy shoes, but everything was in disarray and she didn't care one bit. He ran his hands up her legs, caressing the soft skin on the inside of her thighs.

"Look at you. So ready for me. So ready for however I'm going to take you," he said in a low, dirty growl. He reached the apex of her thighs, his thumbs brushing against her slick folds.

She gasped at his touch. "Take me," she whispered.

He was on all fours, bent over her, his face near her hot center, her trussed-up feet under his knees.

"Open your thighs as far as you can," he told her, and she did as commanded, parting her legs for him. In that position, she couldn't spread them in a *V*; instead she opened into a diamond as one knee hit the side of the seat, the other the bottom.

"I love how turned on you get," he said as his gaze returned to the center of her world. She ached. An exquisite, needy ache. He dragged one finger through her wetness, then brought that finger to his mouth. His eyes floated closed as he sucked off her taste, moaning as if she were his dessert.

"That's so hot," she whispered, burning up all over from watching him savor her, from waiting for him to make contact.

He opened his eyes, breathing hard through his nostrils as he licked his lips. "I want to hear you reach those high notes this time. I want you to shout and scream my name. Tell me to taste you. Say it. I want to watch those sexy red lips say it."

"Taste me, Ryan," she said.

He dropped his head between her legs, and spread her open, then licked—a torturously slow lick up her center that had her singing "Oh my fucking God" at the top of her lungs, the music and the partition making the limo their own pleasure zone. He'd worked her up so much already that it wouldn't take long. He looked up. "You like that?"

"Yes, so much."

He brushed his finger against her throbbing clit, and she rocked her hips into his hand. "Kiss me again," she said, so damn desperate now.

"You need to say please," he said, his eyes blazing as he issued an order.

Oh God, they were playing again. She barely knew the rules. She was figuring it out as she went along. "Please don't stop. I'm dying for you. Please."

"That's better," he said. "Now say *don't stop* as I eat you. Say it over and over as I lick your absolutely perfect pussy."

He dived back into her sex, licking and kissing and sucking. Making her tremble. Making her hot. Making her shudder. "Don't stop, don't stop, don't stop," she said over and over, and she meant it desperately. All she wanted was to come. To buck into his mouth, and soar off that cliff of pleasure. To fall apart as he buried his face between her legs. With her arms stretched so tight she couldn't move, her ankles bound by her own panties, and Ryan kneeling over her hot, wet, pulsing center, she thrust upward.

Fucking him so he wouldn't stop.

He murmured and groaned as she moved beneath him. His hands curled around her ass gently, as if he were aware it still might hurt. But nothing hurt now. She only knew pleasure, only understood desire. Lust was their shared language, as his magic tongue drew wickedly wonderful lines up and down, flicking her clit, kissing her pussy. She screamed and writhed, calling out his name, shouting to the heavens that she was on her way to bliss. He sent her flying over that edge as she came hard.

A minute later, he'd untied her purse from the buckle. She lowered her arms to her waist; the strap was still wrapped around her wrists, her bag by her side.

"Sophie," he said, his voice gravelly and deadly serious. "I need something from you now. I'm fucking desperate for it."

"Okay," she said, still loopy from the mind-blowing orgasm.

"You gotta sit up, get down on your knees, and suck me hard," he said as he stroked the thick bulge in his pants.

A fresh round of sparks rained down in her body from his dirty words. "Gladly," she said, so damn eager to taste him. "Want to untie me?"

He shook his head. "Yeah, that's the thing. I won't do that."

Blow jobs were a hell of a good time, but she did a better job at blowing when she could use her hands. "But wouldn't it be—"

He pressed a finger to her lips. "You said you trusted me, right?"

She nodded, even as a small swell of nerves rose up inside her. She could trust him, right? She wasn't being foolish, was she?

"Good," he said softly, running a hand through her hair. "Because I need you on your knees."

Oh lord, how she'd longed to hear those words. How she'd craved to get on her knees for a man like this.

She dropped to the carpet, her hands tethered tightly to her own purse, which dangled in front of her, and she watched as he untucked his shirt and unzipped his pants. Arousal raced through her at the sight of him.

He pushed down his boxer briefs.

She drew a sharp inhale at the sight of his gorgeous cock. Her lips parted instantly, and her mouth watered with want. His dick was thick, hard, and long. He stroked it with his right hand, and the fire inside her roared. "Come here. Take me in," he whispered, and with his free hand, he grasped the back of her head, guiding her to his shaft. A drop of liquid was on the head, and her tongue darted out to taste it.

He grinned. "You like that?"

"I do," she said breathily.

"Well, I love blow jobs, so I have a feeling this is going to be good for both of us," he said, gently tugging her closer. She opened her mouth wide, her lips tightening over her teeth as he fed her his dick.

It was his turn to groan. "Yeah. Just like that, beautiful. Just like that," he said, his voice rumbling.

She'd never done this hands-free, but he tasted so good, the perfect mix of clean and musky—of sex and freshly-showered male—that she let go of her worry about not using her hands. Besides, she had no choice. She had only one instrument. Her mouth.

He gently guided her head up and down, moving her mouth along his cock at just the right speed. All she had to do was suck. She tightened her lips as he rocked into her.

"I pictured this the day I met you," he said on a loud moan.

She raised her eyebrows as if to say, *You did?*

"You were so stunning. In that dress. Those tits. That hair. The whole Marilyn Monroe thing you have going on," he said, roping his fingers through her hair. "I wanted to have you from the second I laid eyes on you."

She sucked harder, listening to him tell the story of wanting her. It thrilled her to be desired like this, in the same way, with the same kinks. To discover they fit sexually was such a high for Sophie. She'd been craving this kind of electric chemistry in the bedroom.

Not only craving it. Needing it.

"I wanted to fuck you from the second I saw you," he

said on a thrust, filling her mouth. "I wanted to eat you," he said, as he curled his fingers tighter around her skull. "I wanted to make you come." He hit the back of her throat and her eyes watered. But she kept going, pushing past the gag reflex. "And I wanted to come in that pretty mouth of yours," he said and inhaled sharply, breathing erratically. He squeezed his eyes shut, grasped her head, and came in her throat.

* * *

He scooped her up and set her down on the seat, still woozy from his own climax. But he wasn't so sex-drunk that he couldn't focus on taking care of her. Before pulling up his briefs, he unknotted her panties from her feet, untied her from her purse, set the bag down on the seat, and held up her wrists.

"How do they feel?"

She shot him a sly grin. "The purse is made of only the finest leather, so they feel quite fine."

He laughed, and dropped a kiss to her forehead, then tucked himself back in. She pulled her panties on, glancing down at them. "Hmm. They are a little stretched. But I don't regret it."

"Neither do I. And I promise to replace them immediately." He tipped his head to the bar. "Champagne?"

"I'd love some. You should have some, too, especially since you don't have to do bone graft surgery tonight. Or so I presume."

"No. I don't. Lucky me," he said, then poured two glasses from the bar, and handed one to her. He clinked his flute to hers then wrapped an arm around her, rubbing her shoulder and her neck as they chatted and drank the bubbly beverage while they drove around the city with no destination and no goal but time together in a long, sleek car.

Later, he had the driver take her to the front door of her building. He stepped out of the car with her, and before she left, he reached for her hand, and kissed the top of it.

"You're beautiful. And dirty. And clever. And you take direction like a very good girl."

She batted her eyes in an over-the-top way as she sidled up against him. "Does that mean I've earned the dog photo?"

He squeezed her ass, savoring once more the way it felt in the palm of his hand. "You have absolutely earned it." Then he let go and looked her in the eyes, surprising himself a bit with the words that escaped his mouth. "So what would you think about a third date?"

For a moment he was nervous. He desperately wanted her yes, even though he was as sure as a man could be that he'd get it.

She shot him that bright, gorgeous smile that could light up a night sky. "I think I'd wonder how you plan on topping the first two, because they've been spectacular. So I'd say yes out of curiosity."

As the driver headed for his house, he tried to keep his mind blank to avoid the litany of questions he wanted to ask himself. But when Johnny Cash greeted him at the door, the questions tumbled free as he petted the dog's head. "What am I doing? What the hell am I doing? Because I am counting down the hours 'til I see her again."

The dog thumped his tail on the floor and whined. A sign he had to pee.

Ryan took him to the backyard and wished he didn't like Sophie so much already.

CHAPTER ELEVEN

from: guywithgreentie@gmail.com
to: Sophiefashionista@gmail.com
date: July 15, 6:37 AM
subject: Rise and shine...

Took this just now after our morning run. Hence, the tongue lolling out of his mouth. And yeah, you can say it. He's adorable.

from: Sophiefashionista@gmail.com
to: guywithgreentie@gmail.com
date: July 15, 8:34 AM
subject: Some of us sleep in

OMG he is so cute. I'm in love with your dog.

from: guywithgreentie@gmail.com
to: Sophiefashionista@gmail.com
date: July 15, 8:45 AM
subject: Did I wear you out last night?

He has that effect on women.

from: Sophiefashionista@gmail.com
to: guywithgreentie@gmail.com
date: July 15, 9:04 AM
subject: Maybe I just need my beauty sleep…

He is so handsome. If he were mine I'd dress him in a cool leather jacket. Or maybe a sweater. A trendy sweater. Like a cardigan. With an elbow patch.

from: guywithgreentie@gmail.com
to: Sophiefashionista@gmail.com
date: July 16, 9:17 AM
subject: You're naturally beautiful

He will never wear clothes. I assure you.

from: Sophiefashionista@gmail.com
to: guywithgreentie@gmail.com
date: July 15, 9:21 AM
subject: Now I'm blushing

What about a vest? I once knit a vest for my cat when I was in high school, back when I thought I was going to be a fashion designer rather than a geek-girl coder.

From his home office, with the AC blasting and his black and white dog crashed at his feet on the hardwood floor, Ryan laughed softly at Sophie's email and the image of her knitting a vest for a pet. His mom used to make jackets for dogs for fun for friends and neighbors. She'd sewn a forest green jacket with a dog bone design on the back and declared it her lottery ticket.

"Someday I will no longer be merely the seamstress to local high school gymnasts and showgirls. I'll make jackets for dogs. This will be my mark on the world," his mom had declared, holding up the small coat proudly.

She'd made her mark on the world, all right. But not in the way she'd intended. Still, she'd asked him to hold onto the pattern for the dog jacket.

"Someday," she'd said as she gave it to him before she left for good. "Hold it for me, my sweet Ryan."

He opened the desk drawer where he kept the pattern, worn around the edges now. He had taken a photo of it, too, so he also had a digital copy. He held onto it not because he believed his mom was going to break free of bars and become a world-renowned dog-clothing maker, but because it was a rare unblemished moment in the memories of her.

It was a moment about hopes and dreams, and about wishes, even though they'd gone unfulfilled.

He closed the drawer, and returned to the present day. To the email banter that he couldn't seem to stay away from.

from: guywithgreentie@gmail.com
to: Sophiefashionista@gmail.com
date: July 15, 9:27 AM
subject: You probably look immeasurably hot blushing

More like a pin-up girl coder. How on earth did the computer science guys get any work done with you around?

from: Sophiefashionista@gmail.com
to: guywithgreentie@gmail.com
date: July 15, 9:31 AM
subject: You are full of compliments. I like it.

I assure you, I was quite geeky in college. I *never* wore skirts and dresses or high-heel shoes.

from: guywithgreentie@gmail.com
to: Sophiefashionista@gmail.com
date: July 15, 9:33 AM
subject: I could go on all day about you…

I refuse to believe you were geeky. Prove it with a photo.

from: Sophiefashionista@gmail.com
to: guywithgreentie@gmail.com
date: July 15, 9:44 AM
subject: Please do

See? Case closed.

He groaned as he stared at the photos she'd sent. They must have been taken ten years ago, and yeah, she had the whole casual Converse sneakers-sweatshirt-knit-cap look going on, the complete opposite of the woman he knew now. Still, she was hot then, and she was hot now, and no matter what, she turned him on. Fucking hell. He was hard already just from a picture.

from: guywithgreentie@gmail.com
to: Sophiefashionista@gmail.com
date: July 15, 9:47 AM
subject: Hot as hell. Gorgeous as heaven. Sexy as Sin.

Just. As. Fucking. Hot.

You are just as fucking hot in jeans and a hoodie as you are in a tight dress.

Everything looks good on you because you look good in anything.

And everything.

And especially in nothing.

from: Sophiefashionista@gmail.com
to: guywithgreentie@gmail.com
date: July 15, 9:52 AM
subject: Same to you.

Nothing… I believe I have that outfit planned for you.

* * *

After a lunch meeting with a new client later that day, Ryan's phone rang. His spine straightened as he headed to the parking lot of the restaurant and answered John Winston's call.

"Hey," he said.

The detective said a quick hello then slid into business. "Mr. Sloan," he began, and Ryan found it vaguely amusing that Winston was so formal in how he talked. "I hope you don't mind, but I had another question for you."

"Sure," Ryan said, as he unlocked his truck and turned on the radio. It was an old habit to have a little background noise during a private conversation.

"Luke Carlton. The piano teacher your mom had an affair with," the man began, and Ryan clenched his jaw, a visceral reaction to that name and that description. There was so very little anyone could say of his mother that was good. She'd had an affair, she was in prison for murder, she'd been a—

But he couldn't even say those words in his head.

"Was he ever at your home" John asked. "Did you mom spend time with him at the house?"

Ryan took a deep breath, letting the air work its way through his frustration at having to discuss the cheating she'd done. As if that was the worst thing. "Not really. She kept it pretty secret."

"Sure. Of course. I get that," the detective said, and Ryan forced himself to keep blinders on, to see John solely as the detective and not as the brother of the woman he'd taken on a limo ride up and down the Strip last night. "Did they ever meet on James Street?"

Ryan furrowed his brow. "James Street? Not that I know of. But that's a pretty long street. Cuts through a lot of town."

John laughed lightly. "Yeah. I know. That's the problem."

"Why are you asking?"

"Just trying to put some things together."

"Man, I wish I could help, but I sure as hell wasn't privy to the details of her affair," he said, though that wasn't entirely true. His mom had told him how much Luke had helped her to come out on the other side of the trouble she was in. But all that data fell under the *don't breathe a word* category. She'd warned him before she left for prison to guard those secrets, and he did—to keep her out of more trouble and to protect her honor, even from behind bars. He hadn't breathed a goddamn word. He'd buried that secret far inside him, like an artifact in a sandstorm.

"Listen, I would really appreciate it if you could give me a call if you remember anything about their relationship."

He shoved a hand through his hair and nodded. "Of course."

The call ended and he banged his head on the steering wheel.

What the fuck was he supposed to say to Sophie? *Your brother called me today to ask about my mom's lover from eighteen years ago?*

The last thing he wanted her to know about was his shit storm of a past. He'd never met a woman he'd wanted to tell. He had no clue how he'd even begin that conversation. He wished, he really fucking wished, that he could just be the man he was now. Not the guy whose family story had been dragged through the headlines in all its salaciousness years ago.

He only wanted the woman, not for the past to spill over into his present with her.

CHAPTER TWELVE

The puck screamed across the ice, streaking right through the goalie's skates and smacking into the back of the net.

Ryan raised his arms and cheered. His teammates echoed his excitement, skating over and clapping him on the back for putting them ahead with five minutes to go in the game. The line skated off the ice and headed to the bench as another set of his teammates jumped onto the rink for the face-off.

Breathing hard, his muscles working overtime from the intensity of the game, Ryan grabbed his water bottle and gulped down some liquid for his parched throat. He momentarily parked himself on the bench with the line change, his buddy Marshall joining him.

"Good job," Marshall grunted with a pat on the knee.

"Gotta keep up with you," Ryan said, since Marshall had scored the first goal for the recreational league team they played on. They'd been playing together for years—since all the way back in varsity, when they went to the same high school together here in Vegas. Marshall was as close to the inner circle as anyone could be.

"Hey, need to ask you a question," Ryan said, lowering his voice as he tugged off his bulky gloves. Their other teammates were fixated on the game, cheering on their guys. Marshall motioned for Ryan to continue. "You told me a few weeks ago about Stefano being questioned by some of your attorneys for other crimes." Marshall had tipped him off before the investigation had reopened, but had been away on a family vacation for two weeks so this was the first time Ryan had been able to catch up on the details.

"Right," his friend said as he tightened his skates. "Some of my colleagues are working on that."

"Do know anything more about it? Because a detective brought me in for questioning a week ago. He talked to Shan, Colin, and Michael as well." Ryan used his sister's given name, since that was how Marshall had always known her. "My grandmother, too. He asked a lot of the same questions that the guy who investigated the first time around did, but some different ones as well. He really seemed to want to know who my mom was friends with and if there was anyone new in her life at the time," he said, speaking as casually as if they were catching up on the latest sports scores. It was damn nice, in a strange way, not to have to dig in and serve up his messy family story to someone. Hell, Ryan couldn't even remember ever having had to tell Marshall at all—he simply knew because they'd grown up together.

Marshall gestured with his clunky gloved fingers for him come closer. Ryan scooted over as the other man lowered his voice to a thread. "Listen, you didn't hear this from me," he said, beginning with his usual caveat when he shared something he wasn't supposed to share. Ryan never violated that trust. "Stefano's girlfriend came to us a few months ago. She told us she had some information."

Ryan's eyes widened. The cops had tried to talk to the shooter's girlfriend at the time of the murder, since she'd lived with Stefano, but she'd skipped town then. No one had found her, and Colin had told Ryan at the time that there were rumors that Stefano had had her killed.

Ryan never believed those rumors. Didn't seem plausible. Skipping town when you found out the guy you loved was going to prison? That was much more believable. Still, her absence had been one of those unsolved mysteries.

"She left town then. But no one could find her," Ryan said. "Where'd she go?"

"Woman's shelter in Idaho, of all places. Turned out she was pregnant. Stayed there 'til the kid was born. Wanted to lie low and keep away from the cops. She has a seventeen-year-old son now. Stefano's kid."

"Holy shit." His jaw dropped. "So that's why she left?"

"Yeah, and that's why he took the job from your mom. Needed money for the kid. She said she didn't know at the time that he was doing *those* kinds of jobs," Marshall said, with narrowed eyes, suggesting he didn't believe that line. "Anyway, once he was behind bars and the investigation was obviously over, she went back to her family in Reno with the baby. But it turns out some of his friends have been keeping an eye on her and the kid. It was a promise these guys made to always look out for each other. So with Stefano in the big house, his buddies looked after the girl-friend, helped out her and the kid, all as a favor to Jerry. But here's the thing. Those friends were in the Sinners."

"Are they still?"

Marshall shrugged. "My guys don't know yet. All we know is Stefano asked them to keep his kid out of the way of the Sinners. He wanted his son to have a shot at a new kind of life, different from his. So his friends protected the kid for a long time, but apparently they haven't done such a good job lately, and he's been getting into trouble. The girlfriend's not too happy about them breaking their promise to keep her son safe from the gang."

Something about Marshall's info aligned with John Winston's questions. If the girlfriend was talking after all these years, maybe mentioning names that had been off the radar during the first investigation, it would make sense that Winston had been asking about any other people in his mother's life. "Wait. Were these buddies involved in my dad's murder?"

"That's the part we don't know. That's the part no one knows. It's not even my case. It's not even at the level of a case yet, to be honest. Just an investigation. All I know is the detectives are looking into it. And you did not get this from me."

The coach slapped the white wood of the bench, and pointed to the ice.

Ryan, Marshall and the rest of the line hopped over and went out on the rink, returning to the game. As Ryan skated, he mapped out a plan. No reason he couldn't try to work the case, too. John Winston might be the lead detective, but Ryan could play that role on his own. It was his family, his life, and his story. He knew how to figure things out, and how to put two and two together. And he had a damn good notion of some of the people that he'd need to go see.

Later that night, he scheduled a piano lesson with a local teacher.

* * *

"Wish me luck," Sophie said as she pushed back from the table after a fantastic sushi lunch with Holden and her good friend Jenna.

Holden stood first and cupped her shoulders. "I know you can do this. Everything is going to go great with Clyde. Just tell him to keep his grandson's paws off my ex-wife," Holden said with a wink.

"If only you'd kept *your* hands on me I wouldn't be worrying about my biggest donor to the community center trying to pawn me off on his grandson," she said and squeezed his arm. Holden swatted her rear with a light touch.

"Like that? Is that what you want?"

"No. Put some gusto into it," Jenna said in her husky, sexy, Australian-accented voice.

Sophie waved them both off. She wasn't sore, per se, from her spanking two nights ago, but she was keeping this patch of bodily real estate for Ryan's possessive hands only. Actually, *all* of her body. True, they'd made no such promises. But after the time they'd spent together, the things they'd done, the messages they'd exchanged... Well, there was no way in hell she wanted to even dabble with anyone else.

"No gusto please," she joked then glanced at her watch. "I'm off. Enjoy your green tea ice cream."

"We will," Jenna said eyeing the dessert dishes the waiter had just brought to the two of them. "Just remind Clyde how important the community center is in and of itself.

And that building the new additions is not dependent on you dating or not dating his grandson."

"Absolutely." She gave a big thumbs-up. She knew what to do. She certainly knew how to handle herself in front of old, rich men, in front of young, rich men, and in front of nerdy, rich men. She'd handled herself just fine when she ran InCode. She'd made pitches. She'd stood up in front of groups of people. She'd asked for funding. And she'd presented on the strength of her vision.

That was what she would do with Clyde. Besides, she didn't feel her romantic life, one way or the other, needed to be a part of her conversations with him. If she were a man, surely no one would expect her to date someone's daughter.

She hopped into her Aston Martin and headed to Clyde's office. He greeted her with a handshake that lasted too long, then a kiss on the cheek that left too much whiskery scratch on her skin. She wished he wasn't so touchy, but she reminded herself the man hadn't crossed any lines. He was simply more affectionate than she would have liked. No crime in that. Just a wee bit of discomfort.

In his office, she reviewed the final plans for the Beethoven concert benefit as well as the community center. When she was through, Clyde smacked his palm in approval on his grand oak desk. "I am delighted to be able to help fund this. It is so great to have a place for young people to be able to go and stay off of the streets and out of trouble," he said, and she couldn't deny that she loved his giving heart and his spirit. He reminded her in some ways of John, and his mission to help make the city safer and better. They each had their own style of going about it, but the goal was the same.

A better Las Vegas.

Clyde stroked his chin. "Say, do you know who's here today?" There was a glint in his gray eyes.

Sophie cringed inside, then she plastered on her best smile. "I can't even begin to guess."

Soon he was escorting her to an office where a young, blond man was bent over his laptop.

"Taylor, my boy. I have someone I want you to meet," Clyde said, and the young man looked up. He was handsome, sported a nice smile, and boasted straight white teeth that could only be courtesy of the best orthodontia money could buy. "This is Sophie, our city's leading philanthropist, who is spearheading plans for the community center fundraiser."

"That's so great. I'm one hundred percent behind that." He pushed back from the desk in his rolling chair, walked over to her, and extended a hand.

He had a strong grip, and Sophie catalogued that as a good thing. "Pleasure to meet you, Taylor. Clyde raves about his favorite grandson, and I promise I won't tell the others he likes you best."

Taylor laughed. "Excellent. I won't tell the other fundraisers that you're his favorite then, too," he said with a *we've got a secret* wink.

"We're in cahoots then," she said, with a cheery smile for the fresh-faced law school graduate. "How are you finding the transition from law school to the corporate world?"

"My grandfather works me hard. The other day, for instance, he only let me take a one-hour lunch to play the cards at the MGM instead of the two hours he gives the senior partners."

"I'm so cruel," Clyde said with a hearty laugh.

After another minute of casual chatter, she said good-bye, and Clyde saw her to the lobby.

"That went quite well didn't it?" he said, a huge grin on his face.

"He is lovely indeed," Sophie said. *Also six years younger than me, and I'm not a cradler-robber.*

"Perhaps the two of you could attend the concert together," he said, then snapped his fingers. "Wait. I have a better idea. Why don't you go out before? Have a nice dinner. On me."

She wanted to put her foot down, but she also didn't want to offend this man who she needed in her court by turning down his grandson. Nor did she want to lie to him. She wanted to live a life free of lies, and free of trickery. She also wanted to operate on her own terms, not conform to the expectations of the men she worked with, whether they were back in the tech world or the titans of industry with fat wallets now.

"Oh, Clyde you are such a darling," she said, stalling for time.

"What do you think about that?" he said, undeterred.

"Why are you so eager to set him up? He's a handsome, smart, sweet man. Seems he could easily find a date on his own."

Clyde lowered his voice. "I want to leave him the firm. And I want to know he's with a woman who's not going to try to take all my money," he said in a *you-get-my-drift* voice.

Oh, she got it. She definitely got it. Because she had money, she wouldn't *need* his. Clyde assumed she was the type of woman who'd sign a pre-nup. Well, maybe she was that type of woman. But still…the notion of *why* she was his top choice made her feel greasy.

"Also, you're the most delightful young woman I know," he added, as if that reason suddenly would hold water. "The two of you could be a wonderful match."

Sophie had other ideas about what made a good match. Besides, who said she was looking for something serious? She was quite content with her life as it was, thank you very much. If she wanted anything right now, it was passion. It was sparks and fire.

It was Ryan Sloan, and the way he commanded her pleasure.

Oh God, just his name in her head sent heat flaring in her body.

Which meant it was time to nip this thing with Clyde in the bud. She'd run a multi-million dollar company for several years, and she hadn't gotten to that position by letting the men she worked with try to set her up.

She touched Clyde on the shoulder with her fingertips. "Clyde, you know I adore you. And I could humor you right now simply to stay in your good graces, but I want to be totally honest. Your grandson is lovely. However, I've started seeing someone, and it's going quite well so far. So I'm not really on the market at the moment."

He frowned. "Is it serious?"

"Clyde," she said softly. "It's not a matter of whether it's serious. It's a matter of choice. I'm choosing to see someone right now, and likely I'll be bringing him to the benefit. I hope this won't affect your support of the center, but it's important to me to be honest with you."

Clyde took a deep breath and nodded, as if he were processing this news. She mentally crossed her fingers, praying she hadn't messed up by being frank. She held her breath, hoping he wouldn't snatch away his funding.

"I've been too presumptuous," he said, contrition in his tone. "And I respect you for saying that. And of course I remain a committed supporter." Then he fixed on a cheery smile. "And I look forward to meeting this man at the event."

Oh shoot. There was *that* little matter. Now she had to deliver Ryan in the flesh to back up her *thanks, but no thanks*. To prove she was an honest woman.

"You will definitely meet him then," she said, her businesslike bravado hiding her worry that she'd been too bold to think Ryan would be her arm candy.

She was going to need to ask Ryan to be her date. The possibility thrilled her, but he seemed to be playing it day by day. Would he even want to plan that far ahead?

As she drove to her next meeting, she ran through the best ways to invite Ryan to the event. What was happening between them was new and tender, and she didn't want to ruin it by asking for too much. Would this type of date imply they were more than merely lovers? Was she ready to state that so boldly?

She shut off the questions momentarily when she arrived at the community center, parking behind a brown Buick. She rushed inside for a quick visit with Elle, who ran the center, updating her on the status of the fundraising.

"So glad it's going well. We are lucky to have you behind this," Elle said, gesturing broadly to the broken-down building and the basketball court with its cracked concrete surface, badly in need of the repair and revamp that they hoped would soon be possible.

"It thrills me to help," Sophie said, as the dark-haired and insanely gorgeous Elle walked her back to her car, passing the basketball courts on the way, where teenage boys played hoops. A few of them stopped to stare at Sophie, and one even catcalled.

"Sweet blonde ass," the guy said with a whistle. She couldn't tell if it was the guy with ink all over his arms or someone else, and it didn't bother her terribly.

But it bothered Elle.

Elle called the guy's name then admonished him. "Watch it. Show a little respect, like we've talked about," she said in a strong voice, and he muttered a low "Sorry."

Elle turned to Sophie. "They're works in progress."

Sophie smiled. "Aren't we all works in progress?"

Elle laughed lightly. "That we are. Lord knows I certainly am." Then she turned more serious. "Thank you again for everything. I know we can do so much more for these kids when this comes together."

"We have great donors behind this. It'll happen."

As she said goodbye, backing away from the Buick then heading in the direction of the Strip, her damn brain went haywire again, trying to figure out what was happening with Ryan. She muttered a curse as she turned onto the highway, dropping her shades over her eyes to shield them from the sun. She gripped the wheel tighter, trying to focus solely on driving. But still her mind whirred and raced as she played out scenarios and cycled through relationship permutations, just as she had with computers.

The questions rattled her brain and drove the tension in her body sky-high.

When she returned to her building, she felt like a radio station tuned in badly—all warped, fuzzy, and off-kilter.

She'd been frazzled by what she needed to do next—push Ryan into something that might feel more serious, when he hardly seemed the type.

But then she shoved all those feelings aside once the front desk attendant told her there was a delivery for her. He handed her a silvery gift bag with slim handles, and instantly she was sure it was from the man she had a third date with. Desperate to open it, she clutched it tightly as the elevator shot her up to her floor.

The second she opened her door, she tore in and found a small white box, tied with a white bow, resting inside the red tissue paper. She pulled off the bow and removed the lid.

Wow. She lifted the satiny fabric. The panties were dark pink with sheer lace in front. But it was the back that knocked the breath out of her. The rear was comprised solely of crisscross satin pieces of fabric that would leave most of her bottom exposed. A cage-open panel, it was called, according to the tag.

She called it a prelude to multiple orgasms.

Sophie owned many pairs of pretty panties, but this was by far the most alluring. This took sexy to new heights. Moments later, her phone pinged with the notification that a message had arrived.

from: guywithgreentie@gmail.com
to: Sophiefashionista@gmail.com
date: July 16, 3:48 PM
subject: Delivery

I hope you'll forgive me that they aren't pale pink.

from: Sophiefashionista@gmail.com
to: guywithgreentie@gmail.com
date: July 16, 3:54 PM
subject: Forgiveness granted

I do forgive you. I forgive you so much I promise to be wearing these next time I see you.

from: guywithgreentie@gmail.com
to: Sophiefashionista@gmail.com
date: July 16, 3:57 PM
subject: Don't test me like that

See you in five minutes then.

from: Sophiefashionista@gmail.com
to: guywithgreentie@gmail.com
date: July 16, 4:04 PM
subject: Don't tease me like that

Good things come to those who wait...

from: guywithgreentie@gmail.com
to: Sophiefashionista@gmail.com
date: July 16, 4:07 PM
subject: Not teasing...

How's 7:00 tonight? If that's presumptuous, I can wait 'til 7:30. But no later.

from: Sophiefashionista@gmail.com
to: guywithgreentie@gmail.com
date: July 16, 4:12 PM
subject: Presume…

You can take me for that drive in my car that you wanted. I'll be out front at seven-thirty.

Looked like that third date would be happening sooner than expected.

CHAPTER THIRTEEN

It didn't matter where they were going tonight or what they were doing.

She was wearing a dress. She was not toying with him today because she wanted what he wanted.

Access.

She adjusted the slim orange shoulder straps as they curved into a tight white bodice that was practically fused to her breasts. Just enough cleavage ensured his eyes would pop out of his head, and then the skirt itself would pretty much blast all his brain cells away. Full and gathered, the white skirt with oranges printed on it swished as she walked. The waist cinched with a slim belt, and she wore matching orange pumps with a strap over her instep. The cotton sateen fabric of the dress wasn't see-through, so she could wear the pink panties he'd sent, no problem.

As if she'd wear anything else right now.

This was a sex date, wasn't it? Sophie's lips twitched up as she answered the question herself. It was. Oh yes, it was, and she wanted it, needed it, and was damn eager to have it.

Ryan was an enticing mix of enigmatic and open, of caveman and gentleman. The combinations she saw inside him intrigued her, body and heart. His quickness with words and the ease of his flirty banter ignited her mind. There was something else in him, too, that simply gripped her—the man had a magnetic intensity. It drew her to him, lured her under his spell.

That was where she wanted to be tonight.

She grabbed a small white handbag, swapped her wallet, lipstick, and phone into it, then realized she didn't have a condom. She laughed when she couldn't even remember how long it had been—not only since she'd needed one, but also since she'd bought one.

It would be up to Ryan, and he sure seemed like the kind of man who came prepared.

One more check of her reflection told her everything was neatly in place, including the soft curls she'd styled into her hair after she showered. She ran a shimmery red lip gloss wand over her lips, then tucked that into her purse, too.

She tapped her chin, cycling through her mental to-do list. She'd been to the office, she'd seen Clyde, she'd visited Elle, she'd confirmed some items for the concert, and then made a number of phone calls for other fundraisers she was working on. There was so much in motion, but right now her plate was clear. Her list was emptied. Time to have fun.

She left her room, swinging her purse in her hand as she headed for the kitchen to grab a glass of water and go. Ten minutes until he'd be downstairs waiting for her. As she drank the cool liquid, she dialed the valet service in her building and asked them to bring her car around.

The sound of a lock in the door caught her attention. John walked in with the weariest look on his face, but the second he spotted Sophie in the kitchen, his tired eyes lit up. "Hey Soph," he said.

"Hey you. Long day?"

He nodded, dropped his keys on the table by the door, and headed to the kitchen. "Too long a day. Got the runaround from everyone."

"The life of a detective," she said, then held up a finger in the air. "But I have just the cure for a long day."

He arched an eyebrow, as she walked over to a black marble table at the edge of her kitchen and held up a sturdy glass bottle. She removed the stopper and poured some amber liquid. She grabbed an ice cube from the freezer, dropped it in, and handed him the glass. "There's never been a long day in the history of the whole world that Macallan can't make better."

John raised the glass and knocked half of it back. "Ah," he said with a satisfied sigh as he set the drink on the counter. "That does make my day suddenly shorter."

She laughed. "See? I told you. Are you still working on that case?"

He nodded. "That one and a few others. Today was like a goddamn puzzle. You know the math problems you can't solve? If a train is going at the speed of—" Then he stopped and shook his head, bemused. "Look who I'm talking to. You never had problems solving math puzzles."

She laughed. "True. So if you ever run into any math or code-breaking with your cases, just let me know."

He took another drink. "And this was over addresses. Fucking addresses from years ago."

"Sounds more like cartography than math," Sophie said.

"Well, both are vexing my partner and me," he said, then furrowed his brow as he glanced at her outfit. "What's with the dress? Wait. You're probably just going grocery shopping like that. Am I right?"

She made a funny face. "Ha ha. And yes, I *would* wear this grocery shopping. But if you must know, I have a hot date."

He covered his ears. "La la la. I don't want to hear it." He took his hands off his ears.

"Why'd you ask then?"

"Like I said, long day. It fries my brain. Who's the date with?"

"As a matter of fact, it's someone I met—"

But her words were cut off when his phone bleated loudly from his back pocket. "Manny," he said. Manny was his partner. "Got to take it."

She waggled her fingers. "Toodle-loo. Don't wait up for little old me."

He rolled his eyes then pressed the phone to his ear. "What's the latest?"

Sophie left for the elevators, headed to the lobby, and walked out the front door into the hot July evening that had coasted into Vegas.

Her breath fled her chest when she saw Ryan leaning against one of the stone columns in the portico, his sunglasses on, a tailored shirt tucked into crisp pants, and a suit jacket tossed over his shoulder. The second he saw her, he strode over and surveyed her from head to toe.

She waited for him to speak first.

"You," he began, and his voice sounded dry. "Are you?"

"Am I what?"

"Are you wearing them?"

She leaned closer, her lips mere millimeters from his as she grasped his hand and pressed her keys into his palm. "Take me somewhere and find out."

CHAPTER FOURTEEN

The car hummed. Adrenaline surged through him as he drove into the dusk, heading for the mountains southwest of the city. There was still unchartered land in that area. Building had just begun, which meant miles upon miles of roads were still bare.

As he shifted on an uphill stretch, the engine roared. The feel of the luxury automobile she owned was absolutely extraordinary, blurring into some kind of gorgeous harmony between car and driver and road.

Not to mention the incredible woman in the passenger seat.

As he accelerated, his chest vibrated with a purpose—find some place and fuck her.

He stole glances at Sophie during the drive, wishing it were possible to stare at her and keep his eyes on the road at the same time.

"Have I mentioned you look good enough to eat?"

"It's the oranges, isn't it?" she asked, running her fingers along the pattern on her dress.

"You had cherries on your dress when I met you. Now oranges. What will it be next time?"

"Do you like peaches?"

"I love peaches. I love peach ice cream. I especially love peach pie."

"Then maybe I'll have peaches on me next time," she said with a sly look in her eyes.

He laughed then tapped the steering wheel as he turned onto a two-lane road at the base of the mountains. "So what's the deal with you and this car?"

"What do you mean?"

"Is this like a James Bond thing you have going on?"

She laughed and shook her head. "He doesn't drive this model. Lately he's been driving the DBS. This is a Vantage GT."

"I know. It just seems very Bond."

"Maybe I'm a spy," she whispered in a sultry voice, winking as she spoke.

"Are you a good spy or a bad spy?"

"I'm whatever kind you want me to be," she said, and the innuendo in her words heated him up. The notion that she'd play whatever role he wanted intoxicated him.

But then, everything she did turned him on, it seemed. His attraction to her ran red-hot, and burrowed deep into his body. It operated on some kind of elemental level that at times he felt powerless to resist or deny. His fingers gripped the wheel harder as lust thrummed through him.

But even so, he remained curious about *her*. The woman who generated all this heat in his blood. He wanted to understand her. "What I mean is," he said, trying again, "what's the story with you and this fancy car, and the gorgeous building you live in, and the way you dress like you stepped off the pages of a magazine?"

"The answers are simple. I give a lot of my money away, and I give all my time away. But I still like having nice things. And I like to reward myself for hitting milestones in charitable fundraising. Like this car—it was a gift I gave myself after my first big event. And this dress I picked up when I started working with the children's wing. Besides, I like dressing nice. Is that a crime?"

He shook his head. "Hell, no. You wear it all well. Do you like being pretty?"

She laughed lightly. "I'm glad you think that about me."

"Answer the question," he said firmly, since she'd just danced around what he considered an immutable truth of the universe—she was beautiful.

"*Ryan*," she said, and he heard her embarrassment in her tone. He was having none of that.

"Sophie," he said in a firm voice. "You're gorgeous. Don't deny it. Now tell me, do you like being so gorgeous?"

"To you—yes," she said, managing once again not to answer completely. But her answer was completely satisfying.

Briefly, he ran his thumb over her bottom lip. "Stunning. You are fucking stunning." He turned his eyes back to the road that curved up into the hills. "Even in that hoodie and hat picture you sent me."

"I told you I was a nerd in college. I mean, total nerd," she said, slicing her hands through the air for emphasis. "I had a weird haircut. I died my bangs blue. I was bent over a desk coding all the time."

"I wouldn't mind seeing you bent over a desk."

She shot him a naughty grin. "Why does that not surprise me?"

"Did you like having blue hair?"

She shrugged. "I did it to fit in. There's a certain geek culture, and I had to work hard to conform to it. Already I had a strike against me being a woman, so I tried to at least look the part of a computer nerd."

If she hadn't sent that photo he'd never have believed it. "And now that you've left that part of your life behind, you embrace this other side of yourself," he said, gesturing to the pinup dress and high heels and the styled hair.

"Exactly," she said, her eyes lighting up.

"Was that part of you untended to? The woman in you?"

She scoffed. "For many years," she said, almost to herself. He was about to follow up and ask what she meant, but she kept talking. "But there are always parts of ourselves that we don't take care of. I could ask you the same. Are you the same person you were when you were in the army?"

As he hugged the side of the road on a turn, he eyed his tailored pants, button-down shirt, and leather shoes. "Well, I don't wear fatigues anymore," he said drily.

"Did you wear fatigues then? Were you actually in battle?" she asked, worry in her tone.

"I did wear fatigues. But I wasn't on the battlefront. I was in Germany. Stationed in Wiesbaden. Not far from Frankfurt."

"I know where Wiesbaden is," she said quickly, a flicker of excitement in her eyes. "I'm having some work done on a new car at a custom shop in Rüsselsheim, not far from there."

"Yeah? What kind?" he asked, figuring she'd say Audi, BMW, or Mercedes—luxury autos with high-end options for the discerning buyer. Like Sophie.

"It's a Bugatti," she said breezily. "I've always wanted one."

His jaw dropped. There was no hotter make or model of car to a *Top Gear* fan than a Bugatti. "Yeah, me too. You're really getting a Bugatti? I thought they were made in France."

"Mine was made there. But I've contracted with a specialty shop in Rüsselsheim to make it more eco-friendly. And the paint job they're doing is divine. It's going to be a lush *green*," she said, stretching that last word out as if it tasted like honey. "It's going to look like an emerald."

"That's pretty hot. Can't wait to see it."

"Me too. I should get it in a few weeks. I bought it when I hit another goal in money raised for charities. But enough about me. Tell me about Wiesbaden. What did you do at the base there?"

"Army intelligence. The 66tth Military Intelligence Brigade. Worked with Captain Jack Sullivan."

She arched an eyebrow. "Should I know the name?"

He laughed. "No. But there's a funny story behind that man. He's a few years older than me so he left before I did, and for awhile after he became known as the soldier-turned-sex-toy-mogul."

Her lips widened into a big smile. "Really?"

He nodded. "Left the army and started a company called Joy Delivered. Sold products like the Wild One and the Lola. Now he's back in Europe with his wife."

"And does the army advertise that career path?" she asked, a sly look in her eyes as she hummed the one-time slogan. "Be all that you can be, find your future…selling dildos?"

He cracked up as he drove. "No. But perhaps they should. He made a lot of people happy."

"I imagine he did. Though I suspect your career path is the more typical one after working in army intelligence?"

"It is. Military to security. Natural fit."

"So perhaps you aren't that different now than in your previous job."

"Maybe I'm not."

"Maybe you're not," she echoed. "Or maybe you are. I don't really know."

"Do you want to know?"

"I want to know what makes you tick now," she said, her gaze fixed firmly on him as he drove. She was so straightforward as they talked, and he couldn't deny that he liked her directness in conversation as much as he liked her willingness to bend to him in the bedroom.

Besides, it was a good question, one he was rarely asked but one he could, reasonably, answer with the truth. "This car," he said, tapping the dashboard. "My dog. My job. My family. Living the life I choose. Keeping people safe. See, I'm not that different than I was before."

"You're like my brother in some ways," she said. Guilt burned through him at the mention of John, and he tried to shove it aside. There was no space tonight for the things he hadn't told her about how they met. "He's got the same focus," she continued, then looked at him, and rested her hand briefly on his leg. "I admire it."

He gritted his teeth. *No, you don't. You can't admire me. I'm a fucking liar and you're a truth teller, and I don't deserve you. But I still want you. Desperately.*

Sophie leaned back in the passenger seat, lowered the window, and let the wind whip through the car until he turned a corner at a lookout halfway up the mountain road and pulled the gleaming silver beast to a stop.

He cut the engine and stared at the windswept woman by his side. Maybe he wasn't a liar. Maybe he was simply a man who hadn't yet told the whole truth. There'd be time for that. When he needed to offer it up. Then it hit him — he was thinking about the next time with her, and maybe even the one after that. Which wasn't like Ryan at all. He didn't move beyond short-term, so why was his brain thinking differently?

He had no answers, only a stark certainty inside him that he wanted this woman all to himself.

"Do you like the way she handles the curves?" Sophie asked, patting the dashboard.

"So fucking much," he said then nodded to her door. "Wait for me."

"I've been waiting for you," she said, tilting her head, locking her eyes with his and saying everything in her gaze. His breath stopped short at the way she looked at him. So guileless.

He never thought he'd been waiting for anyone. Given the walls he'd erected and the foundation of privacy he built his life on, he never imagined he'd be captivated this quickly. But Sophie had him bewitched—from her beauty to her spirit to her wide-open heart.

Maybe he had been waiting for her.

His muscles tightened. Something that felt like fear raced through him—the fear of feeling something.

But goddammit, he didn't want to think about matters of the heart.

The physical was so much easier.

The physical paid better dividends.

He walked behind the car then opened her door, offering his hand.

"Get out of the car and show me," he said, issuing a command. "Show me how you look in my gift."

Sophie's eyes widened, and she unhooked her seat belt in one second. Damn, this woman loved to be told what to do, and he loved being the one to do it.

He tugged her out and spun her around, lining her back against his front. Sex. Contact. Connection. He needed it to wipe his mind of all the dangerous little details he kept locked up. He moved her body closer to the hood of the car. He tested the metal with his palm — warm not too hot. "Bend over."

She placed her hands on the hood, and flattened her back. My God, she took orders like a dream. "Raise your skirt for me."

She reached a hand behind her and grabbed the orange hem. She lifted it up and a groan ripped from his throat when he saw her in the panties he'd bought for her.

The hottest item of clothing in all of creation.

"Nothing has ever looked better on any woman in the world," he said, as he fell to his knees in the dirt, and pressed his face against her rear. He flicked his tongue through one of the crisscross sections that exposed her creamy white flesh, and she gasped. He gripped her cheeks in his hands, squeezing her as he smothered her barely-covered bottom in kisses. Oh, the things he wanted to do to her. The ways he wanted to touch her with his tongue, fingers, and his cock. Lick her, touch her, fuck her, and taste her.

His dick throbbed in his pants, begging to be set free, to be inside her gorgeous body.

"They were made for you," he whispered as he worshipped her ass with his lips, and she squirmed under his touch, rocking her body back into him. He licked the outline of one of the diamonds, flicking the tip of his tongue over her skin, and she moaned his name.

"I bet you're soaked right now," he said, in a hungry voice.

"I bet you're right," she answered in between erratic breaths.

The world around them was dark and quiet. There was only the slightest rustle of an evening breeze. They were all alone on the turnout at the side of the road, and he was going to fuck her good and hard.

He slid his fingers between her legs and groaned when he felt how damp she was. Nothing was better in the entire universe than when a woman responded to a man like this. Her body told him everything—from the way she stretched her arms, to how her belly pressed flat to the metal, to how her ass was raised in the air, the skirt all bunched up by her hips.

She wanted him. She gave herself freely, and he was utterly consumed with a deep and potent longing for Sophie. He'd intended to fuck her, but with his face so close to her sweet center, he decided on an appetizer first. "Don't move," he said, as he pulled the panel of her panties to the side. Keeping her in place would keep him in control of this ravenous desire that raged inside him. "Stay still as I eat you."

"I won't move," she answered, digging her heels into the ground.

He stared between her legs, where she glistened. His breath came fast as raw desire overtook him. "You're so fucking delicious," he said, then licked.

She trembled and sighed sexily. The most enticing sounds floated from her lips as he licked her sweetness. Her clit was a hard stone under his tongue, and with each flick, she trembled but remained still. She'd taken his order to heart and hadn't moved an inch. She followed directions like a perfect student, and she tasted like heaven on earth. He buried his face in her slickness, his hands gripping her luscious ass as he devoured her.

She flooded his tongue and moaned her pleasure. "I'm so close, Ryan. I'm so close. Can I please move?"

Please.

Oh hell, it was like a direct line of desire to his cock. He ached to fill her. That simple word spurred him on, making him want her even more. "Yes," he said roughly then gave her an order. "You have permission to fuck my face now."

She followed it to the letter. He continued his assault on her pussy with his lips, thrusting his tongue inside her heat, as she rocked into him madly. She went from frozen to frenzied in no time. Her thighs tensed, and as soon as he felt her quiver, he slid a finger inside her.

Her soft walls clenched around him, and she cried out into the night as she came on his tongue, his lips, and his chin.

She tasted divine. Absolutely intoxicating all over him, and he was hooked on her, on her taste, her scent, her body. Everything. He lapped up her wetness as the aftershocks moved through her. He placed a palm on each thigh, steadying her as he kissed the backs of her legs, then lapped up a bead of wetness that had slid down her skin.

He stood up and raked his eyes over the gorgeous sight of her bent at the waist, soft and warm from her first orgasm. "I'm just getting started, beautiful. There's so much I want to do to you."

She looked at him and smiled, a tipsy grin that made his heart pound and his dick ache. Rabid desire raced through him again, and the need to take her overwhelmed him. Her feet were planted on the ground. He nudged the inside of her right leg with his foot, then kicked her legs open wider.

"Spread your legs for me," he instructed, and she inched her feet apart into a more perfect *V.*

His fingers traveled along her spine and up her neck to her hair, grabbing it, turning her so she looked up at him. Her eyes were hazy and full of a lust that matched his. "Do you have any idea what you do to me?" he asked harshly.

"I think I do."

"You are under my skin," he whispered, as he kept her pressed against the warm hood with one hand, then slinked his other hand down to her waist, and unfastened the slim, orange belt. "And in my head," he continued as he snapped the belt free. "And I can't fucking stop thinking about you."

"I can't stop either," she said, and in a flash he wrapped the belt around her wrists, knotting it, twisting it, and tying her hands together with her own accessory. She allowed him, offering up her wrists to be bound. She was a willing hostage.

"That turns me on even more," he growled in her ear, as he stretched her tied arms along the silver hood.

"Tying me up?"

"Yes," he said, pressing his erection against her ass. "But what makes me rock hard is the way you let me. The way you want me to. The way you give your body to me," he said as he grabbed a condom from his pocket, unzipped his pants, and pushed down his briefs.

"Take me," she said, meeting his eyes as she lay vulnerable and completely open to him, her face on the side of her car, her body ready for him.

"I'm going to, Sophie. I'm going to take you right now," he said, as he rolled on the condom. Then he placed his hands on that perfect ass, and dug his thumbs into her cheeks, spreading open her sex. He rubbed the tip of his dick against her wet heat.

Lust crashed over him like a wave beating the shore. He returned his right hand to her neck, held her in place, and sank into her in one swift move.

He stilled inside her, inhaling deeply as he savored the intensity of this moment—the feel of her luscious body drawing him in for the first time. He'd craved this from the second he'd met her, and now he knew why.

She fit him perfectly.

"Jesus Christ," he groaned, the lush, hot feel of her gripping him skyrocketing his need for her. "You feel fucking amazing. I knew you would. I fucking knew you would."

She moaned. She whimpered. She cried out his name. "*Ryan.*"

The sound of his name falling from her red lips made him want her more than he'd ever thought possible. She'd seduced him with her willingness, she'd lured him in with her sweet naughtiness, and she'd captivated him with her mind.

He was mesmerized by this woman. Completely spellbound.

And so he did what he came here to do.

He fucked her. Deep, hard, and feverishly. He swiveled his hips and thrust into her, her sweet, snug pussy taking him all the way. He breathed heavily as he stroked, one hand squeezing her ass. She gave him everything he wanted —complete control of her body—and it annihilated his brain. It scorched a path of pure pleasure through him. He was driven with need for her, by the sheer ecstasy of fucking this woman on the hood of her car in the desert, under the sky, under his command.

"I could fuck you all night. I could fuck you all day." He gripped her neck as he pumped.

"It feels so good," she said on a pant.

"Say it again," he told her.

"You feel so good."

"Again."

"It feels incredible."

"So good you're going to come on my cock any second?" he asked on a deep, furious thrust.

"Yes, oh God, yes. I'm going to come on you," she cried out, and screamed his name. The sound of it echoing in the night made his balls tighten and pleasure ricochet through him, sweeping over his entire body, obliterating everything else in his world but this pure and perfect moment with this magnificent woman.

He grunted, calling out her name as he came, then slumped over her back, and wrapped his arms around her.

She sighed happily.

He damn near did the same. "I can't get enough of you. I just fucking can't."

She shot him the sweetest smile. In a soft voice she said, "I'm hungry. Care to take me out for a bite to eat?"

He'd already eaten, but food sounded good.

CHAPTER FIFTEEN

The dry spell had officially ended, so Sophie ordered french fries and a chocolate milkshake.

Because the combination felt like a celebration, and she was celebrating not only the first time she'd had sex in a few years, but also the best sex ever.

Make that – Best. Sex. Ever.

They'd stopped at a roadside diner on the return to the city, and he ate a burger and shared her fries. She reached for one at the same time as he did, and their fingers bumped. He laughed. "We could fight for it. Or I could let you have that one," he said.

"I trust you'll let me have it," she said then snatched the fry in question and dragged it through ketchup. As she brought it to her lips, she peeked to make sure her napkin was spread across her skirt. Damn. She'd missed a loop when she'd put her belt back on. Wait. She hadn't. One of them had split.

That was some hard loving.

"Looks like I ripped a belt loop," she said after she finished chewing.

"I'll have it fixed for you. Pretty sure I'm responsible."

"I'm pretty sure I can fix it easily with some needle and thread." Then she noticed the dress was streaked along the bodice and the skirt. The danger of sex on a car in a white dress. "Oh no. My dress is dirty, too," she said, gesturing to the marks on the front.

He frowned. "My fault, as well. I'll pay to have it cleaned."

She scoffed. "No. You're not paying for my dress." Funny, how she consented so easily to his orders during sex, but the rest of the time she had no problem holding her own.

"But I made it dirty," he said then took a bite of his burger.

"You didn't make it dirty," she said, correcting him. "Fucking you made it dirty."

He set his burger down on the plate and narrowed his eyes, giving her a purposeful stare. "Sweetheart, *I* fucked you. You didn't fuck me."

She grinned wickedly, loving teasing him like this. "I know." She leaned closer to him across the table. "And I loved it. I loved how you fucked me," she said, and even just saying that word—*fuck*—turned her on. Holden had never been one for *fucking*. Bless his heart, but Holden was a *let's make love* type of guy. Then there was her college boyfriend, Zach, her one and only other lover. He was the quintessential two-pump chump. There was no finesse. No attention to detail. And no more than two minutes, tops. Sex with him was all about choking the chicken so he could rush back to work on his startup ideas, which had never amounted to much.

She couldn't even compare Ryan to those guys. He was in a class by himself. Everything about him—that soft brown hair, those dark blue eyes, his hard body, the way he took her—he was fantasy material.

But real.

Add in the easy way they were able to talk, toss in the intensity of the connection, and mix in the sweet little gestures, and she was dangerously close to feeling something more.

Ryan reached across the table and tucked a strand of hair behind her ear. "I've never met a woman like you, one who's so strong and direct in everything else, but able in bed to turn over the reins. It's addictive," he said, his eyes fixed on her the whole time, the look in them earnest and truthful. Her heart swooped in a daredevil loop the loop.

Correction: she was *already* feeling something more.

Which meant she wanted him to know more about her. She brought the straw in her milkshake to her lips and swallowed some of the delicious chocolate ice cream concoction. "Confession—I've never had the chance to be like this."

He arched an eyebrow in question.

She put the shake glass down, keenly aware of the sounds of the diner—the cooks frying up bacon for patrons ordering breakfast for their late-night dinners, the twang of a country tune playing softly overhead, a waitress taking an order a few booths away. "This isn't some big secret. I know you looked me up before the gala, so you might have learned this, but I was married for five years." At this point it would be odd *not* to tell him this fact of her romantic life.

The surprise in his eyes told her he hadn't known this. "No, I wasn't aware. How long have you been divorced?"

"Since I was twenty-nine, so a little more than two years now. Which means I was twenty-four when I married Holden," she said, sharing the details matter-of-factly, because there was nothing to hide. Now, on a third date, after hot sex on her car, seemed the right moment to mention her past marital status.

"That's young. Did you go to college together?"

She shook her head. "We were best friends in high school, and we stayed close. He went to Berkeley and I was at Stanford, so we weren't far away. I didn't date much in college, except this one guy, Zach, who was a computer geek, too. Truth be told, Zach was kind of a competitive ass who thought his tech startup would blow mine out of the water, and he told me as much every day."

"Did it? Blow yours out of the water?"

"As if." She was pleased, and not a bit guilty, to share this next tidbit. "He never even got funded. He actually applied for an engineering job at my company two years after graduation."

"Did you hire him?"

"No. But it had nothing to do with our past relationship. It had to do with him rushing through things, including his work. He was always cutting corners." His work ethic was similar to his sex ethic. "Anyway, we only went out for a few months during college, and even though it wasn't a tough decision to end things, he was quite insulting at the time. Holden was there for me when I broke up with him."

"So Holden was the guy you turned to when things went amiss with others?"

"In that case, yes. There weren't many others, honestly. But Holden was there for me. I was there for him. And soon enough after college, marrying each other just seemed to make sense."

He furrowed his brow, as if marriage didn't truly compute for him. Perhaps it didn't. "Make sense?"

He reached for a french fry as she nodded. "We were great friends. And we actually still are. He's probably my best friend."

He dropped the fry. "I don't get it. How can you be best friends with your ex-husband? If you're that close, why aren't you with him?"

She inhaled deeply. Okay, telling Ryan she'd been married wasn't hard in the least. But explaining why they'd split up was a wee bit tougher. She lowered her voice. "We weren't compatible in the bedroom."

"You mean he's gay?" Ryan asked, so damn straightforward in his assumption that Sophie laughed.

She shifted her hand back and forth like a seesaw. "Sort of."

"Sort of? How the hell are you sort of gay?" he asked with a laugh.

"Um, it's called *bisexual,* Ryan."

He blinked, and shook his head, as if he were processing this information about sexuality for the first time. Maybe he was. Maybe bisexuality didn't occur to him because Ryan Sloan was as straight as they came. If there were a mold for hot, dominant, heterosexual male, he'd fit it perfectly. Hell, he'd probably made the mold. "Okay, I hear you," Ryan said. "So he likes boys and girls."

She nodded. "Yes. And he was interested in sharing me with boys."

He drew a deep breath and straightened his spine. "Did you?"

She studied his face, unsure if the uncertain look in his eyes suggested that a past ménage was a deal-breaker. She didn't want to be judged for her past, even though she didn't have one. She needed to know Ryan wasn't that kind of person. "Would it bother you if I had?"

"No," he said immediately, then waited for her answer.

She shook her head. "I didn't have a threesome. I don't want to be shared."

He pushed away from his side of the booth, stood up, and moved in next to her. Draping an arm around her possessively, he pulled her close, then brushed his finger along her jawline. "If you were mine, I'd never share you," he said, his deep, sexy voice sending goose bumps over her flesh.

"Is that so?"

He cupped her shoulder in his strong hand, his fingers brushing along her bare skin. "I'd never let anyone else touch you. The thought of it already drives me mad. And I'd never stop touching you," he said, then dropped his mouth to her lips and kissed her hard, as if he were marking her.

Her mind went hazy. Sparks raced madly in her bloodstream, all from a kiss.

He pulled away. "If you were mine, you'd only be mine. And I'd satisfy you every night. Every day. Every morning. Every single time," he said, claiming her lips once more. Roughly. So damn roughly that it sent a charge through her. Every kiss was an assertion. Every touch was ownership. His words said *if*, but his body said *you're mine*.

She *felt* like his. It was crazy to feel that way so soon. But tell that to her heart, beating furiously from his posses-sive words. "You would satisfy me every time. You already do," she said in a breathy whisper, her voice feathery soft now, as he crowded her in.

His throat rumbled. "If you were mine, I'd never let you want for anything. I'd take care of you and all your needs. All the time. Anytime. Whatever you needed, I'd give you," he said, and his words set her on fire. They were so hypo-thetical, but so damn appealing. They made her want him again.

They gave her confidence, too, the kind she'd felt when she was running her company. The kind she hadn't always felt with men. She reached for his collar, needing to hold on, knowing this was as good a time as any. "Ryan," she asked carefully, nerves sneaking up on her.

"Yes?"

She swallowed. "There's an event I'm organizing for the local community center. A fundraiser in another week. One of the donors wanted to set me up with his grandson," she said, and he clenched his hand around her tighter as she said those words. His eyes seared her. "But I told him I was seeing someone, and I was hoping that someone would take me to the event."

The corner of his lips quirked up in a knowing grin. That smile settled the anxiety. "And who is this someone you want to take you to the event?" he asked playfully.

She rolled her eyes. "You. Obviously."

"And do you want me to act all possessive, so everyone knows you're taken?"

"Would it be an act?" she asked, countering him.

He shook his head. "No. It's not difficult for me to feel a sense of ownership of you," he said, brushing his hand along her bare arm.

"Do you like owning things?"

"You're not a thing."

"Do you like owning women?"

He moved in closer, which was no small feat in the diner booth. There was hardly any room between them already. "No. I don't ever get close enough to feel that way," he said.

Her heart fell as his words made landfall. There it was—the admission. She'd suspected all along he wasn't a relationship type of guy. He had walls around him. He'd had them from the start. She didn't know why, but she'd sensed they existed. Now she was certain, and she wished she didn't feel like a balloon deflated.

She straightened her shoulders and tried to mentally talk herself down. They were hardly having a relationship anyway. This was a tryst. A delicious, druggy, wondrous tryst. "That's fine," she said, holding up her chin.

He narrowed his eyes, looking at her curiously. "It's not fine. Because nothing about you is just fine. Because you do something to me that drives me wild."

"I do?" she asked, trying to rein in a grin that had resurfaced.

He nodded, his lips parting as he pulled back. "You do. So when I take you to this event—because I will be taking you. You might have asked me, but I'm the one taking you, Sophie," he said, and that commanding tone lit her up. "And when I do, it will be clear to everyone that you're with me."

A fresh wave of longing rolled through. "Am I? With you?"

He nodded. "Yes."

Oh God, her heart galloped. It raced away from her brain, launching a full-on separation from her sanity, from her clarity, from her mathematical mind. Her heart had gone rogue, and there was nothing she could do about it. Even though a part of her was furious—he'd just told her he wasn't a relationship guy and now he was telling her she belonged with him. She hated being toyed with.

"How can you say that? You just told me you don't ever get close to people?"

He took a deep breath. "I don't. I'm not good with serious relationships. I was in the army for five years, and wasn't involved with anyone then, and since I've been back I don't usually make it beyond the third date. But look what you've done to me. We're already planning our seventh."

"Seventh?"

"The way I see it, I'm not going to last a week without seeing you, much less a few days. So if we're going to this fundraiser thing in a week, I'm going to be seeing you at least three times before then. So the fundraiser will be our seventh, and you need to be fully prepared for me to fuck you like I own you over the next three dates."

Okay, so that was pretty epic. She beamed. "I can handle that."

"You can and you will. And do you know what else I would do if you were mine?"

"What else?"

"Fuck you again on our third date."

He tossed some money on the table, and led her out of

the diner. After opening the car door for her, he pulled into the dark corner of the lot, far away from the lights. He cut the engine and grabbed the back of her head, kissing her in a way that heated her up and made her squirm in seconds. His hand traveled up her skirt, brushing against the panel of her panties, feeling her wetness.

That was all he needed. "Backseat. Now," he growled.

She scurried into the backseat, and he followed. "Get on your hands and knees."

She obliged willingly as he grabbed protection, unzipped his pants, and sank into her. Her body flooded with pleasure, with a deep and hungry desire to give herself over to him, to however he wanted her.

Gripping her hips, he drove into her. "Tell me something, Sophie," he said in between thrusts. "Who's fucking who right now?"

Heat licked her veins. "You are. You're fucking me."

He grabbed her hair, wrapped it around his fist, and yanked. "That's right. I'm having you. I'm claiming you. I'm taking you," he said in a hot, smoky voice. "Are you taking me?"

"No," she said, as he tugged tight on her strands. "You're doing it."

"I am. And I'm going to do it again and again and again."

"Yes. Please do it again," she cried out, as electricity roared through her body. She shut her eyes, seeing stars, feeling heaven, and losing herself to him.

He swiveled his hips and claimed her with his cock. He commanded her with his words. He brought her the most bone-deep pleasure she'd ever known as he took her to the edge and came undone with her.

Chapter Sixteen

"Tell me about this event. What should I wear?" he asked, as he turned onto the Strip to drive her home.

"Tux. Do you own one?"

He laughed softly. "Of course I own a tux. Where is it?"

"The Venetian."

"And who are the sponsors?"

"Well, *me*, for one," she said, then rattled off a few names of local companies, including a law firm, an insurance company, and a national sporting goods chain. "And Redwood Mountain Ventures, too. A venture capital firm."

He jerked his head to look at her as he pulled to a stop at a red light. "Redwood Mountain Ventures?"

She nodded. "Yes. Why?"

"That's my brother's firm. Colin's."

"Oh, that's great. I've been dealing with one of the other partners. A woman. I didn't make the connection that your brother the venture capitalist was at this firm. But how wonderful that he's a supporter. It's a great cause. I was at the community center earlier today. They're going to do so much for kids that need extra help."

"Interesting," Ryan said, wondering why Colin never mentioned anything about such a hefty donation. But then again, his youngest sibling had never been one to brag about all the ways that he gave back. "I wonder if he'll be there."

"You should ask him. It would be nice to say hello. I'm hoping John can make it so perhaps you can meet him, too," she said, lightness in her tone, because, of course, she had nothing to hide.

Unlike him.

His chest clenched. He muttered a silent curse as he reached her building. Now would be a great time to admit he'd already met her brother, had been questioned by him at police headquarters about his father's murder, and then received a phone call from him, hunting for more details about his mother's straying ways.

Honestly though, telling her about the connection to her brother wasn't the hard part. What felt insurmountable was what it meant—if he told her he knew John, he'd have to tell her about his parents. He'd have to give voice to how his family had been blasted to pieces one night when he was only fourteen.

He'd never told someone he'd dated. He'd never wanted to.

But here in the driveway of her building, nearing midnight, after the most mind-blowing sex of his life, was not the moment to dive into the past. He needed to figure out how to tell her without fucking everything up. His experience in saying the right thing was terribly limited for many reasons—he didn't get close to people, and he didn't speak of matters no one else needed to know.

Trust was a screwed-up promise.

Intimacy was a lie.

Love wasn't real.

She'd shared so much though, and he had to figure out how to do the same.

He said good night and headed for his home, taking his dog for a midnight run to glean some answers. But an hour of hard exercise under the stars didn't illuminate his own path any better, so when he got into bed with his dog curled up on top of the covers, only one thing was clear.

He was fucked.

Because he liked her more than he'd ever intended. That first night with Sophie he'd gone in armed with every intention of keeping things only physical. The second time, too. Hell, he'd tried to do as much tonight. But his intentions were futile. He wanted this woman with a desire that burned away everything in its path. That consumed his brain cells. That chained up his heart. And for the first time ever, he felt the flicker of something awfully dangerous. So dangerous it made him start to use words.

Words that mattered.

Words that came from that organ inside him that had gone on lockdown many years ago.

Words that could mean the start of something more.

from: guywithgreentie@gmail.com
to: Sophiefashionista@gmail.com
date: July 17, 1:13 AM
subject: You

You are exquisite.

He tossed his phone on his nightstand and dragged a hand through his hair, dreading the moment that was barreling down on him.

He ran a hand between Johnny Cash's soft ears. "Where do I go from here, buddy? Tell me that."

The dog licked his face.

"Ha. Already done that. That's not the problem whatsoever."

CHAPTER SEVENTEEN

Becky waited for him on the front porch, shielding her eyes from the early morning sun.

Ryan cut the engine on his truck, hopped out of the cab, and made eye contact with his dog, pointing to the house. "Go inside, Johnny Cash," he said, and the dog followed the command, leaping out of the front seat and scurrying across the yard. He parked himself at Becky's feet and wagged his tail at rocket speed.

"Aww, you're such a sweet boy. Give me a kiss," Becky said, cooing at the dog as Ryan walked across the yard and joined her on the steps.

"Watch it. He's a crazy kisser. He can't help himself around the ladies," Ryan said, lowering his shades and wrapping his arms around Becky.

"'Course he can't. He has good taste," Sanders said.

Ryan looked up to see Sanders open the door and join his wife on the porch. "Hey. Didn't expect to see you at the crack of dawn," Ryan said.

His dad's friend puffed up his chest in his faded blue short-sleeve button-down with his name stitched on the right-hand side. "I'm still a working man for a few more months. And it's a Wednesday."

"Right. Of course," Ryan said then turned back to Becky. "Have fun with my boy today."

"I will. You drive safely," she said, patting him on the cheek, then headed inside with the dog.

Sanders walked Ryan to his truck. "You gonna be gone all day?"

Ryan nodded. While he could have left his dog home on a day like this—Johnny Cash was well trained—Becky liked having him around from time to time, so the dog-sitting worked for everyone. "Probably won't be back until the evening. I need to take care of a few things in town before I take off."

"You be careful. No speeding," Sanders said with a wink.

"Yeah, yeah, yeah," Ryan said.

"Hey, Donald's coming over later for poker. You can say hi to him when you pick up your dog," Sanders said, mentioning another friend of his dad's. The three men had been close buddies. For a brief moment, Ryan's chest ached with the image of what tonight could have been. His dad should have been joining them this evening, playing poker, smoking cigars, having a beer.

He should have been doing so many things.

Hell, at this point, maybe his dad would even have met a new woman if he were still alive. Found someone else. Fallen in love again.

Ryan scoffed as he drove to the office, wondering how such a ridiculous notion had appeared in his head out of nowhere. Because love was a fucking lie.

* * *

He slapped the contract on his brother's desk. "Boom. Done. Another deal for us," he said, parking himself in the black leather chair in Michael's office. Guitar-heavy rock music pulsed from the laptop. His brother used to play the electric guitar and had dabbled in rock bands in high school and college. A workaholic with little time to play now, he still assaulted his eardrums with his favorite tunes.

Michael arched an eyebrow. "You don't say. Maybe I should keep you around."

Ryan rolled his eyes. "Hey, fifty-fifty, I could say the same of you," he said, meaning their joint ownership of Sloan Protection Resources.

"Yeah, I know. Just giving you a hard time." Michael cast a cursory glance at the pages on his desk. He tapped his index finger against them. "Looks good. I see White Box is getting a full suite of security services. This is the company you met with in San Francisco a few weeks ago, right?"

Ryan nodded. He'd been slated to visit his mom in prison with Shannon at the time, but their mom had gotten the dates wrong, and Shannon wound up going solo. Ryan had been in San Francisco instead, meeting with the head of White Box, a guy named Charlie Stravinsky, and his right-hand man, Curtis. Charlie owned some restaurants, including a once-popular Chinese eatery, but had now converted them to private clubs, the kind that catered to gentleman with big wallets and hearty appetites for both women and bets. That kind of business needed security, and since White Box was expanding from San Francisco to Vegas, the firm had reached out to Ryan and Michael.

"And you said his VP of biz dev is coming in to sign the papers?"

"One p.m. today. Guy named Curtis," Ryan said, tapping his watch. "He's local here in Vegas. It's on you for the final signatures. I worked on that deal all day Saturday and Sunday."

"Aww, poor baby," Michael said, breaking out an imaginary violin and running the bow across the strings.

"Whatever," Ryan said, waving a hand dismissively. "Point being, I'm out of here the rest of the day."

"You going to see 347-921?"

Michael didn't even use their mom's name, just her inmate number. At first it had rankled Ryan, and he'd told his brother as much. *Use her name at least*, he'd said. Michael never did, and Ryan had learned to let it go. Now, he was used to the way Dora Prince had been reduced to digits.

"I am."

His brother made a scornful sound as he shook his head. "Why do you waste your time with that?"

"Why? You're seriously asking why?"

Michael nodded as a guitar riff played through the speakers. Ryan rose, planted his palms on Michael's desk, and stared at him, wondering if he was crazy. How did his brother not get it? "Because I want to know why the fuck the case is open. Don't you?"

"She won't tell you shit."

Ryan stabbed his index finger against his sternum. "But I'm the only one she *might* tell something. That's why I'm going. Because I'm the one who sees her, besides Shan. So if there is something to say, or someone else involved, I'm the one she's going to talk to."

Michael softened his tone but still held his ground. "Look, man. I get it. I understand she did some kind of

number on you and convinced you she might not be guilty
—but she's so fucking guilty, Ryan. Day is day, and night is
night, and our mother had our father killed. Maybe there
was someone else involved, maybe Detective Winston is
sniffing around for a middleman, or something between
her and Stefano, but I guarantee that you're not going to
exonerate inmate number 347-921."

Ryan gritted his teeth as frustration seared his nervous
system, running a wild course through his body. "Here's
the bottom line. Someone knows something about our
family that we don't," he said through tight lips. "I want to
know what that something is, and I'm not going to stop
until I find out."

Michael stood up and clapped Ryan on the shoulder.
"You're a determined bastard. But you're my determined
bastard. So don't speed like Sanders. We need you squeaky
clean here at the company. No tickets, no record, nothing."

"Don't worry your pretty little head. I'm never dirty," he
said with a wink.

Michael tugged him in for a quick hug. "Love you, bro."

"Love you, too," Ryan grumbled.

This. His brothers and sister. His grandmother. His dog.
That was real love to him—the only kind he trusted.

CHAPTER EIGHTEEN

An elderly woman with curly gray hair opened the faded red door of the ranch-style home and waved goodbye to the man inside. "See you at the recital."

"You're going to be great. Your 'Für Elise' is fantastic."

The voice blasted Ryan back in time, like a slingshot to the end of junior high. Luke Carlton, older, grayer, and paunchier, turned to Ryan as the woman ambled down the steps on the way to her car.

"Ryan Sloan," Luke said and extended a hand. He wasn't surprised to see Ryan, nor should he be.

Ryan had made an appointment for a piano lesson. He hadn't used the name he'd had growing up—Ryan Paige-Prince—but Luke clearly knew who he was. He suspected that was a result of the reopened investigation.

Even so, Ryan's legs felt wobbly and his stomach plummeted. It was as if he was having an out-of-body experience and someone else was grasping the palm of this brown-eyed man in khaki slacks and a sky blue Tommy Bahama shirt.

His mother's ex-lover.

"Come in," Luke said, letting go and gesturing to the home he'd lived in for the last five years. Before this meeting, Ryan had run a security check on Luke Carlton. He was only a few years older than Dora Prince, and he'd bought this home with his wife. Ryan didn't know how long Luke had been married, though.

"My kids are at camp," Luke said as they walked through the living room. Okay, he'd been with her long enough to procreate. "Wife's out grocery shopping. I take it you're not really interested in a piano lesson?"

Ryan shrugged a shoulder. "Sometimes I think about taking it up."

"Lots of adults do. Half my business these days is from adults who decide they've always wanted to learn how to play." He guided Ryan through the kitchen. The sink was stacked with plates. Eggs had been served for breakfast. A loaf of rye bread was on the counter, a twist tie keeping it closed. An odd sense of the surreal descended on him. Everything about Luke's home was so…normal. From the blinds that hung on the living room windows, to the beige couch with an indentation on it in front of a large TV screen, to scattered pictures of his kids and his wife, many of them on a beach, playing in the sand and surf.

Luke led him to an office area, with a baby grand piano, a couch, a chair, and a writing table.

"We might as well chat here," Luke said and claimed a spot on the piano bench. He gestured to a wooden chair.

Ryan hardly wanted to sit. He didn't want to stand. He didn't know what to do with his hands. He stuffed them into the pockets of his pants. He was used to talking to clients, to pitching the need for security services, to giving orders to troops in Europe during his days in the army.

But talking to his mother's former lover from eighteen years ago gave *uncomfortable* new meaning. His throat was parched, and his tongue barely worked. But somehow, he found the ability to speak. "My dad's case was reopened. The detective asked me about you and your relationship with my mom." Ryan jumped right in, hitting the key points without mincing words.

Luke nodded. "I am aware of that. I met him, too. Winston. Seems sharp."

"Yeah," Ryan said, simply to say something. "What does he know? Did you tell him how you knew my mom?"

"I told him we were in love, yes. And that it had been a mistake, since she was married," Luke said, clasping his hands together. "I still ask God every day for forgiveness for having fallen in love with a married woman."

"That's not what I meant," Ryan said, because he wasn't here to talk about contrition for cheating. "I'm talking about her drug problem. *The cocaine*. That she got it from Stefano. Do they know?"

This was the first time he'd said those words aloud in nearly twenty years—*drugs. Cocaine. That Stefano was her dealer.* When he was in seventh grade, a year before the shooting, Ryan came home early from school on a half-day that his mom had forgotten about. He found her cutting lines at her sewing table. With a rolled-up dollar bill, she'd leaned in and inhaled a line of white powder off her Singer machine.

He stood in the door, his jaw hanging open. "Mom?"

She raised her chin. Her green eyes were glassy, but the stunned look in them said she hadn't expected him home.

"Please don't tell anyone," she said and started crying. She stood up and clasped her arms around him. "Please, this is my last time. I'm trying to stop. I swear I'm going to stop. I promise."

At that age, you believed your parents. You believed your mom even if she had powder up her nose. What else was he supposed to think? He was barely thirteen then, and all he knew was that his parents had been fighting, they barely had any money, and they lived in a shitty neighborhood.

She'd clutched him as if her life depended on it and begged him to never breathe a word.

In the months that had followed, she'd seemed determined to prove herself to him. She'd told him she was getting help, that she was going to Narcotics Anonymous, and that she had a sponsor for counseling and guidance. "Please, Ry. I'm trying so hard, baby. I'm trying so hard to fight these demons," she'd say to him at night as he got under the gray cover in his twin bed. "Don't tell your daddy please. He'd just worry. And don't tell your brothers and sister. I'm so ashamed, and I want to get well again. I've got a sponsor and I'm going to meetings, and I swear I'm going to kick this habit. I owe some money to the guy I used to buy from, and I'm working extra for the local gymnastics team to earn enough to pay him back. Once I do, I swear I'll be free of this."

"I won't tell anyone," Ryan had said, battening down the hatches, locking up his brain, some sort of self-preservation kicking in. It was all he'd been able to do. Zip it up, keep it quiet, and never speak of what he saw.

He never said a word.

Even when she met Luke at those meetings. Even when she fell for another recovered addict. Even when she was first questioned by police, and it all came to light that she'd not only been having an affair with that former addict at the time of the murder, but that she'd made a string of phone calls for two months to a man named Jerry Stefano. Why was she talking to him so much, the cops wanted to know?

She'd begged Ryan again to stay quiet. She'd shut the door to his room, planted her hands on his shoulders, and given him instructions. "They haven't found the person who shot your daddy. And they're asking me all kinds of questions, and I'm petrified they're going to try to frame me for his murder. You know what we talked about?"

Ryan had nodded as fear rippled through him.

"If the police know I used drugs, if they know I bought them from Jerry Stefano, it will look so much worse for me. They know I've been on the phone with Jerry for months. I'm going to have to tell a lie about all those phone calls. He's been calling to collect money, and if they know I was buying from him, they'll paint me as a druggie, murderer wife."

"But wouldn't they see you're innocent if you tell them about the drugs? Won't it be better to have them know you bought drugs than to have them think you planned a murder?" he'd asked, trying desperately to understand why she didn't confess her secret.

She shook her head. Vehemently. "No. Never. Trust me. It will look worse, and I have to beat this rap. So I have no choice but to lie about Jerry. Luke is the only other one who knows the truth about those phone calls."

Luke and Ryan.

That was all.

Now, years later as an adult, Ryan was asking the only other person who knew if he'd broken their silence. "Did you tell the detective that Stefano was her dealer?"

Luke shook his head, rose, and turned up the air conditioning in his piano room. The sound of the whirring grew louder, as if Luke was using it as a buffer to cover up this conversation. Ryan bristled inside, because he so often did the same thing. He'd cranked up tunes in his car when he'd told Shannon details of the case.

Luke held up his palm, as if he were swearing in court. "I did not say a word. Her last wish before she went away was for me to keep that secret," he said, his voice trembling. "She was terrified of Stefano. You never met him, Ryan, and I pray you never do. You bump into a guy like Stefano on the street and you run the other way." There was rabid fear in his eyes as he offered this strange piece of advice.

Ryan crossed his arms. He didn't want advice from his mom's lover. Besides, he wasn't afraid. Not of Stefano and not of men like the scumbag who'd killed his father. "I'm not scared of men who deal drugs to fucking mothers and children," he said, practically spitting out the words.

Luke's gray eyes widened, and he grabbed Ryan's arm. "She was petrified of what would happen if people knew she was connected to him," he pleaded.

"But their plan didn't work. Their cover-up failed," Ryan said, reminding him that the lies his mom had told didn't save her from jail. The truth would have tethered her more closely to the Royal Sinners, so she'd fashioned a fable. She'd said all those phone calls to Stefano were for tree trimming, and he'd said the same. That was Stefano's day job—a laborer at a tree-trimming company, so when she was asked about the string of calls, she'd claimed she'd hired him "under the table" to clean up some overgrown branches. It was the kind of work she couldn't have her teenage sons do since it required specialty saws and tools. That was all true and completely plausible.

And the tale seemed to work at first for both Stefano and Ryan's mom. For a brief while, their story did the trick. Botched robbery—that was how the murder looked to authorities, and Stefano seemed clean.

Until the detectives found Stefano's fingerprints on the gun he'd disposed of, and the man started singing about how he'd been hired for much more than tree-trimming.

Stefano served it all up, and the lie unraveled.

He told the cops he'd been contracted to kill. He said the calls to Dora weren't to cut overgrown branches—they were to plan the murder and to make it look like a robbery gone wrong. He alleged he'd been promised ten percent of Thomas Paige's life insurance policy if he pulled it off.

The life insurance company went next, supplying more evidence. They confirmed that Dora had called a few months before the death to make a "routine check" on the beneficiary information on behalf of her husband, then six days after the murder to try to liquidate the funds.

In her defense, Dora maintained her husband had asked her to check on the policy and that was why she'd phoned the company months before his death. *For him*, she'd said. He was busy working, and asked her to check up on various pieces of paperwork. As for accessing the payout, she pointed out that if she'd killed him for money wouldn't she have called hours later for the cash? No, she'd waited a week.

A week. She hung her hope on time.

The jury didn't buy it.

She could have admitted to the drugs then, but it was too late for her. The case was so far beyond drugs. The state had Stefano and his testimony, they had the life insurance proof, and they had circumstantial evidence—she was having an affair at the time of the murder.

They had her, beyond a reasonable doubt, the jury said.

Admitting to drug using and buying, to money owed to dealers, wouldn't have done a damn thing to change the fate of either Stefano or Ryan's mom.

"Don't mention the drugs," she'd begged Ryan before she left for Stella McLaren. "It won't make a difference now. I will keep fighting to be free, and it will look worse for me if this gets out. I'll try to find a way to get the guys who really did it. I have to take the fall now, but please know I will be appealing. I will do everything I can to be with my children again."

But why was Luke still covering up?

Ryan shrugged off Luke's grip. "The lies didn't work. So why are you protecting Stefano?"

"I'm not protecting Jerry," Luke said insistently, pointing to the door, waving wildly beyond. "I'm protecting my family—my wife and kids—from Stefano's friends on the outside. His friends protected him, Ryan. That's what a Royal Sinner does. The goddamn ink on their arms says that. *Protect Our Own.* He has friends who have been looking out for his interests, and I am not about to serve up any more details on him and have those friends come after my family now." Luke rubbed a hand across his jaw, glanced away, then turned his gaze back to Ryan. His eyes were softer now. "Look, I made some mistakes when I was a younger man. I made some terrible mistakes. I left town to start fresh after Dora was gone. Moved to San Diego and met my wife there. We returned to Vegas five years ago. My job now is to protect my family, and Jerry Stefano is not a man to be messed with, so I never talked then and I don't intend to now. He told us to never say a word, so I didn't. He made it clear the people we loved would get hurt. That's why your mother kept it quiet, and that's why I did, too. I love too many people to take that chance."

Ryan sighed heavily, a long, deep, frustrated sound filled with years of regret, years of anger, years of locking up all these awful secrets.

There wasn't much else to say, so Ryan thanked him and headed to the front door. On the way, he spotted a framed wedding photo of Luke and his wife. The man didn't look much younger than he did today. "How long have you been married?"

Luke glanced sheepishly at the floor. "Only a year. But we've been together for seventeen. Anyway, don't tell the church I had kids out of wedlock."

"Your secret's safe with me," Ryan said, wishing it was the only secret he shared with that man.

As he headed for his truck, a fresh wave of loathing rolled through him. He was in a pact with the man who'd fucked his mother behind his father's back.

That was all kinds of messed up.

The one bright spot was the email on his phone from Sophie.

* * *

Red. Ripe. Juicy.

The peaches looked mouthwateringly good.

"One pound of peaches coming right up."

"Thank you, Marietta," Sophie said, flashing a bright smile at her favorite employee at her father's former fruit stand at the farmer's market.

"You will love these. They're divine. My God, they melt in your mouth—and in a peach pie," Marietta said, bringing her big fingers to her lips and pressing a kiss to them before setting to work bagging up Sophie's fruit.

"Nothing is ever as good as a pie with summer peaches kissed by the sun," Sophie said as she pushed her big, white sunglasses on top of her hair.

"How's John doing?"

"You know John. He's as busy as ever. Work, work, work. And he has these dang termites, so he's been staying at my place. Talk about cramping my style," Sophie said, in a faux whisper. "But he'll be gone tomorrow night. So I think…" She trailed off to tap her nails against the red-checkered cloth that covered the table with baskets of peaches, cherries, plums, and all sorts of summer fruit. "I think I might invite over this man who I've been seeing."

Marietta wiggled her thick black eyebrows as she wiped a hand across her apron. "You know that's how your mom wooed your dad," she said, winking.

"Oh, stop."

The woman nodded enthusiastically. "It's true. She lured him with the pineapple."

"How many times did my parents tell you that story?"

"Countless," she said with a laugh then tapped the counter. "This stand has some sort of magic to it. I met my husband here, too, and we're going on twenty-five years."

"The magic of fruit," Sophie quipped, then stopped for a second to gaze heavenward. "You know, maybe that's why I have so many dresses with fruit patterns."

"You're trying to attract love," Marietta said. "Draw it to you. I think that's brave and hopeful. Do you want a pineapple? For an offering?"

"You think I'm crazy, don't you?"

Marietta shook her head. "Nothing is ever crazy when it involves love. Go," she said, gesturing to the back of the sprawling white stand with the red stripes on the awning. Her dad had operated this fruit stand for many years, and Marietta had taken it over when her parents had died within mere months of each other.

In love until the day they'd died. Her mother had said it was because they followed the simple rules of love.

"Always talk. Always be honest. Never go to bed angry. Make time for kisses and meals, dance under the stars, and dream together."

That was her mother's advice to her, shared on many nights, especially on the ones where Sophie would peek around the corner to watch her parents dance with the lights drawn low. They were so in love that they'd become the very definition of it to her.

"I miss them," she said, choking up as the images swirled faster in her mind.

"Of course you do. So go. Leave a pineapple at the kissing tree. As an offering."

"Okay," Sophie said conspiratorially, then walked behind the stand and placed the spiky fruit on the ground by the tree where her parents had their first kiss. It was so silly. But her parents had everything, and their everything was all Sophie ever knew and all she wanted.

She thought she'd had that with Holden. But the big difference was that her parents had both love *and* passion.

They held hands, they sneaked kisses, and they took care of her and John together.

A lump rose in her throat, burning her with the sting of memories.

But at least the memories were beautiful ones. Hopeful ones. She was lucky like that. She wondered briefly about Ryan's parents. He'd never said much about them, other than that his father had died when he was fourteen.

That must have been so hard on his mother.

"To love and pineapples," Sophie whispered as a lone tear streaked down her cheek.

She returned to the front of the stand, and Marietta handed her a sturdy brown paper bag. "Go make a peach pie. It's always the way to a man's heart."

Sophie wasn't entirely convinced pie was the way to Ryan's heart, or that she'd ever be able to travel that path in him. But it certainly couldn't hurt to feed him.

from: Sophiefashionista@gmail.com
to: guywithgreentie@gmail.com
date: July 17, 10:43 AM
subject: Know what's really exquisite?

My peach pie.

So exquisite you should come over for dinner and dessert, and peaches and me. Friday night?

from: guywithgreentie@gmail.com
to: Sophiefashionista@gmail.com
date: July 17, 10:48 AM
subject: You. Still you.

Yes, and yes, and yes, and yes.

Her phone rang as she turned on the engine in her car.

"Tell me more about these peaches," he said, and his strong, sexy voice made her belly flip.

"They're ripe, and juicy, and they taste like sin," she said, taking her time with each word, letting them fall from her lips like sugar.

"Mmmm," he said, in a sexy growl. "So just like you, basically?"

"I'll have to take your word on that."

"Oh, you can definitely take my word on that."

"By the way, I fixed my dress, and I cleaned it myself."

"Aren't you little Miss Independent? Not even letting me help," he said, and she could practically see his playful pout.

"Maybe I just wanted to assert myself in that way."

"Maybe I'll assert myself by getting you another dress. That one you said you wanted."

She laughed as she pulled out of the lot. "I highly doubt you would even know where to get one. They are kind of specialty boutique dresses."

"Oh, you challenge me, woman?" he asked, sounding all over-the-top tough.

She laughed, and gave it right back to him. "Oh, yes I do, *man*."

"I am up to the challenge," he answered, and a robotic female voice sounded from his phone. "*You are two hundred miles from your destination in Hawthorne.*"

She furrowed her brow. There wasn't much in Hawthorne. That was a small town with a big prison. "What are you doing in Hawthorne?" she asked curiously, as she pulled onto the road. "Do you do security for the prison?"

He didn't answer at first. "Yeah. Shit, Sophie, I need to pay attention to the road, but I can't wait to see you Friday. I'll be there. It's the only thing making this drive better."

He hung up.

CHAPTER NINETEEN

Halfway there.

The sun glared at him as he played The National on repeat. His favorite band. Dark and moody. It suited him after seeing Luke then lying to Sophie.

He gripped the wheel tighter. What choice did he have? Was he supposed to tell her about his mom on the goddamn phone? He was flying blind when it came to sharing this emotional stuff, this family history. He'd had no training in how to open your heart, or your life, or your past. He wasn't a practitioner of closeness or commitment.

But he couldn't seem to stay away from Sophie.

So he'd need to do it right. Tell her when they were sitting down, face to face, not over the phone.

As the road echoed its sameness for miles, he dialed his sister's number. After a quick hello, he put her on speakerphone and jumped right into the matter at hand.

"Where do I find a dress? You know the kind the women from the fifties wore?"

Shannon cracked up, so damn loud that he thought his eardrum was going to split in half. "Something you want to tell me, Ryan? You're taking up cross-dressing?"

"My, my. Aren't you a funny lady? Anyway, you know the kind the movie stars wear? Like a pinup dress, I think it's called?"

She stopped laughing and turned her voice serious. "Sure. I've got a super hot one that might fit you. I'll drop it off at your house later tonight."

He rolled his eyes. "Make sure it has a petticoat and all."

"Consider it done."

"Anyway, where do I get one as a gift? For a woman."

Shannon whistled. "Is Mr. Always Single dating someone? Or is this like a gift for your assistant?"

"It's for a woman I'm seeing."

"Details," Shannon said demandingly.

"I can't get into them now. I'm driving. Just tell me where I can buy one. Is there a store on the Strip that sells them? She told me they're kind of specialty items."

"Well, they are very boutique-type dresses. You don't really find them at the department store. But maybe Rockin' Bette or Viva Las Vegas might have them. Do you want me to call around for you?"

He breathed a sigh of relief. "That would be awesome. But I want one with peaches on it."

She scoffed. "You're not going to find that off the rack, even at a boutique. You need to go to Etsy and hunt online for something that specific. I'll look for you. Tell me what size to get."

"Um…I don't know what size she is," he said.

"Well, what's her figure like?"

"Perfect."

"You're going to need to be a little more specific. Perfect is in the eye of the beholder."

An image of Sophie's round, full breasts popped into his mind, and he nearly swerved off the road. "She has nice..." He began and then trailed off, not wanting to talk like that in front of his sister.

"*Tits*, Ryan? She has nice tits?" Shannon supplied.

He laughed. "Yeah. What you just said. But they're bigger than—"

"Than mine? Is that what you were going to say?"

He laughed. "Yeah. Sorry."

"Don't be. I like my tits. So does my husband. Anyway. What are we talking in the knockers department? C?"

"That sounds about right. Maybe a big C."

"And is she skinny? Heavy? Average?"

"There is nothing average about her," he said quickly.

"Oh my God, I do not need to hear you wax on and on, even though it is adorable coming from The Ice Man. Just tell me—is she skinny or curvy?"

"She's not a stick. She has hips. She's not heavy or anything. But she's curvy."

"Marilyn Monroe?"

He snapped his fingers as he drove. "Yes. That."

"Fine. Done. I'll see what I can track down for your girl with the nice tits. How's her personality?"

He smiled, a grin that seemed to come out of nowhere, one that he had no control over when he thought of Sophie. "Brilliant, clever, sweet, fun."

"That makes me very happy to hear. Brent and I are coming by on Saturday for lunch, so you can tell me all about her when I see you in person and, hopefully, drop off the dress." She paused before she added, "By the way, have a good visit with Mom."

"Thanks, Shan."

He hung up and, an hour later, pulled past the gates and into the visitor lot at his mother's home.

* * *

Talking to his mom was like trying to capture a hummingbird with a thimble.

"Focus," he told her, as frustration surged inside him. "You're all over the place. I don't want to hear about how the guys in New York State broke out through a manhole, or why Kelsey in the cell next to you can't eat bread because now she's a fucking gluten-free inmate. I love you, Mom. But you gotta fucking focus."

"Watch your mouth," his mother said, narrowing her eyes as she chided him. She wore orange, as she always did, and they talked in one of the stark concrete visiting rooms, outfitted with only a table and chairs.

"Sorry," he muttered. Then he tapped his watch. "But time is running out, and I want some details. I've held onto your pattern; I've held onto your secrets. Can't you tell me a damn thing? The cops won't say a word about the evidence they have. You've got to know, Mom. I'm sure they've been here to see you about the case being reopened."

She nodded and pursed her lips together.

He held his hands out wide, waiting for an answer. "So?"

She shook her head.

He closed his eyes and sighed. "Mom, c'mon. I'm trying to help, but you've got to give me something. Does it have to do with Stefano's kid?"

She snapped her head up. "What?"

"He had a kid. His girlfriend was pregnant at the time of the murder. His friends were supposed to look out for the kid, but they apparently didn't. I think that's why the case was reopened. I don't know for sure, but I've got a hunch she set it in motion. His girlfriend went to the cops because she's pissed at his friends for messing up their end of the deal. That's my take."

His mom lowered her voice to a bare whisper, her eyes fixed on his. For the first time in a long time, he saw an intense *need* in her green gaze as she asked, "Who was supposed to look out for the kid?"

"I don't know, mom. Who do you think is looking out for the kid?"

"Was it T.J. and K. who—?"

Then she smacked her hand over her mouth and dug her fingers into her cheekbones. Shit. She'd done this before. She'd done some variation of this nearly every time he'd seen her lately. She'd start to say something and then physically stop herself.

"Who are T.J. and K.?" he asked, reaching across the table to gently pry her hand from her face. She was a strong woman though, and she didn't want to let go. He was stronger, and soon he'd peeled her hand away.

"Who? Who are they? Who are T.J. and K.? Are they Royal Sinners? Were they involved?"

She shook her head and the focused look vacated her eyes. "I'm tired. I'm so tired. I'm so incredibly tired."

"Mom, c'mon," he said, begging. "I've done everything you asked. I can't help you unless you tell me. You begged me to never say a word about the drugs, and I never did. I never said a thing, just like you asked. I followed your word to the letter. For eighteen goddamn years. But, Jesus Christ, I miss my dad. Okay?" His voice rose as he pleaded with her. "I miss him every day. If you know something you've never told me, now would be a really good time to share it, since there's a chance of getting justice served."

Her lips curved down. She reached for his hand and clasped her bony fingers around it. "I have to protect you. I swore I'd protect you. I will 'til the day I die."

His leaned back in his chair and shoved a hand through his hair. "I can protect myself. I'm not fourteen anymore. I'm not a kid. I'm a thirty-two-year-old man. So tell me. Who are T.J. and K.? Did they kill Dad?"

"I'm protecting you and your brothers and sister," she said, sticking to her own party line.

He tried again, hoping to rattle her this time. Press her buttons. "Then did you do it? They all think you did. Everyone thinks you did. The state sure as hell does. Did you kill Dad?"

She narrowed her eyes. "*No.* I've told you I didn't."

"You better not have lied to me. For years I have believed in you."

"Everything I've done is for all of you. I love you all so much."

"You gave this to me—don't you get it? You gave me this obsession over what really happened," he said, grabbing the sides of his skull for emphasis. "It's like a sickness now in me. You asked me to cover up when the cops were investigating my father's murder, and the details and the secrets eat away at me. It makes it hard for me to have a normal fucking life. Tell me, who are they?"

Her eyelids started to close. "I need to sleep," she mumbled. "I can't sleep at night. All I do is lie awake and stare at the ceiling and wish for the light to come." She rested her cheek against the table. In a minute, she'd fallen into slumber.

And he was hardly any closer to knowing *why.*

Ryan sat there in silence 'til the hour ended, and the sturdy, brown-haired corrections officer returned to the room.

"Hey, Clara," he said to the woman in the beige uniform.

She smiled. "Hey, Ryan. How's it going?"

"Keeping busy. Trying to stay out of trouble. How about you? How's the family?"

"My oldest starts high school in another month. Time flies, huh?"

"I remember when you were telling me about him starting kindergarten," Ryan said, because it had been that long that he'd known her.

Clara patted his sleeping mom. "C'mon, Prince. Visiting hour is over."

Dora raised her head an inch. A line from the table's edge was pressed into her cheek. Her mouth was open and saliva had pooled in the corner of her lips. She blinked. Then she rose and held out her arms to Ryan.

He hugged her. "Bye Mom. Get some sleep."

"Come by again, please. And stay safe. Stay away from the Sinners. Just stay away and you'll be safe then."

"I will," he said and kissed her forehead.

He gave a quick wave to Clara. "Take care of yourself, Clara."

"You, too. Will we see you later this month? She earned some more visiting hours. End of next week, I believe."

He nodded. "I'll do my best. Can't seem to stay away from this place," he said with a wry smile, and Clara patted him on the shoulder.

As he left, he wished he could simply Google "T.J. and K." and know what the hell his mother had been talking about. But as he closed the door to his truck, it occurred to him he could do something else with the information. He was grasping at straws, but maybe someone else could make sense of this. Maybe it was time for Ryan to ask for help, to turn to another person who was trying to solve this case.

He dialed Detective John Winston, and passed on the initials T.J. and K.

"I really appreciate that," John said.

"I don't know that it means anything."

"I don't, either. But it might, and that's what matters. A lead is a lead, and I'll see what I can do."

For the first time in a long time, Ryan felt unburdened.

CHAPTER TWENTY

The scent of roasted rosemary chicken wafted through her penthouse as she turned off the oven and set the roasting pan on top of the stove. She leaned in to the bird, cuddled by potatoes and carrots, and inhaled the delicious scent.

"Mmm," she said aloud, enjoying the savory aroma almost as much as she delighted in the yummy smells emanating from her second oven as the pie baked. She walked to the other side of the sink and tossed the summer salad, then placed it in the fridge to keep it cool and crisp.

She wiped the back of her hand across her chest since she'd heated up from all this cooking, even with the air conditioning blasting its cooling jets on this scorching July day. Still, she couldn't complain. Project Termite had been officially terminated, and her brother had returned to his own home last night. Even though she'd enjoyed bumping into him now and then in the kitchen, it was nice to have her home to herself again, simply because it was possible for her to dress like this.

She wore red lace panties and a matching push-up bra, barely covered up by the flirty apron she had on as she cooked. Neat pleats lined the edges of the apron's mini skirt, and a hint of lace peeked out at the hem that landed mid-thigh. A red satin bow cinched at the waist, and thick red ties were looped around her neck. She wore black, strappy pumps on her feet.

A timer dinged. She hustled to the oven, turned on the light, and checked the pie. Satisfied with its appearance and its mouthwatering scent, she reached one pot holder-covered hand into the oven, removed the dessert, and placed it on a cooling rack on the stovetop. She waved a hand over the dish, inhaling the fruity, sugary, ripe scent. She'd sliced a few extra peaches; they were in a glass bowl on the island and she planned to serve them on the side.

A sultry Billie Holiday number played on her sound system, piped through her entire home and bouncing off the white walls, the floor-to-ceiling windows, and the blond hardwood floors. She loved this place. It was everything she wanted her home to be. Gorgeously appointed, but not cold or staged. Her home was bursting with everything special that she loved, with bright colored pillows on the couch, pictures of her family throughout, mementos from her parents, and gifts from her friends over the years.

A little later, as the great Billie Holliday crooned about these foolish things, her buzzer rang, the front desk likely alerting her that her guest had arrived. She pressed the button to respond. "Hello there."

"Ryan Sloan is here. May I send him up?"

"Absolutely," she said, and soon there was a knock on her door, and the sound made her chest tingly. She was so damn ready to see him.

She opened the door, and he nearly stumbled.

He opened his lips to speak, but no words came. His jaw simply hung open.

She fought valiantly to contain a victorious grin. Inside, though, she wanted to pump a fist for having rendered him speechless.

He had a bottle of white wine and a bouquet of peach tulips in one hand, so she grabbed his free hand, tugged him inside, and shut the door behind them. In seconds, he'd backed her up against the wall, set down the wine and flowers on the entryway table, and placed his hands on her face. "How is it possible that you are more stunning every time I see you?"

She jutted out her hip and winked. "It's the apron," she said, gesturing to her skimpy attire.

He dropped a hand to her back, running it along the bare skin above the waist. "It's not the apron. It's how *you* look in it. Every time I see you you're wearing something that makes me rock hard," he said, yanking her close so she could feel the evidence herself.

"I like you hard, Ryan Sloan," she said, meeting his gaze, and he smiled at her, then grasped her ass, grinding his erection against her belly. "You're all I thought about all day," he murmured.

"What were you thinking about specifically? Wait. Don't tell me." She leaned back to tap her finger on her chin. "Was it the food? You were so damn curious to know what I was cooking for you—admit it."

He shook his head.

"So it was the peaches then?"

Another shake as he rubbed his hard-on against her.

"Maybe it was getting a tour of my home?" She craned her neck, gesturing with her eyes to the living room.

"Nope," he said with a sexy grin.

"Oh," she said, her lips forming an *O*. "Was it this?" She spun away from his grip and ran her hands along her breasts, down to her belly, letting one hand rest between her legs. Then, she took slow, measured steps into the open kitchen that looked out onto her living room.

His eyes prowled over her as he followed, unknotting his tie and tossing it on the floor. He undid the top button on his crisp, white button-down. She reached a metal stool in her kitchen, bumping it with the backs of her legs. His arms darted out, and he grabbed her waist, lifted her up, and set her on the stool. He skimmed his fingers down her bare arms. "Let me just look at you," he whispered, raking his eyes over her figure from head to toe. His dark gaze made her feel not only naked, but dirty. Filthy. Wanton.

His chest rose and fell as he drank her in. He wasn't even touching her, but her skin sizzled. She felt *touched*. Then he brushed his fingertips along her sides. She let her legs fall open for him, spreading herself, as she hooked her heels on to the bottom rung. Pressing her palms on the back of the stool to hold on, she arched her spine, offering her body to him.

Placing herself in his hands.

Giving herself to him.

"Look at you. Just fucking look at you. What you just did. You are killing me," he murmured, as he cupped her cheek in his right hand. "You're all I thought about all day. Seeing you. Touching you. Tasting you. Having you," he said, stroking her cheek. He paused, his voice rough with desire. "And fucking you."

He swept his lips over hers in a deep, devouring, hungry kiss. His tongue searched hers, and she let him lead. When he broke the kiss, she said softly, "Do whatever you want to me."

He pressed his forehead to hers. "Everything," he said. "I want to do everything to you, Sophie. I want to explore every inch of you. I want to taste all of you. I want to fuck you *everywhere*. But right now?" he said, taking his time as if each word tasted magnificent, "I want your sweetness on my tongue."

She gasped as heat raced through her body. "I want that, too."

"Keep your hands right where they are. Behind you," he said, and she nodded.

Dipping his hands under the front of her apron, he tugged at her panties, and pulled them to her ankles, then off. He hooked her high-heeled shoes firmly back into the rung, a clear sign she had to keep them in place. "I need to taste you every day. I can't go this long without you on my lips," he said, kneeling on the floor then burying his face between her legs.

She squeezed her eyes shut and cried out in pleasure, her voice becoming the harmony to Billie Holiday as Ryan licked and sucked and tasted. If she wasn't allowed to move her body, she could use her mouth. She could rely on her voice. She could scream and moan and groan. And so she did, because every lick, every touch, every press of his tongue against her hot, wet pussy drove her wild.

"It's so good," she cried out, and he looked ravenous as he licked up her slickness, as he flattened his tongue against her clit then sucked on that swollen bundle of nerves until she screamed.

Her orgasm crested. She saw it rising up on the horizon.

He moaned against her center then pulled back. "Grab my head. Use your hands. Do whatever you want," he said, giving her a command. Somewhere in her home she heard her ringtone. "Fly me to the Moon." Seemed appropriate.

Her hands flew into his hair, and she laced her fingers through those soft strands, for the first time touching him as he licked her. She'd longed for this chance. She loved being restrained, but she loved his hair, too. She grasped harder, her nails curling into his skull. He groaned, a mad, feral sound as she dug into his head, and she knew, she fucking knew that he wanted her to be rough right now. That he wanted her to show him how she felt about the way he touched her.

She felt like an animal.

Wild and crazed.

She held onto his head, yanking his mouth closer. She was on fire, a white-hot path of flames tearing through her body, burning everything in sight, turning her into an inferno as he fucked her pussy with his lips, his mouth, his tongue, and she rode his face until she saw stars, until the heavens fell from the sky and she came in his mouth.

Shuddering.

Trembling.

Shaking from head to toe.

Clutching his face between her legs as she rocked into him.

Soon enough, she uncurled her hands from his hair. Everything around them smelled like food, and sex, and chemistry, and peaches.

He reached into the bowl on the island, grabbed a slice of peach, and brought it to his lips. He ate it and then said, "It's good."

He grabbed another piece of a peach. He pulled down the top of her apron, exposing her red bra then unhooking it. He dragged the peach slice across her tits. "Let me taste it like this," he said, then dipped his head between her breasts and licked up the juice from her body.

"So good. But it doesn't even compare to you," he murmured against her chest, and she moaned happily from his words and his touch.

She'd never been one for food play, only because she'd never had this type of sex. But Ryan licking the taste of a ripe peach from her white skin felt like the way sex should be. It felt primal, an elemental connection between a woman who wanted a man and a man who had to have her. Nothing else at play but this red-hot, sinful desire that burned between them. She grabbed his head and pulled him to her breasts.

"That's enough of you being able to use your hands," he said, narrowing his eyes as he picked her up and carried her to her dining room table. She'd set it earlier for the two of them. A large wood table, one half of it was uncovered. He set her down on it, and began undoing her apron strings.

"Ryan?" she whispered in a question.

He looked at her, waiting.

"Do you remember what you said at the slot machine, what you wanted to do to me?" She gazed down to her breasts.

He pressed a finger to her lips. "I told you I would never forget your perfect tits. Do you think I have?"

She shook her head.

He dragged a finger between her breasts. "You want to watch me come on them, don't you?"

She inhaled sharply. "Oh God, I do."

"You want me to fuck these beautiful tits?" he asked, untying the red ribbon from her neck as she scooted back on the table.

"So much. I want you to come all over me," she said.

He got on the table and straddled her. "You need to do something first."

"Anything."

"Take off my shirt," he said.

She sat up, thrilled to unbutton his shirt, pushing it over his chest then down his arms, murmuring as she felt how strong he was. He was so toned and muscular, so hard and fit. He shrugged off the shirt, and she splayed her hands across his chest, dragging her nails through the soft little hairs. He breathed deeply as she explored him.

"Unzip my pants," he said, and she raced to unbutton, then unzip them, pushing them down to his ass, freeing his cock. She ran the tip of her tongue over her teeth as she gazed at him. The head was swollen and pulsing, and she was dying to feel him. He returned his hands to her neck, undoing the ribbon, letting the fabric of the ties fall. He pushed the material below her breasts, but she caught the ties and wrapped them around her own wrists.

She held them tight like that, savoring his reaction as he saw her breasts rise up more, creating an even deeper valley between them, from the tug of the fabric and her own hold on the ribbons.

She didn't tie up her wrists. She simply held tight, as if she gripped the leash of a dog, one in each hand, restraining herself.

* * *

She'd fucking tied herself up. Okay fine, there were no knots. But she'd done it. She'd offered her own bound body to him. His dick throbbed, and lust burned through him like wildfire. She was the most enticing woman he'd ever known.

And she was so damn slippery. So fucking wet. He dropped his gaze to her wet cunt once more as a bolt of desire slammed into him from the sight of her sweet pink flesh. So slick and ready. He slid a finger through her folds, then dipped it inside her, watching her thrust up into his hand. Then he brought that finger to her perfect tits, spreading her wetness between them.

Her eyes widened as she watched him prepare her. He could have fucked her without lubrication. He could have taken her and just thrust his dick between those gorgeous globes of flesh, the friction spurring him on. But it would be better like this.

Better wet. Better slippery.

He gripped his dick, sliding a bead of liquid over the head and closing his eyes momentarily as the sensations roared through him. Fuck, he needed to come. He needed release.

He planted his knees by her ribs, then lowered himself to her chest, sliding his hard cock between her lush breasts, as he parked his hands on the table.

Then he ravaged her tits.

He groaned as he felt her soft flesh press against his dick. She'd inched her arms closer to her body, making a warm, snug tunnel for him. Her breasts caressed his cock as he thrust, his balls slapping against her chest. Her mouth parted, her lips open. Such an eager one, she flicked out her tongue, and licked the tip on several thrusts.

"You like that, don't you?" he asked, panting as heat spread through him.

She nodded. "I want to watch you get off on me," she whispered as she held on tight to the ends of the red fabric, her firm grip on the ribbon giving him all the friction he needed. "I've never seen your face when you're coming. I want to know what you look like when you come all over me."

Desire surged in him, like white waters raging, as he pumped between that perfect flesh. He jammed his hands harder against the table. "Tell me how much you want it," he growled, his voice ragged.

"So much," she pleaded, her blue eyes shining with desire. My God, he had unleashed a wild woman in her, and he fucking loved it as she talked dirty right at him, saying, "I want you all over my neck, and my chest, and my tits. Please give it to me."

His spine ignited. His balls tightened, drawing up closer as he rocked through the slick, hot valley of her breasts. That first neon burst of pleasure roared in him, then climbed higher as he pumped. Keeping his dick where it was happiest, he sat up so she could see his face as he gave her what she wanted.

"Now. Fucking now. Watch me come on you," he groaned, fighting to keep his own eyes open, wanting to watch her as she savored the sight of him straddling her chest, rocking into her tits, and spilling hot white streams onto her breasts, all the way up to her neck and her chin, even the ends of her hair.

He shuddered.

A total body release.

She let go of the hold on one of her ribbons, dragged her finger between her breasts and brought it to her lips, licking him off.

"Oh, beautiful. You deserve another orgasm for that," he said then fucked her with his fingers until she came riding his hand on her dining room table.

CHAPTER TWENTY-ONE

Hot water rained down on them in her luxurious shower with glass brick walls. He poured some of her shampoo into his palm then lathered up her soft hair, taking his time working it into her wet strands. She closed her eyes, and leaned her head against his chest.

"Your dinner's probably getting cold," he murmured in her ear as he turned her around and rinsed the shampoo from her hair.

"I know. But that's what re-warming in the oven is for," she said.

He looped an arm around her waist, tugging her soft, wet body against his. "I know this sounds crazy because it was only a few days ago when I saw you, but I did miss you," he said, planting a kiss on her neck, then traveling to her lips, kissing her softly, slowly, taking his time. She whimpered sexily against his lips, and he let go. "That dinner is really going to get cold."

"And I am really going to get hot the longer I stand here in the shower naked with you," she said, and he eyed her all over, keenly aware that this was the first time she'd been completely naked in front of him, and him with her.

He held up his finger. "Let me go get a condom." He turned to the shower door when he felt her grasp his arm.

"I'm on the pill," she said. "And I'm kind of ridiculously clean."

He laughed. "Ridiculous is good. And same here. Clean, that is."

He backed her up against the royal-blue tiled wall, hitched up her right leg around his hip, and guided himself into her.

There were no words to describe how fantastic she felt. So he didn't say anything. He simply moved inside her, getting to know her body even more intimately as twilight fell and she wrapped her arms around his neck and whispered his name.

Soon, she was saying it louder, in an orgasmic shout, and he chased her there.

* * *

Ryan pointed admiringly at the chicken, which had been reheated and was as tasty as she'd hoped. He was polishing off his second serving. "This is delicious. You sure can cook."

"Just wait 'til you have dessert then," she said with a smile as she brought the glass of pinot grigio to her lips and took a sip of the wine he'd given her. The peach tulips blazed brightly in a vase in the middle of the table. She'd changed into a short yellow sundress and had combed her hair into a clip. The ends of his still-wet hair curled up, a look she found made him even sexier than usual, considering what they'd just done in the shower.

Sparks swooped through her, and she was damn near ready for another round. But she also enjoyed talking to him, and they'd had a nice chat over dinner. He'd spotted a wedding photo of Holden and her, and had even remarked how pretty she looked. If he'd felt any tension or jealousy over her friendship with her ex, he didn't let on, which made her happy. He'd asked about Holden's work, and she'd shared more details, mentioning that he was helping with the upcoming fundraiser.

"I'm getting together with Holden tomorrow to go over some details, and truth be told, we'll probably do some shopping, too. We're both partial to the Grand Canal shops," she said, as if divulging a naughty secret.

"This sounds strange even as I say it, but I hope you have fun shopping with your ex," he said, bemused. She laughed, delighted that he could accept her friendship with Holden so easily.

"Tell me more about your company, and what it's like working with your older brother," she said.

As he talked about his work, and both the joys and pitfalls of working with a sibling, a realization slipped to front and center in her mind.

She liked him. A lot.

No, that wasn't it. It was way more than like.

She was falling for Ryan Sloan. That was what the sparks in her belly were. They weren't *sex* butterflies. They were *falling for you* butterflies.

Ryan set down his fork and cleared his throat. "So, there's something I've been wanting to tell you."

Her shoulders tensed instinctively. Nothing good ever came from those words. "You're married?" she asked, panic seizing her. She wasn't sure why that was the first thing that came to her mind. But she was sure something bad was about to come out of his mouth. Especially given where her own mind and heart had just gone.

He laughed and shook his head, and his response made her feel the tiniest bit better. "No. It's about—"

But his words were cut off by a knock on the door. She stood up quickly. "It's probably just a delivery or something. Dry cleaning maybe," she said, and walked to the door. She peered through the peephole and beamed when she saw her brother.

She turned to Ryan as she opened the door. "You can meet John."

Ryan's face froze, and so did her brother's when he made eye contact with the other man in the room.

John said her lover's name like a hiss.

CHAPTER TWENTY-TWO

"You two know each other?" Sophie gestured from her brother to Ryan.

Ryan nodded as John said, "Yes."

John went next, pointing to Ryan. "Why are you talking to my sister?" His voice was accusing. The tone was enough to send hackles up her spine.

Sophie held up both hands. "Wait," she said firmly. "Someone tell me what is going on."

Ryan pushed back his chair, the wooden legs scraping loudly against the floor. "We know each other because he's working on a case that involves my family." He took long strides to her. "My father's murder."

Sophie clasped her hand over her mouth. She shuddered, but then blinked when she realized something didn't add up. "You said you were fourteen when he died?"

"I was," Ryan said, standing a few feet from her. He pressed his fingers against his temple, speaking the next words as if they pained him. "He was shot in the driveway of our home one night. Both the gunman and my mother are in prison for the crime. The case was just reopened."

Sophie's mouth fell open, and the earth ceased rotating as the enormity of his statement rocked through her. Slowly, she let each word soak in. That was a hell of a hand of cards to be dealt. She couldn't even imagine what he'd gone through, living with that kind of tragedy. To think, she'd once pictured Ryan's mom missing her husband, not serving hard time for offing him. This was so much bigger, so much heavier.

"Oh my God, I'm so sorry to hear that," she said, reaching for him, stepping closer, her natural instinct to comfort surpassing all else.

He shook his head. "It's okay," Ryan mumbled, his body language telling her he didn't want soothing.

"I had no idea," she said softly.

"Of course you had no idea. I don't really talk about it," he said, crossing his arms.

"But even so, I feel terrible that this happened to you."

"*Don't.*"

In that one word, she heard a man who didn't want sympathy. Who didn't think he needed it. She also understood all his walls—and oh hell, did he have them.

"We reopened the investigation a few weeks ago due to new evidence," John added, stepping closer to Sophie, flanking her, as if he needed to protect her from Ryan. Perhaps he did.

Because it seemed she hardly knew the man she'd just spent the evening with. But she knew her brother. Her mind galloped over the last several conversations she'd had with John. She spun to face her brother, adding up the clues. "This is the case you've been working on?"

He nodded. "One of them. One of the big ones."

She turned her gaze back to Ryan, and for the first time ever he didn't look in control. He didn't appear cool, or confident, or passionate. He seemed rattled, as if he'd been knocked out of orbit.

He also looked like a stranger.

He felt like one, too.

Something clicked in her head. "*Hawthorne*," she said under her breath. "Is that why you went to Hawthorne?"

John cut in before Ryan could answer. "He visited his mother on Wednesday at Stella McLaren. He actually passed on some info to me later that day that may wind up being useful," John said, a bit grudgingly, but still with some gratitude in his tone.

"You don't do security for the prison like you said?" she asked Ryan as she furrowed her brow. He'd lied. Maybe it was a small one, but it was still a lie.

He shook his head. "The prison's not a client. I went there to see my mom. She's been in since I was fourteen," he said, his voice heavy, laced with shame and sadness.

Sophie felt neither of those emotions. She simply felt... *fooled*. Here were these men, talking to each other, knowing things, sharing intensely personal details, and she hadn't a clue. She *wanted* to experience this moment honestly. She wanted to feel all the things one should feel when learning something like this. But information was coming at her in bizarre ways, rather than through her lover sharing directly, as she'd done with him.

"I have a question, and it's pretty important, as far as I can tell," John said, cocking his head and staring at Ryan. "How long have you been involved with my sister?"

"Over a week. I met her the day I went to—"

"That's why you were at the municipal building?" Sophie asked, crossing her arms. "The day I met you? You were going to see my brother?"

"I didn't know he was your brother then," Ryan answered defensively. "I didn't have a clue you two were connected. All I knew when I met you was that I wanted you."

John cleared his throat. "I left my phone charger in the guest room. That's why I stopped by. I'm going to get that right now," he said then stopped to look at Sophie. "Unless you want me here in this room."

She waved him down the hall. Once she heard the door to the guest room shut, she spoke. "When did you know the detective investigating your father's case was my brother?"

He gulped. "When I looked you up before the gala," he said, and her blood turned to ice. Now that she'd moved beyond the initial desire to comfort him she felt…*used*.

"Did you pursue me to get close to the investigation?" she whispered, dreading the answer.

He shook his head several times. "No. No. No."

That was a few too many *nos* for her taste. "Maybe a little?"

He shoved a hand through his hair and sighed heavily. "Sophie, I can't stop thinking about you. It's that simple. It has nothing to do with your brother."

She held out her hands in question. "Then I just don't understand why you didn't tell me."

He shot her a quizzical look. "Uh, maybe because it's not that easy for me to say."

She barely registered his words as the memory of her own admissions reared to the surface. She'd shared so much with him. He'd shared so little. He'd had so many opportunities to tell her. "Ryan, I just went on and on about John and his work so many times. And you knew who he was. And you even made remarks like *I bet he has some stories about what he's seen*. You said that on the Ferris wheel," she reminded him, her near-photographic memory coming in handy. "I just feel stupid."

"Did you want me to drop this on you on the Ferris wheel?" he asked, his tone turning heated. She could practically feel the frustration burning off him. "That your brother is investigating a fucking murder in my family? Just weave it in as we gabbed about our siblings. *Oh, that's so great that you're so close with him. By the way, he asked me the other day if my mom happened to associate with anyone new at the time of the murder*. Is that what I should have said?" But he didn't give her time to answer. "We don't even use the last names we had when we were growing up, Sophie. Everyone heard of us in this town. It was all over the news. Everyone fucking knew us. Our family story was dramatized on prime-time news magazines. Our mom was the *cold-blooded husband-killer*. And we were the kids left behind—Mom in prison, Dad in the ground, Royal Sinners gang gunman behind bars. We were the poor Paige-Prince kids from the shitty section of town, who everyone felt sorry for," he said harshly, and she let out a surprised squeak.

She'd heard the story when she was finishing junior high. It was one of the biggest news stories in town at the time. It was pure prime-time scandal. It had even been covered by *Dateline*-type shows, reenacting it. "That's you?"

He nodded. "Yes. That's us."

He'd lost so much. So incredibly much. A father. A mother. A normal childhood. Everything. Her need for self-protection took a backseat to compassion, and she tried once more. She wrapped her arms around him, and hugged him. "I am so sorry for what happened to your family, Ryan. I'm sorry for what happened to your dad, and to your mom, and to you and your brothers and your sister," she said softly. He said nothing, but he let her hold him, even leaning into her. He sighed softly, and that sound, that vulnerable sound from this strong, sometimes standoffish man infiltrated her heart and soul. Somehow, in that brief exhalation, she felt him inching toward her.

Not physically. But emotionally. She wanted to be the one for him. She ran her hands through his hair, wishing she could erase the tragedy.

John's footsteps echoed across the hardwood, breaking the moment. He cleared his throat. "Sophie," he said, and she separated from Ryan. "Is everything okay?"

She nodded. "It's fine."

"Do you want me to stay?"

She shrugged. She didn't know what she wanted anymore. Everything that had felt so certain before John knocked on her door had been uprooted in seconds. "No. Yes. I don't know," she said helplessly.

He pointed his thumb at the door. "I'm going to go wait in the hall. Give you some privacy, but I'll be nearby if you need me."

After he left, Sophie looked at the man she'd been falling for. He had the same brown hair, the same blue eyes, the same strong build as an hour ago, but he *wasn't* the same because she didn't know how to see him the same way. "I feel like I barely know you. I don't even know where you live."

In a monotone, he said his address.

But it didn't change anything. Knowing the numbers and the street name didn't give her any greater insight.

Confusion reigned this Friday night. Maybe she was overreacting to this news. Or maybe she was under-reacting. She didn't know what to make of this revelation. Was she supposed to be hurt? Or outraged? Feel sympathetic? Care for him?

She had no notion of what to do next.

This new wrinkle was so strange, and her chest was knotted up, her head fuzzy. "I like you, Ryan. I like you so much, and I am falling for you. And I understand it's not easy to say what happened to your family. I get that, and I wish I could take away the horrors of what you've gone though. But aside from that, when I analyze what's happening with you and me, the reality is this—I've been completely open. I told you at the diner about my marriage. I didn't wait for you to uncover it. I put it all on the table. I told you about my parents, and my brother, and myself. I can't help but wonder what else you didn't share, or didn't say, or didn't want to deal with when I've tried to be forthright with you."

"Look, Sophie. I don't tell anyone. I don't get *close* enough to tell anyone. But I knew I needed to tell you, and it's not the kind of thing I wanted to tell you on the phone, so I was planning to tell you tonight. I was starting to at the table." He waved his hand in the direction of the dining room.

Maybe he had been planning on opening up. But she had no way of knowing if he was being truthful now. She tried a new tactic. "Why was the case reopened?"

"I don't know. He won't tell me. I think he thinks there were others involved."

His words sent her back to the night she left for the gala, and her conversation with John beforehand.

"Talked to some guy today who I'm sure knows something, but he won't let on what it is."

"What do you think he knows?"

"Something that would help me find the other guys I think were involved."

John was her brother, her flesh and blood. He was the man who'd supported her and helped her build her business, who would take a bullet for her. He had a reason to suspect Ryan was hiding something, and she'd be a foolish woman to wave this off and carry on as if nothing had changed.

"I need you to believe me. I wanted to tell you," he added, and she desperately wanted to trust in his words.

But she'd relied on her instincts before, in her marriage with Holden, and those instincts had been wrong.

Maybe she needed to use her head more. Not her heart. Not her body. "I don't really know what to think. I want to believe you, but I need to sort this out. I've been letting my heart lead instead of my head, and my heart feels pretty foolish and stupid right now." She walked over to the dining room table, picked up the peach pie, returned to her kitchen, and covered it in tinfoil. Then she handed it to him.

He shook his head. "I can't take the pie."

"I need you to. I made it for you. I need some space to think, and I can't do it if I'm surrounded by this fruit I wanted to give you."

She showed him to the door.

CHAPTER TWENTY-THREE

His grandmother dug her fork into the pie on her plate. She rolled her eyes in pleasure. Moonlight shone through the kitchen window in her home. The clock next to the refrigerator ticked near ten.

"Let me tell you something. You don't give up a woman who cooks like this."

"Yeah? That's the bottom line, Nana? How she cooks?" he asked, and grabbed a fork from a utensil drawer and stole a bite from his grandma's plate.

She smacked his hand then eyed the pie tin. "Serve your own, young man. This is all mine."

"That's all I wanted. One bite," he said, thinking the sentiment might be apropos for Sophie, too. Maybe all he'd take of her would be the one bite he'd had. Then he'd walk away. It was better like that, wasn't it? Leave before your heart gets mangled. Enjoy it while it lasts, like this dessert. This absolutely scrumptious, amazing, incredible dessert.

His grandma scooped another forkful then answered his question. "When she bakes like this, yes. You don't give her up. This pie is *divine*."

Funny, Ryan had used that same word to describe Sophie.

Divine.

As well as exquisite. Not to mention delicious.

Sophie was peach pie.

He wanted the whole damn pie.

He wanted all of Sophie.

But what was the point? Tonight's argument was further proof that intimacy was too dangerous. He had to protect the secrets he'd locked up. When secrets were cracked wide open, you were left far too vulnerable. And when you were vulnerable you could wind up dead in your own driveway.

"Yeah, it is, but..." he said, letting his voice trail off.

"You like her," his grandma said.

He shrugged. "What does it matter?"

She set her fork down and parked her hands on the counter. "It matters because this is all we have," she said, tapping her chest.

"It's not like that." He tried valiantly to deny that there was anything more to the empty ache he felt right now than missing great sex. "We were just having a good time. Honestly, there's nothing more to it."

She screwed up the corner of her mouth. "If it was just a *good time*, then why are you here?"

"I wanted to bring you the pie."

"You could have eaten it yourself."

"Nah, I can't finish that," he said.

"Sure you could. You're a sturdy man. You can handle a peach pie."

He patted his flat stomach. "Gotta watch my boyish figure."

She shook her head and rolled her eyes. "You're not fooling me."

He held out his hands wide as if to say he was an open book, even though that couldn't be further from the truth.

"Ryan," she said gently, walking around to join him on his side of the counter. "I worry about you. You're so private about everything."

"I'm fine."

"You're not. You brought me this pie because you wanted to talk, and you have never wanted to talk about a woman before. So I'm saying perhaps you should consider talking to *her*. Sharing some of your heart," she said.

"What would I even say?"

"Just talk to her. Tell her why you didn't say a word. Tell her what's on your mind. What's in your heart. Women often like that."

But did they? He flashed back to Sanders's wife and her weird glances at the mention of the speeding ticket. He hardly knew how to do what his grandma was prescribing. "Is it even worth it?"

"Is it?" she echoed. "Only you know the answer to that. But Ryan, you think you have to manage everything perfectly because your life spun out of control when you were younger. All our lives did. Here's the thing you need to see —you can't control everything, and you also don't have to. The only things you can take charge of are the choices you make, and if Miss Peach Pie is a choice you want to make, then you should let her in." She paused then added, "Besides, you've never shown up at my house at ten p.m. to talk about a woman. So think about that, my love."

He wasn't sure he agreed with her.

Hell, he wasn't sure about anything. Except tonight seemed to prove it was a good thing he generally didn't make it beyond a third date.

Just look at the mess he'd made of the fourth one.

* * *

Sophie scrubbed the island for a third time. She would likely go for a fourth, perhaps even a fifth. John finished loading the last plate in the dishwasher. "Look, men are pigs," he said in a matter-of-fact tone.

She shot him a sharp-eyed stare. "That makes you a pig, too, then."

He nodded vigorously. "Takes one to know one. Men are horrible."

She grabbed a dishtowel and swatted him on the shoulder with it. "Stop. You're being ridiculous. Men aren't pigs. Not all of them at least," she said softly. "You're not. Dad wasn't. I don't really think Ryan is either."

John said nothing, and Sophie returned to cleaning the marble countertop of the island, making sure she scoured each section to a spit shine. She wasn't trying to erase the evening, or the man. She was merely trying to keep her mind busy, so she'd be less apt to rely on her heart.

Her heart was a puppy, happily trotting in a field of poppies.

That was the problem.

"Does your silence mean you think he's bad news?" she asked John. She didn't know anybody else who'd even met Ryan. At least her brother had spoken to him.

"I don't know enough about him to say if he's bad news or not," John said carefully as he poured dishwasher soap into the machine.

"You don't trust him, though."

"It's not that I don't trust *him*. I don't trust anyone."

She shoved the sponge roughly back and forth, back and forth. The repetitive motion was strangely soothing. "But is your distrust of Ryan more or less than your baseline level of distrust?" she asked in a clinical manner.

"It's higher, but that's because we're talking about *you*, now. And I don't want you to get hurt."

"You think I'm foolish."

"No," he corrected as he shut the dishwasher. "I think you love easily. Maybe too easily for your own good."

"I'm not in love with him," she said quickly, dropping the sponge and meeting his eyes.

He arched a brow, questioning her with his steely stare. "It sure looked like that. Or like it was heading in that direction."

"When? When did it look like that?"

"When I walked back out and saw you holding him."

She shut her eyes as she slipped back in time to those few seconds that felt like a slice of possibility. Her arms around him. His cheek on her shoulder. She opened her eyes and straightened the kitchen some more, placing the clean roasting pan in a cupboard.

"Also, you believe in love so strongly because of Mom and Dad, and you think you're going to have that," John continued. "But most of the world isn't like that. Some of the world is like Ryan's parents."

"What happened with them? Beyond the news. Beyond what I could find on the Internet," she asked as she put more pans away. She was dying to know. Curiosity had her in its grip.

"Soph," he said in a chiding tone. "You know I can't say."

"But you think he knows something that will help you in the investigation? You said that. You said that the night I went to the gala. I know you had to have been talking about him then."

He huffed. "You're too smart for your own good."

"I'm just a good listener. So what do you think he knows? You don't think he's a suspect, do you?"

He laughed and shook his head, leaning his hip against the counter. "No. Absolutely not. But everyone has an agenda, and I think Ryan Sloan has his own, which for some reason involves protecting his mother."

"But she's in prison. How can he be protecting her?"

"I think he's protecting things she won't tell us. But the good news is he told me something that I think will be helpful, if I can just connect all the dots."

"Can you?"

He shrugged. "That's the million-dollar question. And you know I can't say anymore. If I do I'll compromise the investigation, and all investigations matter, but this one is a big one, Sophie."

She had a sneaking suspicion John wasn't merely looking into an eighteen-year-old murder. She had a feeling he was hunting for something that went much wider and bigger.

"And if you do? You can keep the streets safe?"

"That's always my goal." He nodded to the door. "I should go. Unless you want me to stay."

She shook her head. "I'm fine. Just tell me—is there anything about him that you think I need to know? Would I be a fool to see him again?"

He tucked his finger under her chin. "Sophie, I can't make those sorts of promises or guarantees about anyone. Let alone someone I barely know. What I do know is this —he is focused, and intense, and his mother adores him, and he loved her, too."

Was that such a bad thing? Was there some law that said you were supposed to become a hater if someone you loved killed? Sophie shuddered at the thought. Was the world that black and white? She had no clue how she would feel in Ryan's shoes, which was why she didn't want to judge him.

She said goodbye to John then headed to her closet and rearranged her favorite dresses and fancy shoes.

When she woke up the next morning, her phone bleated loudly—a reminder of her meeting in a few hours with Clyde. She groaned because the man would surely ask her about her date for the fundraiser, and she didn't know if she had one still.

Or if she wanted one anymore.

Chapter Twenty-Four

Pool cue in hand, Ryan stared down the eight ball and the corner pocket. He tapped the ball lightly then followed its path as it rolled across the green felt, hell-bent on its destination and impending victory.

C'mon, he said silently.

The ball veered to the right, bumping the edge of the table, and missing the mark by an inch.

"Damn." Ryan let out a long, frustrated sigh.

Brent pulled back on his stick and knocked the eight ball flawlessly.

"You're killing it today," Ryan said, extending a hand to congratulate his brother-in-law on his third win of the afternoon.

Brent shook then waved his hand as if Ryan's utter demolishment in a game at which he usually excelled was no big deal. "Just lucky today, that's all," Brent said.

There was a time when Ryan hadn't been a fan of Brent Nichols because the man had broken his sister's heart long ago. But that was then, and as Ryan had gotten to know Brent anew these days, he'd let the past go. Brent made

Shannon immensely happy, and he loved seeing his sister like this—*glowing*.

"Go again?" Ryan asked, holding up his cue.

"You're a glutton for punishment, aren't you?"

"Seems that way," Ryan said. But he was determined to right this ship. He never lost three games in a row. Never ever. This was unprecedented, and he had to get his act together, because he didn't like being so off his game.

He racked the balls as Shannon walked into the den, holding up beer bottles for the crew. "Are we ever going to eat lunch?" she asked as she doled out bottles to Brent and Ryan. She had one left for Colin, since he'd texted that he'd be there any minute, and she set it on the edge of the table. "Or are you boys going to play all afternoon?"

"I'll stop when I break my streak," Ryan said, as Johnny Cash barked happily from the other room. He must have spotted one of his favorite lady dogs walking along the sidewalk from his perch staring out the front window.

"Brent, please let him win. I'm hungry," Shannon said to her husband, who simply laughed.

Ryan shot a sharp-eyed stare at Brent. "Play fair and square."

"I'll play."

Ryan spun around to see his brother Colin walk in, with Johnny Cash trotting by his side. "What the hell? You don't knock?"

"Yeah, some asshole who owns this house didn't lock the front door. I was able to wander in and your guard dog greeted me with a big lick," Colin said with a mischievous glint in his eyes as he petted the dog's black furry head. Then he looked at Ryan. "You'd think a man who works in the security business would lock his door."

Ryan rolled his eyes. "Whatever. I know you used your key. Don't even try to pretend that stuff would slip by me."

Colin grinned widely and held up his key. "Ha. Got you. Where's Michael?" he asked, looking around.

"He said he'll be here soon. Just finished up some work on this new client deal we signed this week. White Box. These guys are awesome, and they fucking love us," Ryan said as he clapped his brother on the back in greeting. "How's it going? Haven't seen you in a few weeks."

"Good. Busy. Been training for the Badass Triathlon next month."

"You are hardcore. Is that the one where you do some crazy rock climbing too?"

Colin nodded. "Yup. Was up at sunrise on a climb. Gotta go for it after the other time I tried to do it. We all know what happened then."

"You're gonna do great this time, man."

"I hear you're busy too these days." Colin wiggled his eyebrows. "Getting it on with some new lady."

Ryan swiveled around to face Shannon. She held up her hands. "Ryan, you had me get her a dress. It's not a state secret that you're seeing someone. But I don't even know her name."

"I really don't want to talk about it," he said, cutting this conversation off at the knees. He missed Sophie like a hungry man misses food, and it had been less than twenty-four hours since he'd seen her. He missed every single thing about her, from her clever banter, to her sexy winks, to her giving heart, to her beautiful body that he wanted to ravage. He'd spent the morning burying himself in work, then in Frisbee time with his dog, then in a long swim in his pool. Now he had some of his favorite people to help keep his mind off the woman who'd nabbed center seat in his brain and his heart.

A picture of Sophie in her black cherry dress and white sunglasses, inviting him to the gala, popped into his head then, unbidden.

Tempting and tantalizing, the image of her was like a summons. And he wanted to do nothing more than appear before her. Tell her how he felt. Tell her he wanted her in his life, not out of it. But he was no good at talking. Despite what his grandma had said, he was no more skilled at opening his heart to a woman this morning than he had been last night.

He desperately needed the diversion of this game. "Colin, grab a cue and join us. You're on Brent's team. Shan, you're on mine."

Shannon arched an eyebrow. "You must really want to win, Ryan. You know I can beat the two of you blindfolded." She did have a knack for the game. Their dad had been a bit of a pool shark and had taught all of them to play at a young age. Maybe Shannon would help him regain his mojo.

Shannon handed Colin the remaining beer bottle, the non-alcoholic kind, then she grabbed a stick, leaned over the table, narrowed her eyes, and assessed the best angle for the break shot. She pulled back the cue, snapped it seamlessly, and sent the top of the table into motion, balls scattering, with an orange one landing easily in a corner pocket.

"Nice," Brent said with an appreciative whistle. "Can't even get annoyed because that was such a perfect shot."

Ryan pointed his beer bottle at Brent. "Sucking up to the opposing team—I approve only because it involves my sister, and you should always compliment her."

"And I always do," Brent said with a laugh as he held his beer in an air toast. Ryan lined up the next shot and then proceeded to whack the purple ball neatly across the table, sinking it easily. Shannon held up a hand to high-five him, and they smacked palms. Ryan turned to Colin as Shannon set up another shot.

"Hey Colin, I heard your firm is one of the sponsors for the big fundraiser for the community center. I knew you were a volunteer, but I had no idea you were putting your money where your mouth is too. That's awesome. Another one of your quiet *give back* projects?"

His brother nodded. "Yup. They do great work, and Elle, the director, is passionate about helping. Some of the kids there have had rough childhoods, so the center is all about giving them a place to hang out, and, man, do they ever need the help to refurbish that place."

Ryan tipped his chin. "Proud of you, bro."

"Hey," Brent cut in, setting down his beer. "That reminds me. I heard from my friend Mindy earlier today. I already told Shan, but I wanted you both to know, too. Remember the guy I saw hanging outside her house a month ago?"

The pool game ceased and all eyes turned to Brent. After the murder case was reopened, Brent had mentioned spotting a guy in a Buick idling outside Shannon's old condo. He'd snapped a photo at the time, and while the guy in the car hadn't done anything suspicious, he'd spent far too long doing a whole lot of nothing in the car while staring at her building. Turned out Shannon had seen him at another time too. Shannon was living with Brent now, so she felt safer. Still, Ryan and his siblings all wanted to know more about the guy in the Buick, in case he'd been watching Shannon for some reason.

"Mindy talked to her friends on the force. Asked them if the ink on his arms looked familiar." Ryan flashed back to Luke's comments about the Royal Sinners, and the tattoos that bore their mantra, as Brent continued. "The picture I had of him wasn't perfect, but we zoomed in as close as we could and it looks like one of the tattoos says 'Protect.'"

Ryan's blood chilled. *Protect our own.* "That's the ink of the Royal Sinners," he said, dread laced through his voice.

Shannon moved closer to Brent, visibly shivering, and he draped an arm around his wife. "Are you serious?" she asked.

Ryan nodded. "You need to be careful, Shan. I'm going to get you a security detail right away."

"I can take care of her," Brent said protectively.

"I know you can, man. I don't doubt it for a second. But I'm talking about when you're *not* with her," Ryan added. "And you need to make sure you're carrying, Shan."

"Ryan," she said, chiding.

"These guys don't fuck around. Stefano has friends on the outside. And he had a kid at the time he went to prison. I heard the kid's been getting into some trouble. What if this guy watching us is Stefano's son? He looks young enough. We need to be careful," he said firmly, in a tone that brooked no argument, then turned to Colin. "Same goes for you."

"You're getting me a bodyguard?"

"If you want one, I will."

Colin shot him a look that said *hell no.* "Let me see the picture," he said, and Brent called it up on his phone and passed it to Colin.

He stroked his chin and appeared deep in thought.

"What is it, Colin?" Shannon asked.

"This is going to sound strange, but I think I've seen this guy shooting hoops at the community center." He tapped the screen and spoke to Brent. "Send me this picture. Let me do a little more digging."

Brent swiped the screen a few times then said, "Done. And listen, we haven't seen him around in a month, so my thought is maybe he was just trying to keep an eye on Shan before the case got reopened?"

Luke's warning rang in Ryan's ears.

You bump into a guy like Stefano on the street and you run the other way.

But he didn't need that man's words about the Royal Sinners to take the threat seriously. His father in the ground, courtesy of a gangland shooter, was all Ryan needed to make sure he did everything to keep his family safe. "We're not taking any chances, because we don't know what's going on. That's the issue. We don't know everything that's happening with the investigation. The only one who knows is the damn detective."

They speculated more on the case while finishing the round of pool. When Shannon landed the winning shot, she declared victory for the two of them. Then she raised her cue, tapped Ryan on the shoulder from across the table, and poked him with it. "Now, fess up. What's the story with the woman you had me buy the dress for? I want to know."

"She's pissed at me," he said, heavily. He hadn't heard a word from her since last night, so that was probably the end of Miss Peach Pie. A black cloud engulfed him at the prospect of never seeing her again.

"What did you do wrong?" Brent asked as he knocked back some of his beer.

Ryan parked his hands on his hips. "Now, why do you assume it was me who did something wrong?"

Brent nearly spat out his beer. "Dude. You just said you did. You said she's pissed at you."

"It's a long story," he muttered. "I don't even know if she wants to hear from me again."

Shannon hung up her cue, marched over to Ryan, and stared at him, her eyes saying *we're waiting.*

Ryan gritted his teeth, pressing them hard together, locking up his words, and shutting the details in his head.

Old habit.

This was his way.

This was how he dealt.

Jam all the personal, private information into his mind vise, then crush it and let the tension live in his bones for years, like a coiled spring. The one time lately he hadn't felt like a taut power line was when he'd given John the initials he'd gotten from his mom. Instead, he'd felt a sense of freedom from the weight of the past.

The memory of that feeling was a soft knock on the door. A gentle reminder that he'd gotten in this predicament with Sophie by keeping his secrets airtight.

Maybe it was time to try a new approach.

"So here's the story," he said, then told them about the only woman he'd ever even started to let into his heart. He kept it short and simple, sticking to basic facts.

When he was through, Shannon slammed her hands against his chest. "You ass."

He stumbled into the pool table, surprise racing through him.

Brent cracked up. "She doesn't pull her punches. You gotta watch out for Mrs. Nichols," he said.

"Tell me about it," Ryan said, straightening up.

"Why are you here? Seriously? Go," she said, pointing to the door. "Go find her and tell her you weren't using her, and that she's the first woman you've ever felt a damn thing for, and that you're all sorts of messed up in the head," she said, tapping her temple, "but that you want to try for her. Or maybe do you want to wait ten years for her to come back into your life?"

Brent raised a beer. "Can't think of a better advertisement for going after the woman you want this very second than our example," he said, gesturing from Shannon to himself. "Go get her now, man. Get her now."

Shannon turned to her husband, and the look in her eyes and the smile on her face said it all. They were in mad love.

He didn't know if that was what he was pursuing with Sophie. It felt more like…*possibility.*

And hell, *possibility* seemed worth it. When it came in a package of brains, beauty, and heart, wrapped up in a peach dress, it seemed worth it for sure.

He searched through his mental files, trying to remember where Sophie said she'd be on Saturday. Something about the fundraiser. Doing some work with her ex. Was she at home? At her office? He snapped his fingers when he remembered.

"Fine," he said, then leaned closer to Shannon and whispered, "But can you give me that dress?"

She smiled widely. "Of course. It's in my car."

He turned to the rest of them. "All right. Wish me luck. You gonna stay here and keep Johnny Cash company and eat the sandwiches?"

"We are, and then we're going to spend the day in your pool and wreak havoc," Colin said. "Leave now so we can start this pool party."

* * *

The ballroom at the Venetian was perfection.

Sophie had just walked Clyde through a quick rehearsal of his opening remarks, showing him where he would enter the stage, and demonstrating how the podium would be set up for his introduction at the fundraiser.

She thanked the operations manager for the quick use of the room and then headed to the elevator with the event's biggest donor. Clyde wagged a finger at her as they stepped into the elevator. "I can't wait 'til next Saturday."

"It's going to be a great event," she said with a bright smile she hardly felt.

Inside, her mind was a cluttered mess. She still didn't know what to make of Ryan, or whether she wanted to keep moving forward with him. Too bad relationships weren't math problems with precise answers. They were essay questions in a philosophy class, and they came down to judgement.

She wasn't sure what choice she wanted to make, or even if there *was* a choice anymore. For all she knew, Ryan might have closed the gates on that flicker of possibility she'd sensed last night. Shut it off like a switch. She was willing to bet he was good at that. That the man had a built-in eject button, and could easily parachute himself to a soft landing far away from her.

"That's not what I meant. I meant that I'm looking forward to meeting your gentleman at the event," Clyde said with a wink, mentioning the man in limbo in her life. "The man who has captured the attention of Las Vegas's most eligible bachelorette."

Oh God. She cringed, absolutely cringed from head to toe, and stem to stern, at that designation. The feminist in her wanted to brandish her claws. The shrewd businesswoman in her affixed her best shiny, happy face. "Oh Clyde, you do shower me with compliments," she said as they reached the ground floor. She attempted to steer him back to the matter at hand, so she could avoid the issue of her date, since she might not have one anymore. "I'm glad everything is in order for the benefit. Thank you again for stopping by on a Saturday morning to have a look-see."

He was undeterred. "Sophie, I want to say, if it doesn't work out with this fellow for whatever reason, you have an open door with me to connect with Taylor."

In the blink of an eye, her wishes went from blurry to crystal clear.

She didn't want an open door with Taylor. She wanted Ryan. She wanted the one and only man she'd felt such passion and lust and desire for.

There it was. Her answer. Her choice. This relationship *was* a math problem. Two plus two equals four, and four was Ryan Sloan.

Now she needed to figure out what to do with the result of her simple addition.

"You are so very sweet. And now I have an appointment I must race to," she said, and pointed down the hallway.

Once out of earshot and eyeshot, she breathed a huge sigh of relief and headed to the Grand Canal Shops to meet Holden for a cup of coffee and some much-needed retail therapy. A beat of happiness played in her heart as she neared the cafe—she'd always enjoyed Holden's company, and she needed her best friend even more today. Over lattes and quality time with Kenneth Cole, Coach, and Christian Louboutin, she caught him up to speed on her latest news, showing him Ryan's photo from his corporate website.

"I hope it's not over," she admitted.

"So on a scale of one to ten, how much do you like him?" he asked as she tried on a peep-toe silver stiletto with a strap over the heel.

"One hundred," she said, peering at the red-soled shoe in the mirror of the boutique. "But I don't know where we stand."

He met her reflection in the glass. "Those look amazing. And honestly, it sounds more like you're in a holding pattern."

"I detest holding patterns. I hate uncertainty. Not to mention, the whole thing just makes me feel stupid."

"So tell him as much. Tell him what you need. That he needs to be open with you," he said, as she slipped off the shoes and gestured to the counter so she could pay for them.

"And I feel stupid, too, because Clyde is breathing down my neck. It's like everyone is using me. I'm sorry if that sounds dramatic, but Clyde clearly has his sights set on me because he thinks I'll never try to touch his money. And then I have to wonder if Ryan had his own agenda."

"Did it seem like that?"

As the saleswoman rang her up, Sophie let the reel of her time with Ryan play before her eyes. Date by date. Night by night. Email by email. Moment after moment of intoxicating, inescapable pleasure. Ryan had always seemed focused on her. Only her. Her pleasure, never anything else.

She floated back to the diner and his heady words.

If you were mine, I'd never let you want for anything. I'd take care of you, and all your needs. All the time. Anytime. Whatever you needed, I'd give you.

A current of longing swirled inside her. Of missing. Of wanting.

"No," she admitted, taking the bag from the employee. "I was his only agenda."

"Then," he said, as he patted her shoulder, "it seems you might want to let him know you're falling for him. Especially since I think he's here right now."

"What?"

He gestured to the entryway of the Louboutin store. "I'm assuming the insanely handsome man in the University of Michigan T-shirt, holding a shopping bag and looking just like the guy in the photo you just showed me, is here to see you?"

CHAPTER TWENTY-FIVE

"Hi."

"Hi."

She was too stunned to say much more, but the softness in his voice, and the vulnerable look in his beautiful, dark blue eyes, settled her nerves.

Ryan turned to Holden standing next to her. "You must be Holden. I've heard a lot about you. Pleasure to meet you," he said, extending a hand. "I'm Ryan."

Holden took it. "Likewise. Nice to meet you, too."

"Sophie tells me you're a talented piano player, and that I'll get to hear you next week at the benefit," he continued, and Sophie's jaw nearly crashed to the floor. She'd never expected possessive, jealous, dominant Ryan to talk so easily to her ex. Sexuality aside, most men wouldn't do so well talking to a prior lover, let alone a woman's former husband.

"Thank you. I hope you enjoy the Beethoven."

"I have no doubt I will. That is," he said, returning his focus to her, "if Sophie will still have me."

Holden smiled broadly and dropped a quick kiss on her cheek. "I believe that's my cue to go," he said, then exited the store, threading through the Saturday afternoon shoppers at the Grand Canal Shops.

She was left in the middle of the Louboutin store with the man she'd kicked out of her house last night. "How did you find me here?"

"Don't forget, I was Army Intelligence," he said with a grin.

"And they taught you how to locate women who are shopping?"

He shook his head. "No. But you told me you were going to be here today, and since you're a classy woman, I picked the classiest shoe store as your possible location. That is, after I tried a few other shops." She loved that she was the object of his treasure hunt. "So," he began, rocking lightly back and forth on his feet. "I'm not terribly good at this whole talk-about-feelings-and-stuff thing, as you've probably gathered by now. So I'm just going to be blunt and lay it out."

He took a beat, drawing a breath. Her heart raced as she waited for his next words. "I want to try with you. And I want to take you to the benefit, and introduce you to my brothers and sister, and I'm pretty sure Johnny Cash is eager to meet you."

Her heart tripped over itself. "I want all that, too."

He wrapped an arm around her waist, and she melted, just melted from the simple touch. "I need you to know, I was never using you. I won't lie and tell you it didn't cross my mind that you were the detective's sister, and I won't insult your intelligence by saying I didn't wonder if you knew anything about the case. I *did* wonder," he said, and she nodded, listening intently to his serious tone. "But that literally lasted for a minute, maybe two. And it ended as soon as I set eyes on you at Aria. Because once I saw you again, none of the other things mattered. I wanted you with an intensity I haven't felt before. And the more time I spent with you, the greater that desire became." His fingertips traced soft lines on her waist. "I know we haven't even seen each other that much in the grand scheme of things, but I already feel something for you, Sophie. Something deep and powerful," he said, and those words weaved through her, humming in her body, buoying her heart and her spirit.

"I feel the same," she whispered. "I barely understand how it's possible that I met you a little over a week ago."

"I know." He pressed his forehead to hers. "It makes no sense to me, either. It was pure, one hundred percent lust at first sight, and then it somehow became more. I can't risk losing you by being so damn stubborn." He pulled back to look her in the eyes again. His dark blue gaze made her stomach pirouette, and the way he brushed his fingertips along her arm had her skin sizzling. *Chemistry*—they had a surplus of it, so much they could sell it on street corners, or bottle it and make a mint. Only, she didn't want to sell it. She wanted to hoard it, because this kind of reaction —like and lust, passion and possibility—didn't come around often. She needed to grab it, explore it, and see where its magic took them.

"You didn't lose me. I promise."

"I know I messed up by not telling you more about my family, and I can't promise I won't mess up again. And I don't really know that I'm able or ready to just sit down and tell you every single sordid detail of my life—"

She pressed her hand to his chest, thrilling at the feel of his firm body beneath the light cotton of the T-shirt. "You don't need to tell me everything. You don't have to deliver your biography on a silver platter, Ryan. I already want to see you more. I just want to know more about you. Bit by bit, day by day, as you're ready to share."

He nodded and clasped his hand over hers. "I meant what I said at the diner. I don't ever get beyond three dates because I don't like to share. So you need to know you're the only woman I've ever wanted to get closer to. You do something to me that drives me wild and makes it impossible for me to think about anything but you."

She couldn't contain her grin if she tried. "You're pretty much ever-present in my mind, too."

"Now listen, I'd really like to get you naked, but I also want to get to know you. So what would you say if we did something totally Vegas and took a gondola ride and talked?"

"I would love to get to know you better, Ryan Sloan," she said. He held out his elbow, and she hooked hers through it, walking with him to the gondolier, excitement ping-ponging through her because they were starting something.

Starting over, and starting anew, and starting fresh.

They were going to make a go of this for real, stripped down and bare, hearts and minds.

And—probably pretty damn soon—bodies, too.

But for now, there was a boat, and there was water, and there was a fake skyline that looked like a bright blue summer day, so she settled into his arms and bobbed along the canals inside The Venetian.

"Why don't you tell me more about hockey?" she asked.

* * *

Whew.

That was not easy.

That was like…scaling a mountain.

Lifting a car.

Leaping over a tall building.

But to have Sophie in his arms again, her lush, ripe body snuggled next to him as they floated down the man-made canal? Yeah. Worth it.

Giving voice to emotional truths was exhausting. But she was happy, so damn happy, to listen to him talk about hockey. And he was relieved, so damn relieved, not to have to dig any deeper right now. Fine, he'd probably have to later. But for the moment he explained the basics of a line change, the different penalties, and the puck-before-skates rule.

"So the puck has to cross the blue line before the skates when you move to the opposing team's zone?" she asked.

"Exactly."

"And if the attacker has both his skates across the line before that happens, it's an offside and there's a face-off," she said, as she processed the rules he'd explained while the gondolier crooned a love song in Italian.

"You could be a ref now," he said, clasping his hand more firmly around her shoulder. She wriggled closer, and the boat passed under a brick bridge.

"That's my next calling, I'm sure," she said resting her head against him. He stroked her hair, and this moment was one of the most surreal of all—living in the present on its own terms. "And why do you like hockey?"

He shrugged and smiled. "It's just fun."

"Fun is good."

"Were you looking for some deeper reason? Like it was my dad's sport?"

"No. But was it?"

"Nah. He wasn't a sporty guy. He was all about cards, and cars, and poker, and pool. He loved this town because he loved the little bets. He had a regular card game going with his buddy Sanders and his other friend Donald. They played poker every third Thursday of the month. Never more than fifty bucks," he said. He was tempted to add that his mom used to give his dad a hard time about playing, saying they didn't have the money to spare. He'd respond by telling her that fifty dollars wasn't going to make or break their month. He was probably right on that count. Besides, he was good at cards, and used some of his winnings over the years to pay for night school classes the last year of his life. But while Ryan might be able to share little details of his dad with Sophie, he wasn't ready to delve into the fights his mom and dad had. Letting Sophie into his life didn't mean baring every single tiny detail. It meant *not* hiding the things that mattered. Like his memories of his father. "He was a good guy. A good man. He wasn't perfect, but he took care of us, and he taught us manners and respect, and he never missed a chance to go to the park."

She slinked out from his hold and turned to face him. "He sounds like a great guy. I'm sure you miss him."

"I do," he said with a nod. "I really do."

He sighed heavily, and Sophie must have decided hockey and this admission were enough for now, because she cupped his cheeks and brushed her lips to his. It was a soft kiss at first, and she explored his lips as if she were kissing him for the first time. Soon enough she pressed harder, nipping with her teeth, nibbling and sucking, and making him groan in the middle of the canal, with the stripe-shirted gondolier mere feet from them.

The kiss was a new beginning. A promise of more to share. A hint of what they might become.

And it blurred the rest of the world. Because all he knew, felt, and wanted had been reduced to the soft and sweet feel of her lips, the smell of her skin, and the scent of her hair.

Then she picked up speed, veering out of poetic and into ravaging. He'd never let her lead in a kiss before, but he did now, and she sure knew what to do to him. She knew how to play rough, how to kiss like a tiger, hard and hungry. She'd turned him on well past the point of propriety in a gondola.

He broke the kiss, clasped his hands on her shoulders, and looked her in the eyes. "Spend the rest of the weekend with me. Come to my house. Swim with me. Meet my dog. Play a round of pool. Besides, I have a change of clothes for you if you need one," he said, holding up the bag with the peach dress in it.

She made grabby hands, and he yanked back the bag. "You can have it if you say yes."

Her eyes lit up. She tapped her chin, pretending to think about it. "I feel like you left one very important thing off the to-do list."

He lowered his hand to her ass and squeezed hard. "No, beautiful. That's a given. Fucking you will be the main agenda item."

CHAPTER TWENTY-SIX

He opened the sliding glass door to his deck and stood on the threshold, stopping to drink in the gorgeous sight before him.

Sophie wore a white bikini and huge black sunglasses as she stretched out on a lounge chair by his pool, reading her iPad under a big yellow umbrella. Her skin was so fair, he doubted she was a sun worshipper. But even so, she looked stunning with the rays casting their glow on her legs. Late-afternoon shadows fell across his yard, along with a quiet hush.

The stillness of the moment—both the silence and her beauty—felt like a dream. But the image was too sharp, too crisp to be anything but real.

His real life. His real chance. A real change.

Okay, some things hadn't changed. He couldn't keep his hands off her.

After a pit stop at her condo, since she'd insisted on picking up clothes, he drove her to his house once he'd ensured his family was already gone. He wanted Sophie to meet them, but he didn't have the patience for a get-to-know-you session when he simply had to have her. They'd christened the hallway the second the door had closed. He took her against the wall, with Johnny Cash hiding his snout under a pillow on the couch as if he couldn't bear to watch. Now, his mutt was sprawled on the cool grass under a tree, back legs sticking out behind him like Superdog.

But the woman.

Oh, the woman.

Sophie was all his for the next twenty-four hours. No dropping her off at midnight. No final kiss in front of her building. And no bumping into her brother.

He struck all thoughts of her brother from his brain as he walked across the deck, down the wooden steps, over the soft grass, and onto the tile edging the oval blue lagoon in the middle of his yard. He had two drinks with him, and when he arrived by her side, she lowered her shades to the bridge of her nose, looking exactly like a glamorous movie star on vacation.

"Are you playing my waiter today?"

"Maybe I'm the pool boy," he said as he handed her a mojito.

She laughed. "I don't have pool-boy fantasies, I assure you."

He sat at the end of her chair with his Macallan on ice. "What fantasies do you have?"

She raised an eyebrow as she took a sip of the drink. "I fantasize about a man who can make a drink like this. This is divine. How did you know I like mojitos by the pool?"

He shrugged, quirking up the corner of his lips. "Lucky guess."

She shot him a skeptical glance as she pushed her sunglasses on top of her head. "I'm not so sure that's just luck. I suspect it's more of your military intelligence training."

"You think they teach us how to identify a woman's drink of choice?"

"No, but I think you have a supremely analytical mind and like to piece clues together, and somehow you decided that a woman like me drinks mojitos."

"And what are the traits that would suggest mojito drinking?" he asked, enjoying the banter as the sun dipped toward the horizon.

"You tell me," she said, crossing her ankles. Her toenails were painted violet. He wasn't a man who cared about polished fingers or toes, but somehow this little detail seemed so very Sophie.

"Gorgeous, confident, smart, fun...and likes to enjoy things that taste good."

She made some sort of sexy humming sound in her throat. "You taste good," she said.

His dick leapt to attention, ready to give her a full salute. He dropped a hand to her leg, wrapping it around her calf and squeezing. "Everything you say and do makes me hard. It's like you have a remote control to my dick."

She laughed as heat poured down from the sky. "I actually ordered that remote last week. They sell them at Sharper Image. Can't wait for it to arrive."

Loud peals of laughter ripped through him, and this was a moment he would savor for a long time—the easy way she had with him, how she teased him, and toyed with him, and never backed down. He caressed her warm calf, kissed by the sun, as he tipped his forehead toward the iPad. "What were you reading?"

"A biography of Tommy Lee from Mötley Crüe. I have a thing for rock-star biographies."

"Interesting. Anything to that?"

She pursed her lips together, as if considering the answer. "I think because the lifestyle is so extravagant and extreme. I read them for fun back in college, with a sort of wide-eyed awe, and these people seemed so foreign but so fascinating. They still are—the hours rock stars keep, the crazy things they do, the excess, the conquests, the dangers. It's like a vicarious thrill ride into a world I'd never want to be in but adore watching unfold."

"Are you a voyeur?" he asked with narrowed eyes.

"Ha. Hardly. I just like to see the curtain pulled back," she said, taking a quick drink. Then she set down her glass on the small table next to her lounge chair. "What do you like to read?"

"Business strategy books to stay sharp. Thrillers to keep the heart rate up. And international news to stay educated. That probably sounds terribly prosaic."

She shook her head. "No. Not at all. I love your reasons, too. They tell me more about what matters to you," she said with a sweet smile. "Plus, I think whatever anybody's reading is a good thing. Truth be told, I was actually switching back and forth between reading the Tommy Lee book, and this email exchange with my contact in Rüsselsheim."

His ears pricked. "Your Bugatti?"

A grin stretched across her features, like a very satisfied cat. "I'm going there to check it out in ten days."

He arched an eyebrow. "Are you bringing it back?"

"An import service will. But I want to touch it and feel it and drive it myself before the final sign-off."

An image of Sophie running her hands along the sleek body of a high-end sports car played before his eyes. "What milestone is this one? You said you reward yourself for hitting milestones in giving."

"I like numbers, especially the big fat ones with lots of zeroes, so I decided that since I sold my company for a hundred million dollars that when I hit that goal in money raised for others, I'd get this car."

He whistled in admiration. "To say I'm impressed is an understatement. Both with the sale, but also with what you've raised."

"Thank you. Though that's not all from my pocket. I do give a lot to every cause I raise money for, but my bigger job is simply asking others to open their wallets. I'm lucky to know many generous people I can call on," she added, as if that somehow lessened the accomplishment.

He tapped her knee lightly with his fingertips. "And you convinced them to part with their money for a good cause. It's amazing, however you slice it. Why did you decide to go into philanthropy?"

She reached for her glass and took a long drink. "Because I could."

He brushed his fingers along her thigh, loving the simplicity of her answer. She'd chosen to do good because she was in the rare position of being able to. She could have done anything with her time, her money, and her access, and she'd opted to donate the hours in her day to help others. The choice was a deliberate one, and it said so much about her, in his view, that she'd picked this particular path. "Beautiful answer. I love that. I respect that. Did you ever think about starting another company? So many other entrepreneurs launch additional businesses."

"I had no interest in being a serial entrepreneur," she said, shaking her head. "I know I'm lucky to have had the successful run I had with my company—to start it when I did and sell it when I did. And now I'm lucky enough to use all my business skills to help with things that matter more in the world. I've raised money for animal charities, for sick children, for cancer research, for kids in need, for troubled kids, and so on. I'd much rather devote my time to doing that." Then added, almost apologetically, "Even if it can be just as much work and take just as much management as running my own company."

"I hear you on that. It must be consuming at times. Everyone needing and wanting things," he said, flashing back to the gala and the way the two ladies there practically hunted Sophie down to make their own cases for the children's wing.

"That's true. Which is why it'll be all the more fun to go for a joyride in my new car," she said with a glint in her eye.

Though Ryan could jet off to Europe with her and hole up in a five-star resort on his dime, she could do all those things for herself, too, and then some. Ryan did well for himself, but he wasn't in a position to drop that kind of cash on a car, and she was. Perhaps for the first time he was keenly aware that while he was successful, Sophie was in another class. It didn't annoy him and didn't make him feel any less of a man. But he wanted to make sure she was fine with everything. "There's not much I can give you materially that you can't get on your own," he said, matter-of-factly. "Does that bother you?"

She laughed loudly. "Not in the least," she said then reached for his hand, lacing her fingers through his. Her smile was gentle and tender. "You don't have to shower me with expensive gifts. You don't have to give me presents at all if you don't want to. I loved the peach tulips, and the pinot grigio, and I am in some kind of mad love with the dress you had your sister track down for me. It's beautiful, and it's perfect for me, and I didn't have one like it, and I've been coveting one. So thank you," she said with a squeeze of his hand, then added softly, "Besides, the things I want from you don't cost money."

He tensed for a moment, shoulders tightening and chest burning. He wasn't ready to have a more serious talk about commitment. Letting her in and talking more was all he could handle. "Such as?"

She took her time answering, trailing her fingers along his bare arm. "What I want is for you to take me for a ride in my new car someday."

A groan rumbled through his chest, escaping his lips. My God, she was so fucking giving. He'd struck gold when he met her. She was precious and rare. "Pretty sure I'm the luckiest guy in the world."

"So that means you'd like to get behind the wheel?"

"There's only one thing I want to do in that car more than drive it," he said in a low voice, raking his eyes over her gorgeous figure.

She tapped her index finger against her lips and peered skyward. "Hmmm. You mean you want to see how far back the passenger seat goes?"

"Exactly. That's exactly the kind of test drive I want to give you in your new car."

She gestured to her iPad. "What if I told you I had pictures of it?"

He made a *show it to me now* gesture with his fingers. "I want to see that car," he said then ran his palms up and down her calves, his way of imploring her. She murmured softly, a sound that said she was enjoying his touch. He took advantage of it, digging his thumbs into her ankles, and working his way up her legs, stopping to kiss her calves along the way.

She reached for her iPad, swiped a finger across the screen and then called up the email. "Are you ready to be dazzled by its beauty? Can you handle it?"

"If I can handle how gorgeous you are, this car won't be a problem, because I'm sure it can't hold a candle. But show it to me anyway."

"Flattery will get you everywhere." She turned the iPad around and showed him the photo. His heart skipped a beat. The auto was a thing of beauty. A gorgeous, gleaming, emerald-green sports car that stirred up every desire in him to hug the curves on a downhill, to hear the purr of the engine, to stomp on the accelerator in this sleek ride. He actually pressed his fingertips to the screen and stroked the photo.

She tossed her head back and laughed throatily. "Do you want me to wipe the drool from your chin now or later?"

He snapped her iPad case closed and set it down on the table. Reaching behind her, he lowered the lounge chair, then crawled over her, pinning her with his body. "You think I'm just going to let that impudent comment slide?"

The look in her eyes changed as she moved from that confident, saucy woman to the vulnerable, submissive one. "Are you going to punish me?"

He shook his head. "No. I'm not going to punish you. I'm going to make you work for it."

"How?" she asked, and in that one word he heard the thrill of anticipation. Her own desire to be led like this was her drug.

He clasped her hands, threading his fingers through hers, watching every move she made—the way her lips parted, how her eyes followed his, how her chest rose and fell. He stretched her arms over her head, and gently pushed her hands beneath one of the wood slats at the top of the lounge chair.

"Hold onto the chair the whole time," he said then moved off her to reach for an ice cube from his drink. He held it above her chest, as the first bead of liquid fell from the cube and landed between her lush breasts. Her nipples pebbled through the fabric of her bikini.

He lowered the ice cube closer to her skin. "Are you hot?"

She bit her lip and answered, "Very."

"I had a feeling you might be." He brushed it through her cleavage, and she shivered, gasping out loud at the first contact with the cold. "Does that make you feel better?"

"Yes," she said on a feathery gasp. He ran the ice under her breasts, down her belly, and to the top of her bikini bottoms, picturing the treasure that lay beneath the white fabric—her wet, hot pussy. His dick throbbed in his swim shorts. His need to have her intensified.

He travelled to her sides with the ice, and she squirmed, writhing under his touch. She was a live wire. At every touch, she sparked. She ignited, responding to his words, his voice, his hands, and his body. It was intoxicating. It was addictive. He bent his neck to her, licking the shell of her ear with the tip of his tongue. She moaned softly, whispering his name in a barely audible voice.

It sounded like a plea.

His shorts made a tent now, pitched high. "Do you want me to touch you?

"Yes."

"My yard is big. My neighbors aren't around today," he said as he travelled up her body with the ice cube, watching her shiver as it left a wet path across her hot skin. He reached the hollow of her throat, making circles, watching the ice melt some. He leaned in and kissed the water away. Then he pulled back and said firmly, "Put it between your teeth."

She opened her mouth, and waited for him to insert the cube. She held it in place with her teeth as he ran the back of his fingertips down her arm. "I could untie your bikini straps right now. Take off the top and tie you up with it. Flip you over onto your hands and knees and fuck you from behind on this chair," he said, not looking at her, but instead reaching for his glass, and finishing off his drink.

He returned his focus to her, and the look in her eyes was already glossy, on the path to red-hot desire. "Would you like that?"

She nodded.

Starting at her collarbone, he brushed his finger to the top of her chest, then through the valley of those gorgeous tits, on a fast track to her legs. He danced his fingers along the waistband of her bathing suit, taunting her. "Or I could take these off right now and feel how wet you are. Since you're all nice and slippery, right?"

She bucked upwards, giving her yes. A drop of liquid drizzled from the cube down her chin. He kissed it away.

"Don't let go of the ice," he instructed. "Hold on 'til it melts between your lips."

He moved his hands down her legs, placing his palms on the insides of her thighs. He spread them apart, and stared at her bikini bottom. "Or maybe I'll just torture you by brushing one finger against this wet spot I love so much. Just play with your hot pussy through this bikini until you're moaning, crying, and begging me to take it off."

Her eyes floated closed momentarily, and she lifted her hips.

Desire tore through him, twisting and curling like a wildfire. He was desperate to quench it and bring her to orgasm. But he had to fight that urge and restrain all of his lust for her.

Waiting made everything better.

With her hands stretched above her head, hooked in the slats of the lounge chair, she was bound to him.

CHAPTER TWENTY-SEVEN

Yes. Yes. Yes.

Every single answer was a resounding yes.

She was so wet, so turned on, so slippery, and all she wanted was his touch. She had no idea how long this torture would last. She could bite down on this ice cube now, but that would only prolong the waiting. He'd find a new way to draw out his touch if she defied him. She wanted him fiercely, with an intensity that bordered on criminal.

Lust and desire ricocheted through her body as she gripped the slats above her and writhed her hips on the lounge chair, baking under the hot sun.

Soon. He had to touch her soon.

Mercifully, he looped his hands around her neck and untied her bikini, then unsnapped the hook at her spine. Her first taste of freedom came as he lowered the straps along her arms, taking off the top. His breath stilled as he took in her breasts.

She willed him to lower his mouth to her nipples and suck, bite, and taste. Maybe she could send a telepathic message telling him to touch her; she tried valiantly by arching her back, lifting her breasts closer to him.

He got the message. Oh hell, did he get it. He reached for her mojito. "Let's check how this tastes," he said as he poured some of the drink down her chest. She drew a sharp breath, even with the ice cube melting in her mouth. He buried his face between her breasts, lapping up the liquid. She wanted to moan, to cry out, to shout *yes* to the sun and moon and stars. This was her taste of heaven—his mouth on her skin.

He looked up and ran his finger along the cube in her teeth. "You want this so badly, don't you?" he asked.

She nodded. She didn't even know what he was offering. Whatever it was, she'd take it.

"It doesn't matter what I do, does it? You just want me to make you come?"

Yes. So much yes.

She arched her hips, seeking him out. His eyes roamed over her bikini bottom. She was soaked. Surely, he could see the evidence of her desire through the fabric.

He stood up and ran his hands over the thick bulge in his shorts. Killing her. He was fucking killing her. "You like that, don't you? When I touch myself?"

She breathed a yes around the melting cube.

"How much do you want me to jack off on you right now? To come all over you?"

She nodded vigorously. He was dirty and filthy and she wanted it. She would beg, bargain, or steal for it.

He pushed his shorts down, freeing his cock—his beautiful, gorgeous shaft that she loved. She flicked her tongue against the back of the cube, and started licking it to free herself.

He took his dick in his fist and stroked. She rocked in the chair, as if she could draw him into her with her hips, her eyes.

"Ice is almost melted," he said, cupping his balls in one hand and fisting harder with the other. "This is really making you crazy, isn't it?"

Heat raced through her body, pooling between her legs.

"I know you want me to do this," he said on an up-stroke. "You want to watch me stand here, and get off to your beautiful body, right in front of you. Tell me that's what you want."

"Yes," she hissed around the ice cube.

He let go of his dick, yanked up his shorts, and kneeled over her. He brought his mouth so close to her face she could feel his hot breath. "But I'm not going to. I have something better for you because you're so fucking good." He devoured her mouth, kissing her, taking the last chip of the ice cube into his own mouth, and getting rid of the obstacle between her and pure, unadulterated pleasure.

Then he tugged down her bathing suit bottom, pulled it off, and thrust a finger inside her.

Not a second passed before she started fucking his hand. She was so turned on, so worked up, and so aroused from him. Her hands were twisted inside the slats, the wood rubbing against her wrists, and she didn't care. All she cared about was this pleasure, this incomparable, other-worldly lust racing through her body, flooding every last cell, bathing her brain in ecstasy.

She couldn't even form words.

There was no point to speaking.

She was reduced to only moans and groans and murmurs as he crooked his finger inside her and hit the magic spot no one had ever discovered until Ryan Sloan walked into her life, fulfilling every fantasy.

This commanding, intense, powerful man loved to tease her, and loved to please her, and, oh God, he was doing just that. Her belly tightened. An orgasm insisted on appearing.

He added another finger, then one more, as his thumb rubbed her clit. She cried out *oh God* so loud she was sure California heard it. Her eyes squeezed shut. This was fucking epic. It was wondrous as he completely owned the center of her body, the center of her world, the core of her pleasure.

She gripped the wood as she writhed into his hand, his fingers deep inside her, and she hit the edge, detonating from the intensity that ravaged her.

Before the orgasm even subsided, he grasped her hands from the slats, released them, and threaded his fingers through hers, as ripples of pleasure continued to spread through her body like aftershocks. He'd taken off his shorts, and now he wedged himself between her thighs, and told her to wrap her legs around his hips.

She did as instructed, and then he sank into her. He filled her so completely, and the sheer intensity of him inside her was astonishing. She moaned loudly, her voice carrying across the heat of the afternoon, floating on the hot air as he buried himself deep. He gripped her fingers hard.

"*Sophie*," he growled in her ear as he thrust.

"*Ryan.*"

"I'm so fucking happy you're here," he said. It vaguely occurred to her that this was one of the first times they'd had sex face to face. It occurred to her, too, that she wanted to try every position with him. She wanted to be taken, she wanted to be owned, and she wanted to be his.

Completely his.

"Me, too," she said on a breathy moan as he claimed her with his cock. She clenched around him, her pussy gripping him tight as he thrust into her.

"I love being with you," he whispered, his breath ragged in her ear, his words lighting her up. "*Everything.* Everything about being with you."

"Oh God," she cried out, because he was doing it again. He was taking her there. To the ends of the earth. To the edge of reason. To another fucking world, one stitched with silver and gold and bright, hot sunlight that rained down on her skin, liquid pleasure that flooded her veins, and something so damn close, so immeasurably close, to *more.*

He let go of one of her hands to palm her breast, squeezing her nipple as he rocked into her. He pinched her, and it hurt so good as she came hard around his cock. In seconds, he followed her, biting her shoulder as he reached his own climax, grunting in gorgeous pleasure, the sound of his deep, sexy moans music to her ears.

"It's you," he said, a minute later as he spooned her, holding her in his arms and kissing her neck. "It's only you."

She knew what he was trying to say. She felt it, too, inside her body, and deep into her heart. For the first time, the emotion lived in both places.

CHAPTER TWENTY-EIGHT

"I have a confession to make," Ryan announced, as he set two plates on the kitchen table then opened the cardboard box of pizza.

"Confess." She held out her hand grandly, inviting him to talk – something he was increasingly enjoying doing with her.

He snagged a slice of the cheese pie that he'd ordered from Gigi's, his favorite pizza shop, and placed it on Sophie's plate. With the salad tongs, he scooped out some of the Caesar salad for her then for himself, too.

He sat down, joining her. "You already know my secret about being completely unable to cook." He held up one finger to make a point—a point of self-defense. "Though I am unbelievably proficient at calling the pizza place."

She nodded approvingly. "Gigi's is the best in Vegas. I absolutely approve of your dinner choice. Cheese pie, Caesar salad, and a chardonnay." She picked up her fork and dug into the salad first. "So, tell me."

He took a bite of the cheese pie, rolled his eyes in pleasure, and pointed to his chipmunk cheeks to say *wait just a moment.* When he finished chewing, he made his confession: "I ate the peach pie you made."

She smiled broadly then took a drink of her white wine. "I'm so happy to hear that. It's my mother's recipe. It's divine, isn't it?"

"That's exactly what my grandmother said about it. *Divine.*"

She tilted her head curiously, asking, "Your grandmother?"

"I brought it to her house after you gave it to me. I had some with her."

Sophie's blue eyes seemed to show her processing this information—that he was a man who brought pie to his grandmother. Maybe he'd made a strange choice to go see her last night, but it had made as much sense to him as anything had then. So he quickly added, "She told me that I should never give up a woman who could bake like that."

Sophie raised her wineglass, a toast of sorts to his grandmother. "Smart woman. Sounds like you're close to her?"

"Definitely. She and my granddad pretty much raised us after Mom went to…" He let his voice trail off.

Sophie nodded immediately, letting him know she understood. "And that brought you all closer, I imagine."

"It did. I was almost fifteen when we moved in with her and my granddad, my dad's parents. I guess that kind of thing can either rip you apart or bring you closer," he said, more easily than he'd ever expected to be able to voice such words. Perhaps because the deadbolt was undone. The door was open, and the heavy weight of years of closeting secrets had lightened. His heart felt freer than it had in ages, his head lighter. Funny, how he'd never known that talking like this, to someone who wasn't in the inner circle, would feel oddly peaceful. "In our case, mostly it brought us closer," he said, and took another bite of his pizza, savoring the delicious cheese and the tasty crust.

She took a drink then asked, "Mostly?"

Yes, mostly. Because he knew exactly how his grandmother felt about his mother. The past's hard grip resurfaced, like claws clamping down on his throat, and his newfound voice. The familiar urge to lock up his history kicked in. But he fought back. "I say that because she doesn't know I actually visit my mom still."

"Ah, I understand," Sophie said softly. "I imagine it would be hard for her to accept that's something you want. But it's clearly important to you to see your mom."

My God, it was like morning sunlight streaming in through the blinds. Talking to Sophie was lightness, it was patience, and it was safety. He barely had to explain a thing. She simply understood it all. She got it, and him. But he didn't want Sophie to think he was a liar. "It's not that I hide it from my grandma, per se. And I think she knows on some level, because she's aware that I go there for Christmas and other times. But I don't tell her about all the visits. I didn't tell her I went earlier in the week, for instance. Or that I'm going again next weekend. Guess it just didn't seem like something it was important for her to know."

"How often do you visit?"

"I try to see her once or twice a month. Sometimes more, sometimes less." He sighed heavily. "She gets her hours cut now and then because she acts up."

"Acts up?"

He looked away, focusing on the steady breathing of his dog on the floor by an air conditioning vent, on the regular up and down motion of the Border Collie's chest, his black and white fur fluttering lightly. "She's not...," he said, tapping the side of his skull. "She's..." He let his voice trail off again. A lump rose in his throat. This was so hard to say. "She's not all there," he said, practically kicking the words past his lips.

Not only was his mother branded a murderer, not only was she the orchestrator of a gang-led shooting, she was also barreling down the path to insanity. He saw the evidence each time he visited her.

Sophie reached for his hand, threaded her fingers through his, and held on tight. "It all must be so hard," she said softly, and then she quickly moved on. He could kiss her—for the segue and for knowing one was needed. "Who are you closest to among your siblings? I only have one, obviously, so it's an easy answer for me. But you've got three. That must be a different story."

A small smile returned to his face. He could do this. He'd made it through the harder topic. His brothers and sister were way more manageable. "On the surface, I guess Michael, since we run a business together and we were in the army together. And we are a great team when it comes to the company. But Michael and I don't always see eye to eye. About my mom," he added.

"How so?"

"He never visits her, and he doesn't like that I do. So we're close, but sometimes that causes problems. Shannon has gone with me a bunch of times to Hawthorne, so in some ways, I'm closer to her. She still talks to my mom and gets her letters. But," he said, stopping to take a drink of his wine, then setting it on the table, "that's not what defines us. That's not what our family is all about. I mean, it did for a long time in the eyes of strangers. But we're more than that. We all support each other and love each other and look out for each other. A few years ago, once we were all back in Vegas, the four of us got together and bought our grandparents a house. The one they live in now. It was our way of giving back to them after all they did to help raise us right and make sure we didn't turn out more fucked up than we were," he said, with a light scoff. "We were pretty messed up, Sophie."

She shot him a gentle smile that said she understood.

"We kind of wanted it to be a surprise, but it was hard to buy a surprise house, since we wanted them to like it. Colin's the money guy though, so he was able to get it all going. The idea was his in the first place. He mentioned it to me once when we were shooting hoops. And, back to your question, sometimes it seems like I'm closest to him. He's the youngest, and Michael's kind of taken on a fatherly role. Colin and I feel more like we're equal brothers. With Michael, sometimes it feels like he still thinks he has to look out for all of us, even though he's only two years older."

Sophie laughed. "Let me tell you, I completely understand that older brothers can be a total pain in the ass," she said with a knowing smile, and he matched her grin. Something was changing between them now that the veil of secrecy had been removed. Her brother had once been the cause of a rift, and now she was able to make a joke about the guy.

He held up his hands in surrender. "I'm not going to touch that with a ten-foot pole. I'll keep your brother out of this, so I don't get in trouble again with the woman I want."

"You're not in trouble at all," she said, returning to her pizza.

"Now about that peach pie. It was your mom's recipe. Was she a baker?"

She shook her head. "She was a teacher. But she was an amazing 'pie mistress,'" she said, stopping to sketch air quotes. "That's what my dad called her."

"And he ran the fruit stand?"

She nodded. "What about your dad?"

"Cab driver, then a limo driver. For the last year, he was going to night school. Taking some accounting classes to try to get a better job. Mom was a seamstress," he said finishing off another slice. "And, don't laugh, but she had a dream to make dog jackets." He glanced over at Johnny Cash lying on the floor. "She'd probably make one for him if she could. But they don't let inmates have sewing machines in prison," he said, the corner of his lips quirking up. For the first time in ages he'd managed to make a joke about his sad family history.

After they cleaned up, he pointed to the shopping bag with the dress in it in the living room. "I'm thinking now would be a great time for you to show me that peach dress."

"I would love to give you a fashion show."

She retreated to his bedroom, and while she was changing, he programmed in soft music on his stereo, hunting for the kind of songs she might like. He remembered "Fly Me to the Moon" was her ringtone. She might not want to hear that one again, so he chose another Sinatra number and let the crooner's voice float through his house. He dimmed the lights in the living room. Stars winked on and off through the windowpane.

"What do you think?"

He turned around to see Sophie twirl for him, then stop and strike a pose. She looked extraordinary in a white pinup dress with a peach pattern, and the silver shoes she'd picked up at the Grand Canal shops.

"That you look edible. But I'm not going there just yet. For now, I want to do what we did on our first date," he said, walking over to her and running his fingers through her soft, blond hair. She lifted her chin to look at him.

The look in her eyes just plain melted him as he wrapped his arms around her. He'd never seen a person so happy as Sophie simply to dance with him on the hardwood floors of his living room, as Sinatra crooned.

"I liked talking to you," he said, his lips brushing her hair.

"I liked listening to you," she said as they swayed.

"You make it easy."

"It shouldn't have to be hard. *This*," she said, and he knew what she meant by "this."

"*Us*," he echoed. "And it's not hard. It's incredible."

* * *

As he held her, she flashed back to some of her sweetest memories, her most potent images of love—her parents slow dancing together at night, and her mother's words, too. "*Make time for kisses, and meals, and each other, and dance under the stars and to the music, and dream together.*"

This was her dream, and she was close, closer than she'd ever been, to having it.

* * *

Lick. Lick. Lick.

The next morning, a long tongue slurping across her cheek greeted Sophie. Yawning, she opened her eyes to find a black-and-white Border Collie kissing her face and wagging his tail.

He whimpered lightly, and Sophie glanced at a sleeping Ryan. He was flat on his stomach, face pressed into a pillow, an arm slung over his head.

She turned back to Johnny Cash. "Want to go outside?" she whispered, and he thumped his tail on the floor at the last word.

She slipped out of bed, and headed to the sliding glass door. The door was locked with a regular latch and a deadbolt. It took her a few seconds to wiggle them free, but she managed, and the dog shot out, racing across the grass and lifting his leg on a tree in the far corner of the yard.

For a very…long…time.

Pale pink fingers of light streaked across the morning sky as the sun rose. Taking a deep breath, savoring the fresh scent of a new day, Sophie soaked in the scene before her. Waking up at Ryan's house, spending the weekend with him, exploring all that they felt for each other had been a day and night of rapture, of passion, and, most of all, of connection.

Fine, it had been *only* one night, but she knew with both her heart and her analytical mind that Ryan Sloan was changing. He was opening up. He was sharing.

For her.

She practically giggled at the thought as she watched his dog finish his business then tear across the yard and conduct some morning recon with his snout, checking out the fence, perusing the edge of the pool, and sniffing some bushes. She felt bubbly, effervescent even, because she was close to having that elusive *thing* she'd craved for so long. For her whole damn life. The very gem she'd hunted for and thought she'd found with Holden, only to be proven wrong by the lack of spark. With Holden, she'd let friendship lead, and in return she'd gotten a great friendship. But with Ryan, she let lust, hormones, and desire start the engine. She'd taken a chance by inviting him to the gala without knowing him. That was a risk, but it had paid off. Then she'd nearly lost out the other night.

But he'd reappeared and had come to the table ready. She didn't need to peer into his mind, but she was thrilled by the glimpses of his heart and soul that he'd been offering. She felt special, she felt admired, and she felt madly desired. To have this kind of crazy, kinky, dirty sex with a man she was falling for…it was like finding a diamond on the side of the road.

It was almost too good to be true, and for a brief moment, her heart seized up. What if it all fell to pieces? What if this was just a bubble? A weekend of bliss and loveliness that would be punctured at midnight?

Ryan's dog raced to her side, and Sophie pushed those thoughts away as she headed inside. After a quick bathroom trip to freshen her breath, she returned to the kitchen and decided breakfast for her man would be a fine idea. She rolled her eyes at the contents of his fridge—it was pure single guy. Beer. Mustard. A loaf of bread. She scanned the shelves and drawers for bacon, certain she'd find some. Personally, she couldn't stand it. But what bachelor didn't like bacon?

She found none.

At least he had a carton of eggs and some butter, so she set to work whipping up some scrambled eggs, and as she turned off the stove, a sleepy and sexy Ryan padded out of the bedroom with rumpled hair and a cute yawn.

"Is this a dream? Or are you really waking me up with a homemade breakfast?"

He walked up behind her and wrapped his arms around her waist as she served the eggs. He planted a sweet kiss on her neck, and his breath was minty fresh. "It's real," she said. "If this were a dream, there would surely be bacon. I bet you love bacon."

He shuddered. "Hate it."

She turned and stared at him with one eyebrow raised. "I have never met a man who hates bacon."

"Well, you have now, beautiful. I do not understand the fascination this country has with bacon."

Her heart skipped a silly beat. "I have to tell you something, Ryan." Turning her voice intensely serious, she whispered, "I hate bacon, too."

He cupped her cheeks and kissed her. A quick morning kiss. "You let my dog out to pee and you hate bacon. I knew you were my perfect woman."

"Sit and eat or your eggs will get cold."

After the meal, he pulled her onto his lap in his chair, and thanked her for breakfast. "And now I have a question for you. You told me yesterday you don't have pool-boy fantasies," he said, reminding her of her joke at the pool.

She nodded. "That is true. Nor stable-boy fantasies either, I might add."

"Good." He kissed her earlobe. His voice went low and husky, sending a shiver through her as he asked, "What fantasies do you have?"

That was an easy answer. She pulled back to look him in the eyes. "You."

He grinned wickedly. "You don't have to fantasize about me. You can have me. I want to know what you fantasized about before you met me so I can do it to you."

She widened her eyes and stared at him, then gave the same answer. "You."

He furrowed his brow. "What do you mean?"

"I wanted someone like you. I fantasized about the things we do. The kind of sex we have is the kind of sex I've always wanted to have. Dirty, kinky, rough."

He groaned sexily. "You told me in your car you've never had it like this before. How did you know you wanted it like that?"

"The same way I can code with my eyes closed and one hand behind my back. The same way I can tell which cards are most likely to be played next in a blackjack hand. The same way I know two seconds after I see a dress if I want it. I just know. It's second nature."

"And you just knew you wanted to be tied up? You wanted to be spanked? You wanted to be told what to do?"

She nodded eagerly. "If you're making sure I'm still on board, the answer is yes. I want it this way. But if you want to know why, I think it's because my mind feels so busy all the time. Like mild OCD. I always make sure I've turned off the stove before I leave my home, and I check twice that I locked the door. I've always felt like I have all sorts of information and facts and details clanging around in my head, back when I was in school, and then when I was running the company. And now, even though I love what I do, I feel like I'm juggling one million things. But when you tie me up, I'm living in the moment. And I'm loving the moment. And that's why I fantasized for so long about being on my knees, tied up, or bent over the bed for a man like you. And now, just for you."

He groaned and crushed her lips in a bruising, demanding kiss, giving her exactly what she wanted and erasing anything else in her mind. Just like she asked for. Just like she dreamed about for years. When he broke the kiss, he spoke firmly to her. "I need you to do something right now."

She recognized that tone instantly, and her nipples hardened in response. He was going to give her an order. "Go to my bedroom. Strip down to nothing. Go into my closet and pick a tie. Put it around your neck. I assume you know how to tie a tie?"

"I do."

"Then wait for me, bent over the bed, ass raised high in the air, wearing only a tie. While you're waiting, I want you to get yourself wet," he said, then took her fingers and slid them into her mouth.

"Suck," he told her.

She took her own fingers deep in her throat, moaning as she sucked.

He breathed out hard. "Just like that. I'm going to clean up the table and do the dishes, since you cooked breakfast. When I'm done, I want you to be good and ready for me to fuck you."

* * *

He found his beautiful woman standing at the end of his bed, his green tie nestled between her breasts, the very tie he'd been wearing the day he met her. The fact that she'd chosen that one made him even harder.

Her palms were pressed onto his mattress, her ass lifted in perfect view, her pussy glistening.

"Move closer to the edge of the bed."

She did as told, glancing back at him, awaiting further instructions.

"Lie on your elbows," he said, and she lowered herself, offering up her body even more.

He unknotted the tie from her neck and bound her wrists together, so tight she couldn't move them a millimeter. Running a hand down her spine, he watched her bow her back as he mapped her body, as if he were an explorer and she the territory he planned to claim.

When he reached her round and luscious cheeks, he bent down to flick his tongue between the tops of them, eliciting a sexy moan from his woman. He bit the soft flesh. That earned him a breathy gasp, then she circled her hips, an invitation that turned his dick to steel. Clasping her ass in his hands, he smothered her rear in soft, quick kisses, then dipped his finger between her legs.

The wetness was divine, like a fucking slippery paradise that he needed to feel greeting his cock.

"You are good and ready," he said on a groan. He stripped in seconds, rubbed the head of his cock against her, then sank in, stopping to savor the absolute bliss of her gloriously wet cunt before he set to work on the important matter at hand.

Fucking her furiously.

"Did you fantasize about me fucking you like this?"

"Yes."

He grabbed her ass cheeks, squeezed them as he slammed into her. "You want it harder, right?"

"Please."

He took her savagely, pleasure tearing through him, her moans ringing in his ears. Snaking an arm up her neck, he brushed his finger across her lips. "Get it wet, like you did to your own." She drew him into her mouth and sucked, swirling her tongue around and up and down. "Good," he hissed, then dipped that finger between her slick folds before he returned to her rear, rubbing against her entrance gently at first, then insistently as he kept fucking her.

Her high-pitched pants were his permission to slide his finger inside all the way. "And this too? Tell me. Did you fantasize about this too?"

"With you, yes," she whispered, then her whispers turned into screams of ecstasy as he asked more questions, unearthing deeper and darker fantasies from his Sophie, ones he intended to fulfill, today and beyond.

For now, he took her over the edge, and they came together with her shuddering beneath him.

Later, when evening rolled around, he asked her if she'd consider spending the night again. She said yes.

It was all he wanted her to say.

Once upon a time, he'd wanted that yes for the sex. And he *still* wanted that from her. Oh hell, did he want it, over and over.

But he wanted *more*. He wanted everything else. He wanted the woman, inside and out, body and mind, heart and soul.

For the first time ever, Ryan Sloan was falling.

CHAPTER TWENTY-NINE

The game moved too quickly for Ryan to talk to Marshall about anything more than their strategy on the ice. The opposing team demolished them for the first two periods, rattling his teammates with penalty after penalty. The last period wasn't much better, and Ryan had to hold one of his guys back from starting yet another fight.

"Cool off, man. It's just a game," he told him before the ref threw the guy in the penalty box.

The game ended with a loss for his team, and his guys cursing up a storm, frustrated by their own poor play.

Ryan hardly cared today. Marshall had texted him earlier that he had an update, so when the other men headed to the showers, Marshall pulled him aside. They took off their skates, and then trudged up a few rows, removing bulky gloves before parking themselves on blue plastic seats.

The ice rink was mercifully empty.

"Got some news for you. You told me your brother-in-law had gotten a tip that Stefano wasn't as active in the Sinners at the time of the murder, right?"

Ryan nodded. Brent had shared that detail during the pool game at his house, something he'd heard from Mindy. But everything was hearsay still, and Ryan was hoping that could change soon.

"I think I know why."

"Tell me," Ryan said, and a mix of both desperation and anticipation gripped him. He wanted a fact. He prayed Marshall was dealing in that currency.

"Seems like Stefano had a broker," he began, and Ryan furrowed his brow in a question. Marshall made a rolling gesture with his hand to explain. "Like his guy who set up his hits."

The ice in the rink had nothing on Ryan right now. He was chilled to the bone. His body turned subzero just hearing how that killer operated. "This guy set up murders for hire?"

Marshall nodded. "He brokered them. The Sinners were all about drugs then, and stealing. Fencing stolen goods, some territory battles—the usual gang stuff, to be honest. But, sadly, there's money in murder, too, so the broker started working that angle for his boy Stefano." Marshall shook his head in disgust. Ryan gritted his teeth, trying to tamp down the treacherous ball of rage that lived inside of him at times like this. "Sounds like he's one of the guys the detectives are looking for."

"T.J. and K.," Ryan said in a hiss, the initials slithering out of his mouth. "That has to be them. His friends. His fucking accomplices. Who the hell are they? Do you know their names?"

"That's the problem. They're slippery. They're smarter than you'd expect a bunch of street thugs to be. The Sinners were quiet for awhile, sort of fell apart, but are now rising up again, and the word is this guy has played a role in some serious shit that went down. But we don't have a name yet. Not a real one, at least. Detective would probably sell an arm for a name."

Ryan probably would, too.

* * *

The week flew forward, hurtling toward the benefit in a heady blur of emails and texts, of days and nights, of sex and sleepovers, of dinners and drinks, and time...so much time together and so much desire for more time.

Tonight was the next big step.

from: Sophiefashionista@gmail.com
to: guywithgreentie@gmail.com
date: July 25, 4:58 PM
subject: I'm so not nervous at all.

You swear they don't bite? I ask because, well, you bite.

from: guywithgreentie@gmail.com
to: Sophiefashionista@gmail.com
date: July 25, 5:05 PM
subject: You have nothing to be nervous about.

My brothers better not bite you. As for Shannon, I make no promises.

from: Sophiefashionista@gmail.com
to: guywithgreentie@gmail.com
date: July 25, 5:17 PM
subject: Dress code?

What are you wearing?

from: guywithgreentie@gmail.com
to: Sophiefashionista@gmail.com
date: July 25, 5:22 PM
subject: The usual.

Pants, shirt, tie.

from: Sophiefashionista@gmail.com
to: guywithgreentie@gmail.com
date: July 25, 5:35 PM
subject: Now you're turning me on.

I'll wear a dress. You're shocked, I know.

from: guywithgreentie@gmail.com
to: Sophiefashionista@gmail.com
date: July 25, 5:37 PM
subject: On a scale of 1–10…

How turned on?

from: Sophiefashionista@gmail.com
to: guywithgreentie@gmail.com
date: July 25, 5:41 PM
subject: Zero.

Now I'm nervous again. I need to go get ready. Jumping in the shower. See you soon.

from: guywithgreentie@gmail.com
to: Sophiefashionista@gmail.com
date: July 25, 5:42 PM
subject: Breathe easy, beautiful.

They will adore you.

* * *

She was ready.

After her pulse had slowed to a normal level, and her rapid breathing settled. After she gave herself more pep talks than she had ever needed when pitching to investors or proposing media companies use her compression services. And after taking more deep breaths than she'd ever required before walking into a billionaire's office with her head held high and asking him or her to generously support a cause.

She'd handled those situations without batting an eyelash.

But meeting the people who Ryan cared about most was new to her. She had no clue what to expect as she headed into the Chandelier Bar in the middle of the Cosmopolitan Hotel. Two-story strands of crystals spilled from the ceiling, enrobing nearly the entire establishment. Faint purple lights cast pretty streaks across the bar.

She was decked out in a simple red linen dress with a hip-hugging pencil skirt and a strappy bodice. White piping lined the neck and the hem, giving the dress the retro look she embraced. Her earrings matched, and her lipstick was red and neat.

She'd only checked twenty times on the way from her building to the nearby hotel.

The dark-haired Shannon arrived first with her husband and immediately wrapped Sophie in a big hug. Well, it was a little hug, because Shannon was a pipsqueak.

After the embrace and hellos, Sophie placed her palms together as if in prayer and pleaded, "Will you please tell me everything you have in store for the *Dance All Night* reunion special? I promise I'll be your best friend forever if you do."

Shannon eyed Ryan approvingly and squeezed Sophie's shoulder. "I like her. Keep her around."

"The big secret is…she's bringing me on the show. I have all the moves," her husband Brent said, adding a gyration of his hips like a stripper.

Shannon rolled her eyes. "You wish."

"Hey! I know you!" Sophie said excitedly, pointing at Brent. He was tall, sturdy, and had sparkling brown eyes. "Your late-night show was the best. And King Schmuck cracked me up on many occasions."

Brent nodded at Shannon. "What she said. I second it. I like you, too."

Soon, Michael and Colin joined them, and Sophie understood what Ryan had meant by Michael's intensity. He was like a sheepdog guarding the flock, even in the middle of a chichi Vegas bar. He had that 'my-eyes-are-everywhere' watchfulness in his cool blue gaze. His eyes were lighter than Ryan's but his hair was darker, making for an interesting contrast. Colin was the laid-back one, easy-going, quick with a joke, and even able to hold his own among Brent, the former comedian, as well as two super protective older brothers. He had an infinity symbol tattoo on his wrist, with four interlocking circles in black ink, nearly the same shade as his hair.

Colin also was a kindred spirit, and as a venture capitalist he inhabited some of the same worlds Sophie had trafficked in. "I had my eye on your second round of funding for InCode several years ago," he said. "I tried to get in on it, but it was too late."

"Oh no! Shame on me then," Sophie said, lightly smacking her own hand, admonishing herself.

"Yeah, it's one of my greatest regrets in business. That was a hell of a sale you had."

"Thank you," she said with a wide smile.

"I'm looking at some startups that are playing in the same space. I'd love to get your thoughts sometime," he added, taking a drink of what looked to be iced tea.

"I'd be delighted to talk shop. I haven't had the chance in ages."

"Then we'll make it a date," Colin said with a wink.

"Date?" Ryan asked, arching an eyebrow as he draped an arm around her.

She turned to look at him, and couldn't resist planting a kiss on his cheek. "Just to talk numbers and other geeky things."

Michael whistled under his breath. "And Ryan Sloan gets a kiss in public from the first girl he ever introduces us to," he said, holding up his palm to high-five Shannon, then Colin. "I knew he liked her for real."

Ryan made a *pshaw* sound, then must have decided to say *screw it*, because he grabbed Sophie, dipped her, and kissed her deeply in front of them all. The hooting and hollering intensified. The clapping grew sonic. When he pulled her up, she felt woozy and stunned, and she was sure her lipstick was smeared.

"And we have a winner," Colin declared, smacking his glass lightly on the counter.

Winner. She felt like one tonight. Holy hell, did she ever.

She'd passed a big test.

* * *

"I told you they'd adore you. Every single one of them already texted to tell me how awesome you are. I'm going to keep you around," he said, raining kisses on her cheeks, her shoulders, and her lips as they walked through the Cosmopolitan, his arm wrapped around her.

"You better," she said with a murmur caused by him running a finger through her hair. "Because I think we're already beyond our seventh date. And yes, I'm counting the weekend as more than one date."

"I lost track of how many it is. I'm glad I lost track," he said, as they left the hotel.

When the first blast of hot summer night air pelted them, she turned to him. "Where do you want to go now?"

"You're five minutes away. I'm twenty minutes away. I took the initiative and already asked Colin to go let my dog out," he answered with a wry smile.

"Ah, so you're assuming I want you to come over?"

"I'm not assuming anything," he said, gripping her shoulder. "It's a fact. You want me over because you want what I'm going to give you."

"What's that?"

He stopped in his tracks there on the Strip. She stopped, too. Summer crowds of tourists thronged past them, cameras around necks, sneakers on feet, towering plastic drink holders in hand.

"My thank you for being so amazing with my family," he said.

"It was easy. They're wonderful."

"You were nervous, but you did great. I want to show you how much it means to me that you met them."

"You have a gift for me?" she asked, arching an eyebrow.

"I have something I think you'll like."

She could hardly wait.

When they reached her home, he pushed her against the wall, fell to his knees, and wrapped her hands in his hair. She gasped, half surprised but all thrilled that he gave her free rein to touch his hair, to hold on hard, to dig her nails into his head the entire time he licked and kissed her until she came apart in his mouth.

It was one of the rare times he'd done that without binding her up at some point. She loved the momentary taste of freedom, the *gift* as he'd called it, but she also loved being bound to him.

When he stood up, she was still seeing stars, her body dizzy and drunk on his touch. She looped her arms around his waist and looked up at him. "Let me do that to you," she whispered. "Let me taste you. But I want you on top of me. I want to be under you."

He ran his finger over her lips. "Fucking your mouth," he murmured. His eyes blazed darkly, shining with intense desire as he scooped her up and carried her to the bedroom. He set her down and unzipped her dress, then freed her breasts from her bra, leaving on only her shoes.

"Undress me now," he told her.

Her skin sizzled with anticipation, with the thrill of having access to his body like this. She'd touched him before, plenty of times, but when it was all said and done, she'd spent more time with her hands tied than not, so having the chance to savor him was not one she wanted to miss. She unbuttoned his shirt, spreading her hands over the smooth, hard skin of his chest, then his arms. She moved to his belt buckle, heat tearing through her as she undid it. There was something so erotic about undoing a man's leather belt. It was the moment before. It was the last second until his cock made its appearance, and so she savored the unfastening, knowing what was coming next.

Kneeling, she pushed his pants down over his hard ass, then his boxers, and drew a deep sigh of appreciation as his hard shaft greeted her, the head nearly bonking her nose.

He laughed lightly, as she flicked out her tongue to lick the head. She moaned instantly, savoring the taste of him.

"You said you wanted to be under me, Sophie," he said firmly, reminding her.

"I know, but I just want to touch you for a minute. I hardly ever get to. Let me worship you," she said, tugging his pants off the rest of the way as he quickly removed his shoes and socks. Starting at his calves, she kissed her way up his legs. Fingers, hands, tongue, lips. She traced him, brushed him, as she traveled along his strong body. She kissed his hipbone then rose up on her feet, crouching to press her lips to his belly. His stomach was so toned she could run the tip of her tongue through the grooves in his abs.

He groaned as she mapped his body with her mouth, grasping the back of her head, guiding her over him. She rose and licked his nipples, then bit each one. His cock jumped against her.

"Sophie," he said, like a warning. "You're driving me crazy."

"I want to drive you crazy, Ryan," she said as she returned to her knees, kissing his stomach as she whispered, "I want you to be mine."

He gripped her head tighter. "I am yours. I swear." He lifted her face so she looked up at him, meeting his eyes from the floor. His voice was barren, stripped down to pure need. "I can't belong to anyone else now."

She shook her head. "I can't either," she said, then wrapped her hand around his throbbing cock, loving the silken feel of his steely length in her palm. Heat bloomed between her legs, and she felt a bead of her own wetness slide along her inner thigh. His eyes drifted down her body, settling on that slim strand of her own liquid arousal.

His voice sounded like thunder. "Get on your back now."

She scrambled to the bed.

CHAPTER THIRTY

Her neck was so long and inviting, like a swan, delicate yet strong as she stretched herself across the wine-red bed-cover, inching herself along the sheets until she reached the top of the bed, resting her head on a pillow. She lifted her hands over her head, and wrapped her fingers around the white metal slats on her headboard.

Such a perfect pose for locking herself to the bed.

He followed her, stalking her. She was his prey. She wanted to be hunted. The notion that both of them craved the same things so fiercely set his blood on fire. He straddled her, moving up her body.

Until he reached that lovely neck. Such a vulnerable part of her, and yet she was allowing him to take control. Because she knew he'd never abuse it. Because she trusted him in bed, and she'd learned to trust him out of it, too.

She raised her arm, reaching for his dick. He shot out his hand, catching her wrist in his palm then moving her hand back to the post. He tsked her, placing his finger over her mouth.

"I'm going to feed you my cock."

Her eyes widened with lust. His dick ached. He longed to shove his cock deep in her throat. "Open your mouth," he said. She moaned and opened wide.

He jammed a palm against the wall, holding his dick in his other hand. He lowered the head between her lips. "Lick the tip. Lick it so I can see your tongue flick all over the head."

She squirmed underneath him and did as told, her wicked tongue swirling in circles around the tip. He groaned, a deep, primal sound that seemed to come from the very depths of his body, of his desire, of his unabashed lust for this woman. For *his* woman. His gorgeous, sexy, brilliant, willing woman who would do anything. He wanted to give her everything. More pleasure than she'd ever had. More intensity than they'd ever experienced. He wanted to take her to new heights, to explore every inch of her body, to introduce her to extraordinary bliss. Unmitigated ecstasy.

She deserved it.

Because, fuck. Look at her. Look at those red, ripe lips waiting, eager, to take him in.

"More," he said, low and husky, as he gave her his shaft. "I want to watch my dick disappear into your mouth."

She sucked him in, wrapping those lips tight around his dick, and he moaned so loudly he was sure he just set a personal best.

If he kept those kind of records.

He groaned, and her eyes said *give me more*. "So fucking hot." He already felt his brain starting to lose contact with language. His thoughts were turning guttural and base. They were consisting solely of verbs and curses and swears as he fed her his cock all the way to his balls. And holy fuck. She took it. She took him all the way like that. On her back. Mouth wide open. Her hands grasping the headboard. Her wicked, wild hips starting to arch up. His gaze drifted to her throat as he gave a deep, lingering thrust, watching her swallow him. He could see the outline of his dick in her throat.

One of the hottest sights ever in the whole damn universe.

He began to rock into her warm mouth to build up friction, taking it slow and steady, letting her handle this vulnerable pose. She handled it like a champ, her lips clamped tight around him, sucking hard and without mercy. His balls slapped against her chin as he picked up the pace. The more he thrust, the more she writhed under him. Oh God, he was going to implode. Pleasure crackled along his spine as his Sophie, his fucking classy, sophisticated, genius of a woman, sucked his dick so hard he was not only seeing stars clouding the edge of his vision, but he was watching planets fall out of orbit, galaxies crashing into each other.

"I want to come like this in you," he gritted out. "Just like this."

Her eyes lit up, giving him permission to flood her throat. But then, she gagged. Her eyes watered, and she choked.

Instantly, he yanked his dick out of her mouth and cupped the back of her head. She coughed lightly. "I'm fine," she said. "I'm sorry."

"Shhh. Don't be sorry. I was too rough. It's too much."

"No. I wanted it like that. I wanted *you* like that. I just…let me do it again."

He shook his head. "Beautiful, I'm not going to die if I don't come in your mouth right now."

Then, with a sly quickness, she sneaked a hand between his legs and cupped his balls. She fondled them then met his eyes. The look in hers said she wanted something naughty. Something dirty. Something she'd never wanted before. "Let me lick them," she whispered. "Let me lick them as you jerk off on my face."

A storm of lust took hold of him.

He scrubbed his palm across his forehead.

He was speechless.

Just *speechless* from the filth coming from her mouth. Pure, beautiful filth. His dick answered her, twitching against her neck.

"Yes," he said, returning to the same position, straddling her neck, only this time he lowered his balls to her lips. Her tongue greeted them, flicking over, sweeping across, then she grazed her teeth. A current surged inside him, and burned red hot as she sucked his balls all the way into her beautiful mouth.

Lord have mercy. He had never wanted a woman so much. He'd never needed to come so desperately.

He wrapped his hand around his dick like a glove, jerking it as she swirled her tongue, caressing and sucking at the same damn time. She had him all the way in, and the sight was so fucking hot, and his dick was so fucking hard, and his body was such a lightning rod, that he knew he'd be reaching the edge soon. She loved it, too, judging from the way her hips rocked against the mattress. She had one hand on his thigh, and he turned around to look at her legs and found her other hand sliding between her wet folds.

"You can't wait, can you?" he said, but he wasn't mad. He was fucking impressed with her sex drive, with her intensity, with her passion. Then both her hands were on his ass, and she was holding and squeezing his cheeks as he gripped his dick harder, his fist flying up and down as he fucked his hand. The head of his dick hovered over her face, near her hair. Her tongue worked its magic on his balls, and soon he felt that first tremor of a climax start to bear down on him.

Then, he felt something else.

Her finger.

Her goddamn index finger was under his balls, rubbing *that spot.*

That spot that could make a man beg for it. Hell, *he* was ready to beg as she stroked him between his balls and his ass. His spine ignited, and the start of an epic orgasm began to roll through him. And then all of a sudden, his vision turned white and silver, and unholy pleasure flooded his body as her finger slipped inside him. All the way. Hitting a part of him that had never been touched. He was sure he was going to pass out from the sheer intensity of this orgasm that wracked his body. His climax roared through him as he came all over her face, her hair, and her pillow.

He trembled. He could barely stop trembling. He couldn't stop groaning. The panting was ceaseless. His palm was pressed hard against the wall. His eyes were squeezed shut.

Somehow, he finally opened them, came down from the sky, and moved off of her. "Did you just—"

She nodded, looking like a cat who'd eaten the canary.

"You actually put your finger in my ass?"

She nodded again, but her smile slipped away. "You didn't like it?"

He laughed. He scoffed. He cursed. "Sophie, I've never come like that before. I just did not expect that."

"I didn't, either."

He reached for her hand and pulled her up. "Time to wash up." He led her to the bathroom, where she washed her hands, and he used a towel to clean up her forehead and her hair as best he could right now.

Then he washed his hands. He wasn't sure why he was cleaning his. His hands hadn't ventured in that forbidden zone tonight.

Not yet at least.

But they would. He turned off the faucet, wrapped his arms around her waist, and moved his mouth to her ear. He lowered a hand to her ass, cupping a cheek. "Where do you keep your lube?"

She met his reflection in the mirror. She didn't speak at first, just stared back. "Are you going to do the same thing to me?"

He gripped her ass harder. "I want you to let me do more. I want you to let me put my dick in you."

Her eyes sparkled in the glass. Her voice was low. "I've been hoping you would do that," she said, as if it was a naughty admission, and she shivered against him, goose bumps rising on her skin.

His throat rumbled. "You beautiful, dirty woman," he said in utter appreciation for her gorgeously depraved desires, which perfectly matched his.

"But I've never done it," she said. "I don't want it to hurt."

"I don't want to hurt you, either. It doesn't have to hurt, but if you don't want to, don't worry, Sophie."

She turned in his arms, facing him. "I want to do every-thing with you." She held up a finger. "I just think a glass of wine would help."

A grin spread across his face. "Wine is good. And mas-sage oil?"

She tapped one of the drawers in her vanity. "It's all in here. I bought it last week. Just in case."

He groaned and grabbed her face. He pressed his nose against hers. Out of nowhere, the next words came out. "I'm crazy for you. And not because you bought lube and massage oil. Just because I'm crazy for you."

Her smile was radiant. "I'm crazy for you, too."

* * *

A glass of white wine later, along with some soft music and Ryan's hands all over her back, shoulders, and neck, and Sophie was wholly relaxed. His touch made her moan softly, and breathe deeply, and move in synch with his strong hands. He rubbed the oil on her shoulders, down her spine, and along her arms.

"What if you slip off me? What if I'm too slippery now?"

He laughed softly and leaned in closer to her ear. "I promise I won't let you escape, my little eel."

She laughed, too, and he continued to work his way down her body. He massaged the top of her cheeks, and she wriggled as the pressure sent sparks through her body, settling between her legs, beating a pulse in her very wet, very hot center. He parted her legs more, widening the space between them, and working his fingers lower on her bottom.

She tensed briefly, unsure how this would feel. But then she remembered the time at his house when he'd slid a finger inside her ass and she'd wanted to sing hallelujah.

She raised her ass for him.

"Yeah," he said, all slow and sexy. "Like that, beautiful. Give yourself to me."

She lifted herself higher, and turned her face to the side, watching him as he reached for the lube on the towel he'd spread out across the cover. He squirted some onto his fingers then returned to her rear. He slid his fingers between her cheeks and pressed lightly against her entrance. She breathed softly, letting the air spread through her lungs.

He rubbed his fingertip in circles, and soon she moved in time with his finger, circling her hips, inviting him to penetrate her. He slipped the finger past her entrance, and waited, letting her adjust, then slid it all the way in. "You're so tight," he murmured.

"How am I going to fit you?" she asked, a fleet of nerves briefly reappearing.

"Lube. Lots of lube. And lots of preparation," he said, as he continued to work his finger inside her. She squirmed as he pushed, then he added another finger, and soon she was panting, and her clit was aching, and whatever he was doing to her ass was turning her on. Wildly.

"Oh God," she said, as a spark zipped through her.

"You like it?"

She nodded. "I do. You're doing it so good," she said, as she rocked her rear back into him. The pressure added to the pleasure. The new sensations of all those fingers inside her sent a wave of heat through her body, settling in her pussy. She rocked back into his hand, craving being filled in both ways. Barely aware of what her body was urging her to do, she started rubbing her pelvis against the bed, desperate for attention in her sex.

Within seconds, he looped his free hand around her thigh, hitching her leg up on the bed, giving him access to her.

She breathed a sigh of relief, then a long, low, purr of pleasure as he stroked her hard clit with one hand, while filling her ass with fingers from the other. The double wave of sensations blasted through her core, like a tornado of lust whirling through her. Some deep and primitive part of her gave herself over to this animalistic moment, to this basest of carnal wishes.

She whispered his name. It sounded like pure sex on her tongue, even to her own ears.

"I'm ready," she murmured, then she rose on her elbows and her knees, lifting her ass for him.

Waiting.

He let his fingers slip out of her, and away from her. She inhaled. It was going to happen. She was going to give up a part of herself to him, only him. He was the only man she could ever imagine having in her like this.

But he didn't take her that way.

Instead, he moved next to her, lying on his back. He tapped her leg.

"Straddle me," he said softly.

"What?"

His command didn't compute.

"You're on top," he added.

"But," she said. "Don't you want it from behind? I thought that's how…"

Guys liked it.

"Yeah, I want it that way. I want to fuck your pretty little ass while I watch my cock slide in and out of that tight hole. I want to get you off with my fingers on and in your pussy, and my dick in your ass. And then when you climax so hard you see stars, I want to pull out and paint your body with my come. All over your gorgeous fucking back," he said, his words as dirty as they'd ever been, and she turned wetter and hotter with the image of jets of his hot, white semen marking her spine. Then he clasped a hand around her hips, and tenderly pulled her closer to him. "But I want it to feel amazing for you *first*. And it'll be better for you if you can control it. If you can ride me. If you can set the pace. We'll get there. But the first time needs to be fantastic for the woman I'm crazy for."

She swallowed and took a deep breath, his sweet dirtiness rushing over her. She ran a hand through her hair, trying to calm her overactive heart. How could she be so turned on, so aroused, so ready to do something thoroughly forbidden and also feel on the cusp of falling deeply?

She had no rational answer. So she listened to her body, and she positioned herself over him. He shook his head, and whispered, "Not yet."

She furrowed her brow.

"I told you I'd get you there," he said as he brought the hand that hadn't touched her rear back between her legs, rubbing her swollen bundle of nerves once again.

"Oh God," she said, closing her eyes and running her hands through her hair.

"Remember the night I met you?" he asked as he stroked her clit, setting off fire after fire inside her, like sparklers on the fourth of July.

She nodded on a pant.

"Even then, before you even knew my name, I made you come like this." He circled her clit, sending waves of intense bliss through her body. She shuddered. "I didn't even touch your flesh, Sophie. I made you come through your panties, and it was fucking beautiful," he said in a husky, smoky voice that brought back all her memories of the way he'd owned her body before she knew who he was.

"It felt so good," she said breathily as she opened her eyes. "Just like it does now."

He pinned his gaze on her, holding her captive as he fingered her clit, rubbing up and down in a blur as she rocked into him, wetness spreading to her already slick folds. "Your pussy is like paradise to me. I want you to feel like you're in heaven every time."

"I do, Ryan. I do."

"And this time, beautiful—this time you're going to ride me," he said softly, slowing the pace on her clit to a lingering, lazy speed, taking her step by step to the next event. Moving a hand to her hip, he lowered her center to his hard cock. She gasped in pleasure as he ran the head through her slickness. "Just giving him a little natural assistance," he said with a wink, then reached once again for the bottle of lube. "Do you want to put it on me?" he asked, handing her the bottle.

"Yes. I love touching you. Any chance I get to touch you I'll take."

"Touch me," he said, and she shivered from the sexy sound of his voice, the sheer honesty of his lust.

She poured some into her palm, then rubbed it over his shaft, from the head to the base and back. She set the bottle down, wiped her hands, and gazed at him. He rubbed himself across her pussy before traveling further. To her ass. He pressed the head against her, and she closed her eyes.

She felt precarious. Wobbly. She breathed shakily.

"Put your hands on my chest, Sophie. You need to hold onto something," he told her, and she lowered herself slightly to anchor her hands on his pecs. "Like you're riding me. Like you're fucking me," he said, as he pushed in, his finger lightly brushing her clit once again. Somehow, that contact, that delicious touch on the part of her body that was designed *only* for pleasure was enough to take the edge off. She drew a sharp breath as he breached her then stilled his moves. "Because you are."

His eyes stayed on her the whole time. His gaze guided her. His reassuring look told her this would not only be okay, but that it would be amazing. "I've got you," he murmured, holding her hips and playing with her clit as she started to slide deeper onto him, the pressure sending sharp jabs through her stomach. This was all so...tense...and bizarre. But even through all the foreign sensations, she felt the potential for ecstasy.

He guided her down, down, down. His voice was smoky as he whispered one last command: "Fuck me, Sophie."

He closed his eyes and groaned.

That sound, that primal, thrilling noise raced through her, turning all that strange stretching into something else. Into the start of a whole new world of sensations.

"You feel so fucking good," he said. "I wanted you like this for so long. I've wanted all of you since I first saw you." His eyes were squeezed shut as he uttered his dirty praise of her body, and his own primitive need for it. "You. Feel. Amazing."

And she did.

She felt fucking amazing.

She rocked into him, letting him fill her, letting him stretch her to the limits. Her skin was hot, and her heart felt feverish as she rode him, her ass gripping his cock as a tidal wave of intensity tore through her veins.

He opened his eyes and blinked. "Wow. Just wow."

"It's incredible," she said, riding him as if she was fucking him...and she was. She was fucking her man in a whole new way. She wasn't bound, she wasn't tied, and she wasn't restrained. She was free, and even though she'd happily and greedily be restrained the next time, for this moment, she loved that she could take his dick deep into a new place inside her. That she could explore the far reaches of her fantasies with him.

"You are exquisite," he murmured, his words tripping back to the compliment he gave her after their first time together. "Every single part of you."

That.

That second.

That moment.

That ode to all of her.

It was enough.

She combusted. She was a rocket, and she soared. Every nerve ending fired. Every inch of her skin sizzled. Every cell in her brain buzzed.

"That's why I wanted you on top. I want to touch your pussy and fuck your sweet ass at the same time," he said, taking the reins, thrusting upward as he rubbed. "So I can look at you. All of you."

She gasped as he seized control. She moaned loudly as he set the pace. She cried out in ecstasy as his fingers worked their delicious magic on her wet, hot, slippery center, coaxing the edge of an orgasm out of her.

Then, sheer and unadulterated pleasure pierced her body. It washed over her like a tsunami. As Ryan thrust harder, and faster, and deeper, he sent her deliriously into a new type of climax, the kind that could be felt in places only he had touched.

He felt like the only lover she'd ever had.

He was the only lover she wanted to have anymore.

She shuddered, trembling in exquisite pleasure.

"Can I come in you?" he asked in a ragged voice.

"Yes," she shouted. "Please, yes."

He followed her there. Filling her with his heat. Flooding her with his release. Coming inside her. She collapsed onto his chest, a hot, sweaty, satisfied, elated woman.

CHAPTER THIRTY-ONE

He cleaned her up.

With a warm, wet washcloth, he erased the remnants of what they'd done, tenderly taking care of her, as she deserved. After gathering the towels and placing them in her hamper, he carried her into the bathroom, then set her feet down in the shower. She was so soft and warm, and he savored the chance to wash her hair—and wash himself out of her hair. He soaped her up, her breasts, her belly, and her bottom. Kneeling down on the floor, he cleaned her legs, then handed her the soap and she finished.

After a quick wash himself, he ran a tub for them. Not too hot, since it was July, and even in her cool home, no one wanted to soak in the heat. When it was full, he scooped her up, and brought her into the marble bath, letting the water soothe her. He wrapped his arms around her, and snuggled her close.

"Does it hurt?"

She shook her head. "No, but it might tomorrow."

He kissed her forehead.

"But I'll probably still want to do it again, even if I'm sore," she said, wiggling her eyebrows.

"That's my woman," he said playfully. He tugged her close. "You are my woman. You belong with me."

"I know," she said, resting her face in the crook of his neck. "Do you think everyone at the event will know?"

"That I took your ass tonight?"

She nodded, and splashed water on him.

"As long as you walk like normal, only you and I will know I own your body. But everyone will know you're with me. And that it's much more than it was when you first asked me to go with you."

"It's so much more for me, too," she said. Then she seemed to remember something. "Am I going to spend the night at your house tomorrow or will you come here again?"

He pulled her closer, loving that she assumed they'd be together. He wanted to be with her. "Stay with me. But I have to leave early on Sunday morning. It's a visiting day."

"Ah," she said. "I'll leave early, too, and head home, so you can get on the road." She seemed to drift off in thought for a moment, then she asked, "Do you ever bring her gifts? Can you give her gifts?"

"Only a few things are allowed. She usually just likes company. She likes seeing me, so I go. Why do you ask?"

She screwed up the corner of her lips as if she were deep in thought. "You said she had a dream to make doggie coats. Right?"

"Yeah. She actually gave me a pattern to hold onto," he said with a light laugh. It was absurd. But it was also very much like his mom. "It has a dog bone design on the back."

"Do you have it?"

"I do," he said, turning to look her in the eyes. "Why?"

"I have an idea. Would you like me to make it for her? As a gift. You could bring it to her. I mean, obviously she doesn't have a dog in prison. But she might enjoy seeing the jacket. It might make her happy, right? Just to see it. If that was her dream to make them."

His heart stuttered. It stopped beating for a moment, then it thumped harder against his chest, as if it were trying to fight its way out to get closer to her.

"You'd do that?" he asked, dumbfounded.

"Sure. I can sew. I'm sure I'm not great at it like she was. I couldn't make a living from it. But I know what I'm doing. I still have a Singer machine. I could do it an hour. It's not hard to make a doggie coat if there's a pattern."

"And you'd do that for my mom? Who's in prison? For murder?" he asked, and he was sure shock was etched on his features.

She shifted in the water that was now cooling. Some sloshed over the side of the tub. "I don't judge her. It's not my place," she said softly, her blue eyes so honest, so guileless. "She's your mother, and the only thing that really matters to me is that without her I wouldn't have you in my life. And I want you in my life."

And then his heart managed to break free. It jumped from the steel cage he'd once kept it in and raced to the woman in his wet arms. He belonged to Sophie. He cupped her beautiful face in his hands and memorized this moment. The cooling water. The dark of the night. The still in her home. The racing of his heart.

She'd bewitched him, and he didn't ever want to be without the only person, besides his family, who he'd ever loved. "I'm in love with you, Sophie. I'm so in love with you."

She beamed. A smile broke across her face. "Oh, Ryan. I am so madly in love with you. I never stood a chance of not falling in love with you."

He smothered her in kisses in the tub. Then he lifted her out, dried them both off, and led her to the bed. Holding her close, he planted kisses all along her sweet skin, from belly to breast, elbow to ear. "I'm so in love with you," he said, over and over. It was like a dam breaking inside him, and he couldn't hold back anymore. He'd spent so long keeping all his secrets clutched tight and locked up, and this one truth, this incomparable, all-encompassing fact of his existence, insisted on being heard tonight.

He couldn't stop telling her as he held her tight. "I'm so in love with you I don't even know what to do."

"Just love me," she whispered back, and a tear rolled down her cheek.

"I do. I will," he said, and he kissed the tear away. "Please love me, too."

"I do, Ryan. I do love you so much."

Then, he made love to her as midnight fell across the city of sin. As he moved over her, they were the only two people in the whole wide world.

She'd become his world.

CHAPTER THIRTY-TWO

Something wasn't right.

She'd noticed it when she traced the pattern on paper, and now she was seeing it for sure on the muslin fabric.

Sophie studied the cloth in front of her, trying to figure out where she'd gone wrong. The little doggie neck-to-tail measurement simply didn't line up. Was it a shorter jacket, perhaps? Mid-back? But as she peered at the printout of the pattern again, she reconfirmed that the coat was supposed to cover up the belly and back, as a coat should do.

Bright morning sun streamed through her living room window. It was an early morning for a notorious late sleeper, but her day was packed, especially since she needed to squeeze in this sewing project before she began her final preps for the benefit tonight. Ryan had departed at the crack of dawn to take care of his dog, and she'd dusted off her sewing machine, setting up on the table by the window, ready to tackle this gift.

He'd emailed her a photo he'd taken of the printed pattern, and she'd grabbed some fabric she had on hand from a few years ago when she'd made a mod retro skirt.

Grabbing a new section of fabric, she followed the measurement once again.

Whoa. That definitely was wrong. Wrong size. Wrong shape. Wrong everything.

Had it been that long since she had sewn? No, it was only two years ago when she'd made that skirt. This pattern didn't seem so complex as to throw her off like this, even with a dog bone design on the back.

Staring at the pattern again as if it would reveal its secrets, she spotted something odd in the first row of instructions, then her brain turned it around. A light switch flicked on.

"Ah!" she said, tasting victory.

She'd just reverse a few of these steps to make the pattern work. Easy enough. Grabbing her pencil, she jotted down the correct order of the steps.

She blinked.

She peered more closely at the numbers in the first row. They lined up precisely with the reverse letters of the alphabet.

She counted off in her head, quickly transposing the numbers into letters, her analytical mind easily sliding into coding mode.

James Street.

A hotbed of crime once upon a time.

Studying the numbers more closely, they clicked into place, sliding like puzzle pieces.

This pattern wasn't a dog jacket.

The measurement was wrong because the first row spelled out a street name, then what appeared to be two addresses on James Street. Her mind raced back to a few weeks ago when John had let slip a small detail from the case.

'Today was like a goddamn puzzle. You know the math problems you can't solve? And this was over addresses. Fucking addresses from years ago."

Oh God.

She dropped the paper as if it were on fire. She scrabbled back in her chair, standing up, then backed away from it as if it would curse her.

Could it be? Did that pattern hold the clues to what her brother was looking for in the case? Was this dog jacket pattern from Ryan's mother something else? Something more? Something that revealed…

Breathe in.

Breathe out.

She inhaled sharply, remembering what her brother had told her the very first day, before either of them realized her Ryan was *his* Ryan.

"Something that would help me find the other guys I think were involved."

John was looking for accomplices. He'd thought Ryan was hiding something. But if this pattern unfolded into code, as she reasoned it would, then Ryan wasn't hiding anything at all. He couldn't possibly know there were addresses buried inside his mother's "prize" dog jacket pattern.

Only a seamstress would know this pattern wasn't a pattern. Only a man or woman who attempted to make this jacket would be able to tell it wasn't for a dog.

Pacing in circles in her living room, she tried to settle her galloping heart. She worked to calm her overactive brain. She didn't want to jump to conclusions. She needed to check, and double check. That was what she'd done in school. That was always her strategy. Make certain. Make sure.

She headed to her desk, flipped open her laptop, and started plugging in the two addresses on Google Maps. They showed up near each other in the same neighborhood—a dangerous section of town years ago that had since been gentrified. Sophie wanted to know who lived there. Property records weren't hard to find—everything was online these days in realtor databases. She plugged the addresses into a realtor search. But the records revealed only when the homes were last sold—a few years ago. Nothing showed the owners' names now, or from when this pattern was made, nearly two decades ago.

But she'd spent a lifetime solving problems. Cracking codes. Creating her own damn codes.

Grabbing the pattern again, she started writing out notes, trying to figure out the rest of the rows of instructions and what they meant. But only that first line translated neatly. The code seemed to shift in each row. Something was missing from the next line. Sophie peered more closely, and it seemed a letter had been turned into a symbol. On the next one, a number was simply missing, like a dropped stitch. She'd have to deal with those at another time.

For now, she zeroed in on the first row of instructions, puzzling over how to find out who these addresses belonged to. She could easily call John and hand him this information in its current form. Or she could tell Ryan what she'd discovered. But she'd never been one to turn in her homework half-done. This code was only partially cracked, and her job was to smash it wide open. Whatever she had in her hands—whether it was a cold, hard clue, or a dead end—she was determined to figure it out.

She tapped her fingers against her temple, as if she could coax out the way to find the names of the inhabitants. In seconds, she had it, because she had friends everywhere in this city, including in the county records office—her friend Jenna's aunt worked there.

Ringing Jenna, even though it was early on a Saturday morning, she gave her only the barest details, adding that discretion was key.

"I'll see what she can do," Jenna said, and five hellishly long minutes later, she called back to say her aunt would be home shortly from a hike and would log into her work computer to check the records for those addresses. "Give me an hour."

"I can't thank you enough," Sophie said, then tried valiantly to keep herself occupied.

But fifteen minutes of checking and double-checking that her shoes, jewelry, lingerie, and evening dress were ready for tonight did nothing to cool her mind.

A deep obsession kicked in, telling her to *do something.*

To understand.

To look.

To see.

She tried to shove all those urges away, and simply exist in this state of waiting. Maybe some tea would help. Maybe she should bake something. Maybe another long shower would keep her focus off of waiting for Jenna's call.

But something insistent was knocking around in her skull, telling her not to sit still.

Her mind was a pinball machine, whirring and whizzing with crazy silver flippers, sending dozens of balls in new directions. She weighed her options. She could stay here and wait. Or she could conduct some recon on her own.

Twenty minutes later, she drove along James Street, her sunglasses on, as if that would hide her from the kids playing in driveways, the men and women walking dogs, the average, every-day feel of this suburban stretch of street that had been riddled with crime years ago. Following the path of addresses in her hand, she drove past the two homes from the pattern.

Two clean, neat, modern standard-order suburban family abodes.

They gave no clue as to why on earth Dora hid these addresses in a pattern many years ago. She gritted her teeth, wishing she truly understood what she'd uncovered.

Her phone rang.

She nearly jumped out of the driver's seat, then settled herself when she saw Jenna's name.

Swiping the screen, she turned her phone on speaker, then pulled over near a park and cut the engine.

"Hey girl," Jenna said. "I've got what you're looking for."

"Tell me," she said breathlessly.

"So, eighteen years ago, one was owned by a family named Stefano," Jenna said, and Sophie cringed, squeezing her eyes shut at that name—the name she knew belonged to the shooter. "The second was a rental. Owned by a guy named Carlos Nelson at the time. But he didn't live there. He rented it to his two cousins, T.J. Nelson and Kenny Nelson."

"T.J. and Kenny Nelson," Sophie repeated, as if she could decode the names by saying them out loud.

But they meant nothing to her.

Of course they meant nothing to her. She wasn't investigating a crime. She wasn't the detective. She wasn't the victim's family.

She was, however, the woman stuck between the two.

After she said goodbye to Jenna, she didn't move. She stayed behind the wheel of her parked car, staring ahead at the swing-set, the world around her fading as she realized that she had the names of the two men John could be looking for in the murder of Ryan's father nearly twenty years ago.

Ryan had no idea he'd been holding onto evidence all these years. He'd thought his mother had given him a memento, a symbol of her hopes and dreams for safekeeping. Instead she'd asked him to hide something that was clearly evidence, and managed to do it without anyone being the wiser.

Her insides roiled. Her head pounded with frustration and so much aching sadness. But underneath that storm of emotions was another one, rising up. *Excitement.* She had something in her hands that might help solve the murder.

The trouble was she was stuck, and Sophie understood precisely why she'd been so consumed with the need to keep herself busy for the last hour.

She didn't know who to tell first.

Her head told her John. Her heart said she should call the man who'd given her the clue he didn't even know he had.

She tossed her phone in the backseat and headed home.

CHAPTER THIRTY-THREE

She wasn't herself. Hadn't been all night. Ryan wanted to figure out why, and to make it better if he could.

"Is it that guy?"

Sophie knit her brows and shot him a confused look. "What do you mean?"

"Is that why you're so tense tonight?"

He squeezed her shoulder, then travelled to her neck, gently massaging. "The guy who wanted to set you up with his grandson. The reason you invited me in the first place," he reminded her, as he tried to work the knots of tension from her neck and shoulders. "Is he why you're so tense?"

"No." She shook her head quickly. Then she nodded just as vigorously. "I mean yes. That must be it. Or it's just that I want this whole event to go well."

"It's going great," he reassured her as they stood at the edge of the ballroom, watching the guests mingling and chatting, enjoying hors d'oeuvres that fancy waiters and waitresses offered on trays as they circled. The huge ballroom glittered in the glow of boat-sized chandeliers. A four-piece orchestra played soft classical music from the stage as guests filtered in. "Or do you want me to make you feel better? Sneak into the fancy bathroom for a quickie?" he suggested in a low voice.

She seized up and spun around. "No. I can't do that," she said sharply.

He held up his hands in surrender. "Hey. Don't bite. I've just never seen you so nervous. I want to help. I know this event is important to you."

She breathed erratically then waved her hand in front of her face as if she felt faint. "I know. I'm sorry. I'm just…"

But she didn't finish her sentence.

He eyed her up and down as if he could somehow figure out what was wrong with his normally polished, poised, and outgoing Sophie. She handled crowds with aplomb. She was unflappable, so it was odd to see her off her game.

On the surface, she was as impeccable as always. She looked extraordinary tonight in a violet dress that hugged her curves, a teardrop necklace that nestled between her breasts, and sheer black stockings that he'd peeked at earlier, when he'd tugged up her skirt in the town car on the ride over to see how far up they went—all the way to the lace tops at her thighs. God, there was little better on a woman than thigh-high stockings. Her blonde hair was twisted high on her head, with loose curls framing her face.

He parked his hands on her shoulders. "Breathe, beautiful. Everything here is perfect, including you," he said, then turned her around to let her soak in the room and all the guests—the glitterati of the city mingling and talking. Many of Ryan's clients were here, from casino owners to his new White Box clients. He recognized plenty of familiar faces, too, from the mayor, to a popular magician, to a big-time high roller. Even his brother Colin was here, though he was busy chatting with a pretty brunette at the bar. Sophie's brother John was somewhere among the guests. Ryan had said a quick hello earlier, and it hadn't been as uncomfortable as he'd expected it to be. Maybe John *didn't* hate him.

Sophie bit her lip, then words seemed to tumble out, laced with guilt. "I just feel bad because I couldn't make the pattern," she said, fiddling with a bracelet on her wrist.

He made a scoffing sound. "That's what's upsetting you?"

"I tried," she said apologetically. "It was too complicated."

"Don't worry about it. It's sweet that you even offered."

"I did try. I tried so hard." Her voice sounded as if it was about to break. Then suddenly she plastered on a huge smile as an older man with gray hair strode up to them.

"Clyde Graser," he said to Ryan, holding out a hand, and Ryan spent the next few minutes chatting with the man who was in some way responsible for this incredible woman and him growing even closer. If Clyde hadn't pressured Sophie, she might not have asked him to the event tonight. And knowing they had this date had pushed them faster into each other's arms.

But then, Ryan also believed that he and Sophie were an inevitability. Funny, because he'd never been one to put any stock in fate and love. But he did now, and if this man in front of him played a role in driving him closer to the woman he loved, then he deserved his gratitude, even if it was veiled in the guise of something else.

"I can't thank you enough for all you've done for the community center. It means so much to so many people," Ryan said.

Then Sophie remarked that it was nearly time to bring Clyde on stage with the center director, so Ryan said good-bye to the two of them.

He turned around to look for Colin, but once again his younger brother was quite busy with the brunette.

* * *

Sure, there were other people here. Quite possibly Colin should talk to them. Maybe even interact with his brother Ryan. But Elle hadn't slipped away from him yet, so he remained at the bar with her, club soda in his hand, a glass of water in hers.

"Did you get the new ink you were talking about?" she asked.

"I did. I'm close to the ten percent mark now," Colin said, not looking away from her, because how could he? He hadn't seen her dressed to the nines before, and she was jaw-droppingly stunning in her evening finery. But then, she was hot-as-sin in the jeans, short-sleeve blouses, and the little flat shoes she wore on the days he saw her at the community center, so he wasn't surprised. This dress though—he was sure it had been painted onto her lush figure.

He wanted to tear it off.

She laughed. "No way are you that covered in tattoos," she said, calling him on his fib. She was right—he wasn't ten percent slathered in ink. He had plenty though, and she was an admitted tattoo junkie. Inked herself, the back of her neck boasted a line of sparrows. He'd kissed those birds a few times. Not enough as far as he was concerned.

"Fine. Maybe not yet. But close."

"Are you going to show it to me? The new one?"

He raised an eyebrow and shot her a dirty look, then moved his hands to his belt buckle as if he were going to take off his pants.

"Colin!" she hissed under her breath, her eyes widening. She waved her hands frantically as if to stop him.

"What?" he said, deadpan. "It's on my hip."

Her eyes fluttered closed momentarily. Maybe she was picturing his hip. Or him unzipping his pants. Or perhaps the image of her lips on his new ink had slid in front of her eyes. Good. He had that image working overtime, too.

"So that's a no?" he asked, then lowered his voice to a whisper. "Even if I told you it matches your favorite one on me?"

She'd seen them all, from the ink that covered his right shoulder and sloped to his elbow, to the art on his pecs—even the illustration that started on his lower back and curved to the top of his ass. Hardly anyone knew he had more than a dozen tattoos. He was a suit-and-tie kind of guy, given his job. But when the suit and tie came off, he was the guy with tattoos.

And "the bad boy," as Elle called him. That was why she kept him at an arm's length. Well, not all the time. But enough.

"I do, Colin. But not here."

He gripped her elbow. "Let's go somewhere."

She inhaled sharply and shook her head. "We can't keep doing that."

"Why?"

"Because. I've told you a million times why."

He leaned in closer and fingered a strand of her long, soft chestnut hair. "I could do that thing you like so much."

She jammed a hand against his chest. "You're incorrigible," she said, but she didn't push him away. Instead, she curled her fingers around the fabric of his shirt. "You make me crazy. But Sophie is going to introduce me and then I'm going to introduce Clyde, so you can't do this right now. This flirting thing." She let go of his shirt, then narrowed her eyes and parked her hands on her hips. "And now you've distracted me. So talk about something else, because I don't want to go up there with my mind on your damn hips."

His lips quirked up. "Fine, fine. I've been meaning to show you a picture my brother-in-law gave me of a guy he's seen around. See if you know him. I think he's one of the guys from the center who plays hoops," he said, reaching into his back pocket for his phone. He came up empty. "Ah, shit. I left it in my car."

"Send it to me later, okay?"

"I will," he said, then added, "Along with a picture of my new ink?"

She shook her head, but under her breath she said *yes*.

* * *

"Be an artist. Be an athlete. Be a leader," Clyde said, his voice booming through the mic across the ballroom. "The local community center has a mission to provide all those services to young men and women in our fine city, whether it's shooting basketballs, learning photography, or even getting a healthy meal for dinner. The center has cooking, parties, poetry, volunteer services, and thanks to the fearless director, Elle Mariano, we have wonderful support and counseling for young people today. I couldn't be more delighted to be a key supporter of this very fine center and its services. And I am thrilled that so many other local companies have opened their wallets and checkbooks to get on board with us." Clyde then rattled off the names of other supporters, from Colin's firm to the newest ones in White Box. When he was through, the crowd clapped and cheered, including Curtis and Charlie, who Ryan had been enjoying a drink with.

"Glad to hear you guys on that list. Impressive to see you get behind the local community," Ryan said to the two men.

"Thank you. We were glad to help," Charlie said in a gentlemanly and gracious tone. "As a younger man, I was a bit of a troublemaker. Now that I'm older, I try to stay out of trouble."

"We were all troublemakers one way or the other, weren't we?"

"Indeed we were. We try to do better as we grow older and wiser," he said, like a sage advisor, dispensing wisdom gleaned over the years. "By the way, your security team is doing a spectacular job already with my clubs. I couldn't be more thrilled to be working with you to help keep my business safe and secure."

Ryan flashed a smile. Nothing delighted him more in business than a satisfied client and a job well done. "I'm thrilled."

"Anything you need, you let me know," Charlie said, then gestured to the stage.

After sharing the details of the fundraising goal – an announcement met with cheers and claps – Clyde passed the speaking baton to Sophie's brother. John walked to the podium then gave a short speech about the importance of keeping the streets safe, finishing with a call to support the community center. "Places like this can make a big difference. I believe that if we give young people a chance early on to be involved in something other than gangs, crime, and the trouble they can get into on the streets, we'll have a safe community and a better Las Vegas."

John said thanks and nodded crisply, and everyone cheered. Ryan soaked in the atmosphere in the ballroom, and the sense that maybe there were enough people who cared about change. Who cared about this city. Who wanted the best for this town they all called home.

He was filled with pride, too, over Sophie's work, bringing such a motley crew together all in the name of this cause. He only hoped seeing the support from the crowds would lift that knot of tension she'd been carrying all night. Even as she introduced the orchestra and her ex-husband, then asked the guests to find their seats to enjoy some Beethoven, he could tell she wasn't herself.

He doubted anyone else could, but it was in the small details, from the way she cleared her throat before she spoke to how she briefly fiddled with her hair on stage. Sophie was not a fiddler. Or a throat-clearer.

All the more reason for him to tie her up to a chair tonight, or maybe blindfold her for the first time. Yeah, he liked the image of that. He suspected that was just what she needed to clear her mind, and rid her body of all that stress.

Great. Now his dick was hard in his tuxedo pants.

He excused himself from his clients, found his way to his seat, and waited for Sophie to join him and his hard-on.

When she did, he brushed his lips to her neck then whispered something dirty in her ear about what he wanted to do to her later. She shivered slightly.

Slightly.

That was all.

Something was wrong with his Sophie.

* * *

She wanted to vomit.

She wanted to hurl.

To crawl under the covers, pull them over her head, and pretend she'd never offered to make that damn jacket.

She should have baked a pie instead. Made a homemade card with construction paper. Knit a scarf.

That damn dog jacket was tormenting her. Its secrets hounded her. She repeated the names—T.J. Nelson, Kenny Nelson—over and over in her head all day.

Then the other names.

John. Ryan. Ryan. John.

Like a pendulum she swung back and forth, seesawing between the two men. She couldn't last much longer in this state of suspended secrecy. She hardly knew how Ryan had ever managed to keep things locked inside his head. It was painful. It hurt her skull to have this knowledge that she needed to share sealed in her mind.

Her stomach clenched. Evil butterflies swarmed her belly, the nightmarish, haunting kind.

As the orchestra swelled during the gorgeous piece of music, she clutched her belly. When Holden joined in on the piano, she dropped her head to her knees. Ryan rubbed her back and whispered, "Are you okay?"

She shook her head. She clasped her hand over her mouth then whispered, "I need to go to the ladies' room."

She took off.

In the bathroom, she washed her hands over and over, as if that would somehow give her the answer. Instead, it only gave her exceedingly clean hands. When she pushed open the door to leave the restroom, she found Ryan waiting in the hallway. The sounds of Beethoven playing from the ballroom could be faintly heard.

"You're worrying me. Are you pregnant?"

She laughed. Deeply and maniacally. Oh, but it would be easier in some ways if she were.

But as she met his gaze, the pendulum stopped swinging. She had her answer. It came in his presence here, his pursuit of her tonight, his clear and real concern for her. It came in the facts, too. It was his mother's pattern; it was his family story.

"I lied to you," she blurted out.

He furrowed his brow. "About what?"

She grabbed the lapels on his jacket and pulled him to the end of the cavernous hallway, standing against the gold-trimmed, scalloped wall as she confessed. "I lied to you about the pattern. I *did* make it this morning. But it's not a pattern, Ryan. It's a code. A hidden code of addresses. And those addresses match names of people who lived there years ago. Do the names T.J. Nelson and Kenny Nelson mean anything to you?"

He froze. His face turned white. His lips parted but no sound came. Then, he managed words, and they sounded dry and cold as he whispered barrenly, "What did you just say?"

She repeated the names.

"*T.J. and K,*" he hissed, his eyes full of fire. He stepped back, his hands shooting behind him to grab the wall. As if he needed to hold onto something. "How did you know those names?"

She quickly explained what happened that morning, reversing the steps, then calling Jenna, then finding the addresses from years ago. "I don't know what it means," she said, her voice rising with desperation. Maybe it was nothing after all. Maybe everyone would have a good laugh at Sophie's half-baked code-cracking. "I might be overreacting. Maybe I'm just going crazy. It's possibly nothing at all. But if there's a chance that it means something, if there's a chance that these are the two names that John has been looking for—"

* * *

He cut her off.

There was no question in his mind. There was not a chance in hell he'd enlist Sophie in sweeping this under the rug. She wasn't crazy. She wasn't overreacting. He might be shocked to the bones, but he was dead sure of one thing.

There was no way he was keeping this to himself.

"Let's go get John."

CHAPTER THIRTY-FOUR

Treasure Island glittered across the Strip.

The glass of the window cooled his forehead as he stared at the hotel across the street from the room at the Venetian. Sophie had rented this suite for the event. The orchestra members had used it as a green room before going on stage, and now for Ryan it was a waiting chamber.

The gold-colored hotel shone brightly back at him. Ryan could still remember when Treasure Island opened twenty-two years ago. He'd been ten and his father had taken him to see the towering structure, one of the Strip's first spectacle hotels.

To his young eyes, Treasure Island had seemed majestic, a true giant among its neighbors. He'd gazed skyward with that childlike sense of awe, his father's arm around him as his dad had pointed out the original skull-and-crossbones marquee. They'd wandered down the Strip to a cheap buffet, then returned in time to see one of the nightly pirate battles in Buccaneer Bay in front of the hotel entrance. Canons on the ships had lit up with flames, and swashbuckling pirates had whipped out swords and fenced to the death.

Now the pirate theme had been mostly washed away and the nightly battles had ended years ago, though the manmade lake still edged the property. Ryan had seen so many changes in this city. He'd watched it morph from the Stardust and Circus Circus style hotels to the mega casinos and their star wattage of today. Through it all, the city was his home, and always would be.

And through it all, too, he'd been a fucking mule, carrying secret names in a goddamn dog jacket.

He'd held onto that pattern all through high school, college, the army and beyond. Stowed it safely away because he'd thought it meant something to his mom.

Something real. Something about hope, the future, and another chance.

It was supposed to be her redemption.

What was it really, though? Was it her own notes that she'd never had a chance to toss away? Names of users? Names of dealers she owed money to? Or worse? And if so, had he been simply in the right place at the right time when she was arrested and she'd thrust it into his hands, whispering that he should keep it safe for her?

She knew he'd do what she asked.

He was her favorite.

He was the only one she could ask.

Latent rage roiled inside him, rising and twisting through his veins. He breathed out heavily, an angry plume, like a dragon. The lights on Treasure Island flickered, and he snapped his gaze away, staring at his black leather shoes as his emotions shapeshifted again.

Now, he was flooded with shame—so much shame at having been deceived.

Because dammit. She could have asked him to throw the fucking thing out instead. Lord knows, he would have. He would have crumpled it up on the way to school the next day and chucked it in a trash can. At least then he wouldn't have carried it around like some sad sack year after year. He wouldn't have held onto the patternless pattern like a fool, running his fingertips over it as if it were a symbol of her freedom someday.

When it seemed more like a glaring piece of evidence.

A lie, now exposed.

What else had she told him that was a lie?

He wanted to know so badly his bones vibrated with coiled tension. He wanted to know who those men were. He wanted to know what role they played in his father's death.

The tension in him spiked, and he pressed his fingertips to the dark window.

Eighteen fucking years and counting without the man. This night. The end of the pirate's show. The opening of the Wynn. The rollercoaster at New York New York. The Ferris wheel. They were milestones. They were markers in time. They were all the moments Thomas Paige had missed.

When the door creaked open, he turned around, straightening his spine and lifting his chin, ready to stop guarding the secrets his mother had asked him to keep. John and Sophie walked into the suite.

"Sophie said you had some new details," John began, cutting to the chase as he motioned for Ryan to take a seat on the couch. Sophie sat next to Ryan, and John opted for a chair.

"Thanks for taking the time out of your night," Ryan said, then drew a deep breath, letting it fuel him, letting it feed him as he proceeded to tell John about the pattern that was never a pattern. He traded off with Sophie, and she weighed in, too, explaining her role in the discovery and then sharing the names.

T.J. Nelson and Kenny Nelson.

To say John's eyes flickered with some kind of hope was an understatement. Marshall's words rang in his ears. *The detective would probably give a right arm for those names.*

"Are those the guys you're looking for?" Ryan asked, his body taut with anticipation. John had kept his lips shut the first time they'd talked, holding all the cards, telling him little. Ryan swallowed, hoping the information exchange would flow both ways tonight. "Because you asked me when I first met you who she was associating with at the time. You said you had new evidence and were trying to determine the validity of it. Is this the evidence you wanted?"

"I can't say for sure, but this is as close as we've come, and it lines up with my leads," John said, and Ryan released a deep breath, relieved this wasn't a fool's errand after all. John continued, "I know it hasn't been easy for you, but I really appreciate you sharing this—"

"I did nothing." Ryan pointed to Sophie. "She figured it out."

John cracked one of the first smiles Ryan had ever seen on the detective's face. "I like to say she's my code breaker."

Sophie waved them off. "Hardly. There's more to it, but the other rows are going to take more time to figure out."

"I might need you as a consultant on this case then," John said to Sophie.

"You know I'll do whatever I can, and whatever you need."

"This is a good start and I appreciate it." John turned to Ryan. "I want to let you know we've been looking for Stefano's accomplices, so I'll share what I'm able to." Ryan leaned forward, his elbows on his thighs, his ears eager as John spoke. "We believe that Jerry Stefano did not act alone the night of the murder. We believe he had help. We believe he had both a broker who arranged for his hits, and a getaway driver who, of course, drove him away from the scene of the crime that night. At the time he was questioned, Jerry repeatedly claimed that after Dora Prince hired him, he acted alone in the crime. He steadfastly stuck to this statement for eighteen years and remains wedded to it. But we have reason to believe that he never gave up the names of his accomplices as a sort of exchange. In return for protecting their own, these two men had a pact to look out for Mr. Stefano's child, who was born shortly before he was incarcerated."

Information came fast and furious, like bullets. But they didn't wound him—they didn't nick him. Instead, Ryan dodged them because he understood what they were—facts. Not his heart. "Wow. That's a lot of info," Ryan said, rubbing his hand across his jaw as he took it in. "Do you think my mother protected their names, too, in some sort of exchange?" He furrowed his brow as he tried to make sense of his mother's urging him to stay quiet about the drugs, and if her warning had something to do with the other men involved rather than with her quest to prove her innocence.

"I don't have the answer to that. But this is the biggest break we've had so far in potentially finding the other men that we believe were involved in the murder of your father," John said, and even though Ryan had heard those words countless times over the last eighteen years—*murder of your father*—they took on a deeper meaning then.

They echoed in his bones and resonated in his blood.

For so long, he'd protected the rest of his mother's story. Kept it locked up in case the truth would ever set her free. But this was no longer about her. This was about finding everyone who was responsible for his father's death.

"There's more I have to tell you," Ryan said, steady and even. Strong, too. He looked to Sophie, who'd been by his side the whole time, like a partner, like a rock, like his foundation. She had given him strength to speak the truth to her, and to speak now for his family. Her blue eyes were full of honesty, full of love. She'd said a few minutes ago *I lied*, but that was nothing compared to what Ryan had done his whole life.

The lies of omission.

The lies of protection.

He shucked them off. Shed them all. Everything was coming undone.

Scrubbing a hand across his chin, Ryan unraveled another secret. "I found my mother doing cocaine when I was thirteen. She told me she was stopping. She said she met her lover, Luke Carlton, in Narcotics Anonymous. She also told me Jerry Stefano was her dealer." John arched an eyebrow, tilting his head at that bit of information. Ryan explained more. "She always claimed she'd been framed for the murder because she owed him money. That's why she was taking on more work for the gymnastics team," he said, serving it all up, giving everything to the one man who might be able to exact justice. A sense of freedom rushed through him as he answered each and every question John asked.

When he was done, Sophie excused herself for the restroom.

John thanked him profusely. "I know it's not easy to share all that. But I'm grateful, and this will help. I assure you."

"Find those fuckers," Ryan said, looking him in the eyes.

"That's my goal."

"Are you going to talk to my mom about all of this?"

John nodded. "I will, but she usually doesn't say much."

Ryan scoffed. "Tell me about it."

"And I'll have to coordinate with her attorney, so it'll be a few days."

"I'll be seeing her tomorrow. I'll keep you posted."

"Appreciate that." John extended a hand. "By the way, it's no secret that I wasn't thrilled when I found out you were dating my sister. But she's incredibly happy. And all I ask is that you keep it that way."

"That's my goal," Ryan said, and it was number one on his to-do list.

CHAPTER THIRTY-FIVE

Sophie understood everything now. Why he visited his mom so much. The way the secrets had twisted over the years, like a string running through a labyrinth. Ryan had kept them all inside his head, locked up tight, clutching like a lifeline the wish of his one living parent.

Sophie's place wasn't to judge the guilt or innocence of Dora Prince. The state of Nevada had already done that. But her role, the self-appointed role that she embraced, was to be there for her man.

"I'm proud of you for speaking all those hard and terrible truths," she said, as the town car driver took them to Ryan's house after the event had ended.

"I barely know what to think anymore," he muttered, staring out the window as the streetlights and cars streaked by through his neighborhood.

She dropped a hand to his shoulder. "You were brave to tell him."

"Hardly," he said, mocking himself as he turned to look at her. "If I were brave I would have said something years ago."

She stared at him levelly and shook her head. "You didn't know what you were dealing with. You still don't entirely know. That's why it's brave. You took a chance."

When they reached his home, Ryan took a moment to thank the driver and wish him a good night. Once they were inside his house, she grabbed his shoulders, then cupped his cheeks. "You said something now. That's all that matters."

He swayed closer to her, his eyes floating closed, his hold on gravity seeming precarious.

"Come with me," she whispered.

She took his hand and led him to his couch, holding him close. Johnny Cash leapt on the cushion and curled up at their feet. Running her hands through Ryan's hair, she let him rest his head in the crook of her neck, sensing what he needed right now was a safe landing. She wanted to be that for him. She wanted to be everything he needed.

"I just…Soph…if she…I don't know." His words beat out a staccato rhythm of what was said and unsaid.

"I know." She ran her fingers through his hair. "I know."

He sighed heavily then pressed his lips to her chest. It wasn't sexual; it wasn't the start of something dirty. It was a gesture of the familiar, of comfort, and she was glad he found it in her.

"For so long, she's said one thing to me. She said she was set up. She said she was framed." His voice was low and sad.

Her heart ached. It cried for him—heavy, mournful tears for what he had borne all those years. "So you go see her and you ask her. You tell her you need to know for your own heart."

He shook his head. "She won't tell me. Talking to her is like pulling teeth."

She brushed a kiss on his forehead. "Then you find the answer in yourself," she said, and wrapped her arms around him. He held her tight.

They stayed like that, curled together, him in his tux, her in her dress, nestled snug on the couch, a ball of fur by their feet. They talked more, whispered confessions and admissions, hopes and wishes.

"There were days when everything felt so out of hand. So beyond anything I could ever manage," he said softly, and for a moment she understood that there was something more to his quest for control in the bedroom. With the way his life had spiraled, she suspected some part of his mind needed the solidity of that kind of dominance—sexual dominance. She kept that notion to herself though, not because it was a secret, but because it wasn't her goal to psychoanalyze him. Whether that was his reason, or whether he simply liked it that way, she was happy to be on the receiving end.

"It was hard to manage because you carried so much. The weight of so many secrets. The pressure of so many things you should never have been asked to keep to yourself. Forget guilt or innocence or who was framed and not framed. You were fourteen. You deserved to be fourteen, not a secret keeper," she said fiercely.

Then, when the conversation seemed to unwind, and it was time to move to something lighter, she sat up, straightened her hair, patted him on the leg, and said, "How about you teach me how to play pool finally? I believe that was one of the promises you made when I stayed here last weekend, and pretty much the only one you failed to deliver on."

A sliver of a smile crept across his face. "I failed to deliver on something, did I?"

She nodded. "I'm wretched at pool. Show me how to play."

He stood up and offered her his hand. "Why do I have the feeling that after one game you're going to be a pool shark?"

"If that's the case, then maybe for this first round, we should simply play strip pool?" she said, running a hand between her breasts as if to demonstrate the possibilities.

A groan escaped his throat, and he looped his arms around her waist. He brushed his lips against her neck. She closed her eyes and smiled. All was not perfect. All was not completely right in the universe. There were so many questions left unanswered. But they had moved through something difficult together. Here they were, ready to slide into another moment in their night.

This love between them had ignited one evening at Aria in a flirty, dirty, and naughty way. Over the days, and the nights, that followed, their connection sparked and sizzled, then deepened. Tonight, he had been forced to stretch and twist in unexpected ways. But after all of that, the two of them had somehow managed to return to their core.

Flirty, dirty, and naughty.

They grabbed beers and headed inside his den with the pool table. He took a cue down from the wall and handed it to her, then grasped one for himself.

"Have you played before?"

She nodded. "A few times. All badly. I barely understand how it works. There are stripes, solids and an eight ball, and we hit them in pockets, right?"

He laughed. "Something like that," he said, taking a sip of his pale ale and setting it down on the table. He removed his tux jacket and his tie, and tossed them on a chair in the corner of the room.

"Wait. You're already taking off your clothes?"

"Consider it my handicap," he said, then racked the balls.

He explained the basics to her, and she quickly processed them, since rules and games made fast sense to her. Her challenge lay in the execution. Sophie Winston wasn't known for her coordination.

Still, she was determined, so she pulled back the stick, stared at the ball, aimed squarely, and missed it by a mile. She laughed and brought her free hand to her mouth. "Oops."

Then she removed an earring, tossing it on his pile on the chair.

"Want me to show you how it's done?"

"I do," she said, and he moved to her side of the table, behind her, then pressed his hand on top of hers, his chest along her back. As he positioned the cue just so, she felt him grow harder. She wriggled her rear as he shot the ball.

And missed, too.

"Hey. Take off your shirt," she said playfully.

"That wasn't my shot! I was helping you set up."

"Fine. Help me again," she said in a flirty tone, and he lined himself behind her once more. She couldn't resist. Screw pool. She dropped the stick, shoved all the balls randomly around the table, then turned around in his arms, and laced her hands around his neck. She moved her lips to his ears. "You win. Strip me."

He wasted no time, unzipping her dress in a flurry and leaving it a silky puddle on the floor. She backed up to the table and perched on it, handing him the stick. "Show me where you'd touch me to land the shot."

He gripped the back of her head, and whispered roughly in her ear. "Everywhere. Every-fucking-where on your perfect body," he said, then stepped back to survey her, roaming his eyes up and down.

She wore only stockings, purple sheer panties, and a demi-cup bra that did lip-smacking things to her breasts, judging from how he stared. Cocking his head, he flipped the stick in his hand then lowered the wider end of the cue to her shoulder, touching her bare skin ever so slightly. "I'll start here," he said, then ran it along her arm, tracing a gentle path to her wrist. "Then kiss your wrist."

"Like you did the night you met me," she said, her skin heating up as he bent his head to her hand and placed a soft, sweet kiss that both sent her back in time and rooted her right here, right now.

"Then, I'd pay a visit to those lovely legs of yours," he said, and brushed the end of the cue from her knees to her ankles and back up the other leg. When he reached the top of her thigh, he gently nudged her legs apart, inch by inch.

Scooting back on the table, she rested on her elbows, giving him a view of her bra, panties, stockings and shoes.

"Your belly," he murmured as the cue strayed along her stomach, then up to one of his favorite parts of her. "Those delicious breasts," he said, licking his lips as he stroked a line through her cleavage then darted back down to her waist, tracing along the waistband of her panties. She murmured, and even though being touched by a pool cue was not the same as this man's touch, she still grew hotter.

Then she burned when he brought the cue to the side of her ass, and whacked her lightly with it. She gasped and moaned, loving the way he knew precisely when to spank her and make her want him even more. "There, too," he said, then bent his head to kiss her rear.

Loving, too, that he knew when to kiss the spot he'd marked.

When he raised his face, he brought his mouth to her ear. "Spread your legs wide for me."

Heat raced through her. She let her knees fall open, savoring the reaction in his eyes when he stared at the scrap of La Perla fabric that barely covered her. "And what about here?" she asked curiously, running her hand between her legs.

"I'd play you there so good," he said, his eyes shining with desire. He followed her with the pool cue, lightly touching her heat, her swollen clit. She arched up, angling for more contact, and he began stroking her with the pool cue. "You like that, beautiful?" he asked, his eyes blazing at her as she rocked into him.

"I've told you, Ryan. I love everything you do to me."

"I'm not even the one doing it."

"You are," she said as she unclipped her hair. "You are doing it to me. Only you can touch me like this. Only you can do this to me."

He stroked faster, rubbing her expertly through her purple panties with the pool cue. Her blond curls spilled behind her on the table, and she let her head fall back as he masturbated her with a pool stick. Like a wooden sex toy that he controlled, it set her on fire. Closing her eyes, she caught a perfect rhythm, like a surfer does a wave, and she rode it, rocking her hot center into the wide end of the pool cue, seeking friction with the wood, until her vision turned black and hazy, and she dug her nails into the green felt, coming in her lingerie on his pool table.

She moaned happily, and opened her eyes to find him stripping. He'd set the pool cue down on the table.

"I think I'm in love with the game of pool now," she said softly, running a hand along the wood he'd used to get her off.

His eyes blazed darkly. "I'm not done with that," he said, and her gaze followed him, as he grabbed her hands, lifted them over her head, then pressed the cue into her palms. "Hold it in place. Restrain yourself."

Sparks sizzled across her skin at his command. She gripped the cue hard over her head, as he tugged off her panties in seconds, leaving her stockings, shoes and bra untouched. Pulling her hips to the edge of the table, he lined her up with his hard cock.

"I have never wanted to fuck you so much," he said in a growl.

"Take me, wreck me. You can't ruin me. You can control me all you want. You won't break me. I'll still be here," she said, knowing it was what he needed, and what she wanted, too.

* * *

He slid into her without mercy.

She moaned the second his cock made contact with her heat.

Then he took over for her hands. He gripped the pool cue and clasped his fingers through hers, pinning her with the wood and his weight.

With her restrained like that, flat on her back on his pool table, he fucked her harder and rougher than he ever had before. He didn't hold back as he held her captive. He slammed into her hot pussy over and over, his beautiful woman writhing and moaning, panting and screaming, and completely and utterly giving herself to him.

Arching up. Meeting him. Inviting him deeper.

His body jolted with each thrust, his heart pumping hard and wild, and *this*—this pleasure, this harsh fucking wasn't just control for him. It was a relinquishment, too. He might be restraining her, but in doing so he'd revealed his hand. He'd shown her his cards. They were all for her, every single one turned up *Sophie*.

"It's you," he groaned, and she locked eyes with him, her gaze holding him tight, sending him to another plane of pleasure—one ruled by more than the physical. By the intensity of how he felt for her. By all the love that he saw in her eyes. "It's all you. I fucking love you so much," he said as he took her.

"It's the same for me, Ryan." Her breathing turned ragged, and her words drove him on. The tension in him rose higher in a fury of passion and love, in a storm of mind-blowing pleasure that spiked in him. Because of how he felt for her, heart, soul, mind and body. He didn't look away. He simply couldn't. His eyes were fixed on her the whole time as he took her deeper. Her moans and groans and cries were the sexiest song he'd ever heard, the scent of her skin and the smell of her lust were intoxicating, and the hot, tight grip of her body sent him into a red-hot, fevered frenzy.

He'd never been more turned on, he'd never been harder, and he'd never wanted to come so intensely.

But there was so much more at play than pure desire.

He'd never loved someone like this. He needed more closeness. More connection. No barriers. Nothing but skin and hands and limbs tangled together.

He let go of the stick, then uncurled her fingers from the cue and yanked it away, letting the wood clatter loudly to the floor. "Just you and me," he said. "Just you and me."

Instantly, she raised up and flung her arms around him, clutching his back, digging her nails in, and God, fuck, hell, it was unearthly; it was heaven on earth. His arms snaked around her, and he gripped her, pulling her, yanking her, bringing her as close as she could be. On the edge of the pool table their bodies coiled together like flames, consuming each other with wildfire.

He breathed her name, over and over, like a fucking mantra—the woman he adored.

She cried out, shuddering beneath him as she hit the edge, her glorious sounds the key in the ignition that set him off.

The tension inside of him snapped, and he came hard.

They collapsed in a landslide of pants and moans, of groans and grunts.

And also, something else.

Something that felt like peace in her arms, as he gave himself up to whatever this was with Sophie, because it felt as if it had the potential to be the rest of his life.

"Sophie," he murmured in her ear, as she sighed happily and ran her fingers down his sweat-streaked back. "The way I feel for you is beyond control. And I don't want that to change."

Everything else was shifting. Everything else was cracking. She was his one constant.

* * *

She didn't wake up as he went for a run with his dog. Nor as he showered. And not as he brewed a pot of coffee. She didn't wake up, either, when Johnny Cash barked happily as Ryan let him take a quick post-run dip in the pool. And she barely rustled as he leaned over her, brushing a soft curl from her sweet, sleepy face to kiss her goodbye.

She murmured something then shifted and yawned.

"Hey, beautiful. I need to go," he said, and kissed her cheek.

She stretched her arms over her head. "I better get out of here then, since you're leaving."

He shook his head. "It's okay. Stay. Sleep. You like your morning sleep."

She smiled and her eyes floated closed again. "I do like my sleep. I need to finish packing for Germany though."

"Is that today?"

"Tomorrow morning," she said, snuggling under the covers.

He patted the bed, and his dog jumped up. "Johnny Cash, you keep Sophie company 'til she wakes up and is ready to leave. Tell her to let you out in the yard once before she heads home."

The dog panted his agreement, and Sophie laughed.

"Call me when you're ready to go. I'll send a car or driver or Uber or chariot or horse."

"A horse please. A white one with a braided mane," she said then fell back asleep.

He left a note by the door with his extra key, got behind the wheel of his truck, and prepared for a five-hour drive that he hoped to God would get him the answers that had eluded him for eighteen years.

CHAPTER THIRTY-SIX

He was too cute to resist.

The way he wagged his tail, and dazzled her with his puppy-dog eyes melted Sophie.

"Fine, you win," she cooed, kneeling to scratch Johnny Cash's soft white chin. He lifted his snout for her, letting her rub him. When she rose, she reached for his leash from a hook by the front door.

She spun around, hunting for a key and found a note by the door. "Aha," she said, like a treasure hunter who'd found the X marking the spot. She unfolded the sheet of white, lined paper. Inside it was a key and a short letter. It was her first real note from Ryan.

By now, Johnny Cash is probably trying to convince you to take him for a walk. He's a bit of a junkie, I must confess. He will pretty much do anything to run those little legs. I have a hunch he might be training for an Irondog triathlon somehow.

Please don't feel that you have to give in, even if he bats those big brown eyes. He is a well-trained boy, and he will be fine inside the house during the day. Just take the key, and lock the door behind you.

Oh, I suppose this would be a good time to let you know that you can have the key. I have nothing to hide from you, and my house is your house. If you feel like going for a swim, the fence is high enough that the neighbors won't see you if you swim naked. If you do that, it would be great if you could send me a photo, as I think a shot of you in my favorite outfit would do wonders for me.

Also, I want to see you before you leave, but I don't know when I'll be back. I promise to call when I'm done, and then I'll come see you, no matter how late it is. Because I can't stay away from you, Sophie. I swear, I can't.

I'll be thinking of you. I'm always thinking of you.

Always…

Sophie grinned wildly as her heart beat like a humming-bird's wings. She tucked the note inside her clutch purse from last night. Smoothing a hand over the pink cotton of her sundress, she was grateful that she'd left this outfit behind last weekend, because it was far easier to walk a dog in this little number than in her violet evening dress. She had no change of shoes though, so she'd be walking him in her Louboutins.

She shrugged happily. So be it.

She lowered her shades over her eyes, opened the door, then locked up behind her. Johnny Cash trotted happily by her side for the next twenty minutes as she click-clacked around Ryan's neighborhood, soaking in the wide lawns, the gorgeous houses, and the palm trees that were ever present in their desert town. Her skin heated up from the hot morning rays, and her shoulders started to bake. The dog panted heavily, his tongue lolling out of his mouth. When she returned to Ryan's block she spotted a young man walking up the steps to his house. The guy was wearing jeans and a red T-shirt. He knocked on Ryan's door, then shifted back and forth on his feet.

He glanced around, scanning the porch, tapping his feet as he waited.

Odd. She tugged the dog closer to her.

As she neared the house, the guy was fidgeting, his right hand rubbing up and down his left arm, which was covered in tattoos. He sighed, seemingly in frustration, then muttered something under his breath. His jaw was unshaven.

She narrowed her eyes.

Was he a neighbor? He looked too young to own a home. A deliveryman? He didn't have a box or package with him. The pool guy? No supplies in his hand.

He turned and walked down the porch steps, heading to the sidewalk.

She flashed back to last night, to those names, to the details her brother had shared. Gangs, brokers, getaway drivers. Her pulse jumped. Was he one of those guys?

Oh God. Her skin prickled with fear.

Wait.

Her logical brain took over, and she talked herself down. The people John was looking for were older—much older than this guy who barely seemed old enough to drink.

Still…

His eyes were on his car, and Sophie followed his gaze to a tan Buick parked in front of Ryan's home.

Recognition kicked in. She remembered who he was. She'd seen him at the community center. Her friend Elle had given his buddy a hard time when he'd catcalled Sophie a few weeks ago while shooting hoops with this guy.

She breathed more easily now.

Sophie reached the walkway to Ryan's house at the same moment the young man arrived at the sidewalk. His T-shirt had a basketball team logo on it. She straightened her spine as a flurry of nerves skated over her skin. She was grateful to have the dog by her side. The collie's ears pricked up, and he went on canine alert.

But Sophie didn't entirely feel that she needed protection.

Something about his brown eyes seemed almost…hopeful. He kept running his palm up and down his arm. A nervous gesture, perhaps?

He stopped short when he saw her. Classic deer in the headlights.

"Good morning. Were you looking for someone?" she asked, opting for directness.

"I'm looking for Ryan Sloan. Is he here?"

"You just knocked on his door," she said, pointing to the house. "It seems he's not in. But would you like me to pass on a message to him?"

He shook his head. "No. I'll stop by another time."

He turned toward his car, gripping the handle.

"Wait. I've seen you at the community center. Playing basketball," she said, trying to figure out who he was. "Why are you looking for Ryan?"

"I need to talk to him." He opened the door and got into his Buick.

"What's your name?"

But he didn't give her his name. He yanked the door shut and took off.

Sophie and Johnny Cash waited until his car disappeared around the corner. Her heartbeat slowed down, and she patted the dog on the head, glad she'd had a companion. She had no idea what to make of that young man. Why on earth would he need to talk to Ryan? Then it hit her. He might not be T.J. Nelson or Kenny Nelson, but could he be related to one of those men? A son perhaps?

A chill shimmied through her.

When Ryan returned from Hawthorne, she'd tell him he had an unnamed visitor. For now, he had more important matters on his mind. Once inside his home, she locked the door, then checked again to confirm it was closed, then checked once more. She peered out the living room window, making sure the guy hadn't circled by again. The street was quiet. She called a cab and headed home.

Today was not the best day to go skinny-dipping.

* * *

Surprise her.

That was his strategy. It was a tactic he'd relied on in the military from time to time, and his mother needed to be treated like the enemy today with a sneak attack.

She was always most vulnerable when she didn't expect something. As he turned into the parking lot in

Hawthorne, showing his ID at the gate, his stomach churned. He hated manipulating her like this, but he'd spent the drive fortifying himself, talking back to his fears, and kicking them aside.

Today he was on a mission, and his one and only goal was finding the facts.

Once inside the visiting room, after a hug and a hello, he launched into one of her favorite topics. "Did you hear Anthony Geary retired from *GH*?"

Her green eyes lit up. He hadn't seen them so bright in months. "I watched his final episode. It was amazing," she said, smacking her palm on the wooden table in excitement.

Yup, that did it. Like a fisherman casting a rod, he'd dropped the lure in the water. She was the fish taking the bait.

She chattered on about the show, and because Ryan had listened to a soap opera podcast on the five-hour drive, he was up to speed on which long-lost twin had reappeared, who had been kidnapped and sequestered away in a mansion, and who was pregnant with a secret baby.

Soon, she was laughing, and he'd done it—he'd lulled her into a false sense of security. Tension curled through him, but this was the only chance he had to shock her into stumbling into the truth.

"I think Sonny has to be behind the kidnapping," she said, chatting about the show as he nodded a yes while reaching into his pocket to remove the pattern subtly. Under the table he unfolded it. Then he laid it on the wood surface, jammed his finger against the center of the paper, and interrupted her.

"Who are T.J. and Kenny Nelson, and why are their names hidden in a code inside your prize dog jacket pattern?"

She fumbled her next words as her jaw dropped and her eyes widened. "What did you just say?"

"Mom, I know what this is. Don't lie to me now. Please, God, after all I've done for you, don't lie to me now," he said, desperation infusing his tone. "Who are they and what role did they play in my father's death?"

"I don't know," she mumbled, dropping her gaze to her hands, twisting her fingers together.

"You do, Mom. You do. You gave me this pattern; you asked me to keep it safe. I did that." He tried to keep the exasperation from seeping into his voice. But that was damn near impossible. "I believed it was some kind of sign of hope for your future," he said, brandishing the paper, faded and wrinkled from age. "I kept it safe for you. I was even going to have a friend make the damn jacket for you as a gift, to cheer you up. And when she did, she figured out it wasn't a pattern. It has addresses in it and those addresses correspond to names, and one of those names is the man doing life for murder, and two of the others might be the broker and the getaway driver in the crime." Her face remained stony even as she blinked several times. He pressed on. "Those other two names match the initials you told me last time I was here, when I asked you who were Stefano's friends who were looking out for his son. You asked me if they were T.J. and K." He leaned back in his chair, stretching his arms out wide in a waiting stance. "The initials all line up. Talk to me, Mom."

She pursed her lips together and squeezed her eyes shut. Her face looked pinched, as if she were sucking all her own secrets into her mouth and holding them in with her breath.

Ryan huffed through his nostrils. *Enough.* This was fucking enough. He wanted to slam his fist into the wood. To knock the damn table over on its side. To throw things. But he wasn't that kind of a man. He didn't do that on the ice, and he didn't do it in here. Violence begets more violence. Fear spawns more fear. He had to rely on his head and his heart.

"Don't you dare shut down on me again," he seethed, the words curling out of his mouth like hot smoke. "Don't you try that routine with me. I have a right to know what I've been carrying around for you. It's not a secret anymore. The pattern was made. The names are revealed." He thumped his fingertip against the table. "*Jerry. T.J. Kenny.* They were in *your* pattern, Mom. *Yours.*" He pointed at her for emphasis. "I want to know why the addresses, and therefore the names, of those men were hidden. Because for eighteen years, you tricked me into thinking this was special to you. I kept it safe. Because I fucking love you, Mom."

His throat hitched, and wild tears threatened to rain from his eyes. He stopped speaking, pressed his thumb and forefinger over the bridge of his nose, and pinched, keeping them at bay. "I love you, and I love Dad. I came to see you all the time, even when I was in college, even when I had leave from the army. I'm the one. I came here. I saw you. And I have been a messed-up son-of-a-bitch most of my life because of this. Please, I'm begging you. Tell me something."

She parted her lips and bit nervously on her thumbnail. Her eyes welled up. She dug into her thumb then whispered. "Ry," she said, like a fearful creature. "They told me not to say a word about anything. That's why I gave it to you. To get rid of it. To hide it."

He knit his brow. "Who? Who told you not to say a word?"

"Those men."

"Why didn't you just have me throw it out?"

She glanced from side to side then under the table, as if she were sweeping the room for spies. Leaning across, she lowered her volume even more. He practically had to read her lips. "I thought I'd gotten rid of that stuff already. But then the cops came, and I still had it, and I couldn't have you throwing out something the cops might think was evidence," she said, her lips quivering. "I didn't want to put that on you, or make you responsible for that. I had you keep it knowing no one would ever look inside my sewing pattern."

His chest burned with shame. He'd been played a fool by his own mother. But why? What was she so afraid of? "Why did you have it in the first place? Why did you put their addresses in there?" he asked, pressing on like a cross-examiner.

She twisted a strand of her hair, back and forth, tight against her skull. "They were just my notes. That was all. They were notes about who I was meeting, and I was taking on so much extra sewing work to pay off my debt, so I wrote things down on my patterns."

"But this wasn't *on* a pattern. It was *in* a pattern."

"I know," she said through gritted teeth. "But I didn't want anyone to know I was meeting them." She dropped her forehead in her hands and hissed, "About the drugs. And I told you why. I wanted to try to stay clean about the drugs in case I ever got out, and I fought so hard to have my conviction overturned."

He drew a deep breath. "You put their addresses in a pattern because you were meeting them about drugs, Mom? C'mon. Why would you do that?"

Her jaw was set hard. "I told you. I wanted to keep you all safe from them. I had to protect my babies. I had to."

"So you put the info on Stefano's accomplices in a pattern to fucking protect us? You told me not to say anything about the drugs because you were trying to get out of here, but then you hid their addresses in a pattern. Something doesn't add up."

She flinched, but didn't answer, then brushed something unseen off her shoulder. Fuck. This was spiraling again.

"Or was there something else going on? Did they have something else on you?" he asked, grasping at straws, but hell, he had to try something. Because it made no sense why she would need to shield all those names so badly.

She covered her eyes. "I was scared. That's why I hid the info. That's why I didn't want anyone to know the addresses and who I was meeting."

"Why? What did they have on you? Why were you so afraid of them? What did you have to hide? What was so important about those names that you asked me to hide this pattern? Because if it was that goddamn important, it sounds like it was more than drugs. It sounds like you gave me your own notes to plan a murder. Is that what it was? Was this your goddamn blueprint that you gave me?"

"No!" She raised her voice—the same tone she'd admonished him with when he was a kid. "That is the truth. I put their addresses in there because I needed to remember them. That's all."

But the dots didn't connect. He pressed on. "Were you meeting them to plan the murder of my father?"

"I told you, I didn't do it," she said in a whispered shout. "I told you I didn't kill him. Are you ever going to believe me?"

"I know you didn't pull the trigger, Mom. Everyone knows that," he said, exasperated, as he scrubbed his hand over his chin. "But you've told me other things that have turned out not to be true. So I want to know this—were T.J. Nelson and Kenny Nelson working with Stefano? Were they his accomplices?"

She said nothing.

"Were you? Were you working with these men?"

She gripped the edge of the table, her eyes like glassy pools of desperation. "I didn't do it. I told you I didn't do it."

"Were you involved?" he continued, a dog with a bone, not willing to relent. "Like the cops say you were. Like the state of Nevada says you were."

"I didn't do it."

Wear her down. Just fucking wear her down. "Did you hire Jerry Stefano to kill my father? Did you? Did you hire him and plan it with those three guys? Did you go to their houses and plan the crime down to every last detail with the broker, and the shooter, and the goddamn getaway driver? Did you kill him for his life insurance money like they put you in Stella McLaren for?" he asked, his voice rising with each question.

He ran his hands through his hair, tugging hard on it because he was at the end of his rope, but he couldn't let go. "Don't you understand what this has done to me? I don't trust people. I don't believe people. I don't get close to people. Because of this. Because of what happened," he said, trying a new approach. Go for the heart. Try to pierce that damn organ in her. "But Mom, I finally met someone. Okay? I finally met a woman and, my God, I am in love with her, and it's the best thing that ever happened to me." He softened momentarily as he thought of his sweet, sexy Sophie. He'd come so far with her, she'd shown him so much, and she'd opened so many possibilities in his life and helped him feel wonderful, amazing, incredible things. He hated the prospect of sling-shotting back to who he was before—closed off, shut down, and obsessed.

"I need some clarity, for once. I need it so I can have a normal life with the woman I love. Don't you want that for me? Don't you want me to be happy? Because I do, Mom. I want it so damn badly that I'm here, asking you to just tell me the truth."

He waited. Seconds passed, spooling into minutes as Dora sat like a statue. Finally she broke her frozen stance, uncrossing her arms, and jerking her head away.

He threw up his hands. This was a lost cause. He was getting nowhere. Sophie was right. He'd have to find the answers in himself, because he wasn't getting them from his mother. He pushed back in his chair and stood up to leave. He bent his head to his mom, and kissed her forehead. "I love you, Mom, but I need to go," he whispered.

She grabbed his wrists, her bony fingers circling them. Her hands were papery and rough. "Do you love her?" she asked.

"Yes. So much."

She exhaled. Deeply. It sounded like relief. "I'm happy for you, baby."

"Me, too."

"All I want is for you to be happy. That's all I've ever wanted." She gripped his hands tighter. "They told me they'd hurt you all." Her voice was just a thread. "They told me they'd come after my babies if I said a word."

He blinked. Holy shit. She was talking. He leaned closer, resting his chin on her head. "Said a word about what, Mom?" he asked, anticipation weaving a dangerous path through his blood.

"I tried to stop it."

"Did you start it?"

A nod. He felt the barest hint of a nod of her head against his. Holy shit. "I'm telling you this now because I love you. Because you said you need this to be happy. And all I've ever wanted is for my babies to be happy. But they made me go through with it, Ry. And that's why I did it. I did it for all of you," she said, and then the words rained down. "Please don't stop seeing me; please don't stop coming. I went through with it because I had no choice. They told me they'd hurt you if I didn't go through with it."

Like a wrecking ball to his gut, her admission walloped him. He stumbled and gripped the wall behind him. His head was swimming. It was a roiling sea. Eighteen fucking years were compressed into this moment. Her words echoed across the vast cavern of time, clanging through the days, the months, and the pages on the calendar, stabbing him with a million cuts. His own omissions. His own secrets. Most of all, his foolish hope that his mother wasn't a murderer.

"You had him murdered?" The question tasted like dirt.

"I had to keep you safe."

"Why did he have to die to keep us safe? He didn't have to die." But even as the words came out of his mouth, he knew there was no point to them. The decision had been made eighteen years ago—whether for drugs, for money, for her lover, or from fear. He might not ever know *why* she did it. All he knew now was she did.

"I love you and your sister and your brothers so much and I do, I still do. I swear I love you so much. I love you, baby. I love you, Ryan." She began weeping, a deep, dark keening sound like a bruised, battered thing heaving itself onto the shore, defeated.

Like Ryan.

He'd travelled here hoping for an answer, but never expecting to get one.

Instead, he'd received her confession.

CHAPTER THIRTY-SEVEN

His legs were lead. His head was concrete. His heart had mutinied. It was somewhere lost in time. It was listening to Johnny Cash with his father before his dad's friends came over. It was watching the end of the pirate show. It was wandering up and down the Strip without him.

He made a beeline for the exit, pushing past Clara and the other correctional officers, putting blinders on to avoid the rest of the visiting families. The second he left the facility, the door falling shut behind him, he crumpled on the hot stone steps. He didn't care one lick that you could fry an egg on them.

Let him burn. Let him feel. Let the pain erase the foolishness, the shame, the utter shock.

He dropped his forehead into his hand, replaying his mother's last words. Wishing he could go back and redo them, erase them, rewrite them.

Make them make sense.

Not that this—his life visiting a women's correctional center each month—would ever make much sense. He shut his eyes, but all he saw was the blood in the driveway. All he heard were the screams when she found the body.

Were those fake too? Had she practiced them? Did she go to some abandoned house somewhere to rehearse her reaction to finding her husband shot dead?

His stomach seized, and he coughed—a dry, hacking bark.

Then, he flinched.

A hand was on his back, rubbing the space between his shoulder blades. He lifted his head to see Clara. "Rough visit?" she asked gently, kneeling next to him.

"Yeah," he muttered.

She nodded sagely. As if she'd seen it all. "That happens sometimes. Can I get you a Coke from the vending machine? Or a Diet Coke?"

He shook his head then realized his throat was parched. "Coke would actually be great."

Two minutes later, she returned with two cold sodas. With a weary sigh, she settled in next to him on the steps, handed him a can and cracked open hers, taking a hearty gulp.

He did the same, narrowing his focus to the coldness of the beverage and the bubbles in the drink. "She did it," he said heavily as he turned the can around in his hand.

Clara patted his knee. "They all did it, Ryan. That's why they're here."

"Fuck," he muttered. "I really thought…"

"Of course you did. You love her. She's your mother. If you listen to the ladies in there," she said, pointing her thumb at the concrete building, "there's not a guilty one among 'em." Clara shook her head in amusement, her brown curly hair bouncing with her. "Amazing, isn't? A whole facility full of the innocent? *Judge made a mistake. Someone else did it. Framed, I was framed,*" she said, rattling off the stories the inmates told.

The last one seared into him like a cattle brand.

"That one. That was hers," he said. *Framed.*

Sure, there were details he didn't know, like twisty rat tails coiled together, which would likely take years to un-ravel. He didn't know why those men made her go through with the murder, or what their motivation was. He didn't know precisely who played what role. He didn't know how far back in time the planning went, or where the other two men were.

But he knew this much—his mother was involved in his father's murder.

His eighteen-year obsession had an answer.

"You'll still come see her, right?" Clara asked.

He shrugged. "I don't know. I mean, what's the point?"

Clara answered in a plain, simple voice. "That's what we do for family."

"But she did it," Ryan pointed out. The specifics didn't need to be outlined. The who, what, why, where and when could be sorted out by others.

"Right," she said slowly. "But that's not why you come see her. You don't come see her because she's innocent of a crime. You come because you're a good man. Because you have compassion. Because even the criminals of this world need someone who cares about them. Maybe she's in for life, and she'll never have a chance to be redeemed on the outside. But maybe the fact that you come here helps her to be a better person in this place. Maybe she finds her re-demption behind bars, because of you."

"Do they? Find redemption?"

Clara shrugged. "Some do. Some don't. You still gotta come to work every day, right?" she said, then drained more of her soda.

He did the same, then rose. "Better hit the road."

She nodded. "I'll be looking for you around these parts."

He managed a half-hearted smile of acknowledgement. He didn't know if he'd ever be in these parts again. He didn't know where the ground was, where the sky ended, or how to find his way back home after hearing her confession.

The only thing he knew for sure was how to avoid the speed traps, so he turned on an app when he got in his truck.

A little more than four hours later, he'd dodged a speeding ticket, but hadn't been able to stop playing the cruel song on repeat in his head—*they made me do it, they made me do it, they made me do it.*

Did she set the wheels in motion, then try to cancel? But they forced her? How would that even work?

Gripping the wheel tighter, he cursed up a storm. He'd been such a fool. For so damn long he'd clung to a big *what if.* That possibility had tied him up, tethered him, and obsessed him.

Today, he was cut loose. Left adrift and unmoored.

Glancing at the green sign on the highway, he registered that he was five miles from his house. He wanted to see his dog, but he also didn't want to be alone. The closer the truck wheels turned to the exit, the less he wanted to be by himself.

He needed company. He needed someone.

Though he desperately wanted to see Sophie, he didn't want to see her like this. Not when his head was messier than it had ever been, and not when his heart was twisted into tattered strands.

The time he'd spent with Sophie over the last few weeks was like shedding a skin, molting his old self, leaving it behind.

But now?

Hell, he didn't know if he was coming or going. If he was the guy he'd been before or the man he'd become with Sophie.

Limbo. This was the utter hell of limbo. He was stuck in it like quicksand, and he didn't want to drag her down with him.

He needed the three people in his life who'd known him before, during and after.

As he turned on his blinker to exit the highway, he called Shannon, gave her the rundown, and she told him she'd gather the crew.

Then his phone rang, and it was Sophie.

* * *

Passport? Check.

Luggage packed? Done.

Flight checked into? Good to go.

After zipping her suitcase, she left a small toiletry kit on top of it, which she would tuck inside tomorrow morning. Then she called the car service that would take her to the airport at the crack of dawn, to confirm that everything was set for her pickup.

When she hung up, she scrolled across her home screen in case it revealed a missed call from Ryan. It had been ten hours since he'd left, and she was eager to know how his day had gone. The more time passed, the more nervous she became about what had happened in Hawthorne. But she wasn't a teenager debating whether to call a boy she liked. She was a grown woman dating a man, so she dialed his number as she walked into her kitchen to grab a glass of water.

"Hey," he said, his voice hollow.

She had never heard him sound so dead. "Hey to you. So how did it go?"

He sighed heavily. "Let me pull over."

The sound of the car engine stopping greeted her ears as she turned on the tap. Then he told her his mother had confessed. She gripped the counter, and set down the water glass. Words sputtered out. "Oh my God, Ryan. I can't believe she told you that. How? Why? How are you doing?"

"I don't know. I honestly don't know how I'm doing. It's like my world is upside down. Because I believed in the possibility of her maybe being innocent for the longest time, and now it's been twisted and turned inside out. I don't know what to do now, or what to think about anything," he said in that same monotone.

Her heart ached for him, and she wanted to comfort him, and hold him close. She wanted to be the one he leaned on. "Do you want me to delay my trip so that we can spend time together? So I can be there with you as you deal with this? I can easily push my flight back a few days if you need me."

If you need me.

Oh God, she desperately wanted him to need her. Her pulse raced with longing for his yes.

"No," he said quickly. "I can't let you do that."

"I don't mind. I want to be here for you," she said, trying to comfort him.

"It's okay. I need to go see my sister and brothers now anyway."

"Of course," she said, and she understood logically why he'd want to go see them. She just wished her stupid heart didn't hurt the tiniest bit that he hadn't needed her. "Go. See them," she said in her cheeriest voice. He didn't need to detect her worry right now. He had enough on his plate.

"I should probably call your brother, too. I guess I'll see you…" he said, but his voice trailed off.

She picked up the thread, crossing her fingers. "Do you still want me to come by later? Or do you want to come here?" she asked, ready to kick herself for sounding like a lovesick teenager.

"Soph," he said, his voice heavy. "I'm not in a good place right now. I think I just need to give John the news then be with Shan, Michael and Colin. Everything—the visit, the pattern, the stuff she said—it's hitting me hard and fucking with my head again. Let me deal with this and then I'll see you."

She gulped. "Of course, of course. This is a huge thing and you need to talk to them."

"When do you get back from your trip?"

"Next week."

"I'll see you then. We'll do something special. Finally ride the roller coaster at New York, New York together. Okay?" But he didn't sound as if he was looking forward to their reunion. He sounded as if he didn't care.

"Sure," she said, nodding several times, trying to convince herself that he still cared.

"Yeah. I just…right now…"

"You need to take a step back," she said, filling in the gap.

"Not from you. Just from…"

"Feeling so much?"

"Maybe. I don't know. I just need to see them right now."

"You go. Drive safely. I love you."

"I love you," he said, but he didn't sound as if he believed it, and the deadness in his tone made her want to cry.

When he hung up, she let the tears fall, even though they felt selfish, even though they felt like weakness. The tears fell for herself, and for him, too. For all he was dealing with. For this new bombshell dropped in his lap. His family couldn't catch a damn break, and she hated that the tragedy in his past was tearing new fissures in his present.

A little later, after she'd dabbed her cheeks and dried her eyes, she let the reel of the last few weeks play, trying to understand the man. He'd been private and circumspect at first. When pushed, he'd become open and vulnerable. But what if the talking was more of the exception than the norm?

Had he returned to the man he was before?

Three and out. Over and done. Protect your heart. Don't get close to anybody but your family.

Even then, family could stab you in the back. He'd learned the hard way.

Call her overdramatic. Call her a conclusion-leaper. Or call her a cool analyst of the situation.

That very morning, Ryan had left her a note saying he would come see her tonight. *Because I can't stay away from you, Sophie. I swear, I can't.*

She could live without seeing him tonight. She wasn't seventeen. But what worried her was the complete 180-degree shift he'd made in ten hours. He'd left his house determined to find his way back to her that night, no matter what. But when everything changed, so did his desire for her. His family story had prevented him from getting close to her in the first place. His family background wasn't going away. It was only becoming more complicated, with more players, more names, and more threads.

More time.

More space.

More moments to retreat.

Hunting for information, she sank down on a kitchen stool, and called her brother. "I know you can't give me the details of the case, and I'm not asking for them, but I need to know—is this going to end anytime soon?"

John exhaled loudly. "Sophie, you know I don't have an answer. Even if this were an open-and-shut case I wouldn't have the answer. These things can go on forever. Oddly enough, this case was something of a rarity in the first place when his mother was arrested and tried in a matter of months the first time. Most cases go on for a long time, especially when they're reopened, and involve gangs and crimes committed over the years."

Years.

That word clung heavily to the air, like thick smog.

What would that be like? Every time there was a new wrinkle, would Ryan retreat? Would she always be the one who had to step closer to him? To offer the shoulder to lean on?

She'd offered it tonight, and he hadn't taken it.

Would he ever want it or need it? And would she be satisfied if he always turned elsewhere for comfort? Compared to him she'd had an easy life. As he reeled over his mother's guilt, here she was jetting off to Frankfurt to check out her new car, for Christ's sake. But that was all the more reason why she wanted to be the supportive one—because she *could*. She could be here to hold his hand when he needed her. But he didn't seem to want that.

To keep herself busy, she called Holden and met him for a drink at the Mirage.

"I have news," he said, his eyes lighting up after he'd ordered his white wine.

"Do tell," she said, glad to focus on something else.

He leaned in to whisper. "I met someone."

She clapped twice. "Tell me everything. What's he like?"

Holden wiggled his eyebrows. "Actually, he's a she."

"A she? Like she used to be a he?"

He laughed and shook his head. "No. I meant I'm seeing a woman."

"You are?" He nodded, but the answer seemed so strange, even though this had always been a possibility. Somehow, it had been easier to think of him with men than with women.

"What's she like, then?"

"Oh, she's lovely. Natalie is very sweet and friendly." As he waxed on about the new woman in his life, Sophie tried to ignore the strange new sting in her heart from this conversation. Seeing Holden through the lens of a preference for men had been far more manageable for her ego, it turned out. Now, her confidence was suffering another blow, unexpectedly, with this realization that she wasn't the right woman for Holden either.

But there was more to this hollow ache in her heart. A new worry took root—the fear that Holden would slip away from her, too, as he cozied up to Natalie. Because Sophie couldn't help but wonder how this new lady would feel about him being so friendly with his ex-wife, and if this most predictable relationship in her life was about to become unpredictable, too.

She loathed instability.

CHAPTER THIRTY-EIGHT

Colin arrived first, with two six-packs. Ryan side-eyed the beers. "Corona?"

His younger brother shrugged. "That's not what you drink?"

Ryan shook his head, grabbed the beers, and shut the door. "Haven't had a Corona since I was in college."

Colin shrugged. "What do I know about beer?"

"Nothing. As you fucking should. I'm all out of that near beer shit. Want a soda?"

"Always," Colin said, and they headed for the kitchen. Ryan handed him a can of Diet Coke, then opened a Corona and took a long swallow. It tasted like spring break.

"Guess you don't hate it that much," Colin said pointedly.

"Guess I needed a drink after my day."

"So what's the deal? Shan said Mom confessed to you?" Colin made a keep rolling motion with his hand. "What the hell?"

"Yup," Ryan said, taking another drink then setting the bottle on the counter and telling him everything that went down in the visiting room.

Colin scoffed. "*Made her do it.* See? Even now, she holds onto the notion that she somehow isn't to blame."

Ryan shrugged. "Yeah, well. That's not what this is really about. That's not why I feel like I'm pretty much having the second-worst day of my life."

Colin yanked him in for a hug. "Yeah, I know," he said softly. "I know, man. You wanted to believe her. You wanted to hold on to a possibility. You wanted that hope that maybe she hadn't done it."

"Can you blame me? Wouldn't you want that too?"

"Sure," Colin said with a nod as he broke the hug, stopping to pet Ryan's dog, who'd wandered into the kitchen. "Of course it would be really fucking fantastic if she didn't do it, Ry. It would be like the greatest thing in the world if our mother didn't have our father killed, right?"

Though there was a touch of sarcasm in Colin's remark, there was also the bare truth. It *would* be the greatest thing.

"But you see, I came to peace long ago with the fact that she did," Colin continued. "Maybe details are still coming to light. Maybe the detective is looking for accomplices. And maybe he'll find them, and they can join Jerry fucking Stefano in the big house where they all belong. The fact is, our mother was into some fucked up shit, from associating with the likes of Stefano, to the ass she was cheating with. She was a messed-up, desperate woman who wanted money, and wanted out so badly she killed for it."

Colin dropped the volume on his voice and draped an arm over Ryan's shoulder. "This shit happens. Just look at the New York prison escapees and how that woman was going to have one of them kill her husband. It's awful, and it feels shocking from a distance, but up close, when it happens to you, you can't believe it. You wish it didn't happen." Colin tapped his chest with his free hand. "I wish that, too. But it did. This is our fucked up story. This isn't the news. This isn't the papers. This isn't someone else's tragedy. It happened to us, and deep down somewhere inside you"—Colin moved his hand to Ryan's chest, tapping his breastbone, searching for his heart—"you know it's true."

Ryan swallowed hard. He scrubbed his hand over his jaw, trying to process the whole damn day, but making no sense of the way the floor beneath him was tilting and cracking. "What do you mean, I know it's true?"

Colin squeezed his shoulder. "You think this confession changes your whole life. You think it changes everything you've believed about Mom. But it doesn't. Deep down, you knew she was involved. Deep down you knew she was responsible. But you hoped, because you're human. Because you wanted to believe in redemption, in basic goodness, in good overcoming evil. You held onto that tiny little kernel of hope," Colin said, cupping his palms together as if he were holding a precious seed. "You held it and you wanted it to become something. You wanted to believe that maybe things were different. It's okay to have hope. It's okay to cling to it. We all wanted that, too. Desperately. The rest of us just let go of it sooner. Now, it's your turn. Let it go," he said, and opened his hands.

Ryan watched the cool, empty air in his kitchen, imagining a dandelion seed falling in the breeze, the wind blowing it away. Was Colin right? Had Ryan truly known in his gut, in his heart, all along? Had some part of him known she was responsible, but some other part clung to the idea that she might be innocent simply because hope felt good?

Was that why he held onto the pattern? Why he went to see her every month? Why he nursed the possibility of innocence like a gardener tending to the first buds of spring? Because hope was a precious thing, it was a gift, and when so many things had gone wrong, he'd needed an anchor?

Hope was his anchor.

Hope that the past could be rewritten.

But the past didn't have to be redone. It was still playing out in the present, unfurling new wrinkles every day, and he'd have to roll with them, to dodge, dart, and avoid the punches.

His true anchor was right here with him. His brother. And his other brother Michael, joining them now, along with his sister, Shannon. They were his foundation. They were the ones who'd made it with him through the years.

Today had floored him. But tonight had taught him that he'd been clinging to something he was ready to say goodbye to. "Anyone want to go for a late-night swim?" he asked.

"Hell yeah," Michael said.

* * *

A few hours later, Ryan and Michael were buzzed, Shannon was tipsy, and Colin was hyper on caffeine. They'd also lost track of who was winning the water volleyball match, but who cared? The clock was closing in on two in the morning, and they were having a blast in the turquoise water, lit up from the lights in the pool. They'd talked some, and they'd cried some, and they'd laughed some more.

Through it all, they were together, just as the four of them had always been.

No matter what.

Michael slammed the volleyball out of the water, sending it careening across the dark grass. He swam to the shallow end, and they followed him.

"Let's drink a toast," Michael said when he reached the steps and grabbed his beer.

"You've been drinking all night," Colin said, hopping out of the water to grab a towel and dry his hair.

"No need to stop now," Ryan chimed in as he reached for his bottle, and rested his arm on the edge of the pool. "Besides, you brought us the beer. Your fault."

Colin pushed a hand through his damp, black hair, then tossed his towel on a lounge chair. "I'm sure you had plenty in your fridge. I was just trying to be nice to my sad sack of a brother."

"Hey. Watch it now. I'm still older," Ryan said.

"Yeah, but you're not brighter," Colin said with a wink.

Ryan shot him a look that said maybe he was right. Colin had figured out the hard stuff well before Ryan had.

Michael raised his Corona. "Never let the non-drinker pick beer again, please. Can that just be a rule?"

Colin rolled his eyes and dipped his foot in the water to splash Michael.

Then Michael's expression turned serious and he cleared his throat. "Listen. We've spent enough time talking about her. She had Ryan in her clutches for far too long. Tonight, he's letting go of all that stuff, so let's drink a toast to the man we all love and miss." Michael's eyes started to water. "To Dad. I still remember how he was when I was learning to drive. He bought me a donut the first time I nailed a three-point turn. Said he was proud of me for that small accomplishment. He was always saying that about the little things we did, and always ready to celebrate with a donut," Michael said, with admiration in his tone.

The water lolled gently in the pool. Somewhere in the yard, crickets chirped. Shannon went next. "I remember when he taught me to play pool. He was patient and determined. He told me he wanted his only girl to be able to beat all his sons, and he coached me until I was able to."

"And she does. She schools us all," Ryan said, with a tip of the cap to his sister.

Colin raised his can. "In middle school, I went to a school dance, and when he picked me up he spotted a hickey on my neck. He was cracking up, and I tried to deny it by making up some ridiculous story that the girl had scratched me accidentally during a dance. He went along with it, even though he said, 'Someday you might like it.'"

"And now you do, right?" Michael asked.

"Oh yeah. I love hickeys."

"I remember when he went to work that night," Ryan began, eyes misting over with the memory. "He told me he was taking some kids to prom, and that someday I'd be the guy taking the girl to prom, and that I should be nice to the driver, because girls like that, and because it was the right thing to do. And then he told me he loved me. That was the last thing he said to me. That he loved me."

Shannon clasped her hand over her mouth, and a huge sob fell from her throat. She threw her arms around Ryan, and then grabbed her other brothers and pulled them into another group hug. "I remember love," she whispered in a broken voice. "Most of all, I remember love."

"Me, too," Ryan said, and they all chimed in and echoed with another, "Me, too."

* * *

Later, after they cleaned up and headed inside, Ryan nudged Colin with his elbow. "Hey, what was the deal with that woman at the benefit last night? Is there something going on with you two?"

Colin shrugged as they gathered bottles into a paper shopping bag for recycling. "She's hot and she's cold. Who knows with women?"

Hot and cold. Some women were like that. But some weren't. Some were always hot. And he didn't just mean physically. Some were always clear, always present, always giving. Some put their heart on the line every day, every night. Every second.

Sophie.

His Sophie.

His loving, giving, supportive, beautiful, amazing Sophie.

Who was leaving the country for more than a week come morning.

He'd told her twenty-four hours ago that he *had* to see her that night no matter what. That he couldn't stay away from her. And instead, he'd done the opposite. He'd stayed away from her. He'd told her he was fucked up again, and hell, he felt that way.

But that wasn't fair to her.

Especially when she was always fair. Always open. Always honest.

But him?

He was the hot and cold one. He was scalding and freezing. As he carried the bag of bottles to his recycling bin in the garage, he muttered a string of curse words. He'd been sending her mixed messages. Telling her he had to see her, then telling her he couldn't handle seeing her. Saying he desperately needed her, then not taking the time to properly say goodbye before she left the country for a trip.

Fine, there was no rule that said they had to see each other every day.

But this wasn't about managing a lover's travel schedule. This was about how he talked to her, how he cared for her, how he tended to her needs. She was so even keeled, so reliable, so fucking wonderful, and he'd taken advantage of that. He hadn't been attentive to the woman he loved. Understandable, some might say, given the way his day had gone.

But it wasn't acceptable to him.

Sophie had given him something he thought he'd never have. He had never trusted in love. He'd always believed love could be gunned down. Then she came into his life, and turned everything he believed about himself upside down.

That was the real change in him.

Not his mother's confession, but Sophie's love.

Falling in love with Sophie Winston was the most magical, wonderful, intense experience of his life. When everything around him wobbled, Sophie was the constant.

He shut the top of the recycling bin and glanced at his truck. His buzz had worn off. He needed to see her. To tell her she rocked his world, then tell her again and again and again. The only problem was, it was four-thirty in the morning, and he was pretty damn sure her flight left in a few hours.

But so be it.

He'd simply have to drive over there now, and see her before she got on that plane. Kiss her hard before she left. As he walked back into his house, his mind latched onto something she'd told him by his pool the other weekend.

"The things I want from you don't cost money."

He turned to Colin, dropped a hand on his shoulder, and said, "Little brother, I need a big favor."

He explained to Colin and his brother said yes. Then added, "Hell yes."

Because that was what family did for each other.

He slid open his phone screen and dialed Sophie's number. It went straight to voicemail. She might even be going through security right now. So he sent her a text.

Then he saw she'd already sent him one.

Chapter Thirty-Nine

Shit. Shit. Shit.

Sophie was late.

Sophie was always late.

Sophie was pissed at herself, too, for being so damn late.

Rolling her suitcase behind her like it was a new Olympic event, she ran out of her building at four-thirty in the morning, her sandals flapping against the marble tiled lobby. The car had been waiting for her in the building driveway for fifteen minutes.

"I'm so sorry I'm late," she told the driver as she slid into the backseat, the night still cloaking the sky.

"Nothing to apologize for, ma'am. I will get you to the airport on time," he said, shutting the door.

She turned on her phone, tapping her foot as she waited for it to boot up. She needed to send Ryan a note.

Because she'd made a decision.

She'd spent a restless night thinking about whether or not to reach out. She'd tossed and turned, debating whether to give him the space he seemed to need, or to re-assure him of how she felt. But then she'd recalled her mother's advice: *"Always talk. Always be honest. Never go to bed angry. Make time for kisses and meals, dance under the stars, and dream together."*

Though she was flying across the ocean, the advice about not going to bed angry still seemed to apply, as well as talking, being honest, and making time for each other. She wanted him to know she was here for him. The reality was, he had a more complicated life than she, and if that was what she was signing up for, he was worth it.

Love was a choice, one that sometimes came with rampant uncertainty.

She might never have stability with him. She might always experience moments, and even days, of pure unsteadiness. But what they shared was worth the risk, the anxiety, and the utter unpredictability of his family life. She'd confronted risk head on as a businesswoman, and surely she could weather the ups and downs in a relationship.

For so long, she'd been seeking what her parents had, that perfect kind of love, with passion, support, and security. But she might not ever have security with Ryan Sloan, and she was going to have to buckle up and enjoy the highs and lows, the thrills and drops of loving that man.

The second her phone warmed up, she tapped out a text. *I'll be thinking of you the whole time I'm gone, and I'll be looking forward to our rollercoaster ride when I return. Every second of it. Love, always. Your Sophie.*

There. Done. Said.

It was enough, and she was choosing to believe in the two of them rather than listen to her own fears.

She was about to tuck her phone into her purse when she found a new message from him, just as the car pulled to the curb at Las Vegas International Airport.

The time on her phone screamed at her. She was really late.

Oh God.

Nerves swamped her. She was dying to read his note, but she needed to get inside. *Now.*

Jamming her phone into her purse, she raced to baggage check-in, then on to the TSA pre-screen, making it through security without having to slip off her shoes.

Safely on the other side, she took out her phone.

Opened the message.

And burst into a wild, wicked, happy grin.

I meant it when I said I can't stay away from you.

She spun around, hunting for him, half expecting to see him. He wasn't there, of course. But that was okay. He'd sent this beautiful note. He'd reached out.

These words were all she needed before she left the country—the reassurance that they were fine. After rushing to her gate, she showed her boarding pass to the agent and headed onto the plane, taking her seat in first class in the second row.

From the cool and comfort of her cushy gray leather chair, she started a reply. She stopped typing when she spotted someone standing by her row. Her skin prickled with awareness, just like it had at Aria. Before she even confirmed with her eyes, her body *knew.*

Her gaze roamed up the jeans, the trim waist, the pullover shirt, the day-old stubble, the soft lips, the nose, the navy blue eyes, the golden brown hair.

The face of the man she adored. Her heart danced in mad circles, like a wild bird.

"You're here," she said, stating the obvious.

He gestured to the seat next to her. "This may be presumptuous of me, but is this seat taken?"

She patted it. "Would you like this seat?"

He looked at his watch. "For the next twelve hours, yes."

"It's yours."

He sat down, and didn't say a word. He placed a hand on her cheek, pulled her gently to him, and breathed her name as if it were his oxygen. "*Sophie.*"

The way he said it sounded like a poem, like a love song. He swept his lips over hers. She shivered. She shuddered. She soared.

"Hi," he said when he broke the kiss.

"Hi." She was on cloud nine. She was floating high above the earth and she didn't want to come down.

"Do you want company for your trip?"

"I want your company."

"Good, because I took the liberty to buy a ticket."

"I can tell. But is this really your seat?"

"Mine's one row up. When the person who has this seat shows, I'll convince him or her to swap." He looked her square in the eyes as he ran a finger over her cheek. "You once told me the things you want from me don't cost money. Well, the ticket cost money, but that's beside the point. The point is you told me that you wanted to go for a ride together in your new car. And I'd like to go with you."

She arched an eyebrow. "You're joining me for the car?"

He shook his head. "I'm here for the girl," he said, his voice so sexy, so certain, so full of passion.

Her eyes fluttered closed momentarily and happiness rushed through all the highways inside her body, infusing her heart and soul with joy. When she opened her eyes, she asked, "Are you taking off work for the whole time?"

He nodded. "I told Michael to run the shop without me."

"Where's your dog?"

"Colin has him."

"When did you plan this?"

He looked at his watch. "It's six-thirty now, so, about two hours ago."

She shook her head in amazement. "And you bought a ticket, and took care of all that, and figured out what flight I was on in two hours?"

"There was only one flight to Frankfurt at seven in the morning, so I took a chance. Oh, and don't forget I showered, too," he said with a grin.

"I like when you take chances for me."

"I've spent eighteen years living with uncertainty. There are only a few things in my life that I know for sure right now. I love my brothers and my sister and my grandparents and my dog." He stopped to take a beat and hold her gaze. "And I love you. I'm not going to sit around and wait and wonder and question it. I'm just going to feel it. I don't want to stop taking chances with you, Sophie," he said, brushing his lips to hers once more. He tasted so good. She wanted the kiss to turn into so much more.

But not right here. Not as the flight attendants began their announcements.

Pressing a hand to his chest, she asked, "So that's it? You're mine for the next week and a half? All mine in Europe? You, me, and my emerald-green Bugatti?"

"Yeah," he said with a casual shrug. "If you'll have me for that long."

"I want you all to myself," she said, dancing her fingers up his chest. "I'm greedy like that."

"Be greedy with me. I want your greed," he said, then fingered a lock of her hair, turning more serious. "Sometimes I retreat when things get crazy, but I want to keep coming back to you. I know I'm just figuring this relationship stuff out, and I'm sure I'm not an easy man to be involved with, but I'll do everything I can for you." He kissed her cheek, murmuring her name. "Sophie Winston." Then another time. Softer. Barely audible. "*Sophie Sloan.*"

She wrenched back, and widened her eyes. "What did you just say?"

* * *

What *had* he just said?

"Um…" he started. "Your name?"

She shook her head and pointed to herself. "My name is Winston. Not Sloan."

He shrugged, trying to cover up his unexpected gaffe. "It was a slipup." Then he thought, *Fuck it.* He was on a plane with her, headed to Europe. He might as well tell her the truth. "I was trying it on for size."

Her lips quirked up. "You were? How did it sound?"

"Hot. Sexy. Perfect. Beautiful. Like you," he said, keeping his gaze pinned on his gorgeous woman. "Did you like how it sounded?"

Her eyes sparkled. "I think I did."

"Someday," he said, threading his hands in her hair and pressing his forehead to hers. "Someday, I want to make you Sophie Sloan. Someday soon. Is that too much? Have I said too much?"

"Oh God, Ryan. You're crazy. You're here on a plane with me, and I have never been happier in my life. All I've ever wanted is a love like this and you're here. With me. Don't you get it? You're all my fantasies come true."

He kissed her nose. "Look what you've done to me. You're everything I never knew I wanted, and now I can't live without you. Hell, I couldn't even let you leave the country without me."

Then, the flight attendant told them to fasten their seat belts.

* * *

The dress, the woman, the car.

Any one of them would be amazing. Together, they were a triumvirate of beauty.

He snapped a photo because he wanted to look at this image again and again—Sophie Winston wearing a sapphire-blue pin-up dress and fire-engine red lips as she stretched out her lush body on the shining, emerald-green hood of her sleek, stylish, million-dollar car. They were parked on the side of a road somewhere outside of Rüsselsheim. Trees canopied them from the hillside.

"You like how she drives?"

"I love how she drives," he said, putting his phone away and wedging himself between her legs. "I love everything about her."

"And me, too?" she asked with a wink.

"Yes, you too," he said, laughing. "Now let's put this vehicle to the true test."

It would the first time in her Bugatti, but he was certain it wouldn't be the last. That it would be the start of a countless number of times.

He tugged her up off the hood, and they slid inside the car. God, this car should be classified a sacred space. Everything from the leather seats to the gleaming dashboard to the gorgeous hum of the engine was a dream. But better, because it was real. Sitting in the passenger seat, he lowered it with her in his lap, and kissed the hell out of her, sealing his mouth to hers. She ran her hands through his hair, and sighed sexily as he kissed her harder. Soon, they were swallowing each other's moans and groans, and she was rocking her hips into him.

He broke the kiss, hiked up her skirt, and tugged her panties to the side, giving him access.

"Take me, Ryan," she whispered.

He unzipped his jeans, pinned her wrists behind her back, and gave her what she wanted.

It was what he wanted, too. Her. And him. Together.

Like this.

Like bliss.

Like everlasting love.

Later that evening, they'd be together in other ways. Eating dinner at a cafe. Making love in their hotel after the lights fell in the town and only stars winked in the sky. Then the next day, too, cruising along the autobahn in a sleek new car, living life to the fullest, loving without limits.

EPILOGUE

Johnny Cash bounded over to him, barreling across Colin's front lawn and into Ryan's outstretched arms on the sidewalk. "Hey, buddy," he said, kneeling down to say hi to his pooch at last.

The Border Collie licked Ryan's face, and whimpered happily as he thumped his tail. Ryan wrapped his arms around the dog's furry neck. He hadn't seen Johnny Cash in more than a week, and even though the time with Sophie had been the best days of his life, he did miss his canine friend.

Colin walked down the steps from his house and joined them on the sidewalk. "Looks like someone missed you," Colin said.

Ryan stood up and gave his brother a quick hug. "Thanks for watching him. I really appreciate it."

"He's easy. Welcome back. How was it?"

Ryan briefly considered the question. He could answer it with patent honesty and say *out of this world, amazing, incredible, fantastic,* or *a dream come true.* Instead, he answered with another truth. "I'm going to ask her to marry me next week."

Colin's dark eyes lit up and his mouth fell open. "Holy shit. Guess you had a great time." He extended a hand and then clapped Ryan on the back.

"Yeah, we did," he said, still grinning over what he had planned for Sophie.

"Congratulations in advance. Couldn't be happier for you. It all happened so quickly."

Ryan nodded. "It did. The whole thing happened so damn fast. But I guess when you're certain of something, you have to go for it."

Colin knocked fists with him. "Couldn't agree more. How did you decide?"

As he pet a happy Johnny Cash, he told Colin the story of how he'd said her name on the plane, illustrating with his hand over his mouth, as if words were spilling out of their own volition.

His brother cracked up. "Awesome. So you just let it slip on the plane that you wanted her to be Mrs. Sloan?"

"I hadn't even thought that far. It just came out, and then I realized I wanted that. She's the best thing that's ever happened to me."

"She is, and don't ever forget it."

"I won't," Ryan said, then walked to his car, and opened the front door to let his dog jump in. A nearby engine rattled, then stopped quickly. He turned in the direction of the car.

The hair on his neck rose. The Buick. Parking outside Colin's house. "He's back. Looks like he knows where we all live," Ryan hissed. "Sophie told me he stopped by my house more than a week ago."

He straightened his spine, kept his eyes on the guy, and waited, arms crossed, feet planted wide. The guy walked around the back of his car, then stopped short when he saw them.

"Hey," he mumbled.

Ryan lifted his chin. His eyes were narrowed. Colin had said something on the phone to him earlier this week about this guy, but Ryan didn't like that he kept showing up, no matter what Colin had told him. "What's the deal? My fiancée told me you stopped by my house the other day. Just man up and tell us what this is about."

The guy walked closer, inhaling and exhaling with each step. He stopped a few feet away. He was younger than Ryan expected, maybe even a teenager. He had a tough-guy edge with the boots, jeans, the tattoos that snaked up his arms, and a stubbled jaw, but his eyes were young.

And something in them looked eerily familiar.

Like Ryan recognized them. His blood froze, and all the hair on his arms stood on end.

"Marcus?"

Ryan snapped his gaze to his brother, whose jaw had fallen open as he'd said the name.

"You know him?" Ryan asked.

Colin nodded, eyes wide with shock.

The guy cleared his throat and cut in. "I want to talk to both of you," he said, his voice steady, but as if he were forcing that evenness. "We all have something in common."

"Why are you here?" Ryan asked, adrenaline surging through his body, like a fighter poised. "Who is he?" he said to Colin.

But nothing could have prepared him for the next words.

"My name is Marcus. I was born seventeen years ago at the Stella McLaren Federal Women's Correctional Center. My mother is Dora Prince. I'm your brother."

THE END

Stay tuned for the final two books in the SINFUL NIGHTS series! SINFUL LONGING is the love story of Colin Sloan and Elle Mariano and it releases in November and can be preordered here! SINFUL LOVE is the final book and it is also available to preorder!

If you'd like to receive an email when my
new titles are available, please sign up for my
newsletter: laurenblakely.com/newsletter

Check out my contemporary romance novels!

The New York Times and USA Today
Bestselling Seductive Nights series including
Night After Night, *After This Night*,
and *One More Night*

And the two standalone
romance novels, *Nights With Him* and
Forbidden Nights, both New York Times
and USA Today Bestsellers!

Sweet Sinful Nights, the first book in
the New York Times Bestselling high-heat romantic
suspense series that spins off from Seductive Nights!

21 Stolen Kisses, the USA Today
Bestselling forbidden new adult romance!

Caught Up In Us, a New York Times and
USA Today Bestseller! (Kat and Bryan's romance!)

Pretending He's Mine, a Barnes & Noble and
iBooks Bestseller! (Reeve & Sutton's romance)

Trophy Husband, a New York Times and
USA Today Bestseller! (Chris & McKenna's romance)

Playing With Her Heart, a
USA Today bestseller! (Davis and Jill's romance)

Far Too Tempting, an Amazon
romance bestseller! (Matthew and Jane's romance)

Stars in Their Eyes, an iBooks bestseller!
(William and Jess' romance)

My USA Today bestselling
No Regrets series that includes

The Thrill of It
(Meet Harley and Trey)

and its sequel

Every Second With You

My New York Times and USA Today
Bestselling Fighting Fire series that includes

Burn For Me
(Smith and Jamie's romance!)

Melt for Him
(Megan and Becker's romance!)

and *Consumed by You*
(Travis and Cara's romance!)

ACKNOWLEDGEMENTS

Thank you so much to all the amazing people who played a role in this book getting in yours hands. I am immensely grateful to Sarah Hansen, Steph Bowers, Jesse Gordon, Kara Hildebrand, Kelley Jefferson, KP Simmon, Jen McCoy, Kim Bias, Helen Williams, and Lauren McKellar, just to name a few. Thank you to the amazing bloggers who spread the word and share their love, to the readers who make everything possible, to my author buds who keep me sane, and to my family who puts up with me. Love, hugs and kisses to all of you. You are beautiful.

CONTACT

I love hearing from readers! You can find me on Twitter at LaurenBlakely3, or Facebook at LaurenBlakelyBooks, or online at LaurenBlakely.com. You can also email me at laurenblakelybooks@gmail.com.

45161966R00220

Made in the USA
Lexington, KY
20 September 2015